Every

Picture

Martin Lloyd

Queen Anne's Fan

First published in 2008 by Queen Anne's Fan
PO Box 883 • Canterbury • Kent • CT1 3WJ

ISBN 9780 9547 1505 2

Set in New Baskerville 10 on 11pt.

Printed in England

Queen Anne's Fan

EPISODE ONE

That girl was back. Short flaxen boyish hair pushed under a floppy denim cap, her blue eyes liquid with a mysterious, searching melancholy. She was back, staring at those same three paintings again. That makes it the fifth time in eight days. He wondered uneasily whether he ought to tell someone.

From his attendant's stool in the art gallery, over the last ten years Arthur Northgate had seen all kinds of customers – students who came in every day to copy some famous painting or other; ladies in tweed jackets peering through opera glasses; bent old men smelling of cheap pipe tobacco looking for a dry place to sit; schoolchildren giggling at the nudes; he had seen them all but none had intrigued him as much as this girl.

He had first noticed her early last week. Heaven knows anybody would have been noticeable at the moment for the exhibition was not popular. It was the annual offering from the local art colleges. Not his type of thing at all. Arthur Northgate did not really bother himself with art, but he did like a picture. Something pretty to look at or something with a story in it. Most of the student stuff was a bit too daubish and modern for him. Judging by the poor attendance it was also unattractive to the usual patrons for they regularly shunned these two weeks every year. It made Arthur's life easy of course. He could move his stool out of the alcove and doze discreetly in the pool of morning sun which seeped through the skylight, never quite reaching the walls.

He had been day-dreaming about his holiday in Malta when he had heard the gentle clicking of heels in the next room. He now even recognised the sound of her approach. Always the same. She would drift slowly around the room, standing before each picture for a short time before moving to the next. It was at her third visit that he had realised that she was not seeing the other pictures. Just looking at them. To him there was an indefinable sadness etched into the minute smiling lines around her blue eyes. But she always stopped before those three pictures at the west corner, staring intently at each in turn; sometimes stretching impatiently onto her tiptoes to scrutinise an elusive detail. Her fresh face would gaze eagerly up, as if expecting something, some reward, some signal. Then her half-open mouth would gently close to obscure her smiling teeth, her eyebrows would lower to a flat line of disappointment and her whole body would assume a slouch of dejection.

Why she came he did not know. Each to his own taste, he supposed. Give him something pretty to look at, or a picture with a story in it – that was what he liked.

Magdaline O'Neil frowned hard at the canvas but the girl in the silver-blue ball gown gazed sedately back at her with a muteness completely devoid of insolence.

'Help me! Oh please, I need help.' Magdaline addressed the picture, 'I can't do it on my own. You can tell me. You must know something. Explain. Please, please.' No answer. 'Just something, anything. Give me a lead.' Her gaze wandered around the canvas, examining and questioning details but the folds and falls of the satin, the fine broderie anglaise on the bodice gave nothing away. It was the portrait of a rich girl on her way to, or just having returned from a society ball. She was perched on the edge of a chair in a pose of frightening precariousness but one in which she managed to communicate an elegant serenity, as if she had been sitting thus all her life.

Suddenly Magdaline caught her breath. The girl had given her something after all. She stared hard at the small feet which were protruding from the hem of the gown.

'Yes! But why? Tell me why! Oh please! Why are you bare footed? You cannot dance in bare feet.'

She put her hand to her head as the blood began to pound in her temples again. The warning sign. She should stop. You cannot dance in bare feet.

'Richard, must you dress like that? You have some beautiful clothes. Clothes that a handsome young man should be proud of and yet when you deign to visit your family you come looking like a tramp!'

The Right Honourable Richard Albermarle d'Ennessy, eldest

son of Alfred Ewin d'Ennessy, the Earl of Wisdene, kept any display of sentiment from his clear brown eyes; he simply pushed a finely formed hand through his untidy bush of brown hair and from his six feet two inches, silently looked at his mother, the countess. His frank and handsome face, glowing with years of good nourishment and healthy exercise did not betray his irritation. At twenty six he considered that he was old enough to decide for himself what he should wear.

'They are called "jeans" mother and everybody is wearing them.'

'It certainly looks as if everybody has worn yours. I almost feel as if you should be using the North Alley, not the drive. Dress like a tradesman...' She left the observation unfinished as if there were a hidden threat behind it. 'You should consider your position Richard. Do you think it is fitting for Viscount Churle, the prospective heir, to be seen running the estate dressed like that?'

'Mother, I am not running the estate. Father is as strong as an ox and has neither the need nor the intention of handing over the running of the estate to me. He has Courtney who is a fully competent estate manager and who, as I am sure you know, wears jeans on his days off.'

'We are not discussing what the staff do on their days off. That is their affair. Your father and I have always maintained a tradition of broad-mindedness with regard to our staff.'

'Lucky staff.'

'Did you say something?' She peered at him through her lorgnette and her silver grey chignon bobbed disapproval.

'Mother, you look ridiculous with that thing. Do get yourself some contact lenses.'

'And why can you not spend more time here at the Hall?' The countess smoothed down the lap of her haute couture gown and adeptly changed subject as she felt the initiative slipping away from her. 'That *taudis* you purchased in, where is it? Battersea?...'

'It's Piccadilly, mother. Just off Half Moon Street.' She knew perfectly where it was.

'Do you consider it fitting to a man of your standing?'

'It is not a *taudis* mother, it is a converted mews.'

'A mews! Why! If you had wanted to live as a chauffeur you could have moved in with Winston here. You and he have always been as thick as thieves.'

'Mother...'

'And this ridiculous art college idea. How long do you suppose that will last? And what good will it be to you? You are just wasting your life Richard. What good will Art be to the estate?'

Richard d'Ennessy ambled slowly across the room and peered blandly into an alcove which was partially hidden by a pilaster. 'Grandfather bought this painting from Monet didn't he?' He nodded at the small framed impressionist landscape hanging in its niche. 'I understand that grandfather knew him as "Claude" at the time. How much is it worth today mother? His knowledge of art certainly did the estate no harm.'

'Don't be insolent Richard. Thank goodness Charles has a sense of proportion, unlike his elder brother.'

'Charles wanted to study agronomy mother, you know full well he did. He has always wanted to do something like that. I have always been drawn to... other things.'

'You never stick at anything for more than two minutes... Yes John?'

It rankled with the Countess of Wisdene to employ a head butler whose surname was also a perfectly good Christian name, but the manner in which she enunciated his name ensured that it could never be misinterpreted as a display of unsavoury intimacy.

'Mrs. Littlewood is here ma'am.'

'I'll see her in the blue room. Bring sherry in fifteen minutes.'

'Very good ma'am.'

'I shall leave you to your work mother.' Richard flicked his hair from his face and kissed her forehead. She held his wrist.

'You know I don't like you doing that Richard.'

'Yes you do mother.'

'Are you going straight back to town?'

'Shortly.'

'Do try to be here for our "at home" this weekend. Vanessa will be here.'

'Good old Vanessa,' Richard mumbled to himself.

'Yes, Good old Vanessa.' His mother's ears were like radar. 'She will not wait for ever Richard.'

He stood on the south terrace and looked distractedly across the park. High on the opposite hillside a small herd of deer was moving in and out of sight as they browsed the Long Covert. Down on the lake the September mist lay motionless over the black water like a diaphanous blanket. Four hundred acres made the park, eight thousand the farm, not counting the two hamlets, the countless hundreds of acres of woodland leased out and several hundred commercial properties in the centres of the county's major towns – witness to his father's acumen.

It could all just jog along without him. He scraped his sneakers on the grey stone and worried a weed which had niched itself in the step. He could hear footfalls scrunching on the gravel and, around the corner of the South Wing ambled Blase, the head gardener. Richard nodded at him absently and Blase touched his cap and came over to him.

'It's going to be a mild winter Master Richard,' he pronounced solemnly as he bent and, gripping the weed with knurled, arthritic fingers, twisted it from its forbidden lodging with an expert jerk of his wrist.

'Is Winston in the mews?'

'Yessir. Washing that *auto-mobile* of his and letting the soapy water run all over my prize rhubarb.'

'I'm sure that must be the secret ingredient that wins you all the rosettes, Blase.'

'Yessir,' he grunted, unconvinced.

Winston was leathering the windscreen of Richard's garish yellow open top two-seater as if he expected it to give birth imminently.

'Fancy a spin Winston?' Richard suggested mischievously.

'Bless me no sir.' Winston lowered his corduroy bottom to the running board of the Daimler. 'It's a long time since I was a lad.'

'How old are you Winston?'

'Old enough for that question to be an impertinence even from you, Master Richard.'

Richard grinned sheepishly. 'No, I suppose you would not know what to do with a car like mine.' He patted the high black bonnet of the limousine. 'You stick to your tank.'

'Do you think that I've never driven a sports car, Master Richard?' Richard's eyebrows rose in surprise. Winston chuckled. 'I'm not completely senile. The twin tailpipes means it's probably got the Rover V8 engine in it. Right?' Richard nodded. 'So it's a pig in the corners even with those tyres.' Richard was astonished at the old man's deductions. Winston chuckled and leaned forward. 'I used to hill climb in an Austin Seven Special when I was your age.' Richard suddenly felt very foolish. 'Don't write me off Master Richard just because I drive a 1937 Daimler.'

'No I won't.' Richard looked down at his sneakers. Winston

always had this ability to bring him down nicely. 'How long have you been with us Winston?' Winston shuffled sideways to make space for him on the running board.

'I served your grandfather for ten years. This was his car. He said to me, "Winston, if you are going to be my chauffeur you've got to choose the car you will be happy to live with. And I mean live with." And he poked me in the chest with the stem of that pipe of his. So I said to him, "If it's all the same to you my Lord, your comfort is paramount. I would suggest the Daimler with the fluid flywheel." "Winston," he says to me, "I was thinking only of my comfort. The Daimler it will be".' Winston chuckled. 'Selfish bugger, your grandfather.'

Richard laughed. 'Is that why we have never sold it?'

'We have never sold it because it still works perfectly, Master Richard. There's too much of this planned obsolescence for my liking.' He flicked a speck of dirt from the polished brown leather of his shoes with the corner of his chamois. 'Spending a lot of time in the big city Master Richard,' he said without looking up. 'Got a girl up there have you?'

Richard felt himself flushing. 'No Winnie I haven't and that's the truth.' The man waited patiently. 'I don't know what I want to do yet.' He looked at the warm red brick of the yard, the trickle of soapy water wending its unerring way to the rhubarb. He recalled the hours he had spent playing here as a child, under Winston's uncomplaining feet, losing his tools, putting sticky fingers on the newly cleaned glass. 'Sometimes I feel I don't belong here. Not really. It's alright for Charles – he takes to nature and growing things and all that palaver like a horse to its nosebag, but lately I have felt sort of unsettled.' He looked across at the ruddy face and the silver hair. The old man said nothing. 'So I am going to live in London and study art. Go to college. Do it properly.' He put on a brave face.

'Your grandfather was a one for pictures, you know. You shan't go wrong. And you'll be back. There's people here who will be awful glad to see you, Master Richard, you mark my words.'

Jennifer Pye hated the tube. She hated being hemmed in but when you are only five feet three inches tall there is not much you can do. She sometimes wore her heels, which made her five feet five but merely gave her a close-up view of the next button higher up the shirt. And when you wear your golden brown hair loose, down to the small of your back, a day in the tube renders it lank and grimy. Struggling with an art folder on the escalator usually degenerated into a thin parody of the classic circus act with the plank as she turned this way and that to avoid hurrying passengers but merely succeeded in obstructing others.

'Excuse me. Excuse me please.' She began pushing towards the door as the train screeched into Sloane Square. 'Excuse me. Could you let me off please? Look I want to get off.'

'Got big feet for a little girl ain't yer?'

'I'm awfully sorry. Could you please just... Excuse me. Excuse me.'

She looked despairingly at the red and blue backpack which towered above her. Why did these people have to travel at rush hour? Couldn't they wait just a little while before starting their holidays?

'No good talking to him, he's a Kraut. He won't understand. Give 'im a shove.'

Jennifer reached up and shook the bulging canvas. She might just as well have been a tick on an elephant's back for all the response she elicited.

'Oh please, please could somebody just....'

'Mind the doors!'

The mass of travellers jolted as the train moved off. The German backpacker trod heavily on her foot.

'Ouch!' She kicked back as hard as she could with the toe of her plimsolls. The youth turned. 'Now let me get to the doors!' she ordered angrily and elbowed him roughly in the ribs. He ambled aside like a dozy cow in the milking parlour.

By the time that the train had crawled into the next station, Jennifer Pye had wormed and squirmed her way to the very front of the automatic doors. More screeching of brakes, and commuters gripping armrests, pressing involuntarily against their neighbours. She stared stupidly at the doors. They did not open. Wrong side of the carriage for the doors. She thought they changed sides at Victoria, perhaps it was South Kensington. Why did things like this always happen when she was in a hurry?

'Excuse me. Getting off! Getting off!'

'Not you again. Make up your mind!'

She forced her way through the knot of commuters by tucking her art folder under her arm as a lance and then squealed in shocked surprise as someone pinched her bottom whilst she was squeezing through the closing doors.

'Pervert!' she mouthed through the glass at a grinning face as the carriage drew away. She had no idea if it was the culprit and cared less.

Buckingham Palace Road was thronging with people intent on their own selfish purposes to the exclusion of all else. Buffeted and baulked, she fought her way along the pavement. It would take her an extra twenty minutes now to reach her destination. By the time she arrived at the Sloane College of Art & Design she would be well down the queue for enrolment. What a way to start the academic year!

'That's just what I could do with,' she muttered grimly as a bright yellow two-seater coasted down the street, its powerful motor burbling softly. She watched the rather dishy young man searching vainly for a parking space. 'Perhaps not,' she decided. 'All right for the back roads of Nottinghamshire. That's where it would be really fun.'

The car testily shot down a side street and out of sight; Jennifer Pye was seeing it still but with herself lounging in the passenger seat as it zipped along the lanes back home. But of course Steven would have been driving it. She could remember his strained face on the platform as the train had pulled out of Nottingham Midland. He should not have bothered to have come, it had been all over by then, irrevocably. His presence had given her no pleasure, not even the perverse one of knowing that he had had to leave that girl's bed in order to be there.

'Will you write?' he had said.

'No.' And she had kept her word. But she had cried all the way to London.

London. Sometimes she hated the place. Most of the time she hated the place. Dirty, noisy, smelly, busy, friendless. Perhaps she should have insisted on going with her parents but then the temptation of starting out in the world to make her fortune at the age of twenty two had been too great...

'Jennifer luv, yer Mam and I want to talk to you.'

'What is it Dad?'

'Come and sit on the arm of me chair luv. Well I, that is, yer Mam and me have made this decision and it's right you should know straight away.'

'Will I like it Dad?'

'We're going to live in Spain, luv. We're moving.'

'Spain! I thought you only went there for holidays. Where will you go for a holiday when you live there?'

'It'll be holiday every day, luv. You know the sun is good for your Mam's joints. We're going to buy a little place down there. What with the money they gave me when they shut the pit and the bit we'll get for this place we shall be all right for the rest of our lives. I've seen the pension people and they say they can pay us direct down there, so we won't want for nothing.'

'What'll I do Dad? Where shall I live?'

'You've always been an independent girl, Jencie. And you're the only treasure we've got so yer Mam and me decided that you could have the money from our endowment that comes up in six months. Set you up in whatever you want to do. You've always had projects haven't you Jencie?'

And so they went to Spain and Jennifer moved into a bedsit above a pet shop and began looking for the property she needed. This was when Steven had come on the scene.

'Miss Pye?'

'Yes.'

'It's Steven Hadden from Rowbotham's.'

'Yes?' She fiddled with the telephone cord absently. She had vaguely noticed Steven Hadden as the office junior at the estate agents; she had not realised that he dealt with the clients.

'You asked us to look for a small boutique with flat over...'

'Yes that's right. Have you got one?'

'We have a selection of properties which might suit you.'

'Brilliant! I'll be straight round.'

'No.' His voice was sharp with a discreet anxiety. 'No, Miss Pye, in circumstances such as these it would be more appropriate if we discussed this over lunch, our compliments of course. Shall we say the King's Head at one o'clock?'

Steven exuded confidence and soon became a valued business adviser with an answer for everything. Jennifer thought that the boutique was too expensive, it would take all her endowment but, as Steven explained, it was on an important through route with lots of passing trade. Once she had bought it, she could mortgage it and use the money to buy the stock. She would be saving money of course by not having to pay herself rent for the flat over. She would have realised none of this had not Steven been there to guide her.

The next few months were a whirl of painting and papering, carpeting and carpentry as they converted the former greengrocer's into 'Fashion Pye' the newest and trendiest boutique in Nottingham City. Well not quite in the City but near enough to the centre, Steven assured her.

She came to rely upon him more and more. He was there when the man came from the council and started asking about why she had not applied for 'Change of Use Permission.' Steven had taken the papers away and done his magic and she knew she need no longer worry. It was Steven who had found the builder for her late one Sunday night when she had discovered the rain dripping into the stock room through the old porous lead flashing on the chimney.

And eventually, inevitably, it was Steven who had climbed into her bed one afternoon when he should have been at the office and she in the shop. He was dynamic, he was energetic, she was trusting, she was blindly in love.

When Jennifer had discovered that working in your own business meant no free time, Steven had found Julie, his sister's friend, who 'could do the job standing on her head'.

When the hoped-for customers had not materialised, Steven had found an agent to finance the loan necessary to buy the new season's stock. Whatever she needed, Steven was able to provide it. How could she have been so stupid?

Popping into the shop, unannounced, one afternoon, she had not even questioned Julie's flushed face as she had hurried down from the stock room. It had not occurred to her that Julie might not have been alone.

When the enforcement order had arrived from the Council's Planning Department, explaining that she should sell vegetables or close the shop, she had realised that the council must have made some kind of bureaucratic mistake. Had not Steven already sorted this out?

Then one afternoon when she sat alone, wondering where Julie had got to and unable to contact Steven at the office; alone in a deserted shop before which Steven's 'passing trade' passed but did not stop, a shop crammed full of stock which nobody wanted to buy but for which she was paying an outrageous rate of interest, the building society's bailiff called and within an hour she was out.

The Right Honourable Richard d'Ennessy, Viscount Churle, had felt neither right nor honourable as he had dodged the early shoppers in the King's Road. He had not been right to use his car in London at this time of the morning and had committed a dishonourable act in parking it in a private road near the Embankment. And now that he was inside the towering black brick monstrosity which proclaimed itself to be the Sloane College of Art & Design he felt distinctly out of place.

All of the students and most of the lecturers appeared to be years younger than him. He had never thought of himself as old at twenty six. They also all knew where they were going and what they were supposed to be doing. They had no time for somebody who did not understand directions like, 'The reg. list is by the refec.' or, 'Try the sec's. office on the Mez.'

He would have one last try. That girl with the big folder, just squeezing through the doors. She looked as if she knew what she was doing. He would ask her.

'Excuse me, could–'

'Oh shit! My best jeans! Just look at that will you?' She fingered the loose flap of her pocket where the door latch had ripped it. 'I shall sue the college for a million pounds.'

'I am sure you would win,' he observed with feeling. He felt his breath had been taken away by this little bundle of energy.

'Hold that a minute!' The art folder was thrust into his arms and he watched her fresh face frown and pucker in concentration as she fished a safety pin from her bag and twisted around to repair the rent. A neat body, Richard observed as the denim tightened across her pelvis. A bit Botticelli – heavy around the abdomen. And that cascade of golden brown hair...

Poor lamb looks a bit lost. Jennifer eased the pin through the welt of the denim. Nice dresser, those clothes must have cost him a packet. Long legs, cosy and snug in corduroy, broad shoulders casually wrapped in a lambswool rollneck. Cultured talking voice, I wonder what subject he teaches?

'Thanks duck!' She grinned impishly. 'First day at school?'

'Yes, I am rather lost.'

'Where should you be? What's your department?'

'I'm doing the Art Foundation Course. What are you doing?'

'Advertising and Fashion Design. Second year.' He felt her eyes sweep him from head to foot with a detached curiosity. 'Art Foundation Course? Oh you'll want the Daubers' staff room. Down the end of the corridor, up the stairs, blue door on your left.'

He returned her art folder, a little confused. 'I don't think I'm looking for the staff room. I am looking for Enrolment.'

'Enrolment? What for? You mean you are a student?' He nodded self consciously as if being addressed as a student in the corridor of a college of further education were somehow incongruous. 'I thought you were a lecturer.' She gave a little grunt which defied interpretation. 'Follow me.'

EPISODE TWO

Jennifer ran her long nails along the cat's spine, making it arch its back and purr with contentment.

'What do you know, pussy?'

The cat butted its head into the palm of her hand and then stopped and began to wash itself as Jennifer's pace took her past the garden wall and onto the black and white tiled garden path.

Mrs. Emily Crowther had 'taken in ladies' for as long as the other residents of Cordoba Crescent could remember. The house seemed to have just grown into the role for which it was eminently suited, it being a crumbling damp Victorian orange brick pile with draughty sash windows and whining geysers. Ealing was peppered with such edifices.

Jennifer stood by the hall table for an instant, her interest arrested by the evening sunlight dappling onto the light wood as it played through the coloured glass on the door. A letter for her, from Spain. She tucked it into the top of her shoulder bag and began climbing the stairs.

'Is that you Miss Pye?' Mrs. Crowther's reed-like voice fluted out from the front room.

'Yes, Mrs. Crowther. Just me.' Just me, unaccompanied, she thought.

'Did you see there was a letter for you?'

'Yes, I did. I've got it thank you Mrs. Crowther.' Jennifer stopped on the stair and turned. 'How is Sandy?'

The parlour door opened and Mrs. Crowther appeared – a short wisp of a woman with watery blue eyes and thin white hair through which her scalp showed pink. She was cradling a Pekinese dog smugly wrapped in her apron.

'The vet said he was probably just feeling a little peeky.'

Jennifer put her hand to her mouth and forced out a quick cough to conceal the guffaw that was bubbling within her. 'You should wrap up more dear. Look at you with your shirt open like that. No wonder you cough.'

'Yes Mrs. Crowther. I am glad Sandy is better.'

Jennifer pushed her door closed behind her with her foot and went quickly to the oven, thrusting the take-away foil container on to the top shelf with one hand and spinning the control knob with the other. She was pulling her sneakers from her feet as she crossed to the window and, having forced up the sash, she threw herself onto the bed and groaned aloud.

Oh Ruth! Why did they have to pair her up with Ruth for the first assignment? Ruth Robey, who dressed like a film star, walked like a fashion model and spoke about the Royal Family as if they all lived down her street. Ruth and she had absolutely nothing in common.

She lay on her back, pummelled her fists on the bed and kicked her legs up towards the ceiling in a mock display of frustration. Then she stopped and inspected her big toe which was poking through a sizeable hole in her sock. She roughly pulled off the sock, spun it around like a propeller and flicked it across the room. Then she made several unsuccessful attempts to grip her parents' letter with her toes and lift it from her bag. She grunted, sat up and fished the letter out.

Dear Jencie,

How are you my darling? We are doing fine here. It's twenty eight in the shade and I am sitting outside the bar writing this. You'll never guess what, in the supermercado we met a couple from Joyce Road yesterday. They even knew Tebbs the milkman. They've lived out here for five years and love it. Your Mam's had a bit of a runny nose this week I tell her she's not drinking enough. How's business? Do try to write soon love, I know you must be busy now you're in London.

All our love, Dad and Mam.

P.S. You must try to get out to see us. Why not Christmas?

She folded it and put it in the drawer with the others.

'Bugger!' she said to nobody in particular.

'Jennie?' a woman's voice called through the door. Jennifer ignored it. A fist rapped on the door panel. 'Jennie!' it insisted.

'Nobody of that name here,' she called out and pulled off her other sock.

'Jennifer!'

She opened the door to a young woman of about her age. Her sturdy hips were squeezed into a plaid skirt and her substantial bosom was fighting its way out of a flesh coloured bra. She flicked her dark hair nervously out of her face and held up both arms. From each hand dangled a jumper.

'Sorry Jennie... fer,' she added quickly. 'I forget.'

Jennifer held one end of the sock to her nose, lifted the other and trumpeted.

'An elephant never forgets! What's your name again?'

'You know it's Cherryl!'

'Right then Cherry, you'd better come in. What's the problem this time?'

Cherryl bustled in and slumped uninvited onto the bed. She gazed out of the window.

'I wish I had this room,' she sighed. 'You get lovely sun in the evenings.'

'Yes and you get lovely sun in the mornings,' Jennifer retorted.

'And pigeons.'

'Well I get the milkman whistling at a quarter to five.'

'I wish a handsome man would whistle outside my window at a quarter to five every morning. He wouldn't have to whistle twice.'

'Have you seen our milkman? The only reason he whistles is because his dentures are cracked. Cherry, you can never be that desperate. What's the problem now?'

'The red or the green?' She indicated the jumpers. 'I never know which looks best. You are good with colours and that.'

'Neither,' Jennifer suggested mischievously. 'Go as you are.' She plucked a silk rose from an arrangement hanging on the wall and pushed it adroitly into Cherryl's cleavage. 'You'll knock'em flat.'

'Oh Jennifer!' Cherryl stood up to go but, catching sight of herself in the mirror, stopped. 'You know... I don't look too bad like that do I?' She arched her back and wondered.

'Stunning but not wise for your first date. Give him the wrong idea.'

'Second date, actually.'

'Oh. Is this the motor bike fiend from Fulham?'

'No. Not him! He dro... I dropped him ages ago. This is Keith. Assistant manager at Safeways.'

'Married,' Jennifer said flatly.

'No he's not. At least, he never said he was.'

'If he's an assistant manager, he must be married. They always are. And in any case, he won't tell you that he is married until he gets to the "my wife doesn't understand me" line. By then it's too late.'

Jennifer bit her lip as Cherryl's shoulders drooped and the light went out of those large doe eyes.

'Cherryl. Come here love.' Cherryl turned. Jennifer slipped an arm around her waist. 'Come on duck, let me do your hair for you, then we'll try out your wardrobe and by midnight you'll have him eating out of your hand.'

'Oh would you Jennie... fer?'

'Sit down there.'

Richard nosed his car into the cobbled yard and, leaving the engine running, jumped out to open the green timber doors of the garage.

'I say! I say!'

Richard looked around for the owner of the voice. A rather foppish looking young man with soft blond hair was leaning from a first floor window opposite.

'I say! You won't forget to close the gates will you?'

Richard waved a non-committal hand. The lad's father owned most of this part of London. Whatever Richard was feeling at the moment, it would never be propitious to be rude to the poor clout.

Richard's bad temper was made worse by the forced admission that it had all been his fault. He had parked the car there. He had known the road was private. The signs were unambiguous. What he had not been prepared for was the large warning notice which had been pasted to his windscreen, decrying his selfishness and threatening him with all kinds of sanctions should he lapse into recidivism.

The threats did not affect him as much as the glue. It had taken him a mortifying three quarters of an hour, scrabbling with his finger nails, frost scraper, car keys – any object which would provide a purchase on the poster in order to clear the screen sufficiently for him to drive the car away. And during this time, he had been captive to the snide and smug comments of the righteous residents. Had he not been warned?

Now, as he surveyed his car in the garage, he realised that he would have to find some kind of solvent to remove the coating. He could not drive a car with an opaque windscreen.

He turned the brass knob on the brick pillar and waited whilst the wrought iron gates silently closed across the mews. He glanced up at the window opposite but his lordship had retreated.

Half Moon Mews had once been the stables and the carriage houses to the six-storey family mansions on the main street. The mews ran like a cobbled gully behind and parallel to them. With the social changes wrought by the first world war – the plunging fortunes of the wealthy classes, the movement of working women from domestic service to the higher rewards of industry – the mews were let to whomsoever would pay a rent. One-man engineering businesses and obscure printing firms had favoured the garage/workshop facilities, often using the rooms above for offices. During the depression of the twenties and thirties the mews had fallen into disrepair and, dilapidated and abandoned, they had become an undesirable eyesore.

It was during the late fifties that far seeing individuals began to realise that a small pied-à-terre with a garage in the centre of London was just what was needed. They began to move in and renovate. Now, Half Moon Mews was a very expensive, select oasis blending Victorian engineering brick and cobbles with double glazing and electronic security.

Richard's cottage had been converted to provide a large garage and two rooms downstairs and three rooms upstairs. Turning the house upside down, he had developed the two downstairs rooms as his bedroom and en-suite and put his kitchen and living rooms above. It amused him to live at first floor level, the light was better and the incongruity, charming.

He touched a button on his hi-fi and the room was suddenly filled with the vibrant tones of a harpsichord. He pulled his sweater over his head in one movement and dropped it to the floor. He unbuckled his cord trousers as he absently flicked at the telephone, drawing open his zip as the number rang.

'Empress – at your service,' a modulated feminine voice assured him.

'It's Richard d'Ennessy. What can you offer me tonight?' His trousers slowly slid over his firm buttocks and crumpled to the floor, unheeded, as he listened attentively to the phone. 'I'll have number one on the menu I think. About eight o'clock. She has my address? Good.'

He stepped out of his trousers and, flipping a silk robe from the back of a leather chair, made his way downstairs towards the bathroom.

Thirty minutes later, scrubbed and invigorated, he lay on his back on the thick Arabian carpet and revelled in the sensation of the tightly packed bristle pressing through the silk onto his naked body. The music sluiced over him like a soul cleanser. He needed it.

He had not been prepared for the sheer squalidness of a common establishment of higher education. Paint peeling from the tall windowed Edwardian doors; wooden parquet, cracked and stained by generations of spills and assaults; hard, unyielding chairs; cramped lecture rooms lighted by harsh fluorescent tubes; crowded students' common room with a smoking corner which stank of stale, cheap roll-ups and the whole invaded by a restless, colourful, busied movement of arty students each trying to prove themselves original in dress and manner. It made him feel very alien and very grown up. But, he had decided to go through with this so he would have to learn quickly. His first lesson had come at enrolment.

'Yes?'

'I am looking for...'

'Enrolment?'

'Yes, I am...'

'Course?'

'Art Foundation.'

'Over there.'

He followed the imperiously pointing pen to the table at the end.

'Course?'

'Art Foundation.'

'Name?'

'I thought that was what it was called. Art Foundation course.'

'Your name?'

'Oh. Richard d'Ennessy.'

'Richard Dennis who?'

'D'Ennessy.'

'Dennis Hee. So "Hee" is your surname is it?'

'No it's D apostrophe E, double N, E, double S, Y.'

'What do you mean, "D apostrophe E?" That's not how to spell Dennis.'

'Ennessy. My name is Ennessy. Richard Ennessy. Just that.'

'Why didn't you say so? Putting on airs and graces. Students! They're always doing it.'

And so The Right Honourable Richard d'Ennessy, Viscount Churle discovered a new identity for himself: Richard Ennessy, student.

As he was passed from one process to the next, he felt himself mentally bruised and battered by the harsh yet puerile brutality of it all. Whenever he heard another voice say 'Art Foundation' he would strain to discover who his fellow students were to be. He could have saved the effort. After a meal of indescribable composition, eaten, thankfully, alone in the refectory, he had joined the other students on his course for an introductory talk in a tutorial room. The most obvious statistic to be drawn from this operation was that ninety per cent of the students were female. At least, he believed them to be female for it was sometimes difficult to tell.

They had then been broken up into their tutorial groups and after Dr. Sullivan had identified himself as their tutor, he had invited them to introduce themselves individually to the group.

'Starting from the left,' he had suggested pleasantly and designated a girl whose thin face and long hair reminded Richard of a saluki.

She blushed crimson and announced haltingly, 'My name is Alison and I... er Alison Barrett that is. And I... I am doing the Art Foundation Course.'

Dr. Sullivan waited, but she had nothing to add.

'Thank you Alison. Next?'

'Yes. Stewart Griffin. I come from Harrow Grammar.' He pushed his spectacles crookedly up his nose. 'I am doing the Art Foundation Course, of course. Ha! ha!... Sorry. I am interested in the history of art and want to become an art historian for an auction house.'

'That is interesting Stewart. A worthy goal to aim for. I am sure the Sloane College will set you well on your way to your chosen career.'

'I am Mrs. Porter.' Mrs. Porter tugged her cerise cardigan around her as if daring anybody to challenge her. She was easily into middle age and was coming back to enjoy an opportunity for education that the bringing up of four children had denied her.

And so it had continued. The only other student Richard had really noticed had been a young man with a mass of tangled red hair and angry red eyebrows.

'My name's Bob Priestman and I don't mind tellin' you I come from Yorkshire. My father owns all the profitable mills in Halifax. You've probably heard of Priestman's.' He was utterly impervious to the blank looks around the room. 'I've had to come down here to get on a fabric design course which should have been available at 'ome but our Education Committee has seen fit to...'

'Thank you Bob. Can we call you Bob?'

'Aye. Yer can.'

And then Richard had realised with a start that everybody was looking at him.

Espousing his new identity with vigour he announced, 'I am Richard Ennessy.' His clear, cultured and confident voice had arrested Dr. Sullivan in the middle of an exploration of his left nostril and encouraged some students to pull faces at each other behind their hands. 'As you can see, I am realising the benefits of tertiary education much more slowly than your intelligent selves. I am coming to college because I...' Why was he coming to college? 'Because I like to paint and think that I should know more about it.'

'All right for some,' a Yorkshire voice had muttered.

'What have I let myself in for?' Richard wondered as he lay on the floor.

A buzzer sounded. He jumped up and peered into small black

and white television screen which provided a view of the gate.

'Empress for Mr. d'Ennessy.'

He pressed the button and watched the narrow personnel gate open.

'Come straight up,' Richard ordered as he pressed another button. 'The door's open.'

'Shall I come up?' a woman's voice enquired uncertainly.

'Yes, upstairs please.' He self-consciously tucked his silk wrap around himself more securely. He was completely unaware that the result was to make his underlying nudity more obvious and this aspect was not disregarded by the young woman who entered.

'Hello. You have not been to me before have you?'

'No sir, I am new.'

'What's your name?'

'Karen, sir.'

'Well Karen, you'll be back here quite soon, I am certain.' He smiled as she placed her burden gravely on the linen cloth and lifted a stainless steel lid.

'One duck with orange, sir. Shall I serve?'

'Would you be so kind? Thank you.'

In Cordoba Crescent, Ealing, Jennifer Pye was burning her fingers as she frantically pulled a carbonised Indian take-away from a forgotten oven.

The refectory buzzed with the traditional eleven o'clock soggy toast and coffee. Richard was not an anti-social creature and during the first few weeks of term he had tried always to mix with his tutorial group. He felt that it was important that they should function in a group as well as individually. He had been down to the pub with some of them one Friday lunchtime and, being aware of the vast rift that must have existed between their incomes and his, had ordered a half pint of beer for himself so as not to appear too wealthy. He need not have worried. Whatever else students pruned and pared, they always seemed to have money for beer. He was the only one drinking in half pints.

In the classroom, he was learning to pretend that he had only seen *La Gioconda* in a book and not in the Louvre, that he had seen the Van Goghs on television and not in Amsterdam and that he had only read about what was in the Prado. And the others had come to accept him in varying degrees. Four of the younger students, three girls and one boy, were madly in love with him. He was completely ignorant of this. Stewart Griffin, the aspiring art historian from Harrow, was intrigued and seemed to suspect an underlying inconsistency in Richard's life but lacked the gumption to tackle him, and Bob Priestman despised him with a venom.

'I am sorry Mrs. Porter, do forgive me, I was miles away.'

And Mrs. Porter saw him as the only other person in the group who was mature enough to be worth talking to.

'Gay. You can call me Gay.'

'Yes of course. Thank you,' he replied absently. 'Isn't this tea awful?'

'I think it's coffee.'

'Oh.'

She followed his gaze. 'Seen someone you know?'

He turned back to her with a smile. 'No. Not really.'

Ruth Robey tossed back her head, let fall a clear tinkling laugh and then crossed her legs high up on the thigh so that the light picked up the sheen on her sheer tights. Her eyes smiled gaily at nobody in particular but in the man's general direction. She posed until she was sure that his attention lingered upon her and then she turned back to the others.

'It wasn't that funny Ruth!' said a girl with wide innocent eyes and a crocheted dress.

'Well I thought it was,' she pouted her elegantly made-up lips.

'Oh rats! There's no sugar in this.' Jennifer nearly spat the coffee out. 'Patsy be a pal and get me some.' Jennifer was wedged into the corner on the bench.

'I'll go,' Ruth declared to the general stupefaction of the group. She stood up and languidly smoothed her skirt down her thighs with the palms of her hands. Negotiating a route between the tables, she was obliged to swivel and sway, a combination of movements which she accomplished with a sensuality finely calculated to churn all the male hormones in the refectory. But there was only one set she was targeting. And he had now definitely noticed her.

'Terribly bad for the figure,' she warned as she dropped the paper sachets to the table top in front of Jennifer.

'When I need advice from a beanpole I'll take up gardening,' Jennifer growled and then regretted the words the moment they were said. It was not the real her. She knew she was unattractive, it was a fact of life. The nearest that she had ever come to a steady relationship had been with Steven but it had transpired that all he had wanted was sex. He had got sex. All the tender murmurings she had shivered delightedly through could now be consigned to oblivion.

'Oh miaow!' Patsy wriggled her crocheted shoulders.

'Sorry Ruth, didn't mean it. Wrong time of the month.'

Ruth merely looked superior, which made Jennifer feel worse.

Richard had noticed Ruth fairly soon after sitting down and had been quite content to glance occasionally in her direction for she was undoubtedly attractive. The result of her behaviour was to draw a more particular attention to herself from Richard and what he saw, nudged him into action.

'Excuse me Mrs. Porter, I have just seen a friend.'

'Oh that's alright Richard, I've got to get on anyway.' She smiled a martyr's smile.

'Who is that gorgeous man?' Patsy's eyes were even rounder than normal.

'Which one?' Ruth enquired and twisted her torso to throw her breasts into greater prominence.

Jennifer glanced across and groaned inwardly. It was that well-dressed drip from enrolment day. And he was coming over to them.

'Oh he's coming this way. I shall die! I shall die!' Patsy twisted her fingers through her crochet in an anguish of excitement and nervously tugged her hem down. Unseen below the table, Ruth surreptitiously eased hers up.

'Oh grow up Patsy! He won't eat you,' Jennifer scowled.

'I'd die if he did!'

'No doubt,' Ruth observed and then added a mystified, 'You know, he is coming this way. Quite a dish isn't he?'

'Well he's wearing trousers if that's what you mean.'

Ruth gave her a look. Jennifer pulled a face at her. Ruth considered every other woman on the planet as competition and Jennifer resented the idea that she herself could ever want the kind of person that Ruth saw as attractive. The concept was grotesque and in any case, Ruth's taste was bizarre. This self assured fellow with lots of brown hair was of no interest to Jennifer and so she was greatly amused at Ruth's consternation when he started talking to her and not Ruth.

'Hello again. Remember me?'

'Oh hi!' Jennifer grinned lopsidedly at him and pulled at the rubber welt of her plimsolls. 'How are you getting on?'

He pursed his lips and made a face at the ceiling.

'It's different.'

Jennifer suddenly wanted to laugh. It was such a silly face. Anybody who could pull a face like that could not be so much of a drip. She was aware of Patsy choking quietly on a mouthful of crochet and Ruth staring at her with an expression near to awe on her face.

'I never actually learned your name,' he admitted, his brown eyes steadily holding hers. 'Mine's Richard.'

'I'm Jennifer.' She nodded across the table. 'This is Patsy.' Patsy squeaked. 'And the one kicking my ankle is Ruth.'

Ruth laid a cool, manicured hand in his and gazed up at him with deep eyes.

She was already dreaming.

EPISODE THREE

'The influence of the designers Vionnet and Chanel on the innovations of Claire McCardell.' Ruth sucked her pen top and looked hopefully at Jennifer. 'It's got to be because her designs were basically, well, you know... sort of...'

'Simple, uncomplicated, comfortable to wear?' Jennifer read from the book before her.

'Yeah. That sounds right.'

'But what were her innovations?'

'Um...?' Ruth glanced vacantly down the library. Getting no help from Jennifer she asked candidly, 'I give up. What were they?'

'Separates, of course,' a male voice informed her. 'Don't you ever take notes Ruth?'

'Oh hello Colin.'

Colin eased his stoutish figure around the table and sat in the chair next to Jennifer. 'Hello Jennifer.' He smeared his lank hair carefully back on top of his head.

Jennifer sighed quietly. 'Hello Colin.'

'So what was so new about separates?' Ruth looked at her paper and tapped a nail on the table top, as if expecting the answer to jump out at her.

'What about tomorrow?' Colin asked.

'To be frank, Colin, football's not really my thing,' 'There's a vintage Vincent Price on late at the Big Screen on Saturday night,' he suggested hopefully. 'There always is.'

'Do people still go to the cinema?' Ruth was astonished. 'Go on, Jennifer, get some horror into your life.'

'Are you talking about the film or Colin?' Jennifer quipped. Colin squirmed uneasily and Jennifer patted a gentle hand on his forearm. 'Just teasing, duck.'

'Jersey,' Colin said suddenly.

'What?'

'That was the innovation. McCardell copied Chanel's idea of using jersey. Chanel did it first but not for separates. McCardell used it for separates and the Yanks thought they were fantastic.'

'Hang on, hang on. I can't write that fast.'

'Up until then, separates had been daytime casual or sporty wear but she made them good enough for evening or smart dress. Skirts were usually black.'

'How do you know all this?' Ruth gasped as she scribbled.

'I listen to teacher.' He stopped reading from his lecture notes and turned to Jennifer. 'So what about tomorrow night?'

'I'm not sure, Colin. I'll ring you.' She flipped through the designs in the book. 'What about this one?' she said to Ruth. 'It shows a skirt and top.'

'O.K. I'll write this up and then the drawing can go in there.' She indicated the bundle of papers which were growing to make their first joint assignment.

Under Colin's admiring gaze, Jennifer whipped a sheet of paper from her pad and started quickly sketching the outlines of the design in pencil. As she became more engrossed, the tip of her tongue began to protrude from her lips and she shuffled on the chair and sat on one ankle.

'You're a quick worker aren't you?' he observed as she finished the inking-in.

'Oh I don't know.' She licked her thumb and then smeared it expertly down the sketch in several places to make a wash contrast to the highlights. She pulled her long hair away from the back of her neck and let it drop again. Once a week she vowed that she would have it all cut off so that she would not have to put up with it nearly pulling her head from her shoulders all day long, but she was fooling herself, she knew she never would.

Ruth had finished her frantic scribbling and now her involvement in the joint venture was dwindling fast. She pulled a glossy magazine from her bag and titillated her real interest – the behaviour and misbehaviour of High Society as photographed at the various social functions of the previous week.

'Just what does she think she looks like?' Ruth turned a scandalised face to Colin and swivelled the magazine around. 'She would make a Dior dress look like a potato sack.'

'Some of them already do,' Jennifer muttered without looking up from her work.

'She should never have put that shawl with that bag. And look at the way she is standing!'

Colin passed a practised eye over the photo.

'Oh I don't know,' he said. 'It's not all that bad. Anyway I think these photographers are paid to try to find an awkward angle. I can't believe that all these women really go to these do's with their tits hanging out and their hems around their waists.'

'Typical male point of view. That's all you think of.' She studied the next picture. 'And look at the conk on her! She looks like a weather vane!'

'Typical female point of view. If you can't join them, slag them off. I bet she's someone in the aristocracy and that nose has been handed down for generations.'

'I'd hand it back if it was given to me.'

'Go on then. Who is she? I bet you a million quid she's a Lady Something or other.'

Ruth read the caption. 'The Honourable Vanessa Clewe-Harting, eldest daughter of Lord Harting of Plethero.'

'What did I tell you?' Colin said triumphantly. 'Just sour grapes, that's all! You owe me a million quid.'

The Honourable Vanessa Clewe-Harting dropped her crop and riding hat onto the stand and strode across the hallway just as John emerged from the service door.

'It's alright John. I know where he is, he waved to me through the window.' She pulled off her gloves.

'Very good ma'am. Shall I...?'

'Don't bother, John, I know the way,' she said as she handed him her gloves. 'Left the gee-gee with Barker.'

'Very good ma'am.'

John watched her silently. This autonomy amongst the youth was not to be encouraged – it could put him out of a job.

Vanessa Clewe-Harting was not what one would describe as 'beautiful', more, 'serviceable'. She was long-limbed and had a tidy waist, which, with her tan jodhpurs, tended to enhance the contours of her bottom. She was one of those young women who had 'big-boned aristocracy' written all over them. Her features were at once large yet dainty. Her hands were as big as a man's yet the fingers were slim, giving the overall effect of elegance. Her bosom was heavy and full, something which favoured men friends had discovered with surprise for its real dimensions were overshadowed by the size of the chest it belonged to. Her voice was a mid tone of depth between effeminate man and masculine woman; the timbre of voice that could sound either sexy or jaded, depending upon the mood of the listener. And then there was her nose. The 'Harting Hooter' she wryly called it. Strong and angular, it projected from her face like the dorsal fin of a shark, unfairly drawing attention away from a mass of lustrous brown hair and a pair of prettily expressive grey green eyes. Eyes which sometimes misted with sadness when she reflected upon her chances of marriage now that she was twenty eight.

Richard heard the door open but did not turn from his easel. He had encountered unexpected difficulties in matching the tints for this painting.

'Ahoy there! What are you doing Boy?'

'Hello Nessie.'

'Just thought I would pop over and see how the Van Gogh of Wisdene Hall was getting along.' She kissed him on the cheek. 'So what are you doing?' She peered short-sightedly at the canvas. 'That looks good. Quite clever aren't you? But copying a picture? Unlike you, Boy. Where's your artistic originality? Still, I suppose it's easier than making it up yourself.'

'You could not be more wrong, Nessie old prune. It's the devil's job. If I were painting this for myself I would look at that brown there,' he shoved his palate at her, 'and be quite happy. But, it is not the brown that Monet used. See what I mean?'

'Who is going to know?' Vanessa sat on an ottoman.

'I am. And the light is not too good in this alcove. That's why I've had this brought in.' He waved at an angled standard lamp whose light he had directed onto the painting.

'Why don't you move the painting to the window?'

'Screwed to the wall.'

'Insurance regulations?'

'Safety. It's holding the Hall up.' He turned and looked at her. 'Oh I'll give up for now. Ring for coffee whilst I stow this easel.'

Vanessa rang the bell and then came and stood by Richard

whilst he closed his oils.

'You're serious about this Art aren't you Boy?'

'You know me Nessie, when I get serious about something.'

'Yes, I know you,' she said quietly. 'So why are you copying a painting?' She gestured at the folded easel with the canvas leaning against it on the parquet.

'Homework.' Richard smiled and his eyes at once sparkled with a boyish mischief. 'We... that is, my fellow students and I, each have to copy a painting by a well known Master. It is supposed to be good discipline for observation and instrumental in developing an appreciation of technique. So whilst the others swanned off to the National or the Tate I thought to myself, 'why not paint a Monet in the comfort of your own home?"

'You don't treat the Hall as your home much nowadays Boy.'

'Don't you start Nessie! You've known me too long.'

'A long time, Boy, but not too long I hope.'

'Drink your coffee and then–'

'Yes?' Vanessa raised one eyebrow knowing that it always made Richard laugh.

'And then you can help me find something for drawing class.'

'What kind of thing?'

'Something interesting to sketch. We take it in turns to bring along a prop for the model and then we all sit around in a circle and sketch.'

'How exciting!'

Richard looked sideways at her.

'You're taking the pi... mickey aren't you?'

'Richard!'

'The average age of the students in the class is about twenty. So it is frightfully important to bring along something avant garde, as a sort of personality statement.' Richard smiled wearily. 'Accompanying the human form, I have sketched an appliance which I believe was designed for toasting sandwiches, I have sketched an elephant's foot umbrella stand artistically garnished with plastic lilies and last week we decorated the poor fellow with two orange cones and a length of red and white striped ribbon stolen from the road works in the Kings Road and smuggled into college under cover of darkness.'

'Who sits for you?'

'Other students mostly. It adds to their pocket money.'

'Nude?' Vanessa asked, with an ostentatious, wide-eyed innocence.

'I understand, Miss Clewe-Harting, that we will be sketching the nude human form at some time in the future.'

She pursed her lips in mock disapproval. 'I see.' Then she surveyed the room. 'What were you thinking of taking, some Chippendale, Chinese Lacquer, Crown Derby or Rennie Mackintosh?'

'I knew I could rely upon you Vanessa.'

'What a fool!'

'You or me, Nessie darling?'

'Listen Boy. The lumber room. You still have that haven't you? Remember, where we used to play?'

The lumber room was a treasure cave for children and a nightmare for adults. Broken toys lay against grimy, framed ancestors, rolls of partly worn carpet were stacked like giant cigars and the whole was permeated by a dusty, forlorn, forgotten air.

Vanessa and Richard entered the room as adults but soon reverted to children – a reversion reinforced by their having to stoop slightly under the mansard.

'Oh heavens, my castle. I had forgotten all about that. Winston made it for me out of an old wooden box. Look you can see where it says *"Pratt's Motor Spirit"* on the inside.' He turned it over and a lead soldier dropped to the floor.

'What about Queen Sheba?' Vanessa wiggled her broad hips sensually at him. 'Remember the stone bench by the yew tree, the one we used for Queen Sheba's throne?' She twirled herself around in a length of curtain netting and then sneezed violently as the disturbed dust assailed her.

Richard laughed and picked up a wooden sword and made a few passing thrusts with it. 'Silly girls' games,' he said and then advanced upon her, swiping wildly with the sword. 'Away you dragon! St. George is never afeared! Unhand her!'

'Unhand? For a dragon?' She sneezed again.

'Unclaw her, then. Pedant!' He slipped the blade into her curtain and flipped it open. 'Ah my beauty. A bosom to die for.'

Vanessa shrugged off the gauze, reached up and opened two buttons of her shirt.

'For shame, sir, would you take advantage of a poor

serving wench?' She arched her back in provocation.

'I would.' Richard threw down the sword and placed his hands on her shoulders.

'Oh spare me sir!' she shrilled.

'Never!'

He pulled her shirt down in the true manner of a bodice-ripping lecher. Her firm breasts bounced up in their sensible sporty bra. He felt himself stirring in his trousers and thought it rather odd with Nessie, after so long. His gaze was drawn slowly from the rise and fall of her tanned bosom, up her neck, to her slightly parted lips. Those grey green eyes glinting with the same devilment that he could remember from long ago in the orchard. Without a word, she moved, her eyes holding him, their bodies closing hard. Her tongue found his in a frank and passionate kiss whilst his hands slid down her broad back to where the material of her jodhpurs was drawn tightly across her sturdy, horsewoman's buttocks. She shivered slightly to his touch, pressing into him and making his hardness kick into her.

'Don't women wear anything under jodhpurs nowadays?' he murmured as he explored the smooth curves of her bottom.

She hooked her thumbs in the back of his waistband and pulled him gently away.

'What women wear under jodhpurs, a man can discover for himself. What a lady wears under jodhpurs, no gentleman would ever raise in genteel society.'

He bent and gently kissed the top of each breast. 'We've come a long way since the orchard,' he said quietly.

She slipped her hands up to his shoulders. He could feel her powerful grip on his collar bone.

'You were the first, Boy.' A tinge of irony slowly invaded her smile. 'I've stumbled at a few fences since then, you know.' He nodded. 'There's only going to be one more jump for me now, Boy, and I've got to make sure I sail clean over it. No faults.'

'Oh come on Nessie, you're not on the–'

She put her finger to his lips. 'You wouldn't know, Boy. You're not shopping.' She pushed him with playful roughness. 'Now what do you want to draw?'

They staggered amongst the artefacts of their past, turning them over, holding them to the musty light, considering them; trying to imagine them in the centre of a studio drawing circle.

But the inspiration had left them.

'This is hopeless.' Richard said as he collapsed onto a leather portmanteau. 'I suppose I shall have to go out and steal a rubbish bin or some such thing.'

'Get up Boy,' Vanessa ordered him peremptorily.

'Slave driver.'

She ignored his moaning, unbuckled the leather straps and threw open the portmanteau. 'There you are,' she said. 'Perfect. This will make a change from sandwich toasters.' She lifted from the chest a ballgown of silver blue silk with a broderie anglaise bodice. She held it against her. 'What do you think Boy?'

Richard laughed. 'It looks like a tutu on you. It must have been Hattie's. She's the only midget in the family. Hey! I can't take all that, it will never fit in the car.' Richard eyed with alarm the bundles of pale blue net underskirt which Vanessa was pulling out of the depths.

'Oh you must have the underskirts, it gives the shape. See?' She draped it artistically across the yawning leather jaws of the chest.

'It looks like a hippopotamus eating a meringue. Still, as you say, it's better than a toaster. Bring it down and I'll see if John can find a grip that will take it.'

'And so Rupert...'

'Who?' Jennifer interrupted.

'Rupert Tort. The Honourable Rupert Tort, I should say. You know, I told you, son of Lord Tort.'

'Yes of course,' Jennifer said quickly. She always found it difficult to follow Ruth's accounts of the goings-on of the upper classes. She listened to the clacking of Ruth's high heels on the pavement and wished herself already in college.

'...He jumped up on the table and took two mandarins and a banana–'

'Mandarins? Where did he get the mandarins from?'

'From the fruit bowl. They have everything at the Savoy.'

'Oh.'

'...and he stuffed them down the front of his trousers.'

'Why?' Jennifer was mystified. She only ever half listened to Ruth.

'Two mandarins and a banana,' Ruth repeated as if the very

emphasis would provide elucidation. 'Think of them. Down the front of his trousers. Two mandarins and a banana. And he did a little dance. Very suggestive.' She giggled.

'It sounds as if your cousin doesn't need paying for working at the Savoy with all the free entertainment she gets.'

Ruth was about to reply when the sharp rapping of a coin on a shop window attracted their attention. It was that rather nice man from the first day. What was his name? Richard? Through the coffee bar window she could see him at a table, lounging casually in a green wax jacket and check shirt as if he had just come out of the woods.

'Ah, your friend Richard,' Ruth said. 'And he's calling us in to join him. Come on.'

'Oh Ruth, I can't be bothered... Ouch!' Jennifer jumped as Ruth pinched her forearm where it was hidden by her bag and propelled her firmly towards the door.

'He's going to buy us both coffee,' Ruth smiled through gritted teeth, 'and that will warm you up. I'm fed up of hearing you complain about being cold.'

It was purely by chance that Richard had been sitting by the window of that particular café. He had not quite got the hang of the Underground yet and when he found that he had arrived too early, he decided to kill time in a local café.

He smiled to himself as he watched Ruth protectively take her little friend's arm and steer her to the door. Ruth was wearing a dark raincoat which was swinging, unbelted, to show a brown woollen skirt and mustard coloured high necked top, set off by a string of pearls. Jennifer had tucked her golden brown mane inside her anorak, wound around her neck like a scarf. He could see where she had neatly repaired the tear in her jeans.

He stood up. 'Good morning Jennifer. Good morning Ruth. Please join me for coffee. Little Jennie looks frozen.'

'Jennifer,' Jennifer growled but for some intangible reason he found himself affecting not to notice.

Ruth quickly slipped onto the bench, leaving Jennifer the chair opposite.

'This is cosy.' She smiled. He could feel the warmth of her hips against his. 'My little hands are frozen. Feel those.' She put the backs of her hands on his cheeks and he held them there momentarily. Breathing in, he could smell the perfume on her wrists.

'Coffee, Ruth?' She nodded. 'Jennie?'

'It's Jennifer. My name is Jennifer not Jennie.' She scowled at him.

He pulled a face at Ruth. 'Right, Jennifer,' he said carefully. 'Would you like a coffee?'

'No thank you.'

'Two more coffees please miss,' he called to the waitress.

'I said I didn't want one... Dick.'

'I didn't believe you. And my name is Richard.'

'Oh touché,' Ruth said tartly. 'Don't mind her she got out of bed on the wrong side this morning.' She turned towards him, the movement was slight but served to highlight the other girl's isolation. 'What did you do at the weekend Richard?'

'I painted.' He stole a glance at Jennifer. She was trying hard to disregard Ruth's body language and she was not altogether succeeding. He casually laid his arm along the back of the bench behind Ruth. 'Us beginners have to copy a Master – I expect you've had to do it.' Ruth looked blank. Jennifer looked out of the window. Richard looked at Ruth. 'So I decided on Monet.'

'Monet? Of course we don't have much to do with... er...'

'"The Impressionists," is what you are trying to say I think Ruth,' Jennifer prompted as she dragged a wiggly finger through the condensation on the window.

'I know,' Ruth said sharply. 'So you spent all weekend in a gallery? I didn't realise they let students in to paint at the weekends.'

'Well no, actually, I am very lucky I didn't have to go to a gallery, we've actually got a...' He stopped. They had both turned to look at him curiously. He suddenly realised that he was on dangerous ground. 'We've got an acquaintance who has a... or, rather, has access to a Monet. Privately, that is.' He laughed easily. 'Well he says it's a Monet anyway. I am sure Dr. Sullivan will not mind. What did you do Ruth?'

Jennifer sat back and played idly with the teaspoon in her coffee as Ruth began to recount how she had stayed with her cousin at the Savoy, being careful to avoid mentioning that her cousin was a domestic and that she had slept on the floor of her room, strictly against house rules. She watched him devouring

Ruth with his eyes and knew that Ruth was loving it. Once, to emphasise a point, his hand rested briefly on her shoulder, a movement which drew them momentarily closer together. Jennifer watched Ruth as she accompanied her speech with studied graceful movements, fiddled coyly with her pearls and leaned her head briefly on his shoulder to laugh easily at some inanity he had no doubt just uttered.

Jennifer knew that her own movements were like a startled sparrow most of the time, she could not dress them up; she did not possess a string of pearls and if she had, she would probably have either broken it or pawned it by now. She laughed to herself – if she tried to lay her head on Richard's shoulder she would need to kneel on the seat.

So, Richard had an acquaintance who could get access to a Monet, had he? How Ruth would love that!

And what should she say if he asked her what she had done at the weekend? 'Spent Friday evening at the launderette, queuing for everything and they still hadn't found my blue sock. Saturday morning I went down to the vets to get some pills for Sandy, trod in some dog shit on the way back and walked it all through the house and into my room; spent two hours cleaning and disinfecting the carpet so that the house then smelled of pine and dog shit; went to the supermarket on the corner just before it closed to get the reductions before the weekend; helped Cherryl wash and set her hair although, heaven knows, she has far less hair than I have; messed around with some fabric colours whilst trying to decide what to eat...' She sighed. She supposed she would have to admit to this. 'Went out to the phone box and called up Colin and asked him if he was doing anything; went to the pictures and spent most of the time with my hand in front of my eyes; found that when I went to bed I then had nightmares; slept badly and got up grumpy; slummed about in my pyjamas all morning; ate some cold rice pudding out of a can whilst watching an old black and white film on the telly...'

But she knew she was safe. He would not ask her. She looked at groomed Ruth and began to pick absent-mindedly at the top seam on her jeans.

'Ruth. We ought to be going.' Ruth looked at her watch. 'Thanks for the–'

'I'll come with you.' He got up. 'I should have left ages ago.'

Ruth and he walked side by side down the street, talking and laughing about something or other. Jennifer trailed behind, trying to avoid stepping in the dog mess.

'You should have seen her!' Cherryl dangled her bare feet from Jennifer's bed and listened open-mouthed. 'It was revolting,' Jennifer continued. 'She was all over him.'

'Some girls are like that.' Cherryl bit at her piece of toast and brushed the resulting crumbs onto the counterpane.

'And then, of course, after he had asked her out she was even more unbearable. They're only going to the Corot Retrospective at the RA.'

'The what?'

'They're only going to look at pictures. Honestly Cherry, you would think that they were going to Ascot the way she went on. "What shall I wear? Is my frilly black blouse too much for a first date? Should I get some higher heels?"'

'Why?'

'Why what?' Without waiting for clarification Jennifer leaped from the chair and yanked the grill pan out. The toast was burning with lazy flat yellow flames. She puffed them out. 'I can scrape it a bit.'

'Why did she need higher heels?'

'Are you burning the house down Miss Pye?' Mrs. Crowther's voice warbled up the stairs.

Jennifer pulled open the door. 'Just a piece of toast Mrs. Crowther,' she called down. 'Nothing to worry about. Sorry.' She closed the door. 'She must have a nose like a smoke detector.'

Cherryl fished in the drawer for a knife and began to scrape the toast over the sink. 'So what is he like then?'

'Oh you know... Nothing much. Ruth goes for anything in trousers.'

'I'll even go for them without their trousers,' Cherryl declared boldly. 'So?'

Jennifer took the denuded slice of toast. 'I haven't really noticed him.'

'Oh.' Cherryl could have been disappointed but it was hard to tell from the tone of that one syllable. 'What colour hair?'

'Brown.'

'Short?'

'Down to his collar. Masses of it. Untidy, like artists are supposed to be.'

'Is he short? I meant.'

'No. No he's not. He looks to be over six feet. But then everybody looks over six feet to me.'

'Eyes?'

'Two.' Cherryl pulled a face and threatened to stab her with a shard of toast. 'Brown,' Jennifer said quickly. She thought of Richard in the corridor on the first day. 'Always looks lost.'

'Hands?'

'Nice nails. Looks after them. He touches people when he talks to them.'

'Voice?'

'Very nicely spoken, you know. Not *fraightfully* posh but definitely upper class.'

'Snobbish?'

'No. Not at all.' She smiled to herself. 'You should have seen Ruth's face when he first came over to our table in the refec. She had been flashing her thighs, as usual and thought he was coming to talk to her. But he just wandered over and said "hello" to me. And he dresses well. Cor! I think Daddy might be well off. His clothes are good. You know? Really good. Not showy, but well made.' Jennifer hugged her knee and gazed into space.

'So you didn't really notice him at all then?' Cherryl observed shrewdly. 'Do you fancy him?'

'No I do not!' Jennifer snapped.

'Thought you did,' was all Cherryl said.

She could be maddening sometimes.

EPISODE FOUR

'Can you put my dyes away Patsy? Be a darling! I've got to rush.' Jennifer slung her bag hastily over her shoulder, sweeping a bottle from the table top. 'Oh banisters!'

'Jennifer look what you've done!' Patsy was staring aghast at the pool of purple spreading across the tiles.

'Why does it always happen to me?' Jennifer pleaded. She dumped her bag on a cleared table and ran for the mop whilst Patsy made ineffectual dabs with paper towels to try to contain the perimeter. 'Whenever I am in a hurry...' Jennifer swabbed and squeezed into the bucket. '...whenever I need to be somewhere in a hurry, the Gods always conspire against me.

'You try to do too much at a time Jennifer, that's why.'

'Oh that's all I needed!' Jennifer moaned in dismay at the sight of the threads of purple being drawn up the frayed denim legs of her jeans.

'Oh dear!' Patsy felt as upset as Jennifer. She suspected that these were Jennifer's best jeans but then, suddenly, despite herself, she found herself laughing. 'You always wanted to be at the forefront of fashion, Jennifer. Everybody in college will want a pair of those when they see them.'

Jennifer stopped and stared at Patsy. It was so unlike her to make fun of somebody's misfortune. Then she found a ridiculous giggle bubbling up in her and she threw one arm around Patsy's neck and announced to the world, 'Jennifer Pye, fashion designer, took the world by storm with her invention of denim jeans with varicose veins!'

'Please choose your preferred papers according to your medium – pastels, ink, pencil, charcoal – whatever.'

Adrian Peene waved vaguely at the paper cupboard and scratched at his beard. His beard was one of his characteristics. The growth on the lower half of his face was abundant, profuse and widespread. It was one of those beards which did not move when the owner spoke, they had to speak through it. His mouth was small and his lips very red and surrounded as they were by an untidy tangle of black, when he spoke, the effect reminded Richard of a hungry fledgling in a hasty nest. Adrian Peene's other characteristic was his paunch. As a staunch supporter of real ale, he considered that the size of his gut was a totem in direct proportion to the depth of his beliefs and the height of his status in his chosen field. In order to maintain his prowess, he regularly 'slipped out' at lunchtime for what he called 'a swift half'. Such is the hyperbole of life that this operation was never swift and never involved half pints and yet convention admitted it as verity.

'What I would like you to do, Richard...' Richard stopped dragging his easel and waited. '...is to treat this as a sketch for painting.'

'I see.'

'You did say that you were interested in portrait painting didn't you? It was you?'

'Yes, it was me. So...' Richard thought back to the views expressed in one of Adrian's earlier tutorials, 'I should be using pencil and coding colours and shades, recording detail. Things like that. Not trying to produce a finished drawing.'

'Exactly, exactly.' Adrian turned to the class which was slowly metamorphosing into a ragged circle around a skinny girl in a tee shirt and camouflage trousers. 'Now class, choose your position but don't all work on top of each other. You can draw wherever you like, whatever you like, you don't have to get all of the model... er, Tracy is it?' The girl nodded. 'You don't have to get all of Tracy in your composition; you may choose head and shoulders, you may choose her left ear lobe but whatever you do, concentrate on a strong composition. And don't forget tonality. Very important.' He turned to Richard. 'You've brought along a prop for Tracy have you?'

'I have indeed.' He unzipped his enormous holdall and pulled out the ballgown. Several of the girls 'oohed' and 'aahed'.

'Ye...es,' Adrian said enthusiastically. He had never really espoused the philosophy of the traffic cones, but students will be students. This, however, was something different. Bit of a dark horse was Richard Ennessy. 'We should be able to do something with this.'

'It's a girl's party frock!' The scorn in Bob Priestman's voice was undisguised and rabid Yorkshire. 'You want us to draw a girl's frock?'

'Yes,' Richard said levelly. 'Unless you would prefer to do something else with it.'

'What do you mean? Eh? Eh? Just what do you mean?'

'Well I think it's a lovely idea,' said Mrs. Porter. 'Thank you Richard.'

'Ah'm asking him just what he meant.'

'Oh do grow up little man,' Richard muttered to himself as he pushed his holdall out of sight on top of the lockers.

'All right class, settle down, settle down.' Adrian pushed up the sleeves of his baggy jumper and wondered just what had got into the college this year. He had never had this sort of animosity in a drawing set. 'Think group dynamics' he said to himself. Group dynamics – that's what. 'Well Tracy, what can you do with that?'

Tracy picked up the ballgown by its delicate shoulder straps and held it at arm's length.

'Well I certainly can't wear it!' she snorted.

'No, no I wasn't thinking of that. More a sort of cameo arrangement or freeze-frame shot of you doing something with the dress,' Adrian suggested vaguely. 'Something you will feel comfortable with.'

Mrs. Porter could not resist leaving her easel to help her. She fussed around it, plumping it up and pulling it out and letting it drop.

'It really is lovely, Richard. What beautiful material!' Bob Priestman sighed heavily and began to tap his pencil on his stand. 'Where on earth did you get it from?'

'Well it's not mine,' Richard smiled pointedly at Priestman who bridled at the attention. 'Someone lent it to me. A lady.'

'Tracy, if we put the petticoats underneath to give it shape... we could bring that chair... Could somebody bring that chair over? Yes that one, thank you. And then...'

'And then I can stand at the side,' Tracy suggested, 'as if I have just... put it there. Sort of, just taken it out of the wardrobe and now I'm looking at it.'

'Yes... or...'

Richard adjusted his board up high. Then he laid out the small emery board which he used to sharpen up his pencils. He glanced over the board. Mrs. Porter and Tracy were still lifting up bits of net petticoat and trying to imbue them with a life or shape of some sort. Suddenly the door burst open and into the room hurtled a little bundle of energy. She spun around to slam the door and her long hair swung sharply and smacked hard against the woodwork.

'Sorry I'm late. I got held up.' Just as suddenly the fizz died. 'Oh, hello Tracy. You beat me to it.'

Adrian stepped forward. 'Can I help you miss?'

'Jennifer Pye. I phoned you about modelling for the drawing class.'

'Oh yes,' Adrian agreed vaguely. He looked at the legs of her jeans. She was obviously on a Fashion Design Course of some sort. He sighed. The things these students get up to in the name of fashion! 'I'm sorry Miss Pye. As you can see, we already have a model.'

'Yup. O.K.' She nodded. By getting there first, Tracy Winters had just done Jennifer out of a new pair of jeans – the fee for modelling would have provided that nicely. 'Well, if you need me...' She shrugged and looked around. 'Oh that is so lifeless!'

Mrs. Porter started in surprise. 'Well we thought that we had arranged it rather well. If you think you can do any better...'

Jennifer dropped her bag on the floor. 'Of course I can. That looks awful. Have you never dressed a window?'

'Well no, as a matter of fact.' Mrs. Porter managed to make window dressing sound like stealing from the offertory.

'Got any pins? You've flattened the life out of this...'

Jennifer stopped with her hand on the skirt. This was silk, she could recognise silk when she felt it.

'We've got some...'

'Shush!' she said irritably, 'I'm thinking.' She lifted the skirt and turned back the hem. She ran her little pointed fingers along the seam. Hand sewn silk, double stitched. Minute, even, perfect. She traced the design of the broderie with the balls of her fingers. Everybody in the room was still. Nobody spoke.

Absolute silence as they watched this diminutive girl examine the dress but she was completely unaware of this. She knew that this dress was no ordinary party frock. She gently pulled out the label: *'Christiane, rue St. Augustin, Paris.'* It must be worth a fortune.

'This is beautiful,' she breathed as she held it up. 'I've never touched anything so beautiful in my life.' They all looked at it. 'Where on earth did you get it?'

'Mr. Ennessy brought it,' Adrian said.

'S'only a frock! Tch. Women!' she heard a Yorkshire voice mutter somewhere in the background.

'It's not just a frock, Yorkie!' She bridled at such ignorant masculine jingoism. 'I bet this is the nearest you will ever get to Parisian couture of this quality.' Priestman opened his mouth to speak but the shock of being addressed as "Yorkie" by this slip of a girl had bottled up any crushing retort in his throat. 'Who is this Mr. Ennessy? I'd like to meet him some day,' Jennifer declared, half under her breath.

'No time like the present.' She vaguely recognised the voice from behind a drawing board. 'Hello Jennie.'

'You!'

'Richard Ennessy at your service ma'am.' He swept her a comic bow.

'My name is Jennifer, I've told you before.'

He smiled as if her correction did not matter. 'So you can dress windows can you?' His gaze fell briefly to her purple fringed trouser legs. The jeans she would not now be able to replace. 'New fashion?' he enquired.

She looked down and realised with dismay that the purple dye had even been drawn part way up one of the laces of her sneakers. She felt herself blushing at the contrast presented by his elegantly casual suede shoes. She tossed back her head.

'Well, I must go.' She was firm but his hand gripped her forearm to restrain her and she found herself looking up into those slightly mocking bown eyes.

'I've just had a brilliant idea.' The corners of his mouth were turning up slightly, giving him an impish air.

'Oh yes?' You and your brilliant ideas I can do without.

'Why don't you put it on? You must be just the right size.'

'Oh yes Jennifer, put it on.'

'Yes do, be a sport!'

She looked around her. Adrian was scratching his beard in bemusement, Tracy was carefully studying her fingernails, Mrs. Porter was nodding vigorous encouragement, various of the girl students' faces shone with a sort of expectation. And from his six feet plus, Richard Ennessy, as she now knew him to be, was smiling down at her with those clear, challenging eyes.

'I dare you,' he said and gave her arm a gentle squeeze.

Up came her chin. 'All right duck, I will!' She stuck out her tongue. 'Then you'll see me in all my beauty.'

She took the ballgown and walked towards the screens at the end of the room.

What am I doing? I shall make a laughing stock of myself. I should not have let him get at me like that. I'll show him. I'll show him. Thinks he can make a laughing stock of me, Huh! That's what he is hoping for. Better take my socks off, I can't wear sneakers with a ballgown. Oh God, have all my socks got holes in? Oh and flowered panties, don't they look daft with a dress like this? Thank goodness nobody can see. Step into the petticoats. Now the dress. This is some dress. Richard Ennessy has got interesting friends; private Monets, Parisian silk ballgowns.

'Do you need a hand?'

'Hi Tracy. Yes, could you zip me up? And for heaven's sake don't rip it.'

'There. Turn around.' Jennifer turned slowly. 'You know, it fits you like a glove.'

'Thanks poppet. Oh my hair! I can't leave it down like this, I shall look daft. Quick, give me that bulldog clip.' With several twists of the wrist, Jennifer wound her hair up into an impressive chignon and clipped it at the back with the sprung metal clasp. Then she stepped out from behind the screens.

Richard Ennessy stopped adjusting his paper on the easel. Somebody whistled, some clapped, but Richard Ennessy just looked. Jennifer acknowledged her public with a bow and an embarrassed grin.

'Well this is what it looks like with someone in it, folks.' She spun on her bare feet so that the skirts flew out and the gown showed its full exotic shape in shimmering silver blue silk icing on a cake of pale blue tulle. 'Satisfied?' She stopped and the skirt continued for half a swing and then surged back before her again.

'Oh lovely!' said Mrs. Porter.

Jennifer parodied a curtsey to Richard. He inclined his head and raised his pencil to her, mutely saluting her parody of his earlier insolence.

'Well I've got things to do,' she said.

'I wonder...' Adrian was surprised at the strength of authority in his own voice. 'I wonder if you would stay and model for us?'

'But you've got Tracy. She was here first. It's only fair.'

'No competition luv,' Tracy grimaced. 'But I'll race you next week.

'Oh well...' Jennifer turned, undecided, towards the chair in the circle. A new pair of jeans loomed on the horizon. 'I suppose–'

'Allow me,' a soft voice said and Richard Ennessy took her arm. 'It would be a pleasure.'

'Right,' said Adrian, 'I'd like you to arrange yourself...' But he stopped immediately when Richard held up his hand.

'I'll do it,' was all he said. 'I know how.'

Jennifer could feel his strong hand under her arm. He walked her to the chair as if they were crossing a dance floor. His movements were sinuous and flowing. She could feel the bulk of the underskirts moving against and between her legs. The sensation made her want to walk bow legged. However did they manage in real life? Would she ever know? He turned her and held the chair. Flouncing out the skirt, she sat down and waited. It was against all her instincts and desires and customs but somehow she knew that it was expected of her. He exuded that kind of authority. She could feel her heart pounding in the bodice as he bent his head towards her and a discreet waft of an expensive fragrance floated over her.

'Listen to me. You wanted to come to the ball,' he whispered instructions in her ear, his breath tickling her hair. 'You were forbidden to come to the ball...' She caught her breath. '...but you were not going to be beaten and so you came just the same.' She set her jaw. He glanced down at her bare feet. 'They tried to stop you by hiding your dancing shoes and so here you sit, serenely triumphant. You went to the ball but... nobody can ask you to dance because you have no shoes.'

Richard left her there and returned to his easel. Sketches for painting a portrait was what he required. He eased his bottom onto the stool, picked up a pointed 2B and looked over the board at her. It was not by chance that he had positioned her so that he had an unimpeded frontal view of her. His pencil flicked lightly across the paper.

The face. The most important part of any portrait was the face. Now matter how you arranged the model, no matter what he or she was doing, the viewer's eyes would always inexorably be drawn to the face.

A round face surmounted by a corkscrew bouffon of glowing hair like a steam pudding with golden syrup dripping down it. How had she managed to produce that effect so quickly? One minute her hair was swinging about like a syncopated pendulum, the next it was piled up like Marie-Antoinette's.

His pencil scratched on.

An open forehead supported by slightly curved eyebrows like the long open arches on the bridges over the Loire. Blue eyes, fulgent with a sad serenity and bolstered by cheeks of an English Rose pinkness. A small mouth with pale lips not quite covering the teeth.

He put the sheet aside and took a clean one.

Just a head portrait? He sat back and allowed his eye to run from her neck down to her bust. She certainly filled the gown better than Hettie ever would have done. It appeared to have been tailored on her. Head and shoulders perhaps?

His pencil began to quickly define the general sweep of her torso and his eyes lingered on the paradoxically soft curves of her firm breasts until he realised that he was no longer thinking of drawing. His eyes flicked guiltily to hers but she was not looking at him. Not at anybody.

Down as far as the waist might make a good frame.

His pencil dawdled over her abdomen as he watched the silk rhythmically filling and emptying with the movements of her diaphragm. It would be a pity not to include the waist for, unlike so many girls nowadays, she actually possessed one. And you cannot form a waist without drawing hips. And hips exaggerated by layers of underskirt would look silly chopped off at the knees.

Take it to the hem.

He smiled. He would have to go further than the hem. He would never forgive himself if he did not include those two bare feet, peeking cheekily out from under the mountain of haute couture.

So, a full length portrait then. He took a fresh sheet.

A composition with a hidden tension in it – perched as she is on the chair's edge. There's a story in it somewhere.

He looked at the clock. Tonality.

He defined the limits of the shades and coded them. The silver blue taking a greyish tinge in the shade; the top of the bust, glowing, underlighting the neck beneath the chin; shades of pink and ivory; so discreet, so gentle, so English. And everything genuine. Not a trace of make-up or lipstick or mascara.

Jennifer Pye is the real Mc.Coy.

New sheet. Back to the face. Must get that expression on paper. Absolutely imperative. He looked deep into the sadness in her eyes but she did not notice. She was at the ball. She could see the couples swirling around, the gowns shining in the chandelier light, she could hear the music, but she could not dance. The frustration had brought her to the front of the chair but she must not let anybody see her disappointment. She must appear happy and contented. Nobody must know how sad she was inside. You cannot dance in bare feet.

Arthur Northgate shuffled on his stool and the creaking resounded around the gallery until it was lost within its own echo. He examined the girl again. Something was wrong. She was holding her head. Perhaps he should ask her if she was alright. She looked a mite pale, probably not eating enough. That was the trouble with these girls nowadays. They'd starve themselves to death just to get into a size smaller clothes. Might just be a headache. She could get aspirin and such things from the shop at the entrance if she needed them. He'd tell her if she asked.

Magdaline O'Neil noticed the attendant looking at her so she smiled to convince him that she was alright. Then she moved along to the next picture. She should not be doing this. She should stop now. She pushed the balls of her fingers into the top of her forehead, hiding her face from the attendant and massaging hard into the throbbing. She knew that what she was doing was probably exactly what the doctor had told her not to do. But she had to know. They could not imagine what it was like for her. She was sure that she was near to the answer. She drew her hands slowly apart and looked through them as if they were a curtain parting.

She felt sure that it was the same girl as was in the ballgown. It had to be. But now she was reclining on a red velvet drape in a classical pose which had her propped up on one elbow, turning her nude back to the artist. Despite the nudity, her modesty was assured by a ruck of velvet which providentially fitted snugly up into the hollow between her lower buttocks.

Magdaline O'Neill allowed her eye to follow the curve of the girl's spine, down her back, down between her plumpish buttocks and along her thighs to her ankles. She squinted at the suggestion of the profile of her face. If only the artist had painted her front instead of her back.

It had to be the same girl! In the ballgown, her hair was drawn up in a bun and now it was hanging loose down her back, but it was the same glorious colour. Was that the same curve on the cheek? Difficult to be absolutely certain. And yet...

'Now that's interesting,' Richard said.

'What is, Richard?' Ruth was finding Corot hard going. She squeezed his arm a little too much and pulled herself closer to him. Men liked that.

Richard tried faintly to disregard the gentle pressure of her bust on his chest.

'The Belfry of Douai,' he indicated the painting. 'I always thought that the point about old Jean Baptiste–'

'Who?'

'Corot. I thought that the point about his paintings was that they were flat. He did not use perspective.'

'Oh.'

'Not that I know much about landscapes. But there is definite perspective in the Belfry of Douai isn't there? Look at that street.'

'Well...' Ruth floundered. Richard looked at her. She was pretty, she was sexy, she looked good, she made a man feel like a million pounds and yet... He threw her a lifeline smile.

'I did promise you tea didn't I? How remiss of me. You must be fainting for lack of sustenance.'

'I could murder a cup of coffee.'

Ruth had only felt moderately nervous when he had met her outside the refectory after the lunch break. She had decided that her black blouse was too much for a first date and far too dressy for her to attend college so she was wearing an austere two-piece in greyish tweed over a dark brown jumper which, she felt, set off her eyes to their best. She had loitered there, trying not to look as if she were waiting for someone, until suddenly his warm voice had said 'Hello Ruth' in her ear and made her jump like a silly girl. And there he was, leaning casually against the notice board and grinning at her. When he ran his hand through his hair his jacket parted slightly and Ruth was quick to recognise a tailor's label from Savile Row and an exquisitely cut casual shirt.

She knew that the Royal Academy was in Piccadilly because Jennifer had shown her the nearest tube station on a map but Richard Ennessy had calmly walked her up to Sloane Square and taken a taxi from the rank. Perhaps it was this that had made her a little nervous, she was not sure.

He was attentive to her as she expected any man to be but she somehow could not get onto his wavelength. It was almost as if he considered her conversation to be just inconsequential chatter. He had shown a polite interest when she had pointed out the Queen's jewellers to him and the private hospital where Prince Charles had undergone his operation but she had been quietly upset by his discreet refusal to be impressed by the catalogue of important and influential people whom she had met whilst helping in her mother's charity work. This ired her to the point where, contrary to the good judgment which had served her so well in the past, she found herself embroidering her social tapestry heavily. It was more galling to Ruth for she knew in truth that although she could talk about 'Nigel this' and 'Lady Sarah that', the intimacy implied by her form of address just did not exist; the people themselves had no idea whom she was. It was all so unfair. She was as good as they were. It was only an accident of birth that put them there.

'It's a bit chilly isn't it?' she remarked. It was not particularly cool but having said it, she was able to then hold his arm and cuddle closer to him as they walked from the Royal Academy into Piccadilly. Must not let him forget she was there. Keep up the pressure.

He looked at her with surprise. He was obviously not cold at all but she noted with some satisfaction that he did not move away from her. He must quite like her being close to him like this.

'Where would you like to have coffee?' he asked.

Where to have coffee? They walked along, Ruth dragging him to a halt from time to time to look in a shop window and he acquiescing with gallant good grace. Where to have coffee?

'So?' he asked. 'Any preference for coffee?'

'Oh I don't know.' Ruth decided to be outrageous. 'Let's go to somewhere swish.'

'Hmm.' Then his brown eyes twinkled at her. 'I know just the place. Come on.' He grabbed her hand and started to run.

'Oh Richard, stop! Stop! I can't run in these shoes.' Ruth hung on, desperately trying to keep her high heels on her feet as she clattered along the pavement.

He stopped under an arcade and she leaned against a pillar to regain her breath. He moved close to her. This is it, she thought, he's going to kiss me. Me, panting like a greyhound and my hair all over the place and he chooses this time to kiss me. Some Lochinvar! She closed her eyes. She could sense that he was looking at her.

'My, you are out of trim!' he observed facetiously. She opened her eyes in surprise. 'Recovered?' She nodded. 'Is this swish enough for coffee?' He took her arm and led her past the uniformed doorman into the chandelier-hung hallway.

Christ! It's the Ritz. What does he think he is doing? You can't just walk into the Ritz and ask for a cup of coffee. Can you? The man there, I suppose he is the hall porter or something, is showing us over to the room at the left. Potted plants, crystal chandeliers and suddenly we have a table. He is holding the chair for me.

'Richard. Are you mad? This is the Ritz.'

'So it is. It will have to do, I couldn't find a MacDonald's.'

'I've always wanted to go into somewhere like the Ritz.' She realised her mistake as soon as she had uttered it.

'So have I,' Richard smiled at her.

She stretched her arm across the table and laid her hand on his. 'You must be mad!' she said. But she was smarting within. So he thinks I normally spend my time in MacDonald's does he?

Richard was beginning to wonder whether or not he was a little bit mad. Across the other side of the room he had just recognised Harry Chatham, a professional who ran a successful series on television for golfers. Richard had occasionally been teamed up with him to play golf when they had been at school together in Westminster. Richard had never liked either golf or Chatham but more importantly, the last thing that he wanted now was to be recognised. He suddenly realised his stupidity in bringing Ruth into an area where his two worlds could overlap.

The waitress was approaching.

'What kind of coffee would you like, Ruth?'

'Er... black, no sugar.'

Richard opened his mouth to speak but the waitress smoothly devanced him.

'We have Colombian, Kenyan, Blue Mountain...'

'I think you prefer the Kenyan don't you Ruth?' Ruth nodded gratefully. 'And the same for me, and er... bring a selection of sandwiches please.'

Ruth knew that she was blushing under her make-up. She felt like an ignorant country cousin, not the suave, well travelled socialite she aspired to. How could she be expected to know that he meant 'what blend of coffee' did she want? And how did he know that the waitress would offer all those coffees? He just gave her the order as if he had been coming to the Ritz all his life. Well two can play at that game. She gazed casually around the room, noting the potted palms, the chandeliers, the mirrors. Then her eyes alighted triumphantly upon a figure in the corner behind Richard. She would wait for the right moment.

'I didn't know that Harry took tea at the Ritz,' she observed casually. See what you make of that.

Richard gulped his coffee.

'Do you know Harry Chatham?' That's all I need.

'He's a friend of my mother's. Taught her to play golf.'

That's shaken him a bit and it's not exactly untrue. Harry Chatham showed Mum how to putt at a charity fete once.

'Really? I didn't know that he did private tutoring.'

'Well he doesn't really... but as a special favour to my mother, you know how these things are.'

Richard raised his eyebrows and said nothing. This was a side of Harry Chatham that he was ignorant of.

Warning signs had begun to ring in Ruth's head. She took a sandwich from the proffered plate and occupied herself with it whilst she thought quickly. Some little detail had been niggling her from the moment that she had mentioned Harry Chatham to Richard and now, with a sickening lurch, it slipped ominously within her grasp: when she had called his attention to Harry, Richard had already known without turning around that Harry Chatham was sitting behind him over on the far side of the room. How had he known? To recognise someone by the back of their head, the instant you enter a room, implies a certain intimacy. With a stultifying dread, Ruth glanced over Richard's shoulder. Harry Chatham was striding towards them.
'D'Ennessy!'
'Oh hello Chatham.'
Just my luck.
'Bit of a *rara avis* in this habitat, D'Ennessy.'
'Yes, look I think you know Ruth Robey.'
'Can't say that I–.'
'Ruth Robey. You coached Mrs. Robey. When was it Ruth?'
Ruth froze speechless in her chair.
'Me?! Coaching? Got the wrong Harry, old boy! Not my line of business at all.'
'Sorry. I thought you two knew each other. Another sandwich, Ruth?'

EPISODE FIVE

'Are you sure this will be alright Jennifer?' Cherryl's anxiety was puckering her brows.

'No.'

'Oh.' She watched with a delicious horror as the orange dye settled in a pool in the baking sheet on the floor. 'Only I was thinking that Mrs Crowther might be upset if... if...'

'If her lamb chops turned out bright orange? She won't know. It won't stain steel.' Jennifer straightened up from the floor and cast a critical eye over the trayful of orange liquid. 'That should do it. Now for the jeans.'

'Keith says that—'

'Keith?'

'You know, Keith,' Cherryl insisted.

'Assistant manager, Sainsbury's?'

'Safeways. Keith says that everything stains steel. There is no such thing as stainless steel. At the supermarket they have fridges and meat benches and they are always having to scrub them to get them clean.'

Jennifer listened cross-legged on the floor and began to pull at the hem that she had previously unpicked.

'How is it going with you and Keith then?' She had not heard any sobbing in the bathroom since Cherryl had been going out with him. That had to be an improvement. 'Is he treating you right?'

'He's a real gentleman,' Cherryl affirmed.

'Has he kissed you yet?'

''Course he has! 'Did that in the car park on our first date.'

'What else?'

'Don't be nosey, Miss Nosey Parker,' Cherryl scolded her and then sighed. 'No, not yet,' she added quietly. 'He's very mature.

Very considerate. Always opening doors and things and he looks very serious sometimes. Don't you think it's nice going out with somebody with a bit of maturity?'

Jennifer thought briefly of Colin, popcorn and Vincent Price.

'Yes, I imagine it is.' She looked at the frayed leg of jeans in her lap. 'Decision time,' she announced bravely.

'Oh Jennifer I am worried for you. Are you sure you want to do this? Look you could stop now and just wear them as they are. What will you do if it doesn't work?'

'Cry.'

'I'll cry with you lovey.'

Richard had done his best. He stood back from the easel and studied the canvas. It was the nearest to Monet that he could get. He had left his painting up there for several days and had returned to it from time to time to inspect it in different lights. He drank the coffee slowly from his beaker and at the same time his eyes drank in his version of *Les Arbres à Toten*. From his hi-fi, a Mozart symphony provided a discreet acoustic background. He smiled wryly. It should have been Grieg, of course, not Mozart, for the Trees at Toten had been painted by Monet in Norway and had been bought from him by Richard's grandfather during a visit to France in the twenties.

Here in his flat Richard had not, of course, got the original to refer to and so he had disciplined himself to resist the urge to alter or titivate any part of his version. He carefully lifted the canvas down and slotted it into its carrying case. Today was the day when the students had to submit their work.

He could not but help feel a little nervous for in his group there was some undoubted talent. Alison Barrett, the girl who looked like a saluki, had emerged as a budding sculptress; her thin, fine fingers shaping clay into remarkably accomplished likenesses of other members of the group and Bob Priestman was concealing behind his aggressive Yorkshire chauvinism a deep and knowledgable love of architecture. His pencil study of the dome of St. Paul's which had fallen from his portfolio one day had been pounced upon and pored over by Dr. Sullivan with an enthusiasm which had made the Yorkshireman blush to the roots of his red hair. Richard wondered whether he had any talent himself or whether it was merely a case of his being lucky.

He wandered through to the kitchen and dropped the beaker into the sink. It was time to go. He took a canvas from its position against the wall and gently placed it on the easel ready for when he came home. This was his relaxation; it amused him. The face was completed but the rest was still only an outline. He felt a special thrill at having captured that melancholy expression. His sketching must have been quite accurate after all. What was her name? Pye, that was it. Jennie Pye, the barefooted dancer. No no! Not Jennie. Jennifer Pye. He remembered her touchiness with a grin.

'See you later Jennifer.'

He threw her a mocking salute as he left down the stairs with his imitation Monet.

The room was buzzing nervously as the students laid out their works with a certain amount of self consciousness. In muted tones, in ragged groups, they appraised each other's efforts whilst awaiting Dr. Sullivan's scrutiny.

Dr. Sullivan was pleased to note that the standard overall was good and in some cases it was excellent.

'Tell me why you chose this particular Turner, Kirstine,' he prompted a girl with long black hair and tight black jeans. 'Was it the dreamlike mix of colour he uses or...?'

'Yer what?' Kirstine stalled on her chewing gum. 'It was the one nearest to the loo. It's freezing in that place, real brass monkeys.' She nodded confirmation to herself and kickstarted her chewing.

'Quite, quite,' Dr. Sullivan muttered and passed on. He had learned long ago to judge students only on their work. Whichever reason had nudged Kirstine it was in fact, irrelevant, for he would never understand it and in any case, the realisation of her work was competent.

He had been looking at student's work now for as many terms as he could remember and had long ago given up the expectation that he would ever be surprised. Rather like the lecturers who could quote from the standard works verbatim and give the page number and who could recognise all the references used by their students without flicking to the bibliography or footnotes, so Dr. Sullivan knew every piece of art that was likely to come his way in this exercise. He could almost predict what they would produce.

Sometimes the proportion changed but the general effect was always the same. Yes, he knew them all.

Except for this one. An impressionist, by the look of it. At first sight rather sombre and bleak. Trees, lots of brown and black. Sinister looking water. Assuming it is not a practical joke, this makes me look rather ignorant.

'That's a painstaking work Richard.'

A useful innocuous comment; should give me a lead.

'I'm sorry?' Richard turned away from appreciating Mrs. Porter's attempt at a Gainsborough to give Dr. Sullivan his attention. He had not been following his progress around the room for he had surprised himself to discover that he had a genuine interest in the other students' achievements.

'Your painting. You prefer oils always? Do you never use acrylics?'

'Monet used oils so I felt myself obliged to do likewise but yes, I do prefer oils.'

'Of course.'

Monet? Monet? I don't know of a Monet even remotely resembling this. It does look like his technique though. I think our smooth Mr. Ennessy has been fooled. I shall have to commit myself.

'I don't know the work Richard...'

'*Les Arbres à Toten*, if you will excuse my French accent, it means "The Trees at Toten".'

'Thank you,' Dr. Sullivan said drily. 'And where did you find it? Which gallery? I have to confess myself stumped on this one.'

Stewart Griffin, the aspiring art historian, sidled over to inspect the painting, a discreet move which brought him into the circle of the conversation.

Richard thought quickly. Could he use the same subterfuge as he had used for Ruth and little what's-her-name... Jennifer? They were perhaps more easily diverted than Dr. Sullivan would be. Worth a try though.

'It is not in a gallery,' he said carefully.

'You cannot have copied that from a print. And in any case, that is not the point of the exercise.' Dr. Sullivan tried not to sound sententious.

'Oh no, it was from the original but it was not in a gallery, it was... in a friend's house.'

Dr. Sullivan's eyebrows rose in surprise and two or three more students began to congregate, sensing a scandal. 'In a friend's house?' He left the expression hanging for Richard to embellish. 'Well, a friend of my parents,' Richard specified easily. 'I don't know them that well but they were quite happy for me to copy it.'

'And they said it was a Monet?'

'Oh yes, there's absolutely no doubt of that. Apart from the signature, they know it is a Monet.'

'Intriguing.' Dr. Sullivan looked again at Richard's painting. 'It certainly is in his style but the colours; brown, black, so dark and brooding, they are not what I think of as typical Monet.' Richard said nothing. 'Toten?' Dr. Sullivan read.

'I believe it is in Norway.'

'Ah yes...' Dr. Sullivan sighed vaguely. He knew details of the lives of most of the painters whose works he had encountered but somehow could not see Monet in Norway.

'I suppose it is a Monet?' Stewart Griffin asked as he peered intensely through his spectacles at the canvas.

'What's going on?' someone said at the back of the group.

'Questioning Richard's painting. They don't think it's a real Monet.'

'I can assure you that it is,' Richard said quietly.

'I was wondering,' Stewart Griffin was trying to develop his art historian's nose, 'whether it was a forgery.'

'Well...' Dr. Sullivan said, 'it could be what we call an "in the style of".'

'It was signed by Monet and I have every reason to believe the owners.'

This could become a little unsavoury, Dr. Sullivan thought. 'Whatever the credentials of the work, the important factor for our assessment is your representation of it and I am very satisfied with the execution of it.'

'Thank you, Doctor.'

'Only, I was thinking that if it was "in the style of" but signed, *"Monet"*, that would make it a forgery,' Stewart Griffin concluded with enthusiasm. 'And then—'

'Thank you Stewart,' Richard laughed easily, 'You will make a superb art bloodhound I am sure.'

'Yes well, I was only trying to help.'

'I know,' Richard said gently. 'I know. Thank you.'

Jennifer did not need Horny Harry standing behind her whilst she was bending over the screen running the squeegee over it. She was aware of her bottom sticking out and guessed that he was waiting for her to take an unexpected step backwards into him. Dirty old man, but he did know all there was to know about silk screen printing. He was still a dirty old man. Well if he wants an unexpected move he will get one. She transferred the squeegee to her left hand and pivoted away from the screenbed on her right foot.

'Oops! Awfully sorry Harry! Didn't know you were there!' She solicitously pulled the dripping squeegee away from his chest.

Harold Menton gasped in shock. This was just too much to take for a middle-aged lecturer like him. One minute he was dreaming about what he would like to do to her gorgeous bum in those jeans and the next he was staring aghast at the canary yellow sausage imprinted on his polyester shirt.

'What the hell do you–?'

'I said I was sorry. You shouldn't have been standing so close. Anyway, you always make us wear an apron. Why don't you?'

'Well I don't expect... Oh for Heaven's sake, it's dripping on my shoes now!' He skipped backwards and impaled himself painfully on the iron handle of a guillotine. 'Oh! Just... just carry on class for the moment.' With an exasperated grunt, he strode angrily from the workshop.

The door banged behind him and an ironic cheer sounded from all corners of the shop.

'Brilliant, Jennifer, brilliant!' The tall masculine girl clapped her on the back. 'I wish I had the guts.'

'He's been asking for it for weeks; dirty old lecher,' another girl said.

Jennifer dropped the offending weapon into a plastic bucket and grinned wickedly.

'I suppose I could branch out into shirts as well,' she laughed to Patsy. 'I'm just going to nip along the corridor with these jeans for Esther.' She untied her hair from under her cap and let it fall down her shirt.

'Oooh let's see them.' Jennifer dragged a plastic carrier bag out from under the bench and pulled out a pair of jeans. The bottom of the legs were fringed in bright orange in a random pattern which crept up the legs where she had teased the cloth apart prior to dyeing them. 'Fantastic!' Patsy enthused, 'You are clever, Jennifer.'

Jennifer leaned over and gave her a peck on the cheek.

'It was your idea, duck, not mine.'

She had sold the other pair before lunch to a girl in the first year and as soon as she got the money from Esther for this pair, she would have made enough profit to be able to buy herself something decent to wear. Or... she could use the money to buy another five pairs, dye and sell those and that would give her enough for twelve or thirteen pairs and then she could sell those... She hummed to herself in the corridor as the progression began to indicate a possibility of astronomical wealth.

The clay exasperated Richard. He could not believe that any medium could be so devious. He could not understand why he was able to control paint on a brush but not clay in his hand. He just could not understand clay. His pot collapsed onto the wheel where it lurched like a drunken flamenco dancer on a round-about. He combed his hand through his hair leaving another streak of clay to stiffen and whiten in time.

Alison Barrett moved over and stood beside him as he frowned in despair at the wobbling blob.

'I can't get the hang of this, you know Alison, I just can't,' he admitted. She gave a nervous little laugh. 'Got any ideas?'

She sucked her bottom lip and looked for all the world as if her pale thin face were going to break into uncontrollable sobbing.

'Try it this way,' she said and stamped on the switch. They waited whilst the wheel slowed to a stop. She scraped the wheel clean and then scooped out another handful of clay from the bin. She stepped on the switch again and waited for the wheel to gather speed whilst her hands worked the mass confidently into a ball. 'Are you right handed?' she asked.

'Yes.'

'So am I. Try throwing with your left. You've got less control so you just aim and let the weight of the clay do the work.' She chopped her left hand down and released the ball. It thudded onto the middle of the wheel.

'Bullseye!' Richard said. 'Well done!'

Alison blushed. 'You try,' she said, glancing up at him. Then she started to giggle. Blushing deeper at her boldness she exclaimed, 'Have you seen what you look like with that clay in your hair?' Then she put her hand to her mouth as if to stop the words from coming out.

Her sudden burst of uncharacteristic intimacy surprised Richard but when he caught sight of the reflection in the oven door of the spiky white locks which had been his brown hair, he smiled.

'I think I'll just go and tidy myself up.' He stepped into the corridor and gasped as the breath was nearly knocked out of him.

'If you drove like that, they would take your licence away!' a familiar voice scolded him as he bounced off the door jamb. 'Why can't you look where you're going?'

It was that Jennifer girl again. He opened his mouth to respond but she had the breath and he did not.

'My, my, Mr. Ennessy isn't it?' She peered grotesquely at his hair. 'The Einstein look! What is it – the latest fashion?'

'I...'

'Close your mouth duck, you'll scare the little children.'

His jaw closed with thoughtful slowness as he watched her hair swinging saucily across her receding back.

Dr. Sullivan relished the free periods in his timetable. They seemed to him like stolen time; a time when he could relax and tinker with the little jobs that somehow never seemed to get done otherwise.

He sat with his feet up on the staff room table as he flipped through the directory and sucked noisily on his empty pipe.

'Good God! The Doctor reading a book!' a lanky man exclaimed flippantly as he sprang through the doorway.

'At least I can, Battersby.'

'No need to flaunt your newly acquired skill. I'll keep it quiet for you.'

'What do you know about Monet?' Dr. Sullivan asked.

'Foreign chap who painted water lilies. Obsessed with them wasn't he? Hmm. I suppose it was because underneath it all, he could not escape from the feeling that he was a Frog.' Battersby wafted across to Dr. Sullivan's shoulder and peered at the book.

'Oh ho! Small writing as well. You are doing well.' Battersby snatched up a cardboard box and made for the door.

'I'm surprised you have lived so long, Battersby,' Dr. Sullivan threw at the swinging door.

He closed the volume and put it none too gently onto the table. The Trees at Toten had eluded him completely. He closed his eyes, interlocked his fingers above his head and cracked the joints noisily. 'And that will probably give me arthritis,' he added gloomily. 'Come!' he shouted at the knock on the door. It was Stewart Griffin.

'Could you spare me five minutes Dr. Sullivan? It's about Richard Ennessy's Monet.' He was grasping some untidy papers in his hands.

'Ah, the mysterious Monet. Yes, come in.'

He closed the door carefully behind him.

'I've been doing a bit of sleuthing. It's good practice for me,' he explained in case Dr. Sullivan thought him a little unkind.

'So have I,' Dr. Sullivan pointed at the book on the table, 'I cannot find it in his list of works; it's not in the Jeu de Paume, it's not in the Met., it's not in Boston, it's not in the Marmottan, and it isn't in Chicago. I suppose it could be in a private collection. Not that I doubt Richard Ennessy for one minute. I am sure he believes that he has copied a Monet.' Stewart Griffin was quietly bubbling inside. 'Go on then Stewart, what have you found out?'

Stewart Griffin smoothed a crumpled print on the table top and pushed his spectacles back up his nose.

'I got it from the micro-fiche in the library. This is from the catalogue of the Pushkin.'

'Moscow!' Dr. Sullivan exclaimed.

'They have some sketches attributed to Monet. Look. *"Toten Wood, Norway – study for painting (never executed)".'*

'Yes... Of course. Mont Colsaas.' Dr. Sullivan turned to the directory on the table and flipped through to the entry on Monet. 'Mont Colsaas, painted in Norway during 1895.'

'You see he was in Norway,' Stewart said breathlessly.

Dr. Sullivan was thinking. It was possible, quite possible. Occasionally unknown works by famous artists had turned up in private collections.

'It says *"never executed"* but I think the painting was executed.' Stewart was excited by the deduction. 'I think it exists. I think he did it. I think we have discovered an unknown Monet.'

'Now Stewart, hold your horses. If you wish to be an art historian, the first thing you have to learn is not to jump to conclusions. You will only make a good name for yourself with deductions which are drawn from patient and diligent research. Unsubstantiated guesswork makes one a laughing stock and will destroy a reputation before it has had time to establish itself.' He was aware of the paradox in his argument but he felt that Stewart would know what he meant. 'It is far more likely that some enterprising artist saw the sketch in Moscow and decided to attempt his version of the painting.'

'Oh... do you think so?'

Dr. Sullivan peered benevolently down on Stewart Griffin's crestfallen face.

'Yes, I think so,' he lied.

'Horny Harry must believe we are all giraffes.' Jennifer stretched up to read the notice board. 'When did this go up?'

'Whilst you were down the corridor,' Patsy said. 'He just rushed in, pinned it up and then told us to carry on till the bell and leave the place tidy.' She sniggered in a most unbecoming manner. 'He had made a mess of his shirt. He had rubbed yellow all over the front.'

'You ought to get a medal, Jennifer,' Amanda said. 'I think he pinned this up so high to punish you.'

'Are you saying I'm short?' Jennifer poked her in the ribs.

'No dear,' she replied, and affectionately patted the top of Jennifer's head.

They studied the notice. It announced the availability of places on a three day residential course at Bristol covering a spectrum of disciplines, from advanced oil and spatula technique through the plastics to textile dyeing and printing processes.

'What do you think then?' Jennifer said.

'If I could get the money together I'd like to have a bash at the batik workshop.' Amanda absently twirled a piece of her hair around her fingers. 'What about you?'

'I fancy the dance on the Saturday night and the optional trip to Cheddar Gorge on the Sunday,' Ruth declared scandalously.

Jennifer turned around. 'Oh, I just bumped into your boyfriend down the corridor,' she announced. 'I don't know what you got up to with him at the RA but his hair was standing up in spikes and it had gone completely white.'

'I don't know what you mean,' Ruth said stuffily. 'Richard and I are just good friends.

'Oh Ruth, I am sorry,' Patsy said with great big eyes.

'It was probably Corot,' Amanda said obscurely. 'He can have that effect on people. What are you going for then Jennifer? Jennifer!'

'Sorry, I was busy reading something else. I fancy the silk screen printing course.'

'Oh yes, you would be good at that!' Patsy said.

'If I could afford it,' she added distractedly. Until a few moments ago, she had not been seriously considering any part of the course but then her eye had fallen on another, smaller, notice pinned at her level which seemed to widen the opportunity for her. It informed those interested that for the post Christmas series of life-drawing classes, nude models would be required and that the rate paid would be five times the usual.

Richard was still musing upon his bizarre interview with Dr. Sullivan as he let himself into his cottage. He had given up on the clay and had been making his way to the refectory when his tutor had buttonholed him and invited him into a vacant room.

'I was intrigued by your impressionist offering this morning, Richard.' Richard had waited, not knowing what to say, unsure what this was the overture to. 'Yes, very intrigued. A Monet you said?'

Ah, so that was it. We were back on the track of grandfather's Monet were we? What was so special about it?

'Yes, that's right. Presumably not a very well known one,' Richard had observed, keeping the tone of his voice neutral.

'Quite. Indeed, I had great difficulty finding it in any of the directories. Has it ever been in a gallery do you know?'

'No, never,' he had said glibly.

'You seem very sure of that.'

That had been a mistake.

'Yes,' he had said. Dr. Sullivan had waited for him to expand his affirmative. Richard decided to take the bull by the horns. He had looked the tutor directly in the eyes and smiled disarmingly. 'How can I help you, Dr. Sullivan?'

Dr. Sullivan had relaxed and confided. 'I think that your friends have an unknown Monet in their possession.'

'Oh it is not unknown. They know it is a Monet.'

Dr. Sullivan had cleared his throat.

'Quite, quite. But it is unknown to the world of art. It would be a great discovery, if it were a genuine Monet.'

'Yes?'

'Yes. These friends of yours. Would they, perhaps, allow me to examine the painting with a view to confirming its authorship? It would be a great honour for me.'

Oh so that was it! Self glorification. We were talking about reputations, were we? Richard had smiled discreetly.

'No doubt,' he had said. 'But in agreeing to allow me to copy it they imposed a condition on me of preserving their anonymity. I'm sure you can understand that, Doctor.'

'Oh, quite, quite. I was merely thinking that should they want expert confirmation...'

'Oh they have it already.'

'Oh?'

'One of their ancestors bought the painting from Monet. They were chums apparently. The painting is accompanied by a friendly note addressed to him and signed *"Claude".*'

'Haa....!' Dr. Sullivan's breath had escaped from him.

'Was there anything else, Doctor?'

Richard had left him standing there, shaking his head.

He stifled a laugh as he entered his living room and kicked off his shoes. It was nice to know that Dr. Sullivan was not immune from the common defects of the human race.

Then he saw Jennifer Pye waiting for him. What was it she had said? 'Close your mouth duck or you'll frighten the children'. Or something like that. Duck? Now that was a peculiar expression. He remembered how utterly foolish he had felt, standing there in the corridor, with his hair standing out in white spikes and his mouth agape, watching her beautiful golden hair swinging as she had marched away from him. He turned to the canvas.

'You're a cheeky monkey, Jennifer Pye!' Then he looked into her eyes and saw the mixture of pride and dejection. 'But you have been sad in your life, Miss Jennifer Pye.'

He sat on his stool and looked for a long while at Jennifer Pye.

The light in the room faded on her poignant face and the ghostly glow of the mercury vapour coach lamp on the mews wall opposite took over. He knew now that he had to complete this painting.

EPISODE SIX

Dear Jencie,

How are you love? Hope you are well. Mam and I are sorry you can't come out for Christmas but we understand how you must be busy. What is this about college? Are you running the shop and studying? We always knew you would do well.

We can't quite get the hang of being able to sit out on the balcony in shirt sleeves in December. And how we are going to eat Xmas pud. in this weather I don't know! The Wilsons across the caille (that means 'street') say they always go out to a Chinese restaurant for Xmas. Fancy that! Still, we would have liked to have had our little girl with us.

Be good, love. We don't hear much of Steven, are you still seeing him? He sounded such a nice young fellow.

Write soon, your ever loving,
Mam and Dad.

Jennifer watched the black rain sluicing down the window pane, rippling the street lights of Cordoba Crescent. Steven. She had not thought of Steven for months. She remembered the weight of his body lying on hers, his arms around her shoulders, the way he tugged playfully at her hair whilst they were making love. Steven, the bastard!

She looked across the street. In a yellow-lit cosy room she could see three children decorating the Christmas tree; hanging a coloured bauble on a springy pine finger and then ducking down below the window and reappearing with a trail of silver tinsel or a shiny star. Behind them, coloured paper chains swooped low from the light fitting and Christmas cards hung on ribbons.

A gust of wind blew some soggy leaves down the Crescent. It tugged insistently at the torn tarpaulin which lay across the semi derelict car, rotting in the drive of the house next door: somebody's abandoned hobby project, no doubt. The wind swung a green wooden garden gate on its feeble hinges and flicked spidery branches, shiny with rain, across the beam of the street lamp opposite and made smudgy, random patterns on the wall of her unlit room.

The house was quiet. Not the smug, satisfied, quietness of a house stuffed with somnolent happy residents basking in seasonal goodwill but the empty quietness of a house rejected by all but Jennifer and Mrs. Crowther. Feeling the absence of gentle thumps on ceilings and slipper-clad footfalls in the passageway; of thinly muffled music and mumbling heard through flock wall paper, the house had retaliated with sawing noises in pipework and whining down redundant chimneys, with a creaking of the porch roof and a slap clapping of loose bargeboard.

Abandoned on Christmas Eve, the house was sulking.

When Jennifer opened an eye on Christmas morning it seemed as if the weather had decided also to take a holiday. Nothing was happening. There was nothing to see. The wind had blown itself out during the night and the rain had stopped but this had not produced any startling improvement. The sky was white and featureless, obliterating the sun, dowsing the light. It was not a whiteness which might promise relief by snow, it was not a ragged whiteness with a hope of blue behind, it was an overall cover of a blank, oppressive neutrality.

She took her denim skirt from its hanger and inspected it with her head on one side. She would have to make an effort, Mrs. Crowther would like that. For Mrs. Crowther had taken pity on Jennifer, all alone in the house at Christmas and had invited her to share her Christmas lunch.

It might not have been Jennifer's first choice, nor even her second, but when it was the only choice then it had to be, and if she wanted excitement then at least she would see in the New Year in lively company, or so she hoped, for Cherryl had insisted she take the train out to Ilford on New Year's Eve where Cherryl was staying with her sister who always threw a really big party. They would be able to stay overnight and then in the morning, Cherryl would come back with Jennifer all the way to Ealing. Cherryl had hoped to see some of her Keith that Christmas but, as she had explained, Christmas was his busy time.

There was a voice at her door. It was Mrs. Crowther. 'I was wondering if you would like a sherry before lunch, Miss Pye. Come down at about twelve if you do.'

'Thank you Mrs. Crowther. I'll come down,' Jennifer assured her. Sherry! What next? It did not bear thinking about.

'Don't let Sandy intimidate you Miss Pye,' Mrs. Crowther called from the kitchen. 'He just takes time to get used to people in his room.'

Jennifer eyed the dog which was crouching on the chintzy sofa opposite her, growling every time she moved. She tried not to laugh out aloud at the suggestion that the minuscule Pekinese might intimidate her. 'Woof!' she said to it and it scuttled from the sofa and hid underneath.

This was the first time that Jennifer had really been in Mrs. Crowther's parlour. The odd glimpse through a half open door had given her a fairly good idea of what to expect but the reality was somewhat overpowering. The room served as a gallery of Mrs. Crowther's life. Jennifer suspected that the gee-gaws and knick-knacks which covered all horizontal surfaces in the room, from piano top to mantle shelf, charted and documented every major event of her life. The china cat from Torquay, the miniature Eiffel Tower; each had its story to tell. Where the horizontal planes had been dedicated to artefacts, the vertical had been reserved for the graphic archive. Every square inch of the wall was covered with framed prints, photographs, petit point, hanging three deep, four deep, five deep from the picture rail. The effect of a mysterious and crowded Aladdin's cave was heightened by the feeble wattage of the candle bulbs glowing from the candelabra over the table.

'Can I help at all?' Jennifer's enquiry was convention more than intention for there was hardly room in the scullery for two cooks and in the parlour the table had already been set with table cloth, napkins, glasses, cut glass cruet set ('*souvenir from Folkestone*') and elegant, old fashioned cutlery.

'It's ready Miss Pye. Sit up to table.'

Jennifer dragged back the dark wood chair and took her

place. Mrs. Crowther placed a dish of steaming vegetables on the cork table mat (a view of Windsor Castle) and then returned from the kitchen with a meat plate of roast chicken.

'I never have enough appetite for a turkey.'

'No that's fine, Mrs. Crowther, I quite understand. It was very kind of you to invite me.'

'Help yourself to vegetables, Miss Pye. Well I didn't like the thought of you all alone over Christmas. Such a happy time, a family time.' She gazed vaguely around her framed photographs. 'My sister usually drops in at Christmas but her Reggie is ailing so she hasn't been able to.'

'Oh dear, that's a shame.' Jennifer had never questioned whether Mrs. Crowther had any siblings. It seemed to her that she was so old that she must be the only survivor of a lost generation. She began to realise that there was a whole sub-world of elderly people clinging to their memories and beliefs.

'Do you have no brothers and sisters, then Miss Pye?'

'No, I am an only child. And my Mam and Dad live in Spain, as you know.' The Brussels sprouts were overcooked.

'Yes, Spain. Fancy what people do nowadays!'

'They retired there,' Jennifer explained. 'They always liked it for holidays and they were fed up with the weather in England so they decided to go and live there.'

'And you did not go with them?'

'No.'

'Did you not want to?'

'Not at the time. I was doing other things but now...' She paused with her fork in mid air. 'You know sometimes I think that I could just drop everything and go,' she said energetically. 'You know, switch off the kettle, walk out of the door with just what I stand up in and get on a plane.'

'I hope you would give me my notice, and settle your rent Miss Pye.' Mrs. Crowther patted her bosom as if easing some indelicate indigestion.

Jennifer felt stupid. 'Oh Mrs. Crowther I didn't mean it in that way. It was just a figure of speech. You know I would not walk out on you like that.'

Mrs. Crowther dropped a morsel of chicken into the slavering pocket that was the mouth of the Pekinese.

'That's fine then,' she said a little coolly. 'Oh heavens,' she exclaimed at their empty glasses, 'I've forgotten the wine.'

'I'll get it,' Jennifer volunteered.

'Oh would you Miss Pye? It is in the fridge door.'

Mrs. Crowther uncorked the bottle of Australian white with a facility that suggested a familiarity with a corkscrew and a suppleness of the wrists quite incongruous with the character Jennifer had supposed her to be.

'Mr. Crowther – my Terence,' Mrs. Crowther nodded at a yellowing framed photograph of a young man with slicked down hair which took pride of place over the mantleshelf, 'Terence first introduced me to wine. He was very refined,' she confided, 'worked in insurance.' Jennifer nodded. 'Not the door-to-door variety,' she specified. 'He was in head office. Dear Terence, not very strong physically, but a brilliant brain. Brilliant.' She sipped at the wine. 'A little too cool perhaps, but he would have approved.' She raised her glass and toasted the photograph.

Jennifer lifted hers, decided that it could be disrespectful for her to do likewise, and sipped from it daintily. She was unaccustomed to wine and was not certain that she liked it. It was nowhere as sweet as the sherry she had drunk before lunch.

When the pudding came, Mrs. Crowther asked Jennifer to pull the curtains and switch off the light and then, enwrapped in the gloom of midwinter Victorian suburbia, she warmed the table-spoon of brandy over a match, doused the steaming mound and lit it. Jennifer studied her bird-like face as it dreamed in the bluish wafting flames of the pudding. How many Christmases was she living? How many noisy, happy, warm, family celebrations was she recalling in this gloomy theatre of her past? As the last flame turned yellow and flickered away, she sighed audibly. 'I do like to do that,' she admitted with an unexpected candour.

'So do I,' Jennifer giggled, feeling the effect of the sherry and the wine.

'Will you stay for the Queen?' Mrs. Crowther asked.

Jennifer grasped gratefully at the suggestion, for the difficulty with such an open-ended invitation for lunch was always to know when it would be time to leave.

'I would love to. But then I must go back upstairs and get on with my assignment.' Mrs Crowther had visibly not understood. 'I have some work to do for college,' she explained. 'It is like a big essay.'

Mrs. Crowther drained the bottle into their glasses. 'White wine doesn't keep,' she said, the unconcealed mischief glowing in her pale blue eyes. 'Need to make room for the port and cheese.'

'Oh Mrs. Crowther, I really couldn't!' Jennifer patted her stomach.

'Nonsense!' she smiled and then spooned the last of the brandy butter into Jennifer's dish. 'It would only go off.'

As they stood cheek by jowl, washing the dishes in the small kitchen, Jennifer felt bloated with food but imbued with a warmth toward all mankind. Mrs. Crowther's white head ducked and bobbed over the sink whilst her face appeared a little flushed.

'Got a young man have you dear?'

Coming unheralded upon her, the enquiry caught Jennifer completely defenceless.

'No,' she assured her, as if such a liaison should somehow inculpate her.

'No-one special then?' Jennifer realised that her last date had been to the cinema with Colin but before she could compose a reply, Mrs. Crowther had continued. 'No of course you haven't. You would not be here if you had.'

'Well, I don't always seem to—'

'Pity,' Mrs. Crowther continued. 'Nice girl like you. You should have them lining up for you.' Mrs. Crowther stowed the last article, took the tea towel from Jennifer and hung it over the cooker. 'Go and sit down and rest, dear. I'll show you my photographs whilst we wait for the Queen.'

Jennifer sat onto the sofa which made a determined attempt to swallow her up for its Christmas lunch. She thought grimly that she would need a crane to lift her out now. Mrs. Crowther came in carrying a small silver tray (*'Hotel Metropole, Brighton'*) with two glasses and the bottle of port. She placed it gently on a side table and from the bottom of the sideboard, produced a brown-covered album. Jennifer knew she was trapped, but told herself, it was Mrs. Crowther's Christmas.

At first, Jennifer had trouble distinguishing anything at all in the photographs, unaccustomed as she was to looking at small black and white snapshots, taken with a Brownie Box and now curling with age. She had not realised how the large coloured photographs of nowadays had taken the charm and discussion from memories. 'You see that dress that I am wearing there,'

Mrs. Crowther would point at a grey smudge, 'was a beautiful emerald green to match my hat. Do you see?' Jennifer learned that she had to interpret the grey and invent colour. No doubt the emerald green she saw was different to the actual and different still from Mrs. Crowther's memories; therein lay the charm. A colour photograph would have recorded an incontrovertible version that would have denied them all interpretation.

She paused on a snapshot of a bright young thing dressed in a skimpy bathing costume, posing rather provocatively against a seaside pier booth.

'Yes,' Mrs. Crowther nodded, answering her unasked question. 'That's Emily Saratt in her heyday. Before she met Terence Crowther, of course.'

'But you were beautiful,' Jennifer breathed and then realised the horror of her gaffe. 'I mean—'

'Oh do you think so?' Mrs. Crowther laid a vibrant arm on hers. 'Really?'

'Oh yes. But that costume. Wasn't that just a bit, well... outrageous for the beach?'

'Oh my dear,' Mrs. Crowther patted her arm, 'That was not for the beach.'

'You surely didn't wear that in town.'

'It was for the Pavilion. The pier.'

Jennifer looked blank. 'The pier?'

'Emily Saratt, artiste,' she announced with a dramatic flourish. She pushed the album onto Jennifer's lap and stood up. She flapped her wrists about in the air as if waving frantically to some departing relative. Jennifer watched her, feeling bemused and a little light headed. What was she going to do?

'Emily Saratt, ladies and gentlemen' she quavered and then looked down at her legs. 'The costume.' She gathered up the hem of her dress and began to tuck it into the legs of her drawers. Jennifer began to giggle as her spindly legs appeared below the bunched up dress. 'No giggling in the stalls please!' She wagged a finger at Jennifer whose efforts to contain her laughter made all attempts at seriousness impossible. Mrs. Crowther held up one hand then with a surprising alacrity, skipped across to the fruit bowl (*Feeling Fruity in Skegness'*) and picked three satsumas. 'I crave the indulgence of my audience. It is some time since I have done this.' Jennifer nodded, one hand pressed across her mouth and her eyes bulging. With an imperceptible flick of the wrist, Mrs. Crowther shot the fruit from one hand to the other and then suddenly they were up in the air, turning in the never ceasing loops of the juggler. Jennifer's mouth dropped open as she watched the fountain of orange bubbling up from her deft hands and the restless movements of her eyes as they unerringly followed the circling orbs.

'Oh, brilliant!' Jennifer clapped frantically.

Distracted by the noise, Mrs. Crowther missed a move, caught two of the fruit and flipped the errant third with her elbow. It ricocheted across the room and toppled a china milk jug (in the shape of a Jersey cow) from the piano. As it smashed on the leg of a chair, Sandy appeared from beneath and yapped bravely at the pieces. Jennifer held her breath.

'Never liked that jug – it rained all the time we played Jersey. "Come to the Sunny Channel Isles," my bum!' Mrs. Crowther declared scandalously. She looked across at Jennifer. 'My bum!' she said loudly again, for the pleasure of hearing it. 'Come on gel, I'll teach you. It's easy, any fool can do it.'

Laughing and giggling, they stood side by side in the middle of the parlour whilst Mrs. Crowther put the three up and then tried to inculcate the movement into Jennifer. It would have been a daunting task had they both been in a state of solid and serious sobriety; in their festive excitement, the task degenerated into a frantic and disjointed grappling at fruit. Where two hands had imparted perpetual movement to three fruit, four hands found themselves incapable of keeping the same number of fruit in the air in any sort of order.

'And I used to play the piano...' Mrs. Crowther bragged.

'Oh do, do,' Jennifer took her hands in hers and shook them, pleadingly.

Mrs. Crowther looked at Jennifer as if seeing her for the first time. Her pale and watery eyes stared straight into Jennifer's. 'Shall I?' she said. Jennifer bit her lips and nodded vigorously. 'Right then, I will.' Then with relish she added, 'My bum!'

The old lady walked to the piano with a slightly exaggerated exactness of movement which Jennifer decided to interpret charitably. She lifted the lid and pulled the music stand over it. For a second or two she peered at the notes and Jennifer wondered if she had forgotten what they were for but then she launched into a vigorous, if not very accurate, medley of popular dance tunes of the forties, warbling the verses in a sweet soprano whilst Jennifer tried to join in any refrain. Soon they were pulling music scores from the stool and sorting through them.

'Listen to this, you'll like this one... *You are, the promised kiss of springtime that makes....*'

Jennifer stood at the side of Mrs. Crowther with one arm around her frail shoulders as she leaned over to read the words on the score. The thin bony hands faltered sometimes on the keys and the voices often did not combine but it mattered not. When they had exhausted the playable works from the stool, she began to softly play carols. She shuffled along the stool and they sat, Jennifer's arm around her waist, binding them together as their voices at last coincided in their own Christmas celebration. And when the street lights lit red, slowly turning to amber as the sodium warmed up, Mrs. Crowther whispered to Jennifer's head, now resting on her shoulder.

'We forgot the Queen. There goes my MBE.'

Richard turned a sour eye on John, the butler, as he placed the silver breakfast tray on the table by his bed. Why did silver have to be so noisy?

'Poached as you prefer, sir.' John informed Richard of the constitution of his breakfast and reminded him of the bent of his preferences, all in one concise phrase.

Richard groaned.

'A couple of aspirin would have been more suitable.'

John silently raised a silver egg cup from the tray, tilted it to show him the white tablets and then replaced it.

'Will that be all sir?' he asked without any trace of smugness.

Richard knew he was beaten.

'Yes thank you John. Oh, what's the weather doing? No! No, please don't open the curtains, I'll see for myself.'

'As you wish sir.'

Richard watched the door closing gently and then hauled himself up on his elbow and gingerly picked out the tablets. He swallowed them with a mouthful of water from his night carafe and then poured himself a cup of black coffee.

He swung his feet to the floor and drifted over to the

enormous sash window, prising the heavy curtains gingerly open with his fingers. He looked idly across the park to Home Farm. He could just see the bowing roof of Tithe Barn, its ancient tiles clinging to the uneven undulations like scales on the back of some gigantic reptile.

This was where they held the Feasten, every Christmas Eve. Nobody really knew why it was called the Feasten. It was presumably a relic of feudal times, for it was none other than a gigantic party for all the tenants of the estate. They crowded in to the trestle-tabled barn amidst much joking and ribaldry, and with a lot of drinking and toasting, they demolished spit roast pig and pheasant, with hamburgers and fish fingers for the youngsters and then the tables were cleared away and the dancing began.

Traditionally, a member of the host family began the snowball by choosing a partner from amongst the tenants. They danced one circuit and then at the interruption of the music, split to seek a partner each, and so the progression advanced until the barn was thronged with all who wanted to dance.

Much good natured speculation was always aroused by any choice of partner by the sons of the family; many a girl had had futile hopes raised, she knew they were futile, but all the same, it would have been against human nature, and definitely most unwomanly, not to dream that the dashing heir might conceal within his breast a heart yearning for just one such as her.

When the musicians had struck up, Richard had played the game they all wanted. He ambled gently around the hall, winking at the girls, nodding at the mothers. The men whistled, the grandmothers cackled, the little children played hide and seek amongst the stacked tables in the gloomy wing. Some of the girls looked shyly away, some stared boldly at him, daring him, their lips parted in anticipation. Occasionally one would be playfully thrust forward amongst shrieks and giggles and accusations. 'Oh it wasn't me sir, I wuz pushed.'

Having made a complete circuit of the floor, he stopped as if to recollect, although in truth he had espied his victim, and then he walked purposefully towards a bold brunette who was wearing a heavy country skirt of dark wool pinned to her neat waist by a broad leather belt. She stood her ground as he approached and then at the last minute he switched his gaze to the diminutive girl with a squint, hiding behind her.

'Rose Ann. Would you allow me the pleasure of this dance?' The girl's mouth opened in disbelief and she tried to bury herself but the brunette was having none of it.

'Oh no you don't, Rose Ann,' she said sternly and turned and propelled her into Richard's arms, 'You take him!' she ordered obscurely.

The hall cheered warmly at his choice and Rose Ann, blushing furiously, initially with embarrassment but later with pride, slipped her good arm around his back and waltzed across the quarry tiles. He held the hand on her stunted arm as if for all the world it were normal and she began to believe that it was and when the time came for them to part, she knew she could ask any man to partner her and none would refuse.

But later that evening, Richard had drunk rather more than he had wanted. The men had craftily inveigled him into some sort of a challenge to do with balancing a cricket ball on a bat, the forfeit for failure of which was to quaff a pint of ale. Needless to say, they were far more dextrous than he and the playful nudging of the rabble ensured that Richard got nowhere near success.

He vaguely remembered the cold night air as he had been carried back to the Hall on four shoulders like a coffin, and had understood their undisguised glee when the door bell had been answered and they had left John to deal with an insensible Master Richard. Of such happenings were the myths and legends of The Wisdene Estate constructed.

He grinned to himself and then winced at the thudding in his head. Well, that was him, human in their eyes, safe for another year. Now all he had to do was to get through Christmas lunch.

'Tell me something about her, Charles,' the Earl of Wisdene prompted his younger son whilst he clipped the end of his cigar. Charles sought guidance from his brother with a glance but all Richard could do was to shrug.

'Well father,' he began tentatively, 'She is the daughter of Sir Miles Barton of Barton Agrochemicals – they have most of their factories out Wisbech way. Her mother is from an old farming family in the Fens – arable, mostly root crops, sugar beet.'

The Earl of Wisdene breathed gently onto the glowing end of his cigar. He was a short man of stocky build with a round, ruddy face, twinkling blue eyes and an almost completely bald head.

He looked more like a successful stockbroker or banker than a member of the landed aristocracy but then, the financial success that he had achieved and which had ensured the continuing integrity of the estate in an era in which other families were having to break up theirs, had been in the field of the stock exchange and land investment so it was fitting that he should appear thus. He happily claimed a complete but untrue ignorance of the ways of the soil; this allowed him to invest important and widespread powers and responsibilities in the person of Courtney, his estate manager and also gave himself the freedom to enjoy what he was best at.

The traditional Christmas lunch at Wisdene Hall was an unusual affair in that it was rigorously and exclusively family. The d'Ennessy's had made it known long ago that they received no guests on Christmas Day. They considered it the one day in the year on which their family life was sacrosanct and in order to ensure this, at 11a.m. on Christmas morning, all the domestic servants were dismissed for the day so that they too, could spend the time in the bosoms of their families.

The Countess then donned her apron and finished preparing the lunch which had been set in motion in the small top kitchen that they had had installed some years previously. The sons set the table and cleared away and each served himself from the buffet rather in the manner of a high class cafeteria.

After lunch, the Countess retired to what she termed her 'boudoir' to read, but in reality to doze on the bed, for she always served herself too large a helping, and the three men passed through to the smoking room and talked family business, secure in the discretion of a house devoid of servants. Thus it was that Lord Wisdene requested his younger son to divulge some details of the young lady whom he appeared to be courting.

'...probably develop the animal feeds division to–'

'What colour are her eyes?'

Charles stalled at his father's interruption and then looked helplessly at Richard again. 'Er... blue. I think father.'

'You think they are blue do you Charles?'

'Yes, I am sure they are. Blueish.'

'Find out,' Lord Wisdene decreed with a quiet authority which told Charles that for today, the subject was closed. It also gave him a devastatingly clear insight into his father's opinion of his performance. Richard tried to defuse the tension a little.

'Are you riding to the hounds tomorrow, Charles?'

'As usual.'

'I'll drive the box for you if you like.' It was accepted that Richard did not ride a horse. 'I'll get it coupled up this afternoon, although I expect Winston has already done it. What about you, father? Are you putting in an appearance?'

'I'll come to the hunt breakfast with you in the Range Rover and then walk back down through the Glade. The fresh air will do me good.' He drew on his cigar. 'You will be seeing Vanessa tomorrow then Richard?'

'Yes father,' said Richard, carefully, 'I have not known her to miss a hunt yet.'

Lord Wisdene turned to face Richard from his position in front of the mantle shelf. His bright blue eyes speared Richard with their sincerity.

'I like Vanessa, you know Richard. She is a fine woman. A fine woman. She has a lot of qualities.'

'Greyish green,' Richard said quickly.

'What?' His father was caught off guard.

'Vanessa's eyes. Greyish green.'

'I suppose you only noticed them because of your powers of observation as an artist,' Lord Wisdene sighed, accepting the impertinence as an unavoidable product of a lively mind. 'What are we to do with you, Richard?'

'Let me be, father. Just let me be.'

As Richard had guessed, Winston had prepared the Range Rover and the horse box. They stood gleaming on a patch of wet bricks where they had been washed. He switched on and checked the level of fuel. He need not have bothered.

'There's a tyre gauge in the glove compartment, Master Richard, if you want to check those as well.' Winston was leaning from the first floor window of his cottage above the old stable.

'A merry Christmas to you Winston,' Richard laughed as he turned around.

'And to you Master Richard. Will you come up for a drink? I am just trying Mrs. Puddlestone's sloe and blackcurrant liqueur as I shall not be needed any further today.'

Sitting easily at the kitchen table, Richard sipped the black liquid and pronounced it good. Winston had put his feet up on the other chair and opened his shirt collar.

'Better than her apple and ginger, I feel. I will tell her so when I see her next.'

'How have things been at the Hall, Winston?'

'Quiet,' he said quickly. 'Quiet, with you two mischief makers out of the way.' Richard smiled. 'Courtney had a bit of trouble with poachers the other week. After the deer they were. Brought a van up to the track at the back of Long Covert but got bogged down. Said they had got lost.'

'What did he do?'

'He couldn't prove anything of course. He got Giles to haul them out with the tractor.' Winston chuckled. 'Giles knew what to do. He hitched the chain to their track rod and wrenched them out on that. Bent it like a banana. They drove off at about twenty miles per hour with the front end waggling like a Labrador's tail.'

They both laughed.

Winston looked at Richard and then said quietly, 'You made quite a stir last night, Master Richard.'

'Oh don't remind me, Winnie,' Richard pleaded. 'My head was very tender this morning.'

'Oh you fully deserved that,' Winston declared boldly. 'I wasn't talking about that. It was a fine thing you did, dancing with Rose Ann, Master Richard. You've given her what she needed. I reckon we'll see her married next year. She knows who she wants and he won't get away, I'll tell you.'

'He'd be a stupid fellow to try.'

'He would that.'

EPISODE SEVEN

'Stuck?'

'Hello Colin. Yes I'm stuck,' Jennifer admitted.

'What are you doing?'

'Oh it's something for Pountney. An exercise on copy writing. It's supposed to widen our vocabulary or something.'

'Oh I don't do the advertising option, thank goodness.'

'I wish I didn't.'

'You could always change.'

''Bit late now. I don't think that words are my thing.'

'Do you want some help?'

'Oh I don't know.' Jennifer felt fed up. She gazed listlessly down the college library. 'It all seems so pointless.'

'Oh dear, getting philosophical so early into the new term. That's suspicious. That's what students do before they drop out.'

'No worry about that,' Jennifer said firmly.

'So what are you supposed to be doing?' Colin twisted her paper around to read it.

'Five other ways of saying "exciting". Come on. Quickly!' she snapped her fingers mockingly.

'What have you put down so far?'

'I've got *"bright"*, *"jazzy"*, *"bubbly"*.' She looked at Colin. 'It's not very good is it?'

'Why don't you use a thesaurus?'

'What's that? Some kind of prehistoric animal?'

Colin delved into his bag and rummaged for a while.

'I thought I had mine with me today,' he said.

'What do you feed it on? Perhaps it got out?'

'Ah... Here it is.' Colin ignored her flippancy and pulled a tattered paperback from his bag. 'See.' He ran his finger across

the cover, 'The-saur-us, spells "thesaurus".' He opened the book.
'O.K. Smart alec. Give me five words for exciting.'

'Exhilarating, enervating, provocative, sensational, inspiring,'
Colin read quickly. 'Next?'

'Whoah, hang on.' Jennifer scribbled quickly on her pad. 'I
don't suppose you could lend me that animal for a bit could you?
I'd feed it and take it walks and that.'

'It'd cost you.'

'How much? A jam doughnut?' Her offer made no impression
on him. 'Two jam doughnuts?'

'I was thinking of a date one evening,' he said hopefully.

'Oh.' Jennifer took a deep breath. 'Colin, I think we should
recognise that I like you but we just have no interests in common.
There is nothing we can share.'

'Except my thesaurus,' Colin observed glumly.

'Oh Colin!' She put her arm on his shoulder and shook him
gently. 'I am just not the girl for you. I am not for anyone at the
moment.'

'You can borrow it till Friday if you like.'

She squeezed his arm. 'Thanks. You are a nice person, Colin.
Don't feel so desperate. Something will happen when you least
expect it.'

Colin nodded sagely. 'Are you going on the Bristol thing?'

'Haven't made up my mind yet,' she replied untruthfully. She
had already made up her mind; she intended to go. What she was
still undecided about was how to raise the money to finance it.
'What about you?'

'I don't think there is anything there that I want to do.' He
glanced over Jennifer's shoulder as someone approached. 'What
about you, Patsy? Are you putting your name down for this Bristol
course?'

Patsy slid her bag onto the table and dropped into a chair.
'I feel as if I have walked to Bristol already today,' she sighed. 'If
Jennifer does screen printing I might do the same. We can sit
together on the coach.' She nudged Jennifer tentatively, 'What do
you think?'

'Sounds alright.' Jennifer was non-committal. 'Did you have
a good Christmas?'

'Awful! You?'

'So, so.'

She had decided that she could never talk about her Christmas Day to anybody, they would not be able to understand. It would have to remain a secret between her and Mrs. Crowther. It was not for sharing with others. Mrs. Crowther had not mentioned it on Boxing Day morning when Jennifer had offered to take Sandy out for a walk. She had observed sprightly that she had 'already been out and Sandy had chased a cat, wasn't it a lovely bright day?' Jennifer had stood there with her mouth feeling like the bottom of a parrot's cage and charged with about as much dynamism as a slug, and had had to admit that she had only just dragged herself out of bed.

And Jennifer would not wish to discuss her New Year's Eve with anybody for different reasons. She had alighted from the train at Ilford at the time specified and had then shivered for an hour and a half before being picked up by one of Cherryl's aunts whom she had never met. They had recognised each other by process of elimination. No explanation had been proffered for the delay and so Jennifer had not requested one.

Cherryl's sister, Marian, lived with her husband and two children in a box-like semi detached house on an estate. Once Jennifer had familiarised herself with the size and layout of the house, she had realised that the sleeping arrangements would probably be organised with the same efficiency as had been applied to the train meeting and she would end up fighting for a portion of dry carpet or the upright back of a soft chair.

With the knowledge of this delight awaiting her, Jennifer had passed the afternoon trying to prise apart two children who had fought ceaselessly in front of the ignored television and sporadically offering to help in the kitchen where nothing at all seemed to be happening.

Just before the guests were expected, she had heard the angry voices of Marian and Cherryl raised in a heated discussion which had terminated in the slamming of an outside door and the sound of a car driving away.

Soon after that, the house had been invaded by a varied collection of men and women, couples and singles, neighbours and friends, whose only homogeneity lay in the communal but unspoken desire to get drunk before Big Ben. By eleven o' clock, Jennifer, having been offered no food since her arrival in Essex, realised that she was supposed to survive on crisps, pickled onions and booze. She had decided to take some sensible action and in a kitchen cupboard had found a loaf of bread, in the fridge, some cheese and had applied herself to making a hefty sandwich.

It was when she was stretching up to the top cupboard for the brown sauce that she had suddenly gasped to the feel of two hands pushed up the inside of her jumper onto her breasts and an urgent, lewd pressing of body into her buttocks. Pumping her elbows viciously like pistons she had freed herself and turned to find Marian's husband leering at her.

'Just a bit of fun, girlie. Give us a kiss.' He had made a grab at her bosom again.

Jennifer had not hesitated one moment. She had lifted her knee sharply into his groin and shoved him backwards with all her might. His strangled look of surprise faded backwards as he crashed down amongst cascades of dirty glasses and peanuts. Then she had locked herself in the bathroom with her sandwich and made herself a bed in the bath with the towels.

On the train journey back to Ealing, the two girls had sat together hardly speaking but occasionally one had taken the other's hand and given it a squeeze. There was nothing they could say.

Richard reached the top of his stairs and pushed open the door. Back to college! Away from the marble floors and Dom Perignon and back to linoleum and instant coffee. He dropped his bag and then carefully lowered his art case after it.

He had come back to London a day early because he had bizarrely convinced himself that he had things that needed doing at the Mews. Perhaps he had merely been seeking an excuse to get away early from the Hall. He switched on the light and when he looked across at the easel, he was assailed by a strange feeling of restlessness and then he knew.

'I bet you had a good Christmas, Jennifer,' he addressed the painting. 'I've come back to finish your gown.'

'Well have you ever done it?' Jennifer insisted as she fiddled with the sugar packet and waited for Tracy Winters to swallow her mouthful of coffee.

'You really want to, don't you?' Tracy observed.

'I don't know – that's the point. What is it like?'

'Well the best way to find out is to do it,'

'I don't think I could.'

'Of course you could. Nothing to it. Just close your eyes and think of England.'

'Oh Tracy, that's not helping me one little bit.'

'I never had the guts, to tell you the truth, but I've just seen someone who has.' She nodded at an angular girl with freckles who had just wafted into the refectory. 'Claudia!' she called, 'Come over here, we need your help.'

Claudia turned to locate the summons and then raised a lank hand to acknowledge it. She willowed her way between the tables to their corner.

'Well?' She looked quizzically at them both.

'Shove up, Jennifer, let Claudia sit down.' Jennifer shoved up. 'Claudia, this is Jennifer, Fashion Design Two.'

'Hi.'

'Hi there.'

'She wants to know all about modelling in the nude.'

Claudia passed a cool eye over Jennifer's figure and then crossed her hands on the table top and pursed her lips.

'Piece of cake,' she said. Jennifer, who had been squirming inside at the overt appraisal of her body, had rather hoped for something a little more technical than such a bland assessment. 'Have you modelled at all yet?' Claudia continued.

'Oh yes!' Tracy said quickly, 'And how! Waltzed in and knocked me off my perch, did little Jennifer. I felt a right lemon.'

'I didn't mean to, it just happened that way. It's not my fault I am shorter than you.'

'Size isn't important when you've got no clothes on,' Claudia said loftily.

'What, not even...?'

'Well look at my tits!' Claudia laughed. 'Not exactly a pair of melons are they? They are not looking for a Venus, they just want a body to draw, that's all.'

'But how do you feel when you are sitting there in front of them stark naked? I mean...'

'Superior. I look down on them, my dear! Haughty.'

'But all those blokes and the girls... looking at you...'

'It's no different from when you have got clothes on. You had all those eyes looking at you then. Did it bother you when you were sitting for them before?'

Jennifer tried to think back to the ballgown but she could honestly not recall what she had felt. It had all happened almost in a dream.

'I don't really remember,' she admitted.

'Well it can't have been that traumatic then could it? Right. Now pay close attention. This is what you do. Claudia Crayford, international superstar and model will now divulge all. First, have a good wash, then you know you are clean. It also means that you are unlikely to want to scratch yourself in awkward places. There's nothing worse than trying to sort out an itch in your fuzz when everybody is looking at you. Second, don't wear undies...'

'What?'

'Have you got a long dress? Woollen is best to keep you warm.'

'Erm.. yes I think I could find one. But why no...?'

'Listen and I will tell you. If you want to sit there looking as if you have just come out of a sex slave bondage session, with strap marks and elastic lines across your belly and bum then that's fine but it does nothing for your self esteem, so, the morning you are going to sit, leave everything off. Get a long thick dress and keep yourself covered in that. Nobody will know you're not wearing knickers unless you tell them. You don't know whether I'm wearing any at the moment do you?' Jennifer's mouth opened and shut soundlessly. 'Right. And when you get undressed, do it behind the screens and come out in the drape. You are not there to give them a striptease.

'Thirdly. Choose a comfortable pose – one that you can hold for as long as you need to. Don't let them hurry you. If you are uncomfortable, it makes you wriggle and if you wriggle, things start to wobble and that makes all the lads cross their eyes and legs. Don't worry if they want you to sit with your legs apart – it's actually very comfortable and there is always someone who wants to do all the twiddly curly bits in pencil.

'Fourthly, heating. Never mind your fanny, that's already lagged, you make sure that there is a heater behind your back. If your back gets cold it's death. And you don't want one of those fan things because they blow dust about and cause draughts. A nice infra red or radiant is best.

'Fifthly, half the artists will be behind you and so you will not see what they are looking at. If the ones in front are looking and not drawing, just stare them straight in the eyes. That'll embarrass them into working, don't you worry. And the final and most important point...' She paused.

'Yes?' Jennifer was breathless.

'Think pious thoughts,' Claudia wagged her finger. 'Unless you want them to draw you with nipples like Cleopatra's needle, keep all your fantasies for later. Think of the cat, the canal, the cathedral – anything that isn't going to turn you on. Now, any questions?'

Jennnifer was dazed by such a forthright exposé. She now knew for certain that she could not do it.

'No... I think you have covered everything.'

'All you have to do is uncover everything,'

The fact of having tried, albeit unsuccessfully, to help Richard with the clay, seemed to have given Alison Barrett confidence. Richard noticed that she was now taking a more active role in the discussions and appeared less anxious about what others might think of her ideas. Sometimes the clash of opinions became too brutal and then she would give a little submissive shake of her head and retreat into her shell with a shy smile.

It was nearly the end of January and drawing class had started up again. As Richard walked to drawing class he caught up with Alison whose slow loiter seemed to indicate a crushing reluctance to begin the impending task.

'Cold feet?' he joked as he came alongside her. Her narrow face looked longer in her anxiety. 'What's the matter?'

'I don't... I don't think I can...' she began.

Suddenly a burst of laughter cannoned down the corridor as a rowdy group of girls rounded the corner. Richard nodded to an open room and they stepped out of the throng. The conversation giggled by them.

'But what if it's a feller sitting up there? You know...'

'What does it matter?'

'Well how does he stop his thingey from jumping up and down and waving every time he sees someone he fancies?'

More giggling.

'They take pills and things.'

'And bromide in their tea.'

'Or, just before, they have a bloody good...'

'Mona!' someone screeched, 'do they use both hands when they do that?'

'Can't do what?' Richard prompted.

She fiddled with the hem of her jumper. 'This drawing.'

'Nonsense. You can draw as well as I can.'

'Ooh I can't!' she denied the obvious lie. 'You're really good. I saw that caricature of Dr Sullivan you were doing in the lecture theatre.'

'So did he, unfortunately,' Richard laughed easily.

'Yes well,' Alison laughed, 'you didn't need to put the horns and the tail on him.' She became serious again. 'But this class... I don't think I could draw a girl naked. I shall be much too embarrassed.'

'At the nudity? It's only a human form.'

'Yes I know it is.'

'What about a baby? You would draw a naked baby wouldn't you? No trouble with that?'

'No. None at all.'

'So it's a psychological thing.'

'I suppose so.' She sounded doubtful. 'It's just that... a girl up there, like me but with no clothes on, it seems somehow...'

'What about a man? Would you draw a naked man?'

'Oh yes. No problem with that.'

'Well why don't you pretend it's a man? You never know, she may look like a man!' He stepped out in to the corridor. 'Come on and buck up or you'll get a lousy position.'

'Yes.' She did not sound convinced.

Jennifer had to control a desire to scratch herself. She had not realised how irritating wool could be next to the skin. She would probably find that when she stripped off she was covered with some blotchy allergic rash. She sucked her lips to stop them trembling from fright. Nothing to be afraid of, she told herself. Had she not come all the way to college on the tube with no knickers on? O.K., she had refused to sit down, and she had waited until absolutely everybody had gone up the escalator before she had stepped onto it but she had done it nevertheless. She had walked through Ealing, holding her anorak tightly across her chest, trying to arrest the bounce of her breasts which, she already knew, no one would have been able to see. She had found the movement disconcerting and although her skirt was long, there was an occasional draught which reminded her of her vulnerability. She giggled. It had made her feel rather naughty.

She had found herself worrying about the old barber at the corner, the one who worked in a basement window below street level. She had never really noticed him when wearing jeans but now she was all too aware of angles and mirrors. Those cellar covers made of small squares of pearly glass, were they really opaque? What if somebody was down there? She had skirted around them when she could. In scores of ways she had given herself delicious frights on the route to college but now she was going to do the serious bit and her heart was thumping. She could not do this. She could not sit there with a class full of strangers or, worse still, a class full of students whom she might know, whilst they stared at her nudity.

She had stared at her nudity before deciding. She had stood before Cherryl's dressing table mirror and angled it in every direction. Her skin was, apart from her appendix scar and a few moles, an unmarked white. Quite unusual really. She liked the shape of her legs, even if they were a bit stocky at the thighs. Her bottom, she had had to twist around awkwardly for that, her bottom was fairly heavy but it was firm, it did not droop. Her tummy was a little bit too big perhaps but then that was because she was bending over to look at it, she convinced herself. And her pubic hair was curly and chestnut.

Oh Jennifer Pye, what are you doing?

She had remembered Claudia's outrageous instructions and undressed in a leisurely fashion behind the screens, allowing nobody to hurry her. A quick inspection of her body had told her that she was unmarked. She had breathed in a lungful of air and expelled it slowly and had liked the way her breasts had risen strongly under the wrap. Claudia was right. There was nothing wrong with her figure at all. It made her feel good.

She had taken her time to check that the heaters were where she wanted them, refusing to be affected in any way by the electric atmosphere of expectancy. The tutor had scratched his paunch absent-mindedly and encouraged her to try out various positions to find the most comfortable. She had eventually decided to lie full length along the red velvet which had been draped over the podium of mattress on box. 'Ah, the Odalisque' Adrian had exclaimed. 'Perfect.'

She had settled down. They had waited for her to signal her readiness. She looked up and caught Richard Ennessy's eye as he inspected a pencil point. He had nodded at her and tugged his hair to show that it was no longer white.

'Can you put that heater on the other side?' she had asked Adrian. 'I think I'll lie the other way.' She stuck out her tongue at Richard and turned her bottom to him. Facing her now, Bob Priestman was blushing like a beetroot.

'I'm ready,' she said.

EPISODE EIGHT

'I see we have something in common then Bob?' Richard said as he pulled up a small stool and sat down opposite Bob Priestman.

Priestman looked up, startled from his pint of beer and glanced around the pub as if not wanting to be seen fraternising.

''Ows that then?'

'We're both exhibitionists,' Richard stated and held up a hand to stop the indignant outburst that was imminent from the Yorkshireman. Richard knew that he was being provocative. 'I mean, that we both have our works displayed in the college.'

''Ave we?'

'You didn't know either then?' Priestman shook his head. 'Nor did I,' Richard admitted. 'I just happened to see them.'

'I know nowt about it. What 'ave they put up of mine?'

'Your pencil and wash of Harrods. It's in the corridor outside the Principal's office.'

'Bloody cheek! They never asked me.'

'They didn't ask me either.' Richard laughed shortly. 'I gather that from time to time the principal collars Dr. Sullivan and asks for some wall decoration to show visitors what the students can do and Dr. Sullivan then sits on the first person he can find, in this case it must have been Adrian, and gets them to come up with the goods.'

'What have they put up of yours, then? That imitation Monet?'

Richard ignored the barb. He had decided several weeks back, when they were doing the nude drawing, that his relations with Priestman needed to be put on a more agreeable standing.

93

He had seen Priestman's discomfiture glow from his face as he had tried to draw the front of the model, almost without looking at her. Richard had begun to suspect that Bob Priestman was a victim of circumstance and upbringing and not the boorish bigot he appeared to be.

Richard smiled and shook his head. 'That 'fake' Monet is still causing ripples. No, they put up a painting that I developed from drawing class.'

'Which one?'

'One of Jennie Pye.'

'Not the...'

'No. Not the nude study. I am not sure whether I will convert that into a painting. I have started but...' He paused. He could not explain why he was having difficulty. 'No it was the one in the ball gown. "The little girl's party frock," I think you called it.' Why did Richard feel that he needed to taunt Priestman? It was not helping the situation in any way. So, the man had got under his skin, but this was not his usual way of dealing with such problems. What on earth was happening to him? Bob Priestman's face immediately clouded with the old resentment.

'Aye well...' he began.

'I'm sorry Bob. That was unfair of me. It was quite uncalled for.'

'Eh?'

'I said I'm sorry. It was a silly thing to say.'

'Right... right then. We'll say no more about it.' Priestman was confused by Richard's surrender. It was as if, in his world, men did not apologise.

'Tell me about how you did that study of Harrod's.'

''Ow d'yer mean?'

'Did you do it from a series of photographs?'

'No I did not. I stood there and drew it,' he assured him, and then added diffidently, 'It's not difficult.'

'Yes, but where on earth did you prop your board? It's not a small drawing.'

'I've got a fold up easel, for field-work, like.'

Richard tried hard to imagine the reactions of the shoppers of Knightsbridge at finding a Yorkshireman and easel installed on their pavement.

'But didn't you get people bumping into you?'

'No. I drew in the early mornings before everyone was up. It only took three mornings, then I added the wash at 'ome.'

'I thought it was rather good.'

'Aye, well it's the best I could do.'

Richard sipped his beer thoughtfully. Somewhere around the other side of the bar a gaggle of students were arguing loudly above the electronic sounds of a gambling machine. The barman was trying to quieten them down, calling them "gentlemen" and invoking the comfort of the other patrons. He had managed to make his voice completely devoid of irony, a technique which effectively told every other customer in the pub exactly what he thought of students.

'Well your best is pretty good Bob.' He looked at him. 'It's not much to do with fabric design though is it?'

'Aye well, that's as maybe. I've got responsibilities. Our family 'as been in cloth for over a 'undred years and I'm t'eldest son.' Richard could not help noticing the sudden intensification of Priestman's accent when he spoke about Yorkshire. 'Aye-oop. Looks like trouble for someone.'

Richard suppressed a smile. For all the world he had thought that Priestman was about to utter the classic 'there's trouble at t'mill' but the Yorkshireman was looking over Richard's back to the street door.

'Looks like it's coming this way an' all.' He put down his glass. 'It's that lass we drew in t'drawing class.'

'Mr. Ennessy! I'd like a word with you!'

Jennifer Pye stood over him with her fists on her hips and her feet firmly apart. Her eyebrows were hovering somewhere near the top of her forehead and her nostrils were tinged with white. He deduced that she was angry.

'Ah, Miss Pye.' He tried to sound as pleasant and formal as he could. 'Would you join Mr. Priestman and I?'

'Who gave you permission to stick me up on the wall?' Richard stood up. He told himself that it was the gentleman in him but he knew that he was also taking away the small advantage that little Jennifer Pye had enjoyed over him whilst he had been perched on the stool. Now she was forced to look up at him. 'I never said that you could put me up there for everyone to see.'

He looked at her angry face turned up at him and was surprised to admit that he found the spectacle quite delightful.

He clasped his hands together, rather like a preacher in the pulpit. 'Ah well Miss Pye, now we are discussing those thorny issues of artistic integrity and the rights of–'

'Bullshit!' The oath resounded around the suddenly quiet pub. 'You get that painting taken out of Reception or I'll–'

'I regret to say that it is nothing to do with me, Miss Pye. You will need to talk to the people who put it there.'

''E's right. They've done the same with me. We knew nowt about it.'

She turned sharply on Priestman and her hair flailed Richard's chest. 'You keep your nose out of this, Yorkie! When I want your opinion I'll ask for it.'

'Suit yourself lass.' His unease upset Richard. It was not Priestman's argument. He was too easy a target.

As if to distract attention from the injustice she had committed, Jennifer threw at Richard, 'It's a lousy painting anyway.' She angrily flicked her hair back. 'Nothing like me.'

'In that case, why are you so worried? If it is that bad, nobody will know it is you.'

'Oooh! You think you are so clever don't you Mr. Ennessy...?' She stood up closer to him, her fists opening and closing. He looked down at her face, flushed with excitement, her breasts rising and falling with her enraged breathing.

'I can see you are upset and I think this has gone far enough, Jennie, why don't you sit down and have a drink?'

'MY NAME IS JENNIFER!' she shouted hotly and stormed back to the door. 'You never listen do you!' The door slammed behind her. There was a moment's silence and then the normal business of the pub resumed in a hum and buzz as the customers discussed the recent entertainment. Richard let his breath out slowly and sat down. He felt as if he had just run across a ploughed field in muddy wellingtons.

'You was right,' Priestman observed.

'Oh I don't think she was even listening...'

'Oh I didn't mean 'er.' Priestman nodded at the door. 'I meant you was right when you said we had something in common.'

'Oh was I?'

'Aye. We've both been shouted at by yon lass.' Priestman grinned ruefully. 'Sup up. I'll buy you another.'

Richard put his elbows on the table and held his head in his hands. 'Oh dear, oh dear, oh dear,' he said.

The shortbread finger had been poised before Cherryl's open mouth for several seconds. 'You never did!' she said.

Jennifer nodded contradiction and rocked back on the bed. 'I did. I shouted "bullshit". You should have seen his face!'

'Oh Jennifer, they'll never let you back in there.'

'I wouldn't want to go in there ever again if those two use it. I'd rather...' She stopped, completely at a loss to think of a worse option.

'Rather what?' Cherryl bit the end of her biscuit.

'I would rather... I would rather have another one of your biscuits,' she giggled as her hand dived into the packet.

'Oh Jennifer. You are infuriating sometimes. They are rather moreish though aren't they?'

Jennifer read the name on the side of the packet.

'These are not from Safeways, that's treachery,' she accused Cherryl. 'I'll tell your Keith.'

'He wouldn't mind. "Live and let live" is what he says. Life's too short to worry about things like that. If you want it, go and get it. Anyway...' Cherryl refused to be diverted from the subject under discussion. 'What is this painting like then? Has he given you green hair or purple eyes or something?'

Jennifer sucked her lips noisily. Cherryl had unwittingly hit upon the problem. Everyone who had seen it had said that the painting was good. Patsy had come running up to her to tell her how pretty she looked. 'You look so... wistful. Perched there with no dancing shoes on. You look like a beautiful but sad Cinderella, unable to go to the ball'. She remembered the sitting and the magic of what Richard Ennessy had whispered in her ear. She had gone to the ball, she had been there, watching the colours of the dancers as they swirled under the sparkling chandeliers. She had wanted to dance. She could feel the under skirts chafing her legs, she could feel their bulk hanging around her waist. She had wanted to dance; she had managed to get there despite them but she had been prevented from dancing because they had taken away her shoes. That was why she had been sad. And Richard Ennessy had painted it and now people kept telling her how pretty she was and how mysterious and moving was the look in her eyes.

'Well?' Cherryl insisted.

'The thing is, Cherry... Actually, everybody says that it is good and that I look super.'

'That's great! So why were you so annoyed with him?'

'I told him I thought it was a lousy picture.'

Cherryl was silent for a while. The chiming of the hall clock sounded from downstairs.

'Is it a lousy picture Jennifer?' she asked quietly. Jennifer shook her head.

'No it's bloody good. Oooh, I hate the man!' She blew air into her cheeks, puffing them up, and then expelled it noisily. 'The trouble is... You see, Cherry, this is not the only drawing he has done of me. I've sat for the class since then and I'm worried that he will use that drawing for a painting. I wouldn't want *that* put up on the wall for everyone to gawp at. I think I would die.'

'Why? If he is as good a painter as you say?'

'That's exactly the reason. Although in the drawing session he... happened to be behind me, if he paints me, everyone will recognise me.'

'But what is wrong with...?'

'They'll know it is my bum!'

Cherryl stared at Jennifer and this time the biscuit was lowered away from the open mouth which continued to gape as its owner coped with what she thought she had understood.

'Jennifer,' she whispered, 'you didn't pose without any... you know... in the nuddy?'

'Absolutely starkers!' Jennifer nodded morosely. 'And if they put up a nude Jennifer in the college, I wouldn't... I wouldn't dare go back.'

'Oh Jennifer... With nothing on at all?' Jennifer nodded again. 'Not even panties?'

'Not even a fig leaf. Not even a tea leaf!' She was beginning to find Cherryl's anxiety amusing.

'How long ago did you do this? Perhaps he has forgotten about it.'

'You remember when I borrowed your long dress?'

'Yes, I do. I couldn't think at all why you wanted it. You're not really a dressy person.'

'Thanks duck.'

'Oh you know what I mean.' Cherryl gave her arm a playful smack. 'So why did you need it?'

'Are you prepared for this?' Cherryl hugged a cushion to her chest and nodded. 'I went to college with no undies on – so that the strap marks wouldn't show.'

'Without any... what none at all? You mean under the dress you...?' Jennifer nodded. 'What... on the tube and in the street and everywhere?' Jennifer nodded again. 'Oh Jennifer, you are awful!' she exclaimed in delight and hugged the cushion tighter. 'Now what are you going to take to wear in Bristol? Let's have a sort through your cupboard.'

Across the other side of London, in Half Moon Mews, Richard Ennessy was working skilfully on a canvas. With the events of the day clear in his mind, he had found that the previous intangible difficulty that he had encountered with this project had suddenly revealed itself to be: motivation. Until today, he had not possessed the motivation to paint Jennifer Pye nude, but now... So, it was his fault that her painting was on display, was it? So it was a lousy painting, was it?

He recalled the cheeky way that she had turned her back on him at the sitting, deliberately denying him the view of her front, presenting instead her head of hair, her back and buttocks. With infinite care and a malicious patience he detailed the suggestion of pubic hair which had peeked through the triangle at the base of her buttocks. See how you like that, Jennifer Pye!

The party from the College of St. Mary Virgin must have reached the Hardiman Room. Arthur Northgate sighed wistfully. He supposed it was education of a sort. Although they were two rooms away, he could hear the excited chattering of the girls echoing through the gallery as they goggled at the eight foot high bronze statue of the bowman. His burnished genitalia would be just about level with their eyes.

Soon Arthur would take a stroll down there, his room was empty except for that girl, staring at those oils in the corner. Yes, he would saunter down to the Hardiman Room and time his arrival so that the teacher would be at the far end of the room and he would catch the mischievous stragglers at the near end, in the act of prodding the bronze penis with curous fingers and he would wink at them as he always did and they would blush scarlet. It happened every year. He always recounted the event to his missus and she always said, 'Brazen hussies!'

Magdaline O'Neill was vaguely aware of now being alone. The solitude suited the atmosphere of the third picture that she was studying. Was it loneliness? Perhaps not. The girl was dressed in jeans and a huge jumper and was sitting on a mound, or a rock, difficult to distinguish which. She was gazing away out to the horizon. A suggestion of a horizon, and nothing between her and the illusory line where sea meets sky. Sea meets sky. That was it! She was on a beach. She was sitting on a rock or something, on a beach and gazing... How was she gazing? It wasn't sadly, like in the ballgown. It was... She was serene. She was at peace. And she was snug in his jumper. What did you say? Snug in his jumper. Whose jumper? Magdaline's heart began to pound. Whose jumper is she wearing? Who is he? Where is he?

'Jennifer! Down here! I've saved you a seat.' Jennifer Pye staggered down the aisle of the coach as it lurched away from the kerb and headed for Sloane Square. 'They nearly went without you, Jennifer, where did you get to?'
'I had to hand in an assignment by two today.' She swung around and fell into the empty seat. 'And then at the last minute I found something else that I wanted to put in it.'
'Do you want to sit by the window?'
'No you stay there Patsy. Any seat will do me, I'm shattered.' She pushed her head back into the seat and closed her eyes. 'Are they stopping before Bristol?'
'On the motorway somewhere, in a couple of hours.'
'Good, I'm starving. I had to work all through lunch.'
'Oh Jennifer! You must look after yourself.' Patsy poked about inside her bag and then pulled out a bundle. 'I've got this. It's cheese and tomato. It's a bit squished.'
'Oh thanks duck, you're a treasure.'
She bit savagely into the roll and gazed absently down the coach. 'It's not just our year then?' She had seen a few unfamiliar heads. 'I thought that it was just us.'

'Well it would have been but not enough people put their names down so they offered it to the whole department.'

Jennifer nodded comprehension through a mouthful of roll and then suddenly stopped chewing. She recognised that red hair. It was Yorkie. She felt a funny sort of flip in her chest. If he was here, then Richard Ennessy could also be. She looked around now more intently. Where was he? Sitting in some vantage point from which he could suddenly swoop down on her and ridicule her? She could not see him.

'Who are you looking for?'

'Oh, Ruth.'

'Ruth is just there.' Patsy pointed with an insolent overtness. She had not been fooled one bit. 'I'll lend you my glasses if you like.'

'Humph,' Jennifer remarked and began to study the programme of the weekend.

They were due to arrive at Bristol at about six in the evening. This would give them a short time to dump their things and have a wash in their rooms before dinner. They had all been allocated accommodation in the students' hostel and so Patsy and Jennifer were sharing a double room to cut down the expense. After dinner they would immediately go to their respective assembly groups and be given a quick induction talk relevant to their chosen course and they then had some time to start their first project. Classes finished at nine thirty.

Jennifer turned the sheet around, trying to orientate herself on the building plan so that she would be able to find the silk screen printing workshop.

Breakfast on Saturday was at seven thirty and classes began at nine and continued all through the day, interspersed with meal and coffee breaks, until nine in the evening. From ten till one in the morning, a disco was being run in the main hall, but breakfast on Sunday morning was at a merciless seven thirty and lessons started again at nine. By lunchtime, most of what they wanted to achieve should have been achieved. After Sunday lunch there was a voluntary feedback session and then they were free. The coach would be leaving at seven in the evening. This would allow Ruth her 'optional visit to Cheddar Gorge' Jennifer thought.

'It's not exactly a rest camp is it?' Patsy was reading over her shoulder.

'I should hope not, for what it's costing us!' Jennifer remarked, and then immediately thought that, given the particular means that she had employed to procure herself the money, she did not yet know what the total cost to her would be.

A hand touched her shoulder.

'Jennifer! Jennifer!' a dramatic voice enunciated. It was Claudia Crayford, "international superstar and model" as she had introduced herself at their previous meeting. 'I've just seen your portrait in the reception.' Jennifer groaned. She was getting sick of this. 'Brilliant, absolutely brilliant my dear. You look so... so...'

'Everybody likes it except Jennifer,' Patsy talked across her as if she were not there.

'But why? It's magnificent.'

'Oh, she's just a sourpuss.'

'It's not that....' Jennifer was shocked into speech by Patsy's uncharacteristic disloyalty.

'But my dear, tell me, who was the artist? Oh, he could paint me any day.'

'It were Richard Ennessy,' Bob Priestman was standing behind her. 'But yon lass told 'im it were a lousy painting.'

'Oh you didn't, did you Jennifer?' Patsy was horrified. 'Well I hope you apologise to him.'

Claudia straightened herself and Bob Priestman shot out a quick hand to prevent her from knocking her head.

'Watch your pretty head lass.'

She smiled uncertainly. 'Is this Richard your friend?'

Bob Priestman appeared at a loss for the moment.

'Well I never thought about it really.'

'Is he coming to Bristol?'

'I thought he said he was.' Priestman looked up and down the coach. 'But he's not on the coach so I suppose he isn't.'

'Pity. I should have liked to meet him.' Claudia said.

'And it would have given Jennifer a chance to say sorry, wouldn't it?' Patsy said.

Jennifer huddled down into her seat and tried to make herself very, very small.

'Donkeys, Nessie? A dance for donkeys?' Richard pretended disbelief. Vanessa Clewe-Harting hurled a green satin cushion with a force and accuracy that nearly knocked him from the ottoman. He momentarily unbalanced himself as he parried the missile with his forearm. 'I suppose you often dance with donkeys do you?' he continued. 'What was his name? Cuthbert?'

'You've gone a bit too far now Boy!' Taking advantage of his precarious position she sprang onto him and gave him a hearty shove backwards.

'Oi!' he exclaimed and grabbed at her shirt. It pulled out of her jeans as together they rolled off the ottoman and onto the Persian rug.

'Not *for* donkeys, Boy, *in aid of* donkeys!' Vanessa pinned him to the floor by sitting on his pelvis.

'Gee-gees too big for you now, little girl?' he teased and bucked upwards, knocking her forwards onto him. 'Oh yum yum, lovely tum!' he said through a mouth buried in her bosom.

'Oh you like that do you?' she asked menacingly. She grabbed his head from behind, and, bringing her whole weight to bear, she yanked his body upwards. 'Have some more!' she offered and clutched his face into her breasts. He tried shaking free but her grip was like iron. 'Do you give in?'

'Mmmmf!' he refused.

She started to wriggle her bottom sensually on his lap.

'Do you give in?' she demanded softly. She could feel her technique beginning to have an effect on him.

'Mmmmf!' he repeated.

'Right!' She clutched his head tighter and began to bounce gently up and down on him. Richard frantically tore his head free and shrieked,

'Give in! Give in!'

She stopped bouncing and let him fall back onto the carpet, where he lay and gasped for breath with an imprint of bra cup creased across one cheek.

'I have brought the tea, sir.' John's perfectly modulated voice betrayed no sign of disapproval at finding Viscount Churle lying on his back under a half undressed and gently bobbing Lady Vanessa.

'Thank you John.' Richard pulled a serious face.

'So it's a black tie dance in aid of your pet charity for distressed donkeys and you want yours truly to fork out the shekels for a ticket?' Richard made a resumé of Vanessa's explanation.

'Two tickets,' Vanessa insisted. 'Unless you are going to dance with a donkey.

'I'm not paying for your ticket, oh avaricious one.'

'No you are not,' she admitted. 'You will need to find yourself a partner, oh smug, conceited one.'

He stopped chewing on the cake and looked at her for an instant. 'Gentleman in the wings eh? Oh well done Nessie! Put me down for two tickets. Must have a gander at this one!' Vanessa reached for the cushion. 'Pax!' he said quickly, 'Pax.' He looked at his watch. 'I must go Nessie love.' He kissed her on the cheek. She held his arm and so he kissed her on the lips. 'Send me the bill,' he called over his shoulder as he scooped up his bag and jacket. 'When is it?'

'May,' she replied.

She stood at the window and watched his yellow car bounce down the drive. Behind her, she could hear John clearing away the tea.

Jennifer scowled into the bottom of the plastic cup.

'That tea never saw a tea leaf.'

Patsy was chewing methodically upon a sticky bun.

'I think this bun is rubber.' She had to raise her voice to be heard over the surge of traffic noise as some more unsuspecting travellers entered the motorway restaurant.

'Come on, we'd better get back to the coach,' Jennifer warned. 'I don't want to get a reputation for being late.'

Visible through the window behind her, yet unnoticed by either of them, a bright yellow sports car passed at ninety miles per hour, travelling in the direction of Bristol.

EPISODE NINE

Although Graham Treadsure held a well-paid and responsible position in an industrial textile research consultancy, twice a year he offered his knowledge and skills to the college by running one of the modules on their weekend courses. The fee that he was paid hardly funded the petrol for his BMW but he was quite happy to be able to spend a weekend in tartan shirt and jeans, messing about with the students and sharing with them their excitement as they developed.

He always aimed to give the students a tangible goal to achieve in the short time that they found themselves under his tutelage. It was a useful technique to send them away on Sunday afternoon with something they had succeeded in producing with their own hands. The actual form of the artefact did not matter, the fact that they had been obliged to employ their newly learned skills in order to realise it meant that it would act forever after as an aide-memoire; every time they looked at it they would remember the toil, the frustration, the success and the failure that went into it.

So, within the space of this weekend, they would all design and screen print their own tee shirt. They would have to make decisions on colours and layout, cloths and dyes; they would need to learn the cleanliness and precision to achieve register, and they would have to limit their imagination to what was achievable and what they were capable of making themselves. This was not a fashion design studio, amputated from the production line; here they were design, production and fashion model rolled into one.

Apart from the practical knowledge that Graham Treadsure brought to the students they also gained by working with a man experienced in the industry, they learned to see practices not as academic disciplines but as commercial processes whose eventual aim was production and sale. And the benefit was not one-sided. Graham firmly believed that these sessions were therapeutic to him. They enabled him to cope with the high powered stress which he was subject to in his normal working environment. He felt that keeping in touch with the grass roots could only benefit him, and although his contemporaries often raised a cynical eyebrow at his quasi-charitable activities and sometimes sneered outright, it was noted with envy that he often correctly identified trends far earlier than anybody else.

And occasionally he made a discovery. He was about to make one in the next five minutes. He had been watching her flicking back her long hair and mixing inks with a determination that showed that she knew what she wanted and that nothing was going to prevent her achieving it. He wandered casually over to her table and read her name badge.

'Are they not coming out as you wish, Jennifer?'

'Oh I'm getting there.' She pushed a tray towards him. 'I've got those four. Just this one to do.'

'May I see your design?'

'On top of my sketchbook.' She nodded towards the end of the table. He picked up the piece of paper and studied the rough pencil sketch. He could best describe it as a series of shapeless lozenges which fell diagonally across the paper and then turned abruptly to climb up one side. He was not sure what he was looking at nor how she intended realising it.

'You can't really see what it is with just that.' She put down her pot and picked up her sketchbook. 'It's based on this,' she said, flicking open a page of magic, watery, amorphous, intangible colours.

'I can see why you are having problems mixing the inks,' he said as he carefully took the book from her. 'How does this design fit onto the shirt?'

'Just like that.'

'Off-centre?'

'Yup.'

'Why?'

'Because that is the way it was.'

He had seen designs inspired by flowers or leaves, even animal fur and wood. He could generally recognise the germ but this one escaped him.

'You'll have to explain to me what image source you are using Jennifer.'

'It's the sunlight coming through a stained glass front door and making the colours on the hall table, that's the flat bit, and part way up the wall.'

'Yes,' he said slowly.

'Try squinting,' she said, mischievously repeating some advice that he had given earlier to another student. He did and as the coloured, misshapen lozenges came to life in his imagination, suddenly, the portion of blank white which formed the centre of the design, glowed with an eerie incandescence. It became the sunlight. He was mesmerised. 'Good, isn't it?' the girl said in a voice devoid of any self promotion.

'Yes. How did you come across it?'

'It was like I said – the sunlight shining through the front door at my digs. I sketched it and watched it as it changed.'

Graham Treadsure put down the sketchbook and straightened up. 'I will be very interested to see how it comes out.' He could already see this design on shirts, on a skirt, on a sarong.

Richard pulled the plastic cup from the vending machine and peered doubtfully into it. He could not remember which button he had pressed and the contents gave him no clue as to their composition. He shrugged and moved further onto the landing. Here, the other students of the floor were congregating for coffee in a noisy bustle of exchanged experiences enlivened by gruesome pouts and ecstatic grins.

A knob of red hair drew his attention and he made his way over to Bob Priestman who was standing on the edge of a group.

'Hello Bob, how's it going?'

'Eh... But...? When did you get here?'

'I came down last night.' Richard could not understand his surprise.

'But you weren't on t' bus.'

'No I came down by car.'

'A car eh?' Richard could sense Priestman struggling with his prejudices again.

'Yes I don't use it in London, except sometimes in the evenings or at weekends. It would only get clamped or towed away.'

'Oh aye.'

'What's your room like?'

'It's O.K. Lovely view of the air-conditioning unit on the flat roof.' This was said with such seriousness that Richard had to believe its sincerity.

'Are you sharing?'

Priestman looked uncomfortable.

'No... Er... I don't go in for that sort of thing. I like bein' by meself. Having me privacy.'

'Likewise,' Richard said, uncertain what "that sort of thing" was. 'So, how's it going then? Good course?'

'Better than I'd 'oped.'

'What course are you doing?'

'I'm having a bash at etching and I'm going to try a bit of engraving. I've always liked those engravings that you get in Victorian books on architecture and in the *Illustrated London News* – you know the sort of thing, "Peabody's Marine Salt Works seen on a sunny day".'

Richard laughed. 'Yes I know exactly what you mean. We've got some bound volumes in the library and I used to spend hours as a child, pretending with my fingers that I was opening the doors of the buildings and walking up inside them.'

'Did yer?'

'Yes. I think it was the detail that fascinated me.'

'Aye, it's the same wi' me. I love doing the cross-hatching and shading to make the depth and perspective to a building. It's something people don't do much nowadays. How's your course?'

Richard looked around quickly and lowered his voice.

'Awful,' he said. 'It's partly my fault for allowing myself to be talked into it. I don't really like the Impressionists.' Priestman opened his mouth to comment but Richard pre-empted him. 'Despite the famous Monet, I don't like having to think like an impressionist and apparently, that is just what the technique demands.'

'What course are you doing then?'

'Spatula technique in oils. Compared to the kind of brush-work I normally do, it's like trying to plant a window box with a JCB.' Priestman laughed at the simile drawn from a vernacular that he could understand. 'And the confounded tutor, or "skills co-ordinator" as they call them, will insist on addressing me as

"Dick".' He fingered the name badge which they had to wear. 'It does not say "Dick" on there, does it? I tell him my name is Richard but he doesn't seem to listen.'

Priestman's face was suddenly brightened by a malicious grin. 'My name is Jennifer! You never listen do you?' he said. Richard started at the touching vision of Jennifer's earnest, face, angrily upturned to his as she had vilified him in the pub. 'Remember what that lass said?' Priestman continued, enjoying the irony of the situation, 'Those were her very words.'

'Yes I remember. I remember very well. And you didn't come out of it exactly unscathed... Yorkie!'

Priestman flinched visibly and Richard realised that the veneer that the man had started to build to protect himself was still just that. Before Richard could try to soften the repercussions of his retort, Priestman had scored over him with glee.

'Well, anyroad, the lass is here.'

'What?' Jennifer Pye in Bristol! Little Jennifer Pye, bounding with indignant energy and anger, just about to walk around that corner. Jennifer Pye pulling her beautiful golden hair up from her neck as she remonstrates with her friends in the refectory. He began to recall images of Jennifer Pye that he did not know he had registered. 'Oh, that's the last thing I needed!'

'Aye, she were on t'bus. Took a lot of stick from everyone about that painting of yours.'

'Oh no!' Richard groaned. 'What course is she on?'

'One of the craft type things. She's downstairs in the other block.' Bob Priestman looked carefully at him. 'Don't you want to meet her then?'

'No I do not!' Richard replied with vehemence.

'Funny....' Priestman observed, 'you've gone quite red.'

Richard was stealing guiltily down the corridor when a voice said, 'Smile!'

Intrigued, he turned a questioning face and was blinded by a photographic flash.

'Gotcher!' Ruth Robey said with glee. 'That will be five pounds please.'

'How much to destroy the negative?'

'I'm sorry, I'm still learning how to develop negatives. I don't think they teach us how to destroy them.'

'Aren't you supposed to be in class?'

'For an aspiring fashion photographer, the whole world is the classroom,' Ruth replied with mock pomposity. She lifted her chiffon scarf to cover the lower half of her face and fluttered her eyelashes. 'Mind you,' she added with feeling, 'they didn't tell me I would need biceps like Hercules. Feel the weight of that.' She dumped the camera into Richard's hands.

Richard weighed it up and then inspected it briefly.

'Hasselblad,' he observed. 'A decent little snapshot camera that.' He carefully put it back into her hands. 'Costs about two and a half grand. Three and a half with that lens on it.'

'You're joking!' Ruth was shocked.

Richard shook his head and smiled. Ruth thought that he looked rather handsome when his eyes were all crinkled up like that. And he had been decent about that fiasco at the Ritz. He had never mentioned it. She moved up close to him to allow some people to pass and could smell his fragrance again.

'Where are you off to?' she asked. 'Shouldn't *you* be in class?'

'Ah!' He took her arm gently and turned her back the way she had come. 'You've caught me playing truant. Now run along before they realise you are missing.'

'Not so fast! You're just trying to get rid of me.'

'Perish the thought!'

'Well? What are you up to?'

'I'm going out for an early lunch. My course is a bit of a washout for me, so I thought I would have a pub lunch somewhere and then go to the city art gallery.'

'Sounds tempting...'

'Miss Robey. Ruth, please...?' They both turned to see a harassed looking man in leather trousers gesturing to her frantically from a doorway. 'Please do not leave the studio with the equipment unless you have been authorised.'

He stared at Richard with a suspicious hostility.

'Sorry Mr. Parkinson.' She pouted.

'Make it two hundred then and it's a deal!' Richard called down the corridor after her.

Mr. Parkinson jumped as if electrocuted and looked around but Richard had turned the corner. He could just hear Ruth's indignant protestations fading away as he reached the exit.

Patsy stopped prodding her fish cake and put the fork down on the plastic tray. She took off her spectacles.

'Do you need these again?' she asked.

'Don't be so catty, Patsy. I don't know what's got into you,' Jennifer scolded. 'I can see perfectly well where Ruth is.'

Jennifer was annoyed and this annoyance was directed at the absent figure of Richard Ennessy. Not only did he put her painting up in the college without asking her permission but when she had tried surreptitiously to find him on the coach, Patsy had made that silly gesture with her spectacles. Jennifer blamed Richard Ennessy fairly and squarely for making her feel foolish and uncomfortable.

But her screen printing had gone well. She was really pleased with it. The design was good, she had almost managed the colours but the registering of the design on the screen – getting each colour to appear in exactly the right place – was causing her some headaches. It required a methodical and precise mind and Jennifer was not certain that she had it. But Graham Treadsure had been quietly encouraging to her. He had suggested she try the coarser cloth although she had already identified the finer as being the one most likely to best render the design. 'At this stage in your career Jennifer, you can and must try everything. Later when you have more experience,' he had laughed, 'when you are old and crusty like me, you will be able to discard processes without a second thought but for the moment don't be narrow, go wide!'

It was the first time that anybody had talked about her studies as a 'career'. It had made her think.

'Mind if I join you?' Ruth sat down without awaiting the answer. 'How are you getting on with the screen printing?' Then before they could bore her with technical details, 'What is the lecturer like?'

'Old,' Jennifer said tartly. 'What about yours?'

'He's not that old,' Patsy objected. 'He's only about forty.'

'That's middle aged, Patsy. He's practically dead. All his bits will have dropped off by now,' Ruth declared as she stabbed a yogurt pot with a teaspoon.

'I don't care. I think he's nice. He listens to you and he is polite. And anyway, all his bits haven't dropped off.' Ruth and Jennifer stared at Patsy. 'I mean...' she stammered, 'I think you were exaggerating.'

'Patsy!' said Ruth, 'You haven't been looking at...' She left the phrase unfinished for greater effect.

'Well, what is your course leader like then?' Patsy tried to deflect the attention. She looked up as someone approached the table. 'I'll ask Claudia, she's doing the fashion photography workshop as well isn't she?'

'He's short and frantic, isn't he Claudia?' Ruth asked for confirmation as she moved to make a space at the table for the new arrival.

'Who?'

'Your course leader,' Patsy prompted.

'Oh my dear,' Claudia flapped her hand in the air space above the table, 'He is the limit. The limit. Listen my dears, listen. You won't believe it. He wears a check shirt and leather trousers. I mean – leather trousers? I keep expecting him to say "Howdey pardner" or "I think I'll just mosey down to the old corral". And he stands with his hand on his hip like this.'

'Ouch, watch what you're doing with your elbow,' Jennifer complained.

'Sorry my dear.' Claudia sighed heavily. 'I don't think I will be able to put up with him until nine o'clock tonight. Aaagh!' she exclaimed. 'I've just had a horrible thought. You don't think he will be coming to the disco tonight do you?'

'Oh Lord, I hope not.' As Ruth made the remark, it suddenly occurred to her that there was someone whom she would like to see at the disco tonight and he was in the college.

'No, you're not his favourite person after trying to flog off half the photographic equipment to some passing gypsy or other.'

'Oh Ruth, you never did!' Patsy nibbled the corner of her paper serviette.

'A slight exaggeration, but thank you for reminding me. I'll tell Richard you called him a passing gypsy.'

'Who?' Jennifer sat up with a jerk. 'Who did you say?'

'Richard Ennessy. I saw him in college this morning.'

'What was he doing?'

'Playing truant, he said.'

'I mean what course was he doing?' Jennifer suspected that Ruth was being exasperating on purpose.

'Why do you want to know?' Ruth's voice was syrup.

'So that she can go and apologise to him, I expect.' Patsy put her spoke in the wheel.

'Nothing of the sort,' Jennifer growled.

'Why should she need to apologise?' Claudia was having difficulty chasing the hare she had raised.

'Richard Ennessy,' Patsy explained, 'Painter of portraits of young ladies,' she paused, 'pretty and ungrateful young ladies, in ballgowns.'

'The painter that you declared could paint you anyday... and you called him a gypsy,' Ruth added with malicious glee. 'I can't wait to tell him.'

'Oh my dear,' Claudia finger-marched her hand across the table top towards Ruth. 'How would you like to be wearing that yogurt pot on your nose?'

'Oh do grow up children,' Jennifer scolded them. She was already concentrating on what she was going to say to Mr. Ennessy next time she saw him.

Towards the end of the afternoon, Richard found a long leather seat in the middle of one of the galleries and settled onto it. Around the walls were hung Victoriana in its unashamed purity. Rich merchants posing in an arcadian obscurity, a fleet of trading vessels riding the high seas, a landowner and his wife proudly stiff before the backdrop panorama of their park. Richard leaned back and closed his eyes. He wondered if one day, many years hence, when he had succeeded his father as Earl of Wisdene, he would feel as smugly certain of his role on earth as did these Victorians? Would he want his portrait painted, posing on the crumbling stones of the south terrace with the deer grazing in Long Covert behind him? And who would be his Countess? Would it be some example of noble breeding stock whom he had felt obliged to marry to ensure the strength of line of the d'Ennessys? Would it be some chirpy chorus girl with long legs and a lascivious smile whom he had ogled from his box at the Playhouse? He smiled at the scenario of him bringing home a big-bosomed disco dancer to present to father.

But more seriously, what was to be his role until the dreadful day when he found that he was fatherless and shuffled up the baronial ladder? From an early age, his brother Charles had engaged himself wholeheartedly in the life of a country squire and although he pretended in private to be unenthusiastic in matters rustic, their father actually exercised quite a patriarchal influence over the running of the estate. He could not warm to acres of alfalfa but he could glow to Lisa Dandy's bubbling baby or Wayne Hartop's singing in the Wisdene Arms on a Sunday night. In fact, the more he thought about it, the more Richard realised that he and his father were alike in their attitude to the estate and their responsibilities. Neither of them cared for agriculture but his father ensured that the estate could continue to turn, providing the livelihood for all concerned with it, by making his money where he could and that happened to be in the realms of business. What would Richard do in his place? Sell paintings? Charge millions for portraits of the noble and rich? He was hardly likely to provide a living in that manner.

Was the accusation that his mother levelled at him, really justified? Did he never stick at anything? Had he no sense of responsibility? What was he doing at art college? Why was he there? He pondered for a bit and decided that the answer was that he was getting it out of his system and that at some time in the future he would discover his niche in life and start to produce the responsible millions that were expected of him.

The burgher in the brown coat stared unblinkingly back at him with crackled eyes. Richard started. A thought had just occurred to him. Since he was no longer interested in the course he had come for, there was no reason to continue his stay in Bristol. He did not mind forgoing the money spent and he would certainly be more comfortable in Half Moon Mews. He stood up and looked at his watch. He could snatch a bite of something to eat in the wine bar across the street then go back, pack his bag and hit the road. Nobody would miss him.

As he was climbing the stairs to his landing, he met Bob Priestman skipping down to the final hour of the day's lessons.

'Got no class to go to?' The Yorkshireman seemed full of beans. No doubt he was happy with his engraving.

'No. Well I have, but I'm not going. I've decided to cut my losses and go home. I'm just getting my bag.'

The effect on Bob Priestman was surprising.

'Oh bugger!' He sighed heavily and leaned his back against the wall. 'I was going to ask you to do something, like.'

'Well you can always ask.'

'No... No. That's all right.' He was unable to hide his disappointment. 'You go. It's not... it's not important.'

Richard could not for the life of him imagine what Bob Priestman wanted him to do; a task which required his continued presence in Bristol, but it was obviously important to him.

'What did you want me to do, Bob?'

'No, that's all right Richard. Forget it. I must go or I'll be late for class.' He started methodically down the stairs.

'Yorkie!' Richard shouted. Priestman stopped, his shoulders tensed and he turned. 'I asked you a question. Don't walk away from me.'

Priestman swallowed and looked sheepishly at the black painted handrail. 'Aye, well... It's a bit daft really.'

'Let me decide that. I'm waiting.'

'Well it's the dance tonight... But you're going 'ome so it don't matter,' he finished quickly.

'What about the dance?' Richard asked evenly.

'Were you not going then? To the dance?'

'I hadn't thought about it. It had completely slipped my mind. Why? Did you want me to go?'

'Aye, I did.' Priestman said quickly and then looked up at him as if the admission had caught him by surprise. 'I want to go, like, but, well I'm not too clever at that sort of thing – you know, people an' that, but you are and I thought that if you was going, I could come with you, like and we could go together...'

'Oh well if it's only that!' Richard said, 'I can easily go home tomorrow morning, no problem.'

'Would yer?'

'What time does it start?'

'Ten till one in t'mornin'. In the main hall.'

'I'm in room 324. Call for me when you're ready. O.K.?'

'Aye. That's grand.' He grinned. 'That's right grand.' And he ran down the stairs whistling.

For some intangible reason, Richard felt a strange expectancy. Perhaps Priestman's enthusiasm was catching.

At first sight, the Saturday night disco appeared to be an unusual sort of hybrid, reflecting the heterogeneity of its patrons. And these were a strange mixture, for the weekend courses attracted students from all walks of life and from all generations.

Some of the mature students were in their fifties and sixties and some of the 'skills coordinators' had turned up to enjoy themselves or perhaps to attempt a bonding process of some sort, Richard was not sure.

But they were in a minority, the greater proportion of heaving and writhing was being undertaken by the generation of which Richard, sometimes reluctantly, claimed membership. He leaned against the bar with his pint of beer and surveyed the coloured flashing lights, booming bass speakers and the crowd of gyrating youth giving it the stamp of normality. It was, after all, a typical college disco. Even to the bar lit by harsh fluorescent tubes and almost certainly run by students on the BA Public Admin. course who could never pass up an opportunity to practise getting their hands in the till – an essential skill for later.

He nudged Bob and nodded towards a couple trying to circumnavigate the floor in a rather unpredictable quickstep, dodging around dancers like the Titanic around icebergs.

'Gay Porter is letting her hair down, I see.'

'Who?' Bob Priestman squinted into the multicoloured gloom.

'Mrs. Porter. Over there with the chap in the brown suit.'

'Oh aye. I think that's the registrar. Shall we try and find somewhere to sit down?' Bob Priestman had already had his suede shoes trodden on twice and was worried that someone would now spill beer down his corduroy jacket.

'Good idea. Lead on.'

He followed Priestman as he rashly tried to penetrate the dancing throng. Point number one, Richard thought, 'when carrying a pint of beer, go around the floor not across it'. He would try to drop this pearl of wisdom in Bob Priestman's ear before the night was much older and before he had splashed his mild and bitter down a naked back, or, worse still, a muscular back. He thought grimly of the likely consequences of an inadvertently drenched stud turning angrily on a hot-headed Yorkshireman and wondered why he had agreed to come to the disco. What was drawing him here? It was not a protective feeling towards Priestman however much their relations had improved. He was big enough and old enough to look after himself although, he had looked pathetically vulnerable as he had admitted that he was not good with people. It must have taken a lot of guts to say that, especially to Richard who apparently embodied all the qualities he despised. Bob Priestman must have a really good reason to want to come here. Richard wondered who she was.

'You see, that denim skirt looks good on you,' Patsy sought support from Claudia. 'Don't you think that skirt looks good on her?'

'Divine, my dear.' Claudia flapped her hand in one of her characteristic but obscure gestures.

'You want to look your best,' Patsy explained with a naivety which Jennifer found difficult to resist. 'You never know who you are going to meet.'

'There's plenty of girls wearing jeans,' Jennifer grumbled and glanced sourly at Patsy's green dress upon the sleeves of which, Patsy had painstakingly sewn sequins. That was the trouble with studying anything to do with fashion. Everybody expected you to dress up all the while, to have a complexion like alabaster and legs right up to your bum. 'You're not wearing your horrid jeans and that's final!' Patsy had said forcefully, 'What did you bring that skirt for?' Jennifer could not answer that. Why had she packed her denim skirt? What on earth had she been thinking of? Had her social life become so restricted that she had forgotten how to behave?

'Come on, let's dance Jennifer, that's what we're here for!' Patsy took her hand and dragged her up from her chair.

'Oh all right. Keep an eye on my bag Claudia.

'Certainly my dear. I'll just sit here and bark whilst waiting for Prince Charming to buzz along.'

This is it, Richard thought. He's seen her.

'Eh, I've just seen someone who's dying to meet you.' Priestman turned and spoke to Richard. Richard winced as, quite unnoticed, Priestman's beer passed within a gnat's whisker of a convulsing bare midriff. 'Come and let me introduce you.'

She was thin and angular and had freckles and was sitting alone at a table full of handbags. Her eyes showed only a polite interest at their approach. Priestman stood awkwardly at the table.

'Remember me?' She looked blankly at him and a flush began

to creep into his face. 'On t'bus. We was talking about portrait of yon lass.'

Richard was suddenly cascaded with an avalanche of realisations. That at their previous meeting, the girl had made a far greater impression on Priestman than he had made on her; that Priestman was unaware of this; that she was the reason why Priestman had wanted to come to the disco; that Priestman's Yorkshire accent became more pronounced in times of stress; that his 'yon lass' meant that Jennifer Pye was somewhere near, and the most disturbing realisation of all: that his own heart was thumping fit to burst.

'Oh yes?' she said vaguely.

'Aye. Yer wanted to meet the artist...' Priestman's voice trailed away.

Richard bowed to her. The girl's eyes lit up with an interest she had not shown for Priestman. Why did he allow himself to be put in such an excruciating position? Priestman doggedly attempted the introduction.

'This is Richard...er... Ennessy.' He turned to Richard, 'This is... Oh.' He stopped, utterly perplexed. 'I... I don't know your name.'

She rose from her chair like a well-oiled cobra and fixed Richard with her eyes.

'I'm Claudia. So, you are the portrait painter?' She slipped her arms around his neck. 'Come and dance a portrait with me.' She wriggled him backwards with her hips towards the knot of dancers. 'Oh my dear, look after the bags will you?' she threw at Priestman.

'Aye. I will that.'

Richard saw him drop into a chair.

'We may be friends but I'm not dancing a slow with you, Patsy. Come on, this lot of fellers have been carved out of rice pudding.'

'Shush Jennifer, they'll hear you,' Patsy giggled as she followed Jennifer back to the table.

'What are you doing here?' Jennifer demanded of Priestman. If Yorkie was there then Richard Ennessy must be somewhere around. Not that she cared, of course.

'Appen I'm looking after your 'andbags.'

'Appen you are. Where's Claudia?'

'Dancing... wi' Richard.'

Claudia dancing with Richard Ennessy? The little minx! I bet she's asking him to paint her portrait. Well, if she thinks he'll paint just any old... What am I saying? What do I know about what he thinks? What do I know of what goes on behind those brown eyes? What do I care?

'Oh yes, I can see them, Jennifer, look, over there.' Patsy was excited at the discovery. 'They're dancing very close.'

'Aye... luv at first sight it were,' he said, sourly. 'She hung round his neck and dragged him on t'floor.'

Patsy turned her great anguished eyes on Priestman but he did not notice.

'I think Claudia can sometimes be just a teeny weeny bit too demonstrative.' Jennifer observed. She realised with annoyance that she was trying to keep all inflection from her voice, so that any feelings she might have would remain hidden.

'You can talk! Demonstrative? What about you in t'pub?' Bob Priestman did not care any more what he said.

'What about Jennifer in the pub?' Patsy asked.

'She tore in like a bloody tornado, pardon my French, and laid in to Richard for puttin' her paintin' up in t'college.'

'Did you Jennifer?'

'I may have mentioned it.'

Priestman's face showed disbelief.

'Menitioned it? The whole pub heard yer! I told 'er it were nothing to do wi' im, but she just walked out and slammed t'door.'

'That wasn't very kind Jennifer.'

'Aye, well you can look after your own 'andbags now. I'm going to t'bar.'

It seemed to Bob Priestman that the bar was the only refuge. He had come here to meet that girl whose name was Claudia, armed with his secret weapon, Richard Ennessy, and it had gone off in his hands. Claudia had thrown herself at him. He should have known better than to trust a smoothie like that.

His eyes wandered vaguely over the jumping, heaving mob that was the dance; a pulsing, amorphous, mass punctuated in places by the occasional island of serenity wherein one of the mature couples glided amongst the dancers like a ghostly galleon through the mist. It was always the same when he tried to socialise. He was tongue-tied, awkward and so took refuge at the bar. He looked along the counter. It was all blokes. Tapping to the music, grinning false enjoyment, on their own, blokes. Failures, like him. Standing, waiting for a gorgeous girl to come up to them. He turned to the barman.

'Gi'us a pint mate.'

Waiting for some fantastic bit of stuff to say,

'And a vodka and lime for me please. You're not dancing then?'

Ruth Robey had decided to slay them with her black frilly blouse with the naughty décolleté and her hip-hugging skirt. It was impractical to dance in and it imparted a stifled, mincing gait to her walk but it did get the feller's eyes out on stalks. She had not found Richard but she had spied that red-haired lad whom she knew was on the same course. He would know where to find Richard.

'Aye an' a vodka and lime for t'lass,' Bob Priestman stuttered and tried not to look at Ruth's bosom. 'No I'm not dancin'. I'm er... 'aving a rest.'

Ruth eased herself onto a stool and pointed her sheer-clad legs like twin cannons at Bob Priestman's stomach.

'Cheers... er...?' She raised an enquiring eyebrow.

'Bob. Me name's Bob.'

'Ruth.'

'Cheers Ruth.'

'So where is Richard then?' she asked casually.

'Well, I saw 'im at tea time and he said he were goin' 'ome cos he were fed up.' Ruth froze inside. 'But I persuaded 'im to stay.' She immediately felt herself warming to this chap. 'Bloody fool that I was. He's over there dancing with... dancing with Claudia.'

Ruth noticed the way he had said, 'Claudia'.

'Why don't we go and break them up then? It can't be healthy dancing with the same person all the time.'

Bob Priestman could not believe his ears.

'Shall we?'

'By the time we have finished these drinks, that record will have finished and we will back to the head-shaking and jigging. All we have to do is go and join them. What do you say?'

'That sounds grand.'

The disc jockey was an old hand at this college dance and he worked to a formula whose success he had proven over the years. He started off with lots of noise and beat, to let the kids get it out of their system. It gave them the opportunity to jump about and do all that waving of hands that they liked. Occasionally he would throw in a bit of rock and roll; this meant that the oldies could chance their quickstep, or he would spin them an offbeat slow and they would foxtrot. The kids, of course, would just do their own thing all the while, regardless. As the evening wore on, it would become apparent that the dancers with the sticking power were the over forties. Then he would increase the ratio of waltzes. This pleased those who could dance. Those who could not, well they were past caring, they just needed someone to lean against. By throwing out time he had them all well trained, and in each other's arms. Magic. It worked every time.

'Jennifer!' Patsy hissed. Jennifer stopped searching for her comb in her bag and looked up. 'It's Graham Treadsure, I think he's coming over. He's just nodded to me.'

'You're in luck there Patsy. You are the expert on him, don't forget.'

'Oh Jennifer, don't say such things. Oooh, he is coming over.' Patsy's eyes were round with delicious anticipation.

Jennifer closed her knees discreetly. She must remember that she was not wearing jeans. Graham Treadsure was dressed in a sober grey suit and an outstanding turquoise tie. He looked like the back end of a peacock in the fog, Jennifer thought. But he was quite distinguished in a delightfully mature and worn way.

'Patsy,' he said and extended his hand gallantly. 'Would you allow me the pleasure of this dance?'

Jennifer could not bear to look at the grimaces that Patsy was making in her attempt to tell him that she could not waltz so she turned away and was stung like a slap in the face by the sight of Richard Ennessy sweeping by with a laughing and outré Ruth Robey, falling out of her blouse and clutching at his chest like a limpet. She stood up decisively.

'I'll dance with you Graham. I can waltz.'

'Ah Jennifer, how delightful!' He took her hand. His was quite warm. 'Perhaps next time Patsy? Hmm?' he said over his shoulder and Patsy melted like a jelly on a hot plate.

His waltz was very basic which suited Jennifer since hers was nearly forgotten. What she had not remembered was how close the two bodies had to be to make contact. The last time that a man had pressed himself against her, she had kneed him in the groin. She laughed.

'Share the joke?'

'Not this one,' she grinned as they lurched to one side to allow an apparently octogenarian couple to thunder by in a flash of twinkling feet. 'I hope I can dance like that when I'm their age,' she said with fervour.

'I already am,' Graham said. 'And I can't.'

'Get on with you! You are not that old.'

'I have a daughter about your age.'

'Oh. And a wife?'

'Yes but she's older than you. Now let's talk about serious things.' Jennifer gripped his jacket a little harder, dreading to hear what he had to say. But it was innocuous. 'What are you going to do with your studies?'

'Oh I don't know. Something will come up.'

'Don't you believe it young lady. Something won't come up. Fashion students are ten a penny.'

'That's pretty depressing.' Jennifer tipped back her head to move her hair on her back. It was making her hot.

'Listen Jennifer, you've got what it takes to get to the top. I know. It's my business to know. I was watching you with the screens. I like your design. I like your use of colour.' He fumbled in his breast pocket and pulled out a card. 'That's my business card. I'm not poaching. I will not be interested in you if you don't qualify. Like I said, fashion students are ten a penny, failed ones cannot even be given away free. I want you to get to the top, Jennifer Pye. Ring me when you get your results.'

'Well I don't know what to say...'

The music faded down quickly and the disc jockey's mellifluous voice oozed out of the speakers in a beautifully modulated instruction,

'Change partners. Gentlemen move to their right and off we go for a foxtrot.'

The music faded in again as Graham Treadsure released her gracefully.

'Thank you for the dance, Jennifer. Keep that card and I'll

expect a ring from you.' He inclined his head with an old world gallantry and moved on to the lady on his right.

Jennifer stood there, stupidly looking at his business card as the dance started up again around her. Graham Treadsure was an important person. A seriously important person and he wanted to help her.

'I'm sorry I did not realise that I needed a calling card,' Richard Ennessy's voice said quietly in her ear. She jumped.

'You!'

'Your partner, Miss Pye.' He held up his hand.

Jennifer spun around and started to carve a route through the dancers, 'Over my dead bo... humph!' she grunted as Richard Ennessy's strong hand inserted itself into her waistband and hauled her back by the belt of her skirt. 'How dare you!' she gasped and as he swung her around to face him she brought her left hand up in a cracking slap across his cheek. He instantly slapped her cheek just as hard and as she stood, rooted to the floor by shock, he gathered her into his arms and led her off in a foxtrot.

'It's a Russian custom,' he explained to a pop eyed couple at the side of him. 'She's from Vladivostock.'

'You brute!' she hissed and wriggled furiously to free herself. She could feel hot tears of anger beginning to prick at her eyes and trickle down her stinging cheek.

'Local variation.' He wriggled his hips in consort with hers. 'Gets awfully cold on the Steppes — they do it to warm up.' The couple nodded understandingly.

'Grrr. Richard Ennessy, let me go!' she growled through her teeth but her right hand was in a clamp, her back was in a press and she just had to go where he led. She, Jennifer Pye, had been hauled backwards across a dance floor and been slapped on the face and now she was having to dance with her tormentor. He was abducting her, dominating her, beating her.

'I suppose you think you are so very clever,' she said at last, throwing her head up to look at his rather fine face, his gently laughing eyes, his beautifully soft, smiling mouth.

'Moderately so. But I think I am more lucky than clever.'

'Well you flatter yourself to think you are clever. Will you let me free?' She tugged at his hand again. It was a futile effort. She had never felt so powerless in her life.

'If you promise not to go, yes.'

'That's daft. Of course I'll go. I'll run like hell.'

'Then I shan't let you go.' he said simply and she felt his strong arm tighten around her back, pulling her closer to him. She could feel his thighs against hers. The pressure in her back was a man's arm. She was in a real man's arms and he did not want to let her go. He had said so. The gentle rhythm of the music began to exert a calming effect over her. Why keep struggling? Her left hand, which had been pumping and pressing hard on his left shoulder to keep him away, now began to slowly relax onto his shirt. She was aware of his pelvis moving against hers, guiding her, controlling her in the gentle, undemanding movement of a rhythm foxtrot.

'Richard, could you not hold my right hand quite so tight please?'

His deep brown eyes looked searchingly into hers.

'You'll not run away?'

'No.'

'Promise?'

'Promise.'

He relaxed his grip. To his apparent consternation she removed her hand but quickly opened it to show him the business card. 'I must just put it somewhere safe,' she explained and slipped it into a pocket. She offered her hand. He looked at the little pointed fingers and he took them and held them gently.

'Last waltz, ladies and gentlemen, take your partners for the last waltz.'

Jennifer sensed the change in the music rather than noticed it. Their movements became more gentle as the floor filled with non-dancers, forcing Richard to take smaller steps. Making her snuggle closer to him. Obliging him to put his arm right around her. Encouraging her to bury her nose into the front of his silk shirt. Willing her to inhale deeply the cosy scent of a warm man. Coercing his head to bow till his lips touched the golden crown of her head. Compelling them both to mutely recognise their unspoken awareness, one of the other.

EPISODE TEN

The early morning spring sun was just lighting the enormous chains of the Clifton Suspension Bridge as Bob Priestman shifted his pack from his back and perched temporarily on a rock.

He did not think he would be attending etching class today. He was going to sort out his mind. The memory of Claudia was engraved into it. Claudia, looking baffled as he spoke to her, making his self confidence drain away. Did she not remember him? Was she just being coquettish and teasing him? Yes, that was it! She had known all along who he was but when she had teased him he had been too serious, too stupid to realise and that had confused her. Could he believe that? He tried to believe the lie. He saw her face lighting up when he had introduced Richard Ennessy as the artist. Or tried to introduce him. What an idiot! He had not even found out her name beforehand! And what about the way she threw herself around Ennessy's neck? Hardly a modest overture. But at least Claudia had danced with him when Ruth had broken them up. He supposed Ruth fancied Richard Ennessy, but then, find him some girl who didn't. Well, he supposed, Jennifer Pye didn't fancy Ennessy, except on a torture rack perhaps.

He had walked to this spot from the halls of residence, starting at first glimmer of light. He was accustomed to walking. Back home in Yorkshire he would trudge for miles with his sketch book. He would stay out all day, taking a packet of sandwiches or eating at a pub. Always drawing. Not open moorland and rolling hills but massive woollen mills and warehouses, canals and cranes. The vestiges of the Industrial Revolution were what inspired him.

It was a pity about Claudia, he had rather liked her.

He looked at the turbulent brown water running beside the

path and then gazed up at the span high above him, a fragile link between the two cliffs. Five suicides a year, they had said. Hurtling down from the road into the gorge. Limbs flailing, mouths gasping, bodies writhing. What happened if you changed your mind half way down? The water rushing towards you, getting closer; or the road, hard, non-negotiable.

He shouldered his pack and cast a last glance at the monument to Victorian enterprise above him. That was where he needed to be. Up there. He started looking for the path.

Richard squinted at the clock although the amount of light burning through the thin curtain had already alerted him to the possibility that he might have missed breakfast. Now he knew that he undoubtedly had. A lone footfall clumped along the corridor and then thundered down the concrete stairs at the end of the block. They would all be in class now, Priestman, Ruth, Claudia... Jennifer.

Priestman, terrified that his suede shoes would get scuffed, Ruth, only just keeping her bosom within her blouse, Claudia, my dear, talking nineteen to the dozen about herself... Jennifer.

Priestman would now be on a stool at a bench, his florid brow puckered in concentration as he bent over the engraving plate; Ruth would be mincing about with a camera, telling models in no uncertain terms exactly how to pose and probably adding that she never had this problem with Lord Snowdon; Claudia would be 'my dear-ing' everybody and thoughtlessly waving her hands about in front of cameras; and Jennifer...

He turned onto his stomach, encircled the pillows with his arms and pulled them to his naked chest. She was not very tall, she hardly reached his chin, but she was strong. He squeezed the pillows harder. Try to get away would you Miss Pye? He remembered her body squirming and writhing against his in her desperation to break free. How pretty she looked when she was angry, her face flushed from his slap. At least she could take as good as she gave. Funny little thing, Jennifer Pye. A disturbing little thing.

He suddenly made up his mind. He struggled out of the clinging embrace of the twisted bedclothes, stood up and stretched in his full nakedness. His fingers rapped smartly against the ceiling and he opened his eyes in surprise.

Well, he could go home now, he thought, as he started to shave at the sink. He had done his duty by Priestman for all the good it had done him. He remembered Priestman's dejected look of betrayal when Claudia had swung around Richard's neck. Claudia was outrageous, theatrical and consumed with a passion for herself. She would not notice Priestman on a desert island even if he had the coconut.

He tapped half-heartedly on the roller shutter which was drawn down over the canteen counter. He could hear an orchestral arrangement for pots and pans being rehearsed behind it.

'We're closed!' a woman's voice shouted.

'Are you really closed?' He tried to put an endearing disbelief into his voice.

'Sod off, can't you?'

They were really closed. He would have to go elsewhere.

The blue cloudless sky convinced him that the weather had committed itself for the day. With the hood lowered, he piloted his car, growling menacingly, out of the college car park and onto the road. Breakfast, the Sunday papers, then back to collect his bag and away off home. That was the plan, wasn't it, Richard? He was trying to convince himself.

It had been good to get out of London and all that awful traffic. He changed down fluidly into third gear and felt the reassuring push in the small of his back as he accelerated out of a roundabout and onto a dual carriageway. It was a little after nine o'clock but Bristol appeared to be still in bed. He slowed down hopefully at the sign of a transport cafe but it was closed and desolate with just an empty plastic bag blowing around in a mini cyclone in the lorry park.

He accelerated again and the breeze tugged at his hair and flicked it up behind him. He had a cap somewhere but he could not be bothered to stop and find it. Apart from the occasional milk float glimpsed rattling along a housing estate, or a car laden with bicycles, he had the road to himself.

Well almost to himself. He was sharing it with the police motor cycle patrolman who had just flagged him down.

'Well, did you give him a piece of your mind?' Patsy peeled off her rubber gloves and hung them on a peg above the sinks. 'You were dancing with him for ages.'

'I was not!' Jennifer retorted. 'We only danced the last two dances. I was dancing with Graham most of the time.' She nodded towards the tutor who was back in his jeans and tartan shirt. 'Because you wouldn't,' she added.

'Because I couldn't, Jennifer,' Patsy corrected her. 'I don't know that old-fashioned stuff.'

'I only know the basics. Didn't you learn anything at school?'

'Only manners,' Patsy said obscurely.

Jennifer slapped her craft knife down on the table top, making Patsy jump. 'And what do you mean by that?'

'Oh don't get angry with me Jennifer.' Patsy sucked the tip of her thumb in anguish, 'I didn't mean... I don't...'

'What?'

'Well... did you apologise to Richard last night – about saying those unkind things about his painting?'

'Sort of. We came to an understanding, I think it's called.' Patsy nodded although she did not really know what Jennifer meant. 'Why? What has it got to do with you?'

Patsy looked down sheepishly at the paper stack. 'It's just that I've seen the way he's watched you a couple of times when he could see that you were not looking at him and... and...' She looked up, great big eyes, brimming with anxiety. 'I do so want you to be happy Jennifer. Don't waste it!'

Jennifer slid her arm around Patsy's waist.

'I don't really know what you mean, duck, but thanks all the same. Richard and I said sorry to each other last night and that's all there is to it. Let's go and have a coffee. I need a break. Everything I have tried to do this morning has gone wrong.' She pulled her hair irritably up her back. 'I've even lost my hair clip. I've no idea where it's got to.'

'That big blue one? You forgot it on the table last night and when we left, I saw Ruth pick it up for you. I thought she had given it to you.'

Jennifer pushed Patsy through the workshop door and towards the coffee machines. 'I haven't seen Ruth yet. I'll pop across to the studio after coffee.'

The door to the photographic studio was opened cautiously by a technician in a green lab. coat. He was holding a hamburger in one hand.

'Yeah?'

'I am looking for someone. Can I come in?' Jennifer found herself talking loudly to make herself heard over the music. In a brightly lit area behind him she could see a girl in a sarong moving to the music and freezing for shots.

'Yeah. Come on, come in.' He waved his hand and a ringlet of onion catapulted over his shoulder. 'Who y'a lookin' for?' he asked as he wiped a hand on the front of his coat.

'Ruth Robey.' He looked at her as if he had not heard her. 'Brown eyes, loads of make up...'

'Yeah, yeah, I know Ruth.' He gestured towards a door and sliver of lettuce dropped to the bench like a dead caterpillar. He swept it to the floor with his cupped hand. 'She's in there.' Jennifer made a move towards the door. 'But you can't go in. Red light's on.'

'Oh,' said Jennifer, understanding little.

'It's the dark room. When the light's on it's being used. If you open the door, then it's not a dark room any longer is it?'

'No,'

'She won't be long.' He looked at her unblinkingly. ''You her friend?'

To escape from his unnerving inspection, Jennifer began to idly turn over a pile of black and white photographs which had been untidily dumped on the bench.

'Sort of,' she replied. 'She's got something of mine. I've come to collect it that's all.' She indicated a blurry photo of somebody's left knee. 'Is this the kind of thing they do?'

'Students' practice reels, they are. For gettin' used to the camera and the developing and printing.' He prodded the photo of the knee. 'Camera must have slipped on that one. Probably trying to wind on too quickly.' He pulled another photo from the pile. 'Quite a good one.' Jennifer stared at the photo. 'Good composition but not really fashion. More press photo, that.' He scooped the pile up in his arms. 'All rubbish now though.' He dumped them unceremoniously in the bin.

'Malcolm can you do this reflector for me?' someone called from the other end of the studio.

'That's me,' he explained. 'Malcolm.' He nodded at the dark room door. 'When the light goes out you can knock on it and she'll let you in.' He turned around. 'Coming!' he called.

Jennifer carefully placed her bag next to the waste paper bin which was overflowing with discarded photos. She hoisted her bottom up on to the table and sat with her legs dangling, to await the extinguishing of the red light.

Richard had found a secluded spot down by the river to read the Sunday newspapers. He had folded the electric hood and installed himself sideways across the two front seats. His fingers now tapped absently to Dvoraks's New World Symphony on his car stereo and the back seat, such as it was, was littered with papers and supplements and magazines and glossy fliers. He felt relaxed and fulfilled. Nothing could beat an uninterrupted plough through the Sunday papers.

The police patrol man had been fairly decent with him. Richard had admitted that he had been enjoying himself on an empty road and knew that he was breaking the limit. He had also admitted that it was very silly of him. His candour must have worked in his favour. He was given a severe warning and was required to present his licence at his local police station within five days. Then he had asked the patrolman about his motor bike, how fast it went, what the road holding was like, and as an afterthought, where the policeman could suggest that he should try to get himself some breakfast.

'Only place that will be open at this time on a Sunday is Bill Bait's, near the bus station. You'll get a good fry-up there.'

Richard eructated discreetly as the breakfast made another determined attempt to corroborrate the policeman's assertion.

He had now finished the sport section, read the general news, done the business, rambled through the travel review and thrown the children's comic straight into the bin. A gentle breeze ruffled his hair and he closed his eyes and allowed the sun to play on his face. It was a glorious morning and promised a settled day – a trifle fresh, but sunny and clear. He was in no hurry to go back to London, was he? He opened his eyes and watched a sparrow hopping along the top of a wall. He had intended going straight back after breakfast... Well, actually, he had intended going home last night but then Bob Priestman, God rest his soul, had talked him into going to the disco. But he was all finished now wasn't he? Just the colour supplement to read and then he could go. There was nothing to keep him in Bristol was there?

Fifteen minutes later Richard dumped the entire Sunday version of what was happening in the world into the bin on top of its patronising publication for the younger generation and then drove his car out onto the street. He had hardly covered four hundred yards when, with a grunt of surprise, he pulled in to the kerb.

'Bob?' he called uncertainly. The figure turned around. It was Bob Priestman, walking along with a rucksack on his back. 'What are you doing here? I thought you were in college.'

'I thought you were going 'ome,' he replied laconically. 'So this is your car is it?' He stood back and inspected the yellow convertible. 'It's a bit posh, like. How fast does it go?'

Richard fumbled in the door pocket and waved a piece of paper.

'Fast enough to get me stopped by the police this morning, but if you prefer the bus...'

'I didn't say that. Are you goin' up to t'college?'

'Yes. Do you want a lift?'

'Aye, that'd be grand. I must have walked ten miles this morning.' He lowered his bag gingerly into the car.

'Where on earth have you been?' Richard asked. 'What have you been doing?'

'Drawing... and walking... and thinking.'

'Well there is some lovely scenery around here. Terrific views. Let's see what you've done.'

'Well...' Priestman hesitated.

'Come on Bob, don't be shy. I can stand the shock.' He switched off the engine to emphasise his determination.

'Aye, all right then.'

Bob Priestman reached over the back of the seat and pulled out his sketch book. Richard was not certain what to expect, but he was still surprised by what he saw.

'That's a link on the chain on t'Clifton Suspension Bridge. It's like a great big bicycle chain.'

'Hav you been up to the bridge?'

'Aye, I started up there.'

'What time did you leave this morning?'

'Just as sun was rising – 'bout six o'clock I suppose.'

'What even after that disco? I didn't wake up until half past eight.' Richard admitted.

'Aye, well 'appen I didn't work as hard as you last night.'

'I thought you did very well.'

'You did better.'

'It's Claudia you fancy isn't it?'

'If you bloody knew that why did you keep dancing wi 'er?'

'I didn't have much choice, Bob. If you remember, she did rather throw herself at me.'

'Aye, I bet all the girls do,' he observed with a bitterness in his voice. 'I didn't see you fighting her off.'

'No Bob. All the girls do not throw themselves at me, thank goodness.' He wanted Priestman to know that his prejudice was completely unfounded. 'Some, Jennifer Pye for instance, slap my face and turn their back on me.' He also wanted to thrill himself by saying Jennifer's name.

'Gerr away. She never did!'

'Oh yes, she certainly did.'

'Aye, well I expect you deserved it,' he grinned. 'She's got some spirit 'as that lass!'

'She packs quite a punch,' Richard said and turned a page in the sketch book.

'Ah look now this is right interestin' this is.' Bob Priestman suddenly became all animated. 'I found this empty warehouse down by the old docks and t'door was open. Well, it wasn't exactly open but there were no-one around so I climbed in. It were magic. There were this cast iron hoist right up in t'loft. Look you can see it here, and you could see the rails in t'floor and everything. And it were a hammer beam roof. That's this drawing here. You could stand in t'middle of that shed and it took yer right back to Victorian times. You could imagine it all working. It were like a history lesson.'

'What are you going to do with these drawings then Bob? It's a long way from fabric design.'

'Oh no it's not for that. Those drawing are for me. For my pleasure, not for t'studies.'

'Oh I see.' Richard said as he started the car and began to pull away. It seemed obvious to him that it was not Bob Priestman who had chosen the course he was to study.

'Come on Patsy. We all want to see your elephant!'

'Well I don't know...' Patsy hesitated as she cleared aside her plate and put her bag on the canteen table. 'It's not as good as Jennifer's tee shirt.'

'Show them your elephant, Patsy,' Jennifer encouraged her. 'It is brilliant and you should be proud of it.'

Which is more than I am of my efforts, Jennifer thought sourly, for her own design had translated into a rather drab mess of colours. On the material it had none of the vigour or vitality of the paper. Graham Treadsure had tried to reassure her by telling her that she had learned more by failing than someone who had just simply succeeded. She had discovered that some designs just did not work. It was not that she was incapable of making it work, the fault lay in its conception – it was just not suitable, it could not transfer from flat paper to cloth around a body. 'The thing is, Jennifer' he had said, 'You were brave enough to risk everything on one throw of the dice and you lost. It will happen. One day you will do it and roll a six and then you will have hit the jackpot.'

She was pleased for Patsy. She watched the others as they cooed over her pink elephant and yellow banana and could see her glowing with pleasure. Then she noticed Ruth suddenly stiffen and peer through the window into the car park.

'Just look at that!' she exclaimed and they all goggled. Richard Ennessy and Bob Priestman were standing by a bright yellow sports car and laughing about something. Richard was standing with one hand slipped in the pocket of his linen trousers and the other absently stroking the neck of his chunky Arran jumper. Priestman was pulling a bag from the back seat of the car.

'Flash car. I wonder whose it is,' Claudia remarked.

'I bet it's Richard's,' Ruth asserted. 'Am I right Jennifer?'

'How should I know?'

'Aye, well thanks for the lift. Now I shall 'ave to go an' comb me hair.'

'Are you not getting something to eat?' Richard nodded at the cafeteria. 'I'm going to grab a sandwich. I don't need much else after the breakfast I had.'

'I thought you said you missed breakfast.'

'I did, here. I went to Bill Bait's at the bus station and had a fry-up.' Bob Priestman looked at him closely, trying to decide whether his leg was being pulled. 'As recommended by the local constabulary.'

'Oh right,' Priestman laughed as he pulled his bag from the back of the car. It amused him in a delightfully malicious way to think of Richard being caught by the police. 'Oh heck, watch yer neck. Yon lass is in there.'

'She doesn't worry me,' Richard tried to sound casual. 'We've signed a truce. I think. Anyway, ' he added with mischief, 'I can see Claudia in the gang. Come on.'

Whilst choosing something edible at the counter, Richard tried to identify the owner of the voice which had instructed him to go away when he had endeavoured to obtain breakfast, but he failed. The three women managed to serve them using only grunts and sighs as a means of communication. It was as if they had closed ranks in a conspiracy of silence to protect the matinal transgressor.

When they turned from the counter, Ruth waved them over to join their group and so, with heart a-thumping, Richard led the way over to their corner. He could see the girl Patsy, the one who was always with Jennifer, just wrapping up something in a bag; Claudia was giving an explanation which, unsurprisingly, required much gesticulation; Ruth was opening a folder on the table top and Jennifer was sitting at one end of the table, calm, quiet, and studiously avoiding his eye. Taking the bull by the horns, Richard sat down next to Claudia – a manoeuvre which would force Priestman to sit opposite her.

'Mind if I sit down? I realise that I risk my sandwich being knocked down my throat by one of your gestures but that could be useful – it doesn't look very appetising.'

'Oh my dear, sit down, do sit down and tell us all about your morning. Is that your delicious car?'

'Bob and I have been playing truant.'

'Again!' Ruth exclaimed. 'That's what you were doing when I took your photo in the corridor.'

'Ah yes,' Richard said, 'I was going to talk to you about that. I presume the motive was blackmail was it? How much are you asking for the negative? Is it amongst that lot?' He indicated the spread of photographs which Ruth had been displaying from her folder. They, most of them, featured a young man in tight jeans sitting on a step ladder.

'Oooh Ruth, did you take a photograph of Richard?' Patsy's eyes were wide with anticipation. 'Can we see it?' She glanced quickly at Jennifer who was fiddling with the leaf of the potted plant.

'Impossible.'

'A fiver,' Richard said, taking out his wallet.

'Not even for a fiver. Art is not to be treated as a commodity!' she reprimanded him with mock pomposity.

'A tenner? And a half-eaten egg sandwich.'

'Oh how disgusting! No can do, I'm afraid.' With much apparent glee, Ruth smugly disclosed to one and all, 'You were consigned to the waste paper bin. Your career as a model was over before it started.'

Patsy was horrified. 'Do you mean you threw it away?'

'Not me, Patsy darling, but Malcolm – he's the darkroom technician.' She flicked back her hair affectedly. 'One does not ask photographers to operate the shredder.'

'Shredded? Well that's a relief,' Richard laughed.

Jennifer gazed out of the window and said nothing.

Bob Priestman cleared his throat and addressed Claudia. 'What are you all doing afterwards, like? The bus don't leave till seven.'

Claudia looked down the table.

'Well what are we doing, my dears?'

'I would *love* a ride in your car, Richard,' Ruth said.

Richard glanced at Jennifer. She met his gaze for an instant and then looked away. So that was how things stood was, was it?

'Sorry Ruth, I think I shall have to push off home. I've got things to do.'

'Oh,' said Patsy, as if the disappointment should have been felt by all present. 'Well I would like to go on the excursion to Cheddar Gorge. It's such a lovely day and I have never been there. It seems such a pity to come down here and then miss it.' She looked around the group. 'Who else is coming?'

Jennifer suddenly stirred in her corner. She recalled the noticeboard discussion back in London. 'You said you wanted to go,' she reminded Ruth.

'Yes,' Ruth said vaguely, hoping perhaps that her obvious indecision would prompt Richard into changing his mind. 'What about you?'

'Oh do come Jennifer!' Patsy pleaded.

'Oh alright,' Jennifer surrendered, 'I'll come.'

'In that case, my dears, so will I.' Claudia waved her hands with a flourish.

'I think I will too,' Priestman announced.

Jennifer threw her hair clip onto the bed and then began to tug angrily at her hair with the brush. Cheddar Gorge with Ruth, Patsy, Claudia and Yorkie! Well, she supposed, Patsy was all right. And what was wrong with Cheddar Gorge anyway? She had never been there so she should not judge.

She tugged at her hair again and wished that she was the kind of girl who would have the cheek to ask Richard Ennessy for a ride in his car. Why should she care though? The man was a brute. He had slapped her face and then held her so tight that she could not get away. She hugged herself, wrapping her arms around her shoulders, but it was not the same. She could see his laughing eyes when she had tried to wriggle free. She remembered the frustration, the feeling of utter helplessness as he had held her fast and then obliged her to move to the music. She remembered her surrender. Had he felt it? Had he felt her body soften into his, her cheek lie on his chest?

Patsy was humming to herself as she tried on her teeshirt. She eventually decided that she would be too cold to wear just that and if she had to put a jacket on top then it would lose its effect, so she packed the shirt carefully into her bag, patting it lovingly as she zipped the bag closed.

They carried their bags downstairs towards the car park, having elected to put them in the coach now and not have to bother later. Most of the other students had done likewise and the driver was standing by a pile of bags on the tarmac, waiting to load them into the boot.

'Come on,' Patsy said, 'let's get a decent seat.' And she hurried off to dump her bag alongside the coach.

At that moment a hand closed over Jennifer's and a voice said, 'Carry yer bag miss?'

'Oh Richard Ennessy! You made me jump! Its O.K. I'm not

an old aged pensioner, I can still carry a bag.' With an infuriating ease he calmly unhooked her fingers and took her bag from her. 'I said I can manage,' she insisted.

'No reason why you should have to, though,' he observed as he strode off ahead of her, carrying her bag for all to see.

Jennifer had to hurry to try to keep pace with him for his long legs covered the ground far more easily than hers.

'Look, I said I could manage.' She felt ridiculous trotting along behind, trying to catch him up and with all the students on the coach watching her. 'Thank you, that's fine, just drop....' He walked past the pile of bags, ignoring them completely and disappeared behind the coach. 'Richard, where are you going? Bring back my bag.' She hurried after him. It was happening all over again. He was taking control.

She rounded the corner to see him insolently sling her bag onto the back seat of his car.

'What do you think you are doing?' She bustled up to him.

'Abducting you,' he said, holding open the passenger door. 'You don't want to go to Cheddar Gorge any more than I want to go straight home.'

'I...'

'Get in.'

She looked up at his warm brown eyes and his smiling mouth and she knew that he was right.

'Oooh I hate you,' she lied.

'And I, you,' he laughed as he vaulted over the door and into the car.

Jennifer stole a glance at the coach as they pulled away. Ruth and Claudia were staring open mouthed. Behind them, Patsy waved frantically and gave her an energetic thumbs-up.

She could not believe this was happening. She was sitting in his car and allowing him to drive away with her and she was making no attempt to stop him. She stretched out her legs and then flicked her hair free from her neck.

'Where are we going Richard?' she laughed. 'What will people say?'

'It doesn't matter what people will say, we are both grown-ups. And as for where we are going, I haven't a clue except that...' he glanced at a signpost, '...if Cheddar Gorge is that way, then we are going this way.' He spun the wheel to the right and the car roared off. 'Weston super Mare,' he read. 'Let's go to the sea side.'

'At this time of the year. It will be deserted!'

'Suits me.' He glanced across at her. 'What about you? Do you want crowds?' Jennifer shook her head. 'Weston super Mare it is then.'

Jennifer closed her eyes and then leaned back to permit the sun to reach her face. She had never thought that she would be riding in this car. She opened her eyes with a jerk. She had remembered the first day of term and recalled seeing this very car, and the dishy man with the brown hair and dreaming of spinning through the Nottinghamshire lanes with Steven.

'I saw you on the first day of term,' she announced.

'I know,' he said. 'You pretended to think I was a lecturer to make me feel like a fossil.'

'I did not!'

'You are obviously so embarrassed that you have obliterated it from your memory. Just as well, under the circumstances.'

She sat up. 'You can be so annoying sometimes Richard Ennessy. What circumstances?'

'Do you remember the very first thing you said to me?' he grinned.

'Something like, "what course are you on" wasn't it?'

'Nope. You burst through the door, took one look at me and said "shit".'

'I never did.'

'I am not likely to forget it.'

'Well I wish you would. What I was talking about just now, was the fact that I saw you in your car, in this car, on the first day of term. You must have been on your way to college.'

'Quite possible.'

'You were looking for a parking space. You looked flustered.'

'I was not.'

'Oh yes you were. I could see you quite clearly.'

'Humph. Must have been somebody else.'

'Then in that case it must have been somebody else who said "shit" to you.'

'If you distract me with your quibbling I will lose the slight concentration that I possess, take a wrong turning and we will end up in a quarry or a sewage farm or something.'

'Weston super Mare, left at the roundabout,' Jennifer said promptly. 'You don't think I would calmly sit in a madman's car without checking on the route we were taking, do you?'

'If you promise not to say another word until we arrive, Miss Pye, I will buy you an ice cream.'

Richard parked near to the sands and they sat silently watching the sea. Weston super Mare was deserted. The nearest human was about half a mile away, walking with a dog. Now that he had thrown them headlong into this mad adventure, Richard was wondering what on earth was going to happen. Or had it happened already and this was merely the manifestation of it?

'Come on. You can't go to the seaside without seeing the sea.'

He jumped out. Jennifer stumbled slightly on the steps and Richard's hand flashed out and grabbed her elbow but released it as soon as she had established her equilibrium. Apart from that slight contact, they walked side by side, but untouching, down the beach towards the lazy ripplng of the tide.

'I like watching the sea,' Jennifer said quietly. 'It is so relaxing. It is a great opportunity for humans to put boredom into its proper context.' Richard had no idea what she meant but he liked listening to her voice and watching her hair shake when she moved so he remained silent. Jennifer sat on a rock so he sat on the sand, still maintaining a polite distance between them. She waved her hand at a ripplet, the final exertion of a wave, as it struggled up the sand towards them. 'Boredom,' she continued, 'can you imagine having to do that every minute, every hour, every day of the year? Hundreds and thousands of times and yet, it makes every single wave different.'

'I had not thought of it like that,' Richard admitted.

Jennifer folded her arms around her, clutching her thin jumper to her chest.

'Here, put this on.' Richard pulled his sweater over his head and handed it to Jennifer. 'I don't want you suing me for cruelty as well as kidnapping.'

'No I...'

'Don't argue, Miss Pye.' He languidly tucked his thick cotton shirt back into the waistband of his trousers where it had pulled out to reveal the taut muscles of his abdomen.

'Thank you.'

She pulled the garment over her head, breathing in the mixture of odour of raw wool and scent of man. The sleeves were too long for her and she waved them about like a floppy puppet.

'It's probably the nearest you've come yet to wearing a straitjacket,' Richard said as he discreetly opened his sketch pad.

She flicked a small shell over her shoulder at him and gazed out to sea again, feeling the immenseness of the horizon filling her with calm and tranquillity.

'This takes a lot of beating. A lot of beating. I could sit here all day just recharging my batteries,' she sighed. 'I suppose this must be the Irish Sea is it?'

'I don't know. I'm not too hot on geography.'

'Or the Bristol Channel at least. I don't know the Atlantic side of Britain. We always went to Skeggie for our holidays. Where did you used to go for yours?'

'All over the place. Nowhere special. Have you got brothers and sisters?'

'No. My Mam and Dad took one look at me and decided that one was enough.'

'I can understand that.'

Another shell winged its way over Jennifer's shoulder.

'What about you?'

'A brother called Charles. He's short and hairy and covered with warts.'

'Obviously your younger brother and you envy him his good looks.'

'I like him to believe that.' Richard flicked a shell back at her and missed. 'Where do you come from? I mean, where's home? Where are your parents for example?'

Jennifer gave a short laugh.

'It won't help you if I tell you they are in Spain.'

'Are they?'

'Yes, they retired there, but we originally come from Nottinghamshire. What about you?'

'Oh, Home Counties me, born and bred.' He carefully turned a page and started another sketch detail, coding the colours and textures and marking the highlights. He was getting quite good at this, he realised. 'What did your father do before he retired?'

'What do you think? In Nottinghamshire?'

'I don't know.'

'Guess, dumbo.'

'Er... Nottinghamshire. Nottingham Forest. Outlaw! Robbing the rich to feed the poor?'

The shell hit him on the forehead.

'Coal miner.'

'Oh. Never thought of that.'

'Does your dad still work?'

'Well my father goes in to the office. Whether he ever works there I don't know.'

'What does he do?'

'I suppose he is a sort of businessman.'

'Presumably a successful one, seeing the car that you drive.'

'Oh no, that was a distant aunt who shuffled off her mortal coil and had the decency to leave me a little something.'

'Well don't spend it all at once,' Jennifer gave the advice with feeling.

'Oh no, I couldn't.' One cannot spend a thousand acres of Dorset, he thought.

Jennifer hugged her knees wistfully.

'What would you do if you could lay your hands on a million pounds?' She gazed dreamily across the sea.

Richard realised quickly that he could quite probably lay his hands on a million pounds if he really needed it but he also suspected that disclosing this fact would be the surest way to terminate any relationship that might be forming between him and Miss Jennifer Pye.

'I don't know. I've never really thought about it.' That was honest, he said to himself. 'I suppose I would find somewhere exotic to go on holiday and buy a new car and... buy you a proper jumper of your own. What about you?'

Jennifer wondered whether she would set up a boutique again. No, she would not do that, too much hard work. What about a design studio? But did she have the talent? She was not sure that she had nor that she could find it.

'I would like to do something to bring art to people who don't get to see it normally. Educate people so that they are not scared to go into art galleries and, sort of help those who find it physically or socially difficult. Perhaps organise outings for them and open the gallery just for them on that particular day, so that they have time and are not flustered. Do you see what I mean?'

'Sounds like a good idea. And you should have some left over to buy yourself a proper jumper as well.'

'And a new pair of jeans... and some furry slippers with bobbles on the top like Mrs. Crowther's.'

'Who?'

'My landlady. And... a great big ballgown to cause a sensation at civic receptions. Like when you painted me,' she explained.

'Last time I painted you, you weren't wearing a ballgown at all. You would cause a sensation if you turned up like that.'

'Ooh you beast!'

Jennifer jumped up quickly but Richard had snapped his sketchbook shut and was rising to defend himself.

'Race you back to the car,' he challenged her. 'Last one buys the ice cream.'

The ice creams had been eaten and the sun had now drifted behind a blanket of cloud, precursor to the night.

'Thank you for taking me to the seaside, Richard. I have enjoyed it.'

'Thank you for coming.'

'I didn't have much choice.'

'Perhaps next time, if there is to be a next time, I shall not have to use so much persuasion?'

'Could be.' Jennifer looked at her watch. 'You must get me back to the college now, Richard or I'll miss the coach.'

He nodded.

As they drove back towards Bristol, Jennifer tugged her jacket out of her bag and by a feat of writhing and twisting, which Richard appreciated immensely but would not dare say so, she managed to divest herself of his jumper and slip her jacket on.

'There's should be a cap somewhere in that door pocket if you need it for your hair,' he said.

'What's this?' She held up a piece of paper.

'Don't lose that,' he said quickly, 'I got stopped by the police this morning. That's my notice to show my driving licence. I didn't have it with me.'

'Oh. Were you speeding?'

'Sort of. Ever so slightly.'

'Aren't they going to prosecute?'

'No.'

'Why not?'

'I used my charm on them. You look disappointed.'

'No, just surprised.' Jennifer shrugged and slipped the paper into the glove compartment and fished out a denim cap. 'Oh yes,' she said enthusiastically and pulled it on, tucking her hair up into it like a wimple. 'Just the job.'

'I've been thinking.'

'Good.'

'Why do you need to go back to the coach? You've got all your belongings with you haven't you?'

Jennifer looked about her. 'Yes I suppose I have. And...?'

'Why don't you come back to London with me?'

'But what about the others?'

'Oh I've not got room for them.'

'I didn't mean that! I meant, they'll wonder where I am?'

'They saw you go off with me. That's their answer. The coach won't wait, don't worry, you're not that important.'

She ignored his teasing and thought about the idea. It was very naughty. And he was rather nice. And she did rather like him.

'O.K.' she said.

Richard suggested that they should stop for a bite to eat before joining the motorway and Jennifer, remembering the tea and Patsy's rubber bun, agreed. But when he pulled in to the car park of a rather smart hotel she began to have awful misgivings about her finances.

'My treat,' he said. 'You bought the ices, because you lost the race to the car,' he reminded her. 'Obviously out of trim.'

'Don't worry, I'll make up for it. I discover with surprise that the sea air has made me remarkably hungry.'

And she demolished a sizeable roast dinner and dessert, thinking that that would teach him. Before starting off, Richard pressed a button and an electrically powered hood climbed out of a panel on the boot and stretched itself lazily over them. They were cosy in a little world of their own. A noisy and bumpy world, Jennifer thought, but still rather intimate.

After half an hour on the motorway, Richard said, 'There they are,' and pointed to the lights of the coach ahead.

'Give them a toot, Richard.' Jennifer took off Richard's denim cap that she was wearing and waved it out of the window as they passed. She thought she saw Patsy but was not certain. The car felt very low and the coach windows looked very high.

They drove on, Richard's face softly illuminated by the glow of the instruments. Jennifer studying it, safe in the darkness and thinking what a handsome face it was. She closed her eyes and dreamed to the drumming of the tyres and the humming of the engine.

She awoke with a start to street lights flicking past the windscreen and discovered that her head was cushioned by Richard's jumper that he had somehow, one-handedly rolled up and tucked alongside her neck.

'I must have dozed for a minute. Where are we?'

Richard smiled to himself and then looked across at her for an instant. 'Elevated section of the M4. You've been asleep for an hour and a half.'

'Crikey. It must have been that jam roly poly.'

'Or the run up the beach. Where do you live?'

She thought of Cordoba Crescent, of yapping Sandy and the tarpaulin over the derelict car next door.

'Oh, no need to take me home, Richard, you've been very kind.'

'It's no trouble at all.'

'As soon as we come down off the stilts just drop me at the nearest tube station. It's not far.'

'Don't be silly, the traffic is still very light. It will not take me a minute. Where do you live?'

'I'm not being silly.'

They drove on in silence for a while.

'Well, which way?'

'Up there,' Jennifer said quickly, 'and you can drop me just outside that block of flats.'

'There, you see. That was not too difficult was it?'

Jennifer felt a pang of guilt.

'Thank you for a lovely day, Richard and for bringing me home.'

'My pleasure,' he said as he unloaded her bag onto the pavement. 'Are you going to be all right now?'

'Yes thanks.' She took his hand and squeezed it. 'Good night Richard.' He smiled a sheepish smile and for an instant looked just as he had done on his first day – lost. 'Off you go,' she said.

He looked up at the block of flats and nodded.

'Goodnight Jennifer.'

She waved until his car had disappeared around the corner, then she picked up her bag, crossed the street and descended the steps to the Underground.

EPISODE ELEVEN

'Oooh I like your cap Jennifer, it does suit you.' Jennifer glanced quickly at Patsy but there was nothing other than admiration in her face. 'Where did you get it?'

Jennifer slipped her bag to the floor as casually as she could, aware that Ruth and Patsy were probably bursting to ask her questions about Sunday afternoon and equally aware that she would be loath to answer them.

'It's not mine actually. Just borrowing it. Have any of you got the notes we did on hems? I can't find the stuff about the shell hem and braided hem.'

Patsy began to search in a file.

Colin said, 'Well, the shell hem is just a hand-rolled hem which you pucker at intervals with an overstitch.' He sketched on a rough piece of paper. 'Look, it's like this. And a braided hem is the kind of thing you would find on Worth evening dresses. Obviously it has to be on a net or lace design otherwise the braid would not show through. You tuck the cloth under and make an envelope for it, see?'

Jennifer leaned across the table. Ruth inspected the cap.

'Not only does he take you for a spin in his car but he lends you his hat as well.' She pouted.

'Oh, is it Richard's hat?' Patsy looked up in surprise. Then she folded her arms across her file and shrugged her shoulders. 'Oh do tell us where you went,' she pleaded. 'And what you did. I was a bit worried when you didn't turn up for the coach.'

'I wasn't,' Ruth said. 'I thought you would go off with him. You've been after him for ages.'

Jennifer felt the colour coming into her cheeks.

'I have not! Just because a guy lends me his cap to stop my

hair from blowing about when he takes me home it doesn't mean–'

'Did he bring you all the way home then Jennifer? In his car?' Patsy hugged herself. 'How gorgeous!'

'Yes and just that. It was quicker than going back by coach.' Ruth pulled a long face of insolent disbelief.

'Was this something I missed?' Colin asked innocently.

'You should have come to Bristol – talk about a riot!' Ruth's exaggeration was lost on Colin.

'I couldn't find any course that tempted me and anyway, I told you. It was my mum's fiftieth. We had a big family "do".'

'Oh that's nice,' Patsy said.

'No it wasn't,' Colin said gloomily. 'They all got tipsy on pina colada and Uncle Phil started telling dirty jokes and Aunty Moira couldn't stop him. And what was worse,' he added, completely without humour, 'was that Mum kept coming in with the punch lines too early.'

'That reminds me of the girl who complained that her boy friend knew a lot of rude songs,' Ruth recounted. 'And when her mother said, "he doesn't sing them to you does he?" she said, "no, but he whistles them".'

'It would,' Jennifer observed.

'I don't get it,' Patsy said as she pulled at the lace decoration on her sleeve.

'That is to your credit, Patsy,' Colin assured her.

'What was Cheddar Gorge like?' Jennifer tried to change the subject but realised her recklessness too late.

'It was lovely, Jennifer,' Patsy enthused.

'It was cold and dark and full of morons wearing woolly caps,' Ruth muttered.

'No it wasn't!' Patsy was shocked. 'It was lovely and pretty and you should have come Jennifer.'

'Instead of... Just what did you get up to?' Ruth left the insinuation in the air.

'Oh yes, Jennifer, you haven't told us what you did. Do tell us.'

Jennifer assiduously ignored them as she copied Colin's diagram into her notes. She was not going to tell them about their intimacy on the beach. The quickly grasped elbow when she had stumbled and the celerity with which it had been released; the casually probing questions and the half mumbled replies; the

147

way they had pretended that flicking shells at each other signified anger and not some other emotion; the fact that he had been looking at her and sketching her, thinking that she could not see him, and her realisation that she was flattered more by his wish to conceal the attention he afforded her than by the attention itself. They would not be able to understand that. It was not their business. It was nothing to do with them. Sharing it would only sully it.

Ruth sat back in her chair and lifted her pendant from her cleavage and let it drop casually back onto her bosom.

'No need to put yourself out, Jennifer dear, we can ask him ourselves,' she said and smiled with a smug satisfaction at the way that Jennifer's head jerked up from the paper.

Richard Ennessy had just entered the library. He was wearing rather formal grey flannels and a sports jacket and, Jennifer had to admit, he cut quite a dashing figure even in this conservative attire. He stood at the doorway and looked around, searching for something.

'Over here, Richard!' Ruth waved gaily.

'Oh Ruth!' Jennifer hissed. 'You are the limit sometimes.'

'Coo! Doesn't he look really smart Jennifer?' Patsy observed ingenuously.

Colin said nothing.

'Hello all,' Richard greeted them as he approached, allowing his eye to linger a little longer on Jennifer than on the others. But Jennifer had suddenly found a problem with her hair. 'I've been looking all over for you, Jennifer.'

'Well you've found her and just in time,' Ruth said. 'She was just about to tell us what you got up to on Sunday afternoon but now we can get it straight from the horse's mouth.'

Jennifer scowled at Ruth under her hair. Patsy's mouth fell open and Colin swallowed hard. He was feeling more and more an outsider.

'Ah ha,' Richard laughed smoothly, 'Do I detect a scandal monger here? Well, my motto is "give 'em what they want".' Jennifer cringed, afraid that Ruth had goaded Richard into doing or saying something outrageous. 'So you want to know what Jennifer and I got up to on Sunday afternoon when you all dutifully went off to Cheddar Gorge?'

'Jennifer seems to have lost her memory,' Ruth explained.

'Shall I tell them then Jennifer? Put them out of their misery?'

Jennifer looked up at his brown eyes, dancing with mischief. 'Please yourself.' Her voice was expressionless. She had lost. He was about to destroy the magic. She knew it had been too good to be true.

'May I sit down?' Richard pulled out the chair next to Colin. 'Hello. I'm Richard.'

'I'm Colin.'

'Are you doing the same course as Jennifer, Ruth and Patsy?'

Colin suddenly awoke to the fact that he was getting involved in a conversation.

'Yes. That's right. Yes. Advertising and Fashion Design.'

'Do you have to be able to sew for that?'

'Yes, and spell.'

'I can spell,' Richard admitted, 'but I'm useless with a needle. What about you?'

'Colin is brilliant at stitching,' Patsy suddenly lurched up to the table from her slouched position. 'He's better than I am. Show Richard that gauging that you did. Go on,' she urged him.

'Oh he doesn't want to see that,' Colin was embarrassed. Jennifer stole a glance at Ruth. She was fiddling with her pendant with one hand whilst her other tapped on the table.

'How do you know I don't?' Richard asked. 'I don't even know what "gauging" is.'

Colin studied him for an instant, trying to decide whether or not he was being made a fool of and then decided that it did not really matter either way. He reached under the table and pulled up his bag. From it, he withdrew a roll of cloth which he opened gently to show how it had been ruched delicately in a line of even gathers.

'And this is gauging is it?' Colin nodded. 'What is it used for?'

'Well anywhere you need to gather your dress. Could be the sleeves – you know, puff sleeves – or at the bodice.'

'Is this the kind of thing that they did on girl's dresses in Victorian times?' Richard asked.

Ruth sighed heavily and Jennifer looked at her with a growing amusement.

'Well not really,' Colin replied.

'Of course it is,' Ruth said sharply. 'A "modesty bodice," it's called.'

Colin blinked at her. 'Um... no. They wouldn't use gauging for a modesty bodice because it has no "give". It is not elastic.' He tugged gently at the sample to show her. 'There would be no room for the girl to grow her bumps.'

'And we all like girls to grow their bumps don't we?' Richard observed saucily.

'Ooops! Sorry!' Patsy hiccoughed as a result of holding her breath too long in suspense.

Ruth leaned across the table and fingered the lapel of Richard's jacket, feeling the cloth sensually and purposefully showing her bumps. 'You're very smart today.' She looked across with a thin smile of satisfaction at Jennifer who was beginning to bridle quietly.

'I've been to the dentist's,' Richard replied. Colin coughed as he tried to suppress a laugh. 'He's an old family friend. Awfully formal. Wouldn't dream of upsetting him.'

'I hope he drilled holes in you.' Ruth realised it was her who was being made fun of.

'He said to me, "No more ice creams at the sea-side for you, young man".' Richard theatrically put his hand to his mouth and then addressed Jennifer in a contrite tone. 'Oh, now I've let the cat out of the bag, Jennifer, I do apologise. Now everybody knows that we went to the sea-side and ate an ice-cream.'

'Oh how romantic!' Patsy sighed.

'Don't get carried away Patsy,' Jennifer found her voice at last. 'There was a howling gale and I had to buy the ice cream.'

'Shame on you, Richard!' Patsy scolded him.

'Indeed. Shame indeed. I felt so guilty that I came here to make amends.' Richard watched Jennifer as she gently pushed her hair up into the denim cap. 'I think you should keep that cap,' he said abruptly. 'It looks far better on you than it ever did on me.'

'Richard,' Colin suddenly said, as if making a discovery, 'Are you the Richard who did that painting of Jennifer in the reception?'

Ruth clapped her hands ironically.

'Oh well done, Colin. And the world is round.'

'It's not. It's an oblate spheroid,' he argued.

'All right smart arse... '

Jennifer felt Richard's gaze upon her and slowly raised her

eyes to his in a lopsided sort of way. He indicated the door with a flick of his eyes. She looked at him, puzzled. He repeated the movement. She deftly picked up her bag and hopped from her chair. Richard rose at the same instant and by the time Ruth had reached some sort of fuming truce with Colin, she looked up to see them leave the library together.

'I hate you, Colin,' she said.

'No you don't,' said Patsy. 'You hate yourself.'

This time he did not let go of her elbow. As Jennifer walked down the corridor she was very aware of his hand just touching her arm. As if by accident yet they both knew that it was not so. At last she said, 'Where are we going Richard?'

'Anywhere we can talk in peace.' He guided her into the art shop. 'Let's browse awhile. I want to ask you something.'

Richard was lounging in his leather chair, digesting the thick cheese and pickle sandwich that he had made himself for his tea. The plate was on the carpet at his side and in one hand he held a mug of coffee. As he sipped it, he peeped over the brim of the beaker at Jennifer Pye's bare buttocks. His gaze slowly crept up to the hollow of her back, twisted as it was in her pose, with her vertebrae just showing little lumps through her skin. Her flawless skin. Was it really like that? He had sketched and toned it such but could he have missed something? He had noted one mole on her left shoulder blade but otherwise she appeared unmarked.

He had enjoyed painting the hair. As he had transferred the sketch to the canvas, in his mind the lines had not been monotone, they were already the golden cascades of twisted hair, rippling down her bare back and when he had eventually painted the tresses, he had managed to catch the light so that they assumed an almost three dimensional fullness.

He remembered the cheeky manner in which, once she had spotted Richard, she had blatantly turned her back on him and then he momentarily winced as he recalled her angry outburst in the pub. She certainly had some energy, had Jennifer Pye. As he studied the discreet intimacy of the small area between her lower buttocks, he smiled at the irony of the situation, for it had been her behaviour which had spurred him on to complete this painting and to record her every curl and half curl with a spiteful precision. But the cause justified the effect. This was a good painting.

He put his beaker on his empty plate, stood up and removed the naked reclining Jennifer from the easel and gently leaned it up against the wall. Taking his fresh canvas and with a rising feeling of wellbeing, Richard began to pin up his sketches. Now that he had got everything properly organised, it was all going to be all right.

'And the doorman wore a top hat and a funny coat. It was a really swish place you know.' Jennifer nodded and Cherryl continued, 'And you'll never guess what! We drove up in the car and Keith just handed the man the keys and said, "park it for me, would you?" and in we went.'

'So what was it like inside?'

'Difficult to tell really, because it was all so dim. Atmospheric lighting and all that. But it was plush – velvet cushions and thick carpet. Really luxurious.'

Jennifer eased the biscuit tin out of Cherryl's reach.

'These have got to last another week, Cherry,' she said. 'Doesn't Keith feed you when he takes you out?'

'Oh yes, he wines me and dines me and then that's not all,' Cherryl whispered naughtily.

'You mean he...?'

Cherryl nodded and grinned. 'He's terribly strong.' She pulled her blouse from her shoulder and turned to show Jennifer some scratches on her back. 'And passionate,' she giggled.

'Looks a bit rough to me,' Jennifer observed.

She felt ill at ease with Cherryl's matter of fact reference to her lovemaking. Although it was not in her nature to enquire about such things, she did ask herself where they had done it. Had Keith taken her back to his house? Or had they done it in the car? One thing was for certain, they had not done it here. Mrs. Crowther would not permit any of those sort of goings-on in her house.

Then Jennifer surprised herself to find that she was now wondering what Richard would be like to... What it would be like if they both... If together they... She could not fix the concept in her imagination, all she could do was conjure up brief images and they excited her. Richard's strong thighs pressing against hers.

His fingers running down her naked back – she did not think he would be the type to carve gouges in her. His arms around her waist, easing down her jeans. She gave a delicious shiver and pressed her knees together.

'So how was Bristol?'

Jennifer jerked back to reality.

'Erm, all right. They've got some good equipment there. Oh and the lecturer gave me his card and told me to call him–'

'Oh yes, I've met creeps like that,' Cherryl interrupted. 'All they want is–'

'–to call him when I get my results because he thinks I could go far,' Jennifer took pains to finish her phrase but even as she did so, she realised that it sounded a bit lame. 'He's an important person in the industry. Could help me a lot.'

'You just keep a firm hold of your knicker elastic!' Cherryl warned her.

'You can talk!' Jennifer retorted.

'That was different. We are in a relationship. What did you do in Bristol?'

'I made a tee shirt. Well, I printed a tee shirt. That is to say...' She paused and reflected. 'I tried to put my design on a tee shirt.'

'I get this feeling that you are going to show me a tee shirt.'

'Lift your feet up then, it's in my case under the bed.'

Cheryl lifted her legs and Jennifer scrabbled on the floor.

'Ouch!' she exclaimed as one of Cherryl's hard-soled mules dropped onto her head.

'Sorry,' said Cherryl. 'I'll take the other one off before it–'

'Ouch again!'

'Too late.'

'I suppose your legs are properly bolted on are they? I'm not going to be brained by one of them dropping off?'

'I said sorry.'

'Are you all right Miss Pye?' Mrs. Crowther's enquiry floated up from the hall.

'Yes thank you Mrs. Crowther. Nothing to worry about.'

'Only I heard something drop...' she warbled.

'No damage done,' Jennifer called back and then muttered, 'It was only Cherryl's chastity belt.'

She dragged her case out from under the bed and took out her tee shirt and sketch book.

'This is the tee shirt. Shift your great carcase.' She spread it out on the bed beside Cherryl.

Cherryl looked at it and frowned. Then she looked perplexed at Jennifer. 'Um...'

'Yes?' Jennifer snapped.

'Well it's very pretty.'

'But...?'

'But... what is it?'

Jennifer sighed and pulled out her sketch pad.

'It is supposed to be this,' she said as she flipped open the pad. 'I took inspiration from the light coming through the coloured glass on the hall door, downstairs.'

'And who is this?' Cherryl had scooped up from the floor the photograph of Richard which had been taken by Ruth, discarded and then rescued from the rubbish bin by Jennifer and smuggled out in her sketchbook.

'Oh it's just one of the photographs that they took on the photography course.' She held out her hand for the print. 'It's nothing important.'

'Liar!'

'No honest,' Jennifer tried to assure her. 'Come on Cherry, give it back.' She made a lunge but Cherryl held her at bay with a raised foot and whisked the photo out of reach.

'Who is he?' She studied the picture of Richard caught turning, his eyebrows raised quizzically. 'You don't get it back till you've told me who he is.'

'Well...'

'And his telephone number.'

'I'll tell Keith.'

'I'd forget Keith for this one,' Cherryl vowed.

'Do you like him then?' Jennifer asked casually.

'I think he's sexy.'

'Do you really?'

Cherryl nodded, 'Look at those glorious eyes. And that kissable mouth.' She clutched the photo to her chest. 'Who is this hunk?'

'He's hardly a hunk, Cherryl.' She looked down at her fingers which seemed to have twisted themselves in the tassels of the counterpane. Trying to make her voice sound as disinterested as possible she said, 'His name is Richard. You remember, I told you about the man who got his painting of me put up in the college reception.'

'Oh yes,' Cherryl said slowly. 'And this is him?'

'Yes. One of the girls on the photography course snapped him in the corridor, just by chance.'

'Oh yes?' Cherryl handed back the photograph and watched Jennifer as she put it carefully in the top of her underwear drawer. 'So why have you got it then?'

'Well, he's got a picture of me, I didn't see why I should not have a picture of him. Fair's fair.'

'But he hasn't got a picture of you, it's in the college.'

'Yes he has. He did one when we went to the–'

'Got you!' Cherryl shrieked gleefully and bounced up and down on the bed. 'Oh tell me all about him, do!'

Jennifer's resistance, such as it was, collapsed before the obvious joy of her interrogator.

'We sort of met at the dance on the Saturday night, for a couple of dances and then on the Sunday when we were going to put our bags on the coach ready for the evening departure, he just waltzed up, grabbed my bag and walked to his car with it.'

Cherryl was sucking her bottom lip and smacking her fists together in front of her bosom.

'Go on, go on! What happened then?' she demanded.

'Well I had to go with my bag... he sort of kidnapped me.'

Cherryl sighed. 'Did he take you to his castle and ravish you?' she asked dreamily.

'Nothing of the sort. We went to the seaside. I bought us both an ice cream.' She decided that Cherryl would not be interested in the reason why the purchase had fallen upon her. 'And then he took me to a hotel for–'

'Yes? Yes?'

'No Cherryl. For dinner. I had roast beef, yorkshire pudding, roast potatoes, cabbage, carrots, sprouts and gravy and for afters I had jam roly poly and custard. And that is why I fell asleep in the car on the way home.'

'Did he bring you home? But I saw you walk up the street.'

'He dropped me at the Underground. It was easier.'

'Hmph! I don't call that very romantic. Did he kiss you?'

'No, funnily enough, he did not. But he has asked me over to his flat to pose–'

'Not in the–?'

'No! Not in the nude. To pose for him to sketch out for a painting of me.'

'I reckon he's a bit sweet on you. Will you go?'

'Yes, I probably will.'

'I thought you said you didn't like him?'

'I never said that.' Jennifer shrugged. 'He's alright.'

The rumbling traffic of Piccadilly faded behind Jennifer as she wandered uncertainly down Half Moon Street. She glanced at the directions written on the scrap of paper in her hand. It did say down here, on the left. 'Just a little cottage' Richard had said. How you could possibly have a little cottage in the middle of London she was unable to imagine.

She stopped and looked at the brick arch and the wrought iron gates. *'Half Moon Mews'* it said on the lintel stone. Beyond the intricate whorls and curlicues of tortured iron she could see a wide alley of cobbles and flags, lined on either side by the cottages that Richard had mentioned. Half way down, one of the cottages had been whitewashed and adorned with decorative wooden shutters and window boxes, the latter were already alive with pinks, reds and blues. At the far end, she could see the lower half of an overalled torso, working under the bonnet of an ancient looking car.

Number seven he had said. Well, here goes. She tried the pedestrian gate at the side of the main arch but it defied her every attempt at opening it. This is daft, she thought. How does he expect me to get in? Then she noticed the bank of discreetly illuminated buttons set into the brickwork. No names, just numbers. She pressed 'seven' and jumped when Richard's voice came at her from the speaker.

'Hello Jennifer! I'll let you in.'

'Hi!' she answered faintly. She was still recovering from the shock when something on the gate buzzed and she jumped again. Now what was happening?

'Push the gate, Jennifer, it won't bite!'

She gingerly nudged the gate and it swung open with an insolent ease. As she stepped into the mews, she felt a bizarre and almost intangible unease that she was entering a different world.

'Over here!' Richard called from a doorway. She went to him. 'I'm glad you could get here. It wasn't too difficult was it?'

'It's not the getting here that's difficult,' Jennifer observed, 'it's the getting in that's hard.'

'Yes, it is a bit Fort Knoxish I'm afraid. Come on up.' She followed him up the stairs to the living room. 'Let me take your coat.'

'Wow!' she said, looking about her, 'this is rather smart, Richard. However did you find it? The rent must cost a bomb!' She felt that unease tingling at her but Richard's reply smoothly put her doubts to rest.

'I was lucky. These friends of my parents needed someone to look after the place for their distant cousin or something, I can't quite remember what the relationship was,' he said diffidently. 'Anyway he's off in the States somewhere, and when they heard that I was looking for somewhere in London, they let me have it for a pittance.'

'Lucky you,' Jennifer said as she swept a woman's eye over the expensively equipped kitchen. 'I could do with some friends like that. Are you a good cook?'

Richard grinned. 'Lousy. When I said "dinner" I never said that I was going to cook. I like you too much to want to poison you.' Jennifer felt her heart give a flip at his casual, almost light-hearted declaration of amity. 'There's a super restaurant just around the corner. Are you all right with Thai food?'

'I'm not sure. I've never had any.'

'Well, there's always a first time. Do you want a coffee?'

'I'll tell you what I do want,' Jennifer divulged. 'The loo.'

'I'm sorry, I should have thought. It's downstairs, the door on the right. The house is upside down,' he explained. 'Go through the bedroom to the ensuite.'

Jennifer paused at the bottom of the stairs and looked through the fireproof glass on the door to her left. She could just make out a dim yellow shape in the gloomy garage. It reminded her of the drive to the seaside and the dinner at the hotel and the journey back down the motorway.

She felt that strange unreality again as she opened the door to his bedroom. She thrilled a little at the thought of violating his most intimate sanctum. The carpet was a thick cream and the bed looked enormous. She imagined that she could sleep quite comfortably crossways on it. She wondered who had slept on it. Who had lain alongside or underneath Richard's strong, healthy body? He must have had a few girls. She went through to the bathroom which was decorated in a rather cold marble design laminate. Except that it was not laminate, she discovered, it was marble. She thought back to the coffee shop and the stumbling explanation that Richard had given over the access he had had to a real Monet. Was it 'friends of his parents' he had said? She could not quite remember. Ruth would remember, she thought sourly.

When she came out of the bedroom she caught her foot on the doormat and in straightening it, noticed an envelope standing white against the white wall. She retrieved it and carried it upstairs. Richard was tugging inexpertly at a packet of biscuits as she entered the living room.

'*Viscount Churle*,' she read from the envelope. 'Is that the friend of your parents'?'

Richard's head jerked up and the biscuits suddenly exploded everywhere as the packet tore open in his hands.

'I'm a bit clumsy with these things,' he said. She noticed that his lack of expertise was making him blush. 'What was that you said?' he asked as they crawled around on the carpet, retrieving biscuits.

She pushed the envelope across to him. 'Letter addressed to Viscount Churle. I found it downstairs. It had dropped down by the wall. I just happened to see it.'

'Ah yes,' he looked at the envelope. It was a circular from a company promoting a new magazine for the landed gentry. 'He's always getting things like this.' He casually tore it in half and dropped it in the bin.

'Should you do that?' Jennifer was surprised. 'I mean it is his letter.'

Richard realised his mistake. 'I suppose I shouldn't,' he said. 'But I always do when it is that sort of junk mail. He knows that I always forward his proper mail.'

Jennifer was intrigued. 'Is he a viscount then?'

'I suppose he must be, unless he is putting on airs and graces.'

'I don't really know what a viscount is,' Jennifer admitted. 'It's probably someone who gets the servant girls into trouble.'

'I'll tell him.'

Jennifer's hand flew to her mouth. 'Oh no don't!' She was horrified. 'I didn't mean that he was someone like that.'

'Oh that's all right then. But he could be, for all you know. Come on, lets forget these confounded biscuits.' He pushed them onto a tray and dumped them in the kitchen. 'Dinner! I'll get your coat.'

Jennifer could hardly believe that all this was happening. Here she was, calmly sitting in Richard's rented pad in London, surrounded by reminders of his intimate life, his books on the shelves, his clothes on the chair, his music playing.

She watched him as he absent-mindedly pushed his hair from his face and concentrated all his attention on the canvas before him. Why did he want to paint her again? She amused and thrilled herself with fabricated answers. He caught her eye and grinned at her in a frank, boyish way. She smiled back and she felt the warmth coming from within her to mellow the smile with a deeper significance, one that she could not prevent. His glance rested on her for a split second longer, undecided, then he smiled again and lowered his gaze to the easel.

Why was he being nice to her? She had been treated to a strange but delicate meal, full of exciting flavours and odours in a cosy back street restaurant where, judging from the fuss made over him, Richard had dined several times before. Perhaps he did this with all his girl friends. This reflection shocked her slightly. Was she, then, his girl friend? She wondered where he had taken Ruth. Funny that she had never said.

'Nearly done,' he said.

'Are you using the sketches you made on the beach at Weston super Mare?'

He stopped and looked at her. 'Oh. I didn't think you had seen.' He sounded embarrassed and that thrilled her even more.

'Why didn't you want me to see?'

'I wanted to catch you as you were – natural and relaxed. You looked so... peaceful. I wanted to try to capture that.'

'I was very happy that afternoon Richard,' she said.

He stared at her softly. 'I think I was too.' He wiped his hands. 'You can come and look if you like. I've done all I need. I can see it now. Everything – the colours – everything.'

She slipped off the low stool and moved around to look at the canvas. She was seated on the beach, gazing out to what would be, eventually, the sea. He had caught that three quarters view with the wind tugging at her hair. She could hear the gulls and the murmur of the surf.

'What do you think?' he said, as he moved closer to her.

She could feel her heart beginning to thump in her chest. She could smell him.

'I think it will be a very good painting Richard. As good as the ballgown.'

'What do you think of the curve of your nose, just there?' He pointed with his finger and casually draped his other arm around her shoulder to turn her towards the canvas. Their bodies were drawing together. She sensed his thigh lightly touching her bottom. She could not speak. The blood was pounding in her temples. 'Makes you look a bit like an elephant don't you think?' He laughed awkwardly and lifted the canvas from the easel. She could still feel the warmth where his arm had lain on her shoulder.

'What is the next stage then, Richard?'

'Well I won't need you again, now, thank you. Not for posing.' he added hastily and then looked away and busied himself in arranging the canvas into the stack against the wall. 'I'll probably start with colours next week.'

Jennifer was staring aghast at his stack of canvasses. 'Oh no Richard!' She strode over to the wall. 'You didn't...' She put her hands to her cheeks and looked at her nude figure. 'Oh Richard, why did you...?'

He lifted it from the floor and placed it on the easel. 'I thought it was rather successful,' he remarked with a certain amount of mischief. 'As an exercise, I managed to translate it from sketches to painting with little loss of integrity.'

Jennifer thought ruefully that it was her integrity that was more likely to be lost. Oh why had she done it? Why? Had she needed the money that much? Ironically, she realised that she would not be here now had she not been able to go to Bristol in the first place and that journey had only been possible after she had been paid for modelling nude. But she had never thought that Richard or anybody would use the sketches for anything other than practice, for improving skills.

Richard had undoubted talent. Her hair looked good. Good enough to touch. Was it really that golden? Did the skin at her hips really wrinkle like that when she propped herself up on one elbow? Were her thighs that plump? Suddenly she felt the blood surging up into her face as she studied her buttocks. She had not realised that he could see that much, from behind, as it were. And all done in such intricate detail.

'Oh Richard, I wish you had not have done it in quite so much detail.' Her voice was halting and unsure. 'The hair...'

'Oh I'm rather proud of the hair, Jennifer, it's your best bit.' He stood back with his hands in his pockets and his head on one side. 'One of your best bits.'

'I didn't mean that hair,' she said boldly. 'Oh Richard...' her voice quavered a little. 'It's terribly embarrassing. Why did you have to put in so much detail? If anybody sees that I won't know what to do.'

'It's all in the cause of art,' he tried to reassure her.

'I preferred the ballgown. I felt good in that.'

'You looked good in it.' He lifted down the painting. 'Since it offends your eyes, I shall turn it to the wall, your majesty.'

Jennifer looked at her watch. 'I must go. Thanks for dinner and everything.'

'Thanks very much for coming. That sitting has been really useful to me.' He took one of her hands and held it. 'Look, let me take you back, it won't take a minute in the car at this time of night.'

'No.' She withdrew her hand to fish in her bag. 'I've got my tube ticket already.'

'Well I'll walk with you to the tube.'

'Don't be daft. Just show me how to get out of this fortress, that's all I need. I suppose all your girls have this problem do they? Once ensnared by the spider they can't get out of the web?'

Richard said nothing but looked down to inspect his shoes, a move which momentarily hid his face.

'I'll take you to the gate then,' he said in a neutral voice.

Jennifer stormed up Half Moon Street towards the noise of Piccadilly. She was furious with herself. Why could she not learn to control her mouth? 'I suppose all your girls have this problem do they?' She shuddered and clenched her fists in her coat pocket. She was certain that he would have kissed her but for that!

Richard stood alone in the middle of the room. He had lied to Jennifer about himself. But he had done it because he did not want to lose her. Why did he not want to lose Jennifer Pye?

His eyes fell on the envelope propped up on the mantle shelf. Two tickets for Nessie's charity ball. Jennifer's voice came back to him. 'I felt good in that.'

He still had the ballgown in the cupboard.

'I wonder...'

EPISODE TWELVE

Dr. Sullivan closed Richard's portfolio and moved back towards the display easels. 'I'll be frank, Richard, you are a little thin on the plastics.'

Richard nodded. 'That's a fair comment.' The memory of Alison Barrett showing him how to throw clay came back to him. 'I am just not good with my hands.' Dr. Sullivan looked at him in surprise. 'I mean, not to do that type of thing with my hands. They just don't work that way.'

'It's not in the hands, Richard, it's in the eye.' Dr. Sullivan returned to perusing his paintings.

Richard glanced at the window as a shower of hail rattled against it. A late April shower. Late, for this was already May – the month in which Dr. Sullivan always reviewed the students' progress. Traditionally discussing their work with them and customarily endeavouring to put the fear of God into them so that they would be spurred on to supreme efforts in the last half term before their portfolios went to the assessment board. Dr Sullivan approved heartily of a good dose of fear at this time of year. They would all be getting a little complacent by now. The youth of today needed a little stimulus from time to time.

'Ah yes, I saw the sketches for this in your portfolio, did I not? Drawn from life?'

'Yes that's right.'

'This, of course, is where you make up for your plastics. Very competent portrait, Richard, very competent.'

Richard thought so too. His eyes caressing Jennifer Pye's nakedness, were still those of the innocent artist. How could they be anything else? They had not been lovers. They had not even kissed. He had nearly kissed her but she had said something, he

163

could not remember exactly what, which he had interpreted as a warning to stay clear. Perhaps he had been mistaken.

He looked at that secret part of her lower buttocks, where the curls of hair had so embarrassed her when she had seen the painting in his flat. Well, she would not be embarrassed now. He was glad that he had erased them by painting an extra fold in the cloth. She would be pleased with that when she saw it.

Dr. Sullivan moved on. 'Ah yes, the famous Monet.' He shot a sideways glance at Richard. 'I am not sure how the board will view this, given that they are unlikely to know the original...' Richard shrugged non-committally. 'I wonder whether you should arrange for a viewing?'

Richard slowly shook his head. He had no intention of inviting Dr. Sullivan or anybody else to inspect grandfather's Monet. If they could not count it, then so be it.

'I gave my word.'

'Quite! Quite!' Dr. Sullivan surrendered. It had been worth a try. He turned to the next easel. 'This young lady seems to be a favourite model of yours. It is the same one again?'

'Yes, that's her. On the beach at Weston super Mare.'

'A private sitting?'

'Hardly. We were on a weekend course at Bristol.'

And I danced with her and held her in my arms and we flicked pebbles at each other on the beach and I raced her up the beach and she bought me an ice cream and I bought her an enormous roast dinner and then we drove magically through the darkness, headlights, cats' eyes, road signs and Jennifer Pye oblivious to it all, safe, asleep at the side of me, her head snuggled unknowingly into my jumper, her little fists curled loosely in her lap. And I took her home and she lives in a block of flats just off the M4 in Chiswick. And tomorrow night I shall be dancing with her again.

'Richard?'

'Sorry, I was day-dreaming.' He smiled brightly at Dr Sullivan who was trying not to look sour.

'I was saying that I think on the whole your portfolio is adequate. A little unbalanced but then if all artists were competent at everything nothing great would ever be produced. I assume that you will be specialising in portraiture in your second year?'

'Assuming I get through, of course.'

'Er, yes.'

'I hadn't really thought about it,' Richard said vaguely.

'Well, I suppose you still have some time left.' Dr Sullivan tried to hide the exasperation in his voice. 'I think that's all I need do today. I'll leave you to pack up. Can you be clear in fifteen minutes?'

'Easily.'

Dr. Sullivan nodded and then, for no apparent reason, suddenly thrust out his arm and shook Richard's hand. Then he grunted to hide his embarrassment and left him to pack away his paintings.

'What was it like?' Alison Barrett poked her head around the door. 'Do you want any help?'

'Oh yes please,' Richard said, although did not need help. 'Are you in next?'

'Yes.' She sucked her lip nervously and her face looked even longer and thinner. 'What was it like? What did he say? I mean, what sort of thing was he interested in?'

Richard looked at her and realised that the poor kid was frightened.

'Alison, you've nothing to worry about. Look at that bust you did for the Greek day.'

'I don't know...' She lifted down a canvas and carried it to his case. 'You see, I can't paint like this.' She brandished Jennifer Pye to emphasise her point and then blushed at the nudity.

'No and I can't model or sculpt anything.' He put his arm around her thin shoulders and gave her an encouraging squeeze. 'Dr. Sullivan will huff and puff up and down your display and suck his teeth over your portfolio and then say, "Well Miss Barrett", he doesn't call you 'Alison' does he?' She shook her head. '"Well Miss Barrett, you're a little thin on the graphics but your plastics should just pull you through," which in normal language means you are well on the way to sail through your assessment with flying colours but I can't tell you that otherwise you would stop working for the rest of the term.'

'Mmm... Do you think so?'

'I know so. Come on, buck up or I shan't be clear of the studio before the great Alison Barrett presents her show. If you're quick, I'll buy you a coffee afterwards. Don't keep the doctor talking because I'm going home for the weekend straight after this and I want to miss the traffic.'

When this house is quiet, it is never tranquil, just silent, Jennifer said to herself. She knew that Mrs. Crowther was there because she had heard Sandy yapping a short time ago but now all was still. She imagined that the thumping of her heart must have been audible three streets away. And it always started thumping again whenever she thought about what had happened the previous week when he had asked her.

She had been going in to the refectory when he had appeared at the door, languidly combing his hand through his hair as people do when they are nervous.

'Hello Jennifer. Long time no see.' He had leaned casually against the doorway, one hand in the pocket of his loose fitting trousers. 'Could I have a word with you?'

Very formal.

'Hello Richard,' she had replied, and then found herself colouring as she had turned to Patsy and said, 'I'll catch up with you later, Patsy.'

Patsy had looked from her to Richard and back again and then said, 'Oh right.' Then she had squeezed her arm and whispered, 'Tell me about it.'

She had watched Richard's amused blue eyes following Patsy into the refectory.

'Do you tell her all your secrets?'

'I don't tell anyone my secrets. What did you want to speak to me about?' She was sounding terribly distant but he had started like that and she could not see her way out of it.

He straightened up and now put his both hands in his pockets. She thought how gorgeously handsome he looked when he was unsure of himself. Just like the first day.

'Are you... erm.. What are you doing next weekend? I mean, have you got anything important that you must do? I mean, could you...?'

A weekend. Not 'one evening' but a weekend. Her heart had begun to thump. Trying to sound as relaxed as he was hoping he appeared, she had said, 'I'm not doing anything special. At all.'

'Not washing your hair or anything?'

'Why, does it look awful?'

'I think it looks lovely, it always does. I've got this friend called Nessie...'

'Nessie?'

'Vanessa. She is very heartily concerned with donkeys.'

'Donkeys?'

'Er... yes... Yes. Donkeys. And she...' He had stopped then and looked at her grinning at him and then it had all come out. 'Jennifer will you come to a dance with me. Nessie is having this charity ball for her blessed donkeys and she has given me two tickets and I really ought to go but I can't go on my own. You could come down on the Friday night and we could make a bit of a holiday of it, the ball is on the Saturday night and it will be alright I've got a place we can stay. Two bedrooms, two bedrooms. Ermm... What do you think?'

That was when her heart had really started pounding.

'But where is the dance, Richard?'

'In a private house, near my place.'

'A ball, in a private house?'

'Yes, a country house. Well I suppose it's more what you would call a stately home, really. You know the type of thing – parkland and porticos. I thought it would be a bit of a laugh.'

'But what shall I wear, Richard? These are my best jeans.' At least she was not turning him down.

'Oh I've thought about that. I haven't returned that blue ballgown yet, the one I painted you in. I thought that you looked really good in it and it is a proper ball, all the ladies will be putting on their best... Go on, be a sport!'

Cherryl had listened open eyed to her and then brought her back to earth with practicalities.

'You're not taking that thing.' She had brutally prodded the slumbering bundle of Jennifer's giant tee shirt which she used as a nightdress.

'Separate bedrooms, he said.'

'And you believed him?'

'Yes, of course I did. And I still do.'

'What about getting up for the loo? Or coming down for breakfast? Do you want him to see you in that?'

'I suppose not. But what–?'

'Show me your knickers.' Cherryl had moved towards her top drawer.

'Hold your horses, Cherry, he won't be seeing those!'

'Don't you believe it. Anyway, you should know that what you wear underneath is more important than what you wear on top. It makes you feel good.' She sighed as she caught sight of Richard's photo lying on the top of Jennifer's underwear, then she giggled, 'He's already got his nose in your knickers, what are you worried about?'

'Cherry!'

'Only joking, poppet. Oh Jennifer!' She held up a pair of Jennifer's panties, 'Is this the best you can do? Do you really like flowers?'

'No, but they're cheap and comfortable.' Jennifer snatched them back.

Cherryl had stood up and looked at her watch.

'We've got an hour and a half. Come on, Jennifer, no arguing, Marks and Sparks for you.'

For the hundredth time, Jennifer opened her travelling bag to check that she had not forgotten anything and for the hundredth time she caught her breath at the whispy naughtiness, the brazen nothingness of what Cherryl had made her buy.

Cherryl always slept late on Saturday mornings; by the time she awoke, Jennifer would already be on the train rattling out of Paddington and bound for the small station in rural Berks where Richard would be waiting for her in his yellow car. Cherryl would have to wait until she came back for all the latest news. If at all she was interested, for Jennifer knew that Cherryl was going out with Keith tonight and that would surely eclipse any of Jennifer's adventures.

Jennifer slit open the envelope from Spain and skimmed through the letter from her Mam and Dad. When would she feel brave enough to tell them the truth about it all? About Steven and the shop and Richard, if, indeed, there was to be anything to tell about Richard. 'Your Mam and I are really excited to hear that you're coming over..' I never said that, she protested angrily. I never said that. Oh why don't you read my letters properly? Parents were sometimes so exasperating.

'Now sit still Sandy, you naughty dog.' Mrs. Crowther wiped the dog's muzzle with a cloth. 'We cannot have you going out looking like that. What would my sister think?' She took a comb from the sideboard and scuffed it through the top of his head. 'And if you stay on your best behaviour I shall ask her Reggie to take you to the common tomorrow morning and you can chase the rabbits.' The dog wagged its tail, confirming in Mrs. Crowther's heart that he understood every word she said.

She put on her powder blue coat and placed her matching train case by the door. Then she looked in the mirror and primped up her hair. 'And no barking in the taxi!' she added as an afterthought.

Hearing the front door slam, she peeped out from behind her net curtain. Miss Pye, with travelling bag in her hand, was setting off down the street as if she had not a care in the world. It made an uneasy image in her mind.

By pinpointing the noise of tortured metal, Richard found Winston. He was in one of the garages, using the bench drill. He stood by the door and watched him working. Each time his silver-grey hair fell before his eyes he puffed a burst of air upwards from his lower lip and flicked his head at the same time to clear his vision. Eventually he switched off the drill and stepped back to admire his work.

'You should wear a hair net Winston. I think I'll suggest it to mother.'

'Master Richard!' The surprise and pleasure registered on his face simultaneously. 'You'll do no such thing I trust.' He came forward into the afternoon daylight, blinking slightly.

Richard peered at the metal in his hands.

'Hinge?' he asked.

'That's right, Master Richard. I'm drilling out the holes to take larger bolts. Jeffrey is making me some battens out of some hardwood offcuts he has and then with a bit of jiggery-pokery and a little magic, we should be able to save those garage doors for another generation.'

'I am sure if you spoke to Courtney the estate purse could stretch as far as a new set of doors.'

'That is not the point, Master Richard. Look after the pennies...' He looked around the yard, turning his body more than a supple youngster would have to do. He's getting old, thought Richard. 'Where is that little yellow scooter of yours?'

'Oh I've left it down at the bridge,' Richard said airily, 'I walked up through the park.' Winston's raised eyebrows spoke volumes. 'I thought I would spend the weekend at Bridge Cottage as it is empty. It'll make a change from the Hall and with my parents away.' Winston was studying the workmanship on the hinge. 'Actually, Winnie, I've got a favour I want to ask of you.' The old chauffeur had turned the hinge over and was now studying the burr on the other side.

'You'll have to let Mrs. MacCallum know, Master Richard,' he said without looking up, 'so that she can get the beds aired. Bridge Cottage hasn't been used since the last shoot.'

'Yes, I've done it, I phoned her on Wednesday.'

'I see,' he said, looking up. 'Now what is this dreadful favour you are wanting to ask of me?'

'I've got a friend coming down and we are going to Nessie's ball for the donkeys tomorrow night.'

'Over at Hartlip House?'

'Oh, you know about it?'

'Miss Vanessa did mention it to me some time ago.'

'I was wondering if... I mean I know it's your weekend off and all that with my parents being away but I thought it would be good fun if we could arrive in style. After all, it is a ball and–'

'Perhaps you had better tell me who she is, Master Richard.' Winston set the hinge down and sat on the black wood cabin chest that he had been using as a makeshift door trestle.

'Who?'

'I don't believe you are going to the ball on your own, Master Richard, so who are we trying to impress?'

Richard looked around the mews. The cobbles were bubbling with mirth at him, the orange bricks were roasting with glee, the slates were slyly smiling. He sighed heavily.

'Shove up, Winnie,' he said and Winston wordlessly moved aside on the chest to allow him to sit down. 'Her name's Jennifer. She's a student at college. I've painted her a couple of times, once when she was dressed in an old ballgown of Hattie's and she looked really good so when this ball came up I thought it would be good fun to take her along.'

'What about Miss Vanessa?

'Ah!' Richard announced contentedly, 'Miss Vanessa Clewe-Harting has already told me that I shall have to find somebody else because she has already been spoken for.'

'Good for her!' Winston slapped his knee. 'Too many people take Miss Vanessa for granted.' Richard opened his mouth to speak. 'Including you, Master Richard.' He shut it without a word. 'So you would like me to take you and...?'

'Jennifer.'

'Jennifer, to Hartlip House, in the Daimler I presume?'

'If you would, Winnie, just for me.'

'And wait and bring you home again at some ungodly hour of the morning?'

'No later than one o'clock I promise.'

'In the middle of my free weekend?'

'Well... I know it is an awful cheek.'

'Yes, it is, Master Richard, but I'll do if it will keep you out of mischief.'

'Out of mischief?'

'I don't know what this young lady, Jennifer, is like but she must be a bit special.'

'She's a bit different, I'll admit to that, but thanks Winnie, I do appreciate it.'

'Hmm. I wonder.'

'Oh there is another thing...' Richard began. Winston folded his arms and looked sideways at him. 'Well, this is going to sound a bit silly, but, just for this weekend I'd rather you didn't call me "Master Richard", just "Richard". You see, up at college they just know me as Richard. I'm just another student and this er... Jennifer, well she thinks that I am, well, she knows me as another student, that's all. I don't want her to feel intimidated by all this.' He swept his arm around to indicate the mews, the park and Wisdene Hall.

'But she knows who you are?' Winston asked slowly.

'Not in the sense that you know who I am.' The chauffeur's grey eyebrows knitted in a perplexed frown. 'Look Winnie, if I swanned up to her and said that's where I live and my father's an earl, I wouldn't see her for dust.'

'She's important to you then?'

'I suppose she is.'

Winston shook his head sorrowfully.

'I don't think this is the way to do it, Master Richard, if you don't mind me saying so. If she is that important, it shouldn't make any difference to her.'

'Will you do it, though?'

'I said I would, fool that I am. How do you account to your young lady for the chauffeur-driven Daimler?'

'A friend. Doing it for a laugh.'

'Ah ha. And the cottage?'

'Lent to me by a friend.'

Winston sucked in his breath and said nothing.

The station was unmanned. The benches had been removed but the weeds had been left. Jennifer shrugged at the deserted platform and, slinging her bag onto her shoulder, made for the exit. As she turned the brick corner a body suddenly cannoned into her and then grabbed her shoulder to stop her from falling over.

'Oi!' she shouted as her bag fell to the ground.

'Sorry!' Richard panted, 'thought I had missed you.'

'Oh no, you didn't miss me Richard, it was a bull's eye,' she laughed.

He was still holding her. He pulled her gently to him so that their bodies were touching. His brown eyes, unusually serious, looked down at her.

'I am glad you came. I am... glad.' He kissed her on the forehead and then quickly leapt aside and picked up her bag. 'Come on,' he called and ran through the archway into the station yard.

He kissed me, Jennifer thought as she slowly followed him.

Making sure that her cap, Richard's cap, was firmly in place, Jennifer threw back her head and allowed the wind to catch and tug at her hair as Richard whisked the car through the lanes. A rather watery sun was peering through a hazy sky and the air had a nip in it. Jennifer frowned as she thought of her new undies. She did not want to freeze. What if this stately home was one of those cold draughty places with stone walls and marble floors? She glanced across at Richard who was also frowning but in concentration as he gauged the gap between a van and the narrow bridge. Despite the coolness of the air, magnified by the movement of the open top car, the sleeves of his raw cotton shirt were rolled up, showing his tanned forearms. How had he got tanned? Was he an outdoors type? Or was he a vain type with a sunbed? Her gaze drifted down to his legs when he changed gear, and to the creasing in the cloth of his black jeans as his foot moved across the pedals. She suddenly realised what she was looking at and looked away, feeling herself blush. Separate bedrooms he had promised. Separate bedrooms.

Richard nosed the car between the gate posts of what looked like a rather fancy farm gateway and onto a gravel drive which cut through a park of mature trees. Jennifer looked quickly across at him.

'Short cut?' she asked.

'Wait and see.'

'Oh how lovely!' she exclaimed as the drive wound down to a sparkling clear stream which it crossed on an ancient hump backed stone bridge. Richard ran the car to a halt before the pair of cottages and switched off the engine. Jennifer hopped out and ran across to lean over the parapet of the bridge. She gazed down into the water, watching the emerald green weed waving gently back and forth and the bubbles and ripples breaking the shadowy reflection of herself. At length she straightened up. Richard was lifting her bag from the car.

'What are you doing?' she was mystified.

He nodded towards the cottage. 'We're here,' he said. 'The one on the left – Bridge Cottage.'

She felt her heart give a little leap of alarm.

'Oh Richard! It can't be. It's idyllic.' Her eyes ran over the warm stone mullions and quoins and the red brick; the diamond latticed windows and the neat but intricate twisted chimneys. 'However did you manage it?'

'Friend owed me a favour. Come on.'

She followed him through the front door whose key was nestling ready in the lock. He showed her the kitchen which, unusually, had been built at the front of the cottage to look out over the bridge and the little parlour which gave out to a neat cottage garden at the back. On the table stood a small vase of late spring flowers.

'It's lovely,' she breathed. 'Like a fairy tale.'

He glanced at her quickly and then looked away again. 'Come

on,' he said, running up the narrow staircase and bowing his head at the eaves, 'You can choose your bedroom.' He threw open a door. 'This is the back bedroom.' She crept in across a creaking board floor to the window, the patchwork counterpane throwing colours to the ceiling as the sun flowed over it.

'Oh, it's lovely Richard.'

'Come and see the front room. You'll like it better.'

She did. From the window which was already open she could gaze down over the bridge to the stream and the copse through which they had driven. She drank it all in with her eyes, feeling her batteries being recharged by the tranquil beauty of it all. She sensed him standing behind her and felt his hand on her shoulder.

'This is what England is all about, you know,' he said with a strange certainty in his voice. She stood unmoving whilst his hand absently stroked her neck under her hair and they both gazed at the early afternoon sun dappling through the trees to the parkland sward.

'However do they keep the grass so short all over. They don't mow it do they?'

'Sheep.'

'And is that the big house up there?' She pointed at a huge edifice just visible, sitting astride the hill. 'Who lives there? Anybody important? Anybody famous?'

'Oh just a local family. Look out!' he said and pulled her away from the window to one side. An energetic man dressed in twill trousers and plaid shirt with his countryman's cloth cap pulled down over piercing eyes had suddenly appeared at the side of the bridge, having clambered up an unseen path by the parapet. Jennifer had just had chance to see him stop and glance at Richard's car thoughtfully before turning his gaze towards the cottage when she had been pulled aside.

'What's the matter?' she gasped but further enquiry was swept from her mind as his mouth closed on hers. Her lips parted to his tongue and a tingle ran from her neck down her spine to her buttocks as she felt his strong arms crushing her to him. The ridiculous chant of 'separate bedrooms' ran through her mind, taunting her. She knew that she could give in. She wanted him. He slowly drew from her and studied her face.

'Sorry,' he said mischievously, 'thought I saw someone I knew.'

'Beast!' She punched his chest.

'So you want this room then?' She nodded. And with that nod she discreetly accepted that their relationship was evolving into something more than a casual bond between students with common interests. 'I thought you would. I have already hung your ballgown on the back of the door.'

'Richard.'

'Yes.'

'I need to speak seriously.' He pulled a face at her. 'This cottage. Is it alright us being here? We're not squatting or anything?'

'Good Lord no!'

'Are you sure that you have your friend's permission to use it?'

'Scouts' honour.'

'Were you ever a scout?'

'No. Were you ever a girl guide?'

'No.'

'Well that's all settled then.' He dragged her bag in from the landing. 'Get settled in and then we must find some lunch. What do you fancy? Pub lunch O.K.? We'll be eating tonight. We can always have an afternoon tea here before we go if your stomach starts rumbling.'

'That sounds lovely.'

As he backed out of the door he said,

'You know, I quite like you, Jennifer.'

'I quite like you,' she replied.

Quite like you, she thought as she sat on the bed. Yes, I suppose I do; what I know of you, Richard Ennessy. You're a bit of a mystery sometimes. But then, I suppose, so am I. You know about as much of me as I know of you. I don't think you come from my class. I am certain you don't but that doesn't make you a different person. It is you that I like, your gentleness, your strength, your even handedess, your prejudice, your social ease and your embarrassed discomfort; it is all part of the you that I like. She pulled her clothes from her bag and then glanced quickly at the door in embarrassment as her hand clasped her exotic underclothes. She looked around and thrust them urgently into the top drawer of the small cottage-style chest of drawers by the window.

She looked at the ballgown and then disaster suddenly hit her between the eyes like a searchlight.

'Richard!' She could hear talking outside. Looking from the window she could see him chatting with a silver haired gentleman in corduroys and an open-necked shirt. Doesn't anybody here feel the cold? she said to herself as she pounded down the stairs and out into the drive. 'Richard!' she skidded on the gravel, her long hair flying madly in all directions.

'Careful miss, or you'll do yourself an injury.' The elderly gentleman turned a ruddy face to hers and openly appraised her.

'Winnie, this is my friend Jennifer. Winston is a friend of mine, Jennifer.'

The old man rubbed the palm of his hand on his corduroys and shook her hand.

'Oh,' she said and then realised the importance of what Richard had said. 'Oh is this your cottage? It's awfully kind of you to let us–'

The old man chuckled. 'Bless you, no, it's not my cottage, I live up at the Hall, in the mews.'

Jennifer looked to Richard for explanations since she was now completely lost.

'Winnie has offered...' The old man cleared his throat discreetly. Richard sighed and started again. 'I asked Winnie if he would take us to the ball tonight in his car.'

'But...' Jennifer looked across at Richard's car.

'No miss,' Winston said kindly, 'You would not get into that Yellow Peril in a ball gown.'

Jennifer turned her eyes to the Hall.

'But we could walk up couldn't we?'

The men followed her glance.

'Oh it's not here, Jennifer. We are only lodging here. The ball is over on the other side of the county at Hartlip House,' Richard explained with an ease that suggested that she should have known.

'Richard, I need to talk to you about something,' she said, urgently remembering her original quest.

He looked at her, puzzled and then turned to the old man. 'Excuse us a minute Winnie.'

'Yes Master Richard.'

As soon as they were inside the cottage she turned to him and stuttered, 'I've... I've got no shoes... or bag or anything. I can't go in just a ballgown and sneakers. I am sorry, Richard, I didn't think. I'm not used to...' She stopped, feeling the tears welling up.

'All right. All right.' He patted her shoulder. 'Nothing to worry about, it's my fault really, I should have thought. Of course you need shoes and an evening purse and I know where I can get them.'

'You do?' He nodded. 'But they have to match my gown.'

'They do. They were all together but I only brought the gown to the class. Silly of me. I'll pop up and get them now.'

'Pop up?'

He pushed her gently out of the door. Winston was standing peering at the dashboard of the car.

'Winnie, why don't you take Jennifer for a drive in the park? Take my car, Show her the lake and Long Covert or whatever it's called – where the RAC rally came through a couple of years ago.'

The old man looked at Richard as if trying to read his mind.

'Oh please don't trouble yourself,' Jennifer said.

'Oh it's no trouble at all miss. It will be a pleasure.' He turned to Richard. 'Down by the lake did you say Ma... er Richard?'

'Yes, you know. You are always telling me how pretty the park is. I've just got to run an errand.' He nodded his head vaguely towards the Hall. Shouldn't take more than half an hour.' Winston opened the door for Jennifer. 'If you are lucky Jennifer, you might see some deer.'

He watched them out of sight, Jennifer waving gaily over her turned shoulder and Winston gingerly handling the wheel as the car twitched on the loose gravel. He smiled at the unusual sight of Winston perched on, rather than in, a car for a change.

Ten minutes later he was standing on the South Terrace watching with smug satisfaction the progress of a yellow blob as it stopped and started its way across the park. Winston was giving her the full tour, bless his little cotton socks.

He let himself in by the service entrance, grabbed a bunch of keys from the cupboard and ran up the back stairs two at a time to the lumber room. The shoes and bag were still there at the bottom of the trunk, safely wrapped in tissue paper and chiffon scraps.

'Of course you won't see any deer up here at this time of the afternoon, miss,' Winston admitted, 'I don't know what Master Richard was thinking of.'

'Oh that doesn't matter. It is a lovely park. Have you lived here long?'

'Oh yes. Sorry!' he added as his foot lurched off the clutch. 'The clutch is rather harsh miss, but I am getting used to it.'

'Please don't keep calling me "miss". I would much rather you call me "Jennifer".'

'Well I don't know.'

'And why do you call Richard, "Master Richard"?'

'Oh do I?' Winston prevaricated to give himself some thinking time. His mind was not accustomed to all these complexities of deceit and he was certain that he did not like them one little bit.

'Yes you do. Twice you've called him that.'

'Well it's rather hard to explain Miss Jennifer. It's a sort of long standing joke I suppose.'

'Oh yes, I understand. Some things just cannot be explained easily can they?'

'You are right.'

'My father calls me "Jencie".'

'Does he?' Winston smiled as he swung the car easily around a sharp bend, leaving the tail to wag a bit. He had got the feel of the car at last.

'Wow!' Jennifer giggled and clamped a hand onto her cap. 'Is it supposed to do that?'

'It can do a lot more than that, Miss Jennifer, I assure you. This is where the RAC rally came through that time. They like private land because there are no speed limits on it, you see.' He stopped and pointed at a break in the trees, far ahead. 'You see that gap there, miss?'

'Left of the pylon?'

'That's it. Well those rally drivers could get from here to there in fifty two seconds. I timed them.'

'How long do you take?'

'Well I don't really know that I've ever timed myself...' He stopped as the girl pushed up her sleeve and pressed a button on her watch.

'No time like the present,' she said. Winston looked across at her and felt stupidly young. She was fresh and clear and vital.

If he were forty years younger... 'I'll count you down. Ten, nine...'

He laughed at her and realised that the sound was strange to him. He had not heard himself laugh like that for years.

'Don't be such a temptation, Miss Jennifer, you will get me into trouble.'

'Seven, six,...' She was looking at him.

'Now then Miss Jennifer, behave yourself. What would Mast...?'

'Four, three...' Impish blue eyes watching him.

'But they have proper rally cars.' His foot went to the clutch.

'One, GO!' she shouted and they were off.

The car bucketed and bumped as they raced along the track, raising a plume of dust behind them. Jennifer held up her watch as they approached the pylon. As it flashed by, Winston braked in cadence and veered onto the gravel apron used by the tractors and turned the car on its handbrake to face the other way. He switched off the engine as the dust drifted slowly past them.

'Wow!' she said. 'That was some driving!'

'How did we do?'

'One minute, thirty.'

He gave a laugh. 'I don't think I shall make the team.'

'I can still feel my heart a-beating.' She held her palm flat to her chest.

'I am pleased to hear that, Miss Jennifer, that is quite a relief. I thought you were a bit quiet.' His watery eyes twinkled at her.

'Yes, well I was concentrating on the watch,' she laughed.

'I must return Ma... Richard's car to him. He should be back by now and you will be wanting your lunch.' He started the engine and they drove slowly back towards Bridge Cottage.

Jennifer could see Richard waiting by the bridge. His hands were thrust deep into his pockets and he was kicking at the stone parapet with the toe of his sneakers. He whirled around at the sound of the car. She had never seen his face like that.

'What the devil did you think you were doing, driving like that?' he threw at Winston.

She saw Winston's face register the shock then it set into a strange expression, not of insolence, but almost... subservience.

'The car came to no harm I assure you Master Richard.'

'Never mind the car, you could have hurt... you might have both got hurt...'

'Richard!' Jennifer cried, 'It was my fault. I asked Winston to drive like that. I egged him on, honest.'

'No miss, it was entirely my responsibility.'

'I said I would time him.'

'Driving like that was utterly reckless! Utterly reckless.'

Winston pulled himself slowly up out of the car.

'I'll leave you to your lunch then,' he said quietly.

'Anything could have happened at that speed.'

'Stop it!' Jennifer said angrily and jumped out of the car. 'I asked Winston to drive me like a rally car...'

'Like a...?' Richard was speechless.

'And I'll tell you something, Richard Ennessy,' she poked him in the chest, 'Winston is a damn sight better driver than you are. I feel safer with him than anyone.'

'Better?'

'He would not have even have tried to have passed that van on the narrow bridge when we came from the station. He is utterly safe and I'll tell you another thing, Master Richard Ennessy, if you don't go now and immediately apologise to Winston you'll need to find yourself another partner tonight.' She stormed off into the cottage, leaving him standing there, struck by a cyclone.

EPISODE THIRTEEN

Jennifer peered into the mirror above the tiny dressing table and then carefully applied the lipstick. Very pale pink. She looked at it critically. She rarely wore make-up and was not accustomed to seeing herself thus. She was not convinced that it improved her looks, merely changed them, but Cherryl had lent her the lipstick from her battery of colours. 'One for every occasion!' she had said. 'What's this one for then?' Jennifer had asked her. 'Seduction!' she had replied.

Jennifer pouted her lips and inspected them. Merely the act of pouting made her feel strange. Perhaps it was all a dream. Perhaps it was a fairy tale and in a moment she would wake up in Cordoba Crescent, Ealing to the sound of Sandy yapping at the postman or Cherryl thundering down the stairs.

She turned her head this way and that. She had allowed herself the merest suggestion of eye shadow and the thinnest dusting of face powder. The effect did not displease her. She did not like wearing make-up but it was not startlingly apparent that she was, so that was that. She smiled as she thought how Cherryl made herself up in technicolour – it suited her – but Jennifer had decided long ago that such a dedication would never look right on her. She knew that she had an ordinary, plain face and painting and colouring it would only be cheating.

She could hear Richard whistling softly in his room and wondered just how much they knew of each other. Meeting almost exclusively in academic surroundings meant that a whole gamut of reactions were denied them. She had never seen Richard angry before. He had looked quite fierce, almost as if he had been ready to strike Winston, and she...? Well he had seen her angry before. She remembered the scene in the pub when

181

she had laid into him for having her portrait put up in the college reception. She had been really angry then and he had been teasingly calm and almost amused, but this time it was different. How was it different?

She dropped her hands to her lap and then looked down sharply at how little she was wearing. The underwear was so dainty she could feel her hair through it. The very same private hair that Richard had painted in such embarrassing detail on her nude portrait. Oh how she wished he had not done that!

So this anger, it was different then was it? How was it different? She knew the answer even as she formed the question and she thrilled to the knowledge. She saw Richard's features distorted by his passion, the eyebrows twisted in fury, the skin drawn tautly across his jawbone, the white-nostrilled tension. He was angry because he cared. He cared for her. He, gorgeous, groomed, cultured, sophisticated Richard Ennessy cared for squat little Jennifer Pye. She recalled what he had said. 'You could have hurt...' and then he had corrected himself, 'You could have both been hurt.'

Was that it? Did he really care for her as a man cares for a woman? Was it that kind of caring? You be careful, Jennifer Pye. You made a fool of yourself over Steven, don't make the same mistake again.

She was aroused from her self-examination by a tap at her door and Richard's voice mimicking a backstage messenger boy,

'Fifteen minutes Miss Pye!'

'Go away!' she laughed. 'I'll come down when I am dressed.'

'Spoilsport!'

They had survived the hiccough of the pre-lunch fireworks. Each one probably believing that they had overstepped the mark and had entered dangerous territory, generating feelings and reactions that neither of them wanted to express or even admit to having felt. Richard had disappeared off up the track after Winston; she had seen him from her bedroom window and by the time he had come back she had disguised any evidence that she had been crying on the bed.

They had motored out to a pub for lunch. She had wanted to go to a pretty little pub called the Wisdene Arms which she had seen close by the white gates at the entrance to the estate but

Richard had said that they did not serve food. When she had pointed out to him the boards which advertised that very service he had made a peculiar face and explained that 'you got some funny types in there' and that she would not enjoy it. So they had motored about ten miles through the lanes and just made a country pub menu by the skin of their teeth.

The chill in the air had disappeared by the afternoon and sitting in the garden, they had felt quite warm. Jennifer had almost regretted not bringing a skirt with her.

Then he had taken her to see some woods. Climbing over a fence marked 'private' and scampering under the eerie glow of the light umbrella. The odour of the damp leaves and soil had incited in her a pang of nostalgia but then she had gazed up at the enormous oak and beech trees and observed to herself that the trees of her childhood would look a bit scraggy next to these.

Back at the cottage he had parked her in front of the television whilst he had magically prepared 'just a light tea' to tide them over before the evening. That was when she had first felt the butterflies coming on.

'How many people are going to this dance, Richard?' She had tried to make her enquiry sound casual through the slice of fruit cake.

'It's a ball, not a dance,' he had corrected her absently. 'I don't know. Four or five hundred I suppose. Don't worry, there will be enough food to go around.'

'Oh I wasn't worried about the food. I'm sure I shall hardly need anything tonight.' The thought of eating before an audience of hundreds alarmed her.

'You had better! We must get our money's worth. Those tickets cost me...' He stopped and laughed. 'Never mind what they cost. We are doing it for a bit of fun aren't we?' He looked at her and she nodded unsurely. 'There's nothing to worry about. It won't be a banquet with flunkies behind your chair and everybody afraid to start because they don't know which knife to use.'

'Oh good,' she said with heartfelt relief.

'It will be a buffet. You do a quick reconnaissance down the table, grab a plate and some eating irons and then make rapid incursions at the weak points to grab what you want. Then you find a decent niche with a flat surface for your plate and glass and sit back and watch all the unprepared ballsters trying to stand up, hold a plate, eat with a knife and fork and drink from a glass and still look intelligent. It's great fun.'

'Provided we get somewhere to sit.'

'That's your job.'

'My job?'

'Why do you think ballgowns are so wide? It's so that you can reserve at least three seats by simply parking your bum.'

She looked at the gown, still hanging on the door. It was undoubtedly beautiful. Richard had brought the shoes and they fitted her as well as the gown did, and an exquisite evening purse in black, decorated with a reprise panel in the same blue silk of the gown, and, best of all, he had brought a black velvet cloak which had been fashioned to cover her gown. It fastened at the neck with a diamante clasp that was a startlingly good match for the pendant earrings that Cherryl had lent her. She had taken Cherryl's advice and decided to pile her hair on top of her head, and as that would uncover her ears, Cherryl had pressed a pair of sparkling, costume jewellery earrings on her.

Time to get dressed.

'Winston's here!' Richard called as he went down the stairs. She glanced out of the window, forgetting for an instant that she was wearing practically nothing and then pulled back as she saw Richard's head appear below her window sill as he left the front door.

Five minutes later she gingerly opened her door and passed into the corridor. Her gown bunched itself together and then burst through the doorway behind her. She felt a little tottery in the shoes but the heels were not too high so she was confident that she would accustom herself to them pretty quickly. She could hear Richard and Winston talking outside the cottage and was reassured by the knowledge that the cottage was empty but for her, for she felt deliciously vulnerable coming down the steep cottage staircase in a flounced out ballgown with her Marks and Sparks naughties on underneath. She decided that she would have a stern word with Cherryl when she got back.

She stepped outside the cottage and stopped in surprise. Winston was wearing a chauffeur's uniform and standing by an enormous black car with polished headlamps and chromework. The rear door was open to show a gloomy interior of deep coloured leather and burred woodwork dimly lit by a pair of small orange lamps. Richard stood talking to Winston and it seemed that he had been made for the evening suit that he was wearing. He was in total command of himself and at elegant ease, with one hand in his pocket and a foot on the running board of the limousine. He was strikingly handsome, she recognised, and the butterflies started again. What on earth was he doing with a girl like her?

Both men had now turned to see her and when she found their astonished eyes staring at her she suddenly saw with a sickening reality what a stupid mistake she had made in agreeing to go to the ball. What on earth had been going on in her mind? How could she possibly accompany this highly groomed, distinguished young man to a society ball? She would be a laughing stock.

'Jennifer you look stunning!' Richard moved quickly to meet her and took her hands in his as he looked her up and down. 'Wow!'

'You don't think I am a bit...?'

'An absolute knock-out Jennifer. I never thought...' He shook his head slowly and smiled in admiration. 'Wow!' he said again simply.

Winston found his voice. 'The Belle of the Ball, Miss.'

Jennifer had never seen men rendered speechless at her appearance and so did not recognise the effect.

With Richard's arm curled lazily along the back of the seat behind her they wafted along in a magical world of old fashioned luxury and splendour. It was a dream, ensconced cosily in that cocoon of breathing natural materials; wood, where every panel bore a different pattern and leather which was creased and ruched in a hundred different ways. She watched the world moving silently past them as Winston discreetly piloted the limousine to its destination.

As they turned a corner she felt Richard's bodyweight move against her and she snuggled towards him. He looked down at her and felt for her hand in her lap.

'Everything O.K. Miss Pye?'

'Wonderful,' she whispered. 'It's like a fairy tale.'

'Well be careful not to kiss any frogs this evening,' he warned her and then added, 'In fact, I think I shall stake my claim now before you turn into a pumpkin.' And he tilted her head up to his and kissed her. It seemed to go on forever, his tongue brushing over her slightly parted lips then gently, tentatively moving to touch hers in the briefest of caresses, then returning more urgently for stronger contact as his arms pulled her and held her to him. She surrendered to his blend of strength and gentleness, feeling her heart pounding and excitement tingling in her stomach. Flushed with passion, she pulled away.

'Shh!' she warned and nodded towards the glass partition through which she could see the back of Winston's grey head.

Richard grinned. 'Winston is a chauffeur, Jennifer. They have more discretion than a royal midwife.' He stretched forward his arm and began to wind around a small chrome handle below the partition. 'I'll ask him what he saw, shall I?'

Jennifer realised that the partition was sinking slowly into the polished woodwork and that they could now talk to Winston. She put her hand to her mouth in horror as Richard leaned forward to speak.

'Richard!' she hissed.

'How are we doing Winnie?' He turned back to her and stuck out his tongue. She sighed with relief and then felt a little indignant at the ease with which he had made fun of her.

'Nearly there, Master Richard,' Winston's voice floated back.

'It's very kind of you to drive us Winston. It is a lovely car and you drive it very smoothly,' Jennifer said.

'Thank you Miss Jennifer, but it is my pleasure really. I don't get many opportunities nowadays to show the Daimler off so well.'

Jennifer wondered if, in his genteel way, he was paying them a compliment. One thing was certain. He obviously thought a lot of Richard to do all this for him. She hoped he would not get into trouble for it with his employers.

The approach to Hartlip House had been lighted by lanterns staked out every ten yards. Jennifer's eyes grew wider and wider as they drew steadily closer to the porch of the enormous stone pile of a house. 'It's like a castle,' she thought. Richard saw her gazing at it.

'Yes, hideous isn't it?' he observed.

Jennifer was scandalised. 'It's magnificent, Richard.'

He looked at her and then smiled disarmingly.

'Only joking,' he said.

Jennifer's heart was now beating like a drum solo as she

looked at the smartly-dressed couples walking casually up the steps to the entrance. The cars had been parked somewhere around the side of the house and the occupants were strolling back along a carpet; Jennifer blinked and then confirmed that it was a red carpet which had been laid along the edge of the gravel drive to the portico. A carpet! Outside!

Winston pulled up smoothly behind a white Rolls Royce alongside which a thin chauffeur with a gaunt face was standing.

'That's Harold, Master Richard. He's with Lord Tort.'

The chauffeur raised a silent hand in a lugubrious salute to Winston and then, having discharged his passengers, slid behind the wheel and moved forward.

Jennifer was searching frantically for the door handle when Richard put a restraining hand on hers.

'Don't be so impatient! Calm down,' he said and the door was opened easily by a footman in emerald and gold. He bowed forward and proffered his hand. Jennifer thought that she had to give him the tickets but then she realised that he was 'assisting her to alight from her carriage'. She thought that this was the best phrase to describe it. He was certainly not 'helping her to get out of the car.' Wishing woefully that she had enjoyed a different upbringing – one which had not involved climbing trees and making mud pies – she mustered up as much grace as she could, grasped his hand and stepped down from the car. For an instant she panicked as she felt herself held back by her gown but with in one natural movement the footman slid his left arm behind her and eased the skirt through.

'Thanks ever so much,' she grinned. 'It's a bit awkward.'

'Madam,' he replied solemnly.

'I expect we are all parked around by the Orangery, Master Richard, that is where I shall be if you need me.' Winston said as he moved back to his driving seat.

'Thank you Winston.'

'Enjoy yourself Miss Jennifer,' Winston said seriously to Jennifer and then startled her by adding, 'You'll be easily the prettiest girl there.'

Her mouth dropped open and she felt a blush stealing into her cheeks as she watched the enormous black Daimler as it began to scrunch its way around to the Orangery.

'Ready then Miss Pye?' Richard asked, as he offered his arm.

Jennifer, feeling a rising wave of anticipation and excitement, slipped her arm into his and together they walked up the stairs to the chandeliered vestibule.

As they passed inside, Jennifer felt that she had entered a film set or a theatre or some other false and glittery world. From somewhere within she could hear an orchestra playing a Viennese Waltz, above her, hundreds of candles twinkled on the chandelier and here, around and about her, people were milling, laughing and joking with their friends as they handed their coats to the three cloakroom ladies. The vestibule was marble tiled and footsteps click-clacked back and forth and the dozens of conversations seemed to rise into the stone vaulted ceiling and then descend, scrambled into a melange of intermingled sibilance. It was like a museum or an art gallery on an exhibition day, she thought.

Feeling rather self-conscious, she unclasped her gown and then smiled thankfully at Richard as he lifted it from her shoulders for her. She did not see the glances from the other women and if she had, she would have been unable to interpret them. She only saw Richard, as handsome and refined as any of the men present, handing her cloak over the counter and she felt an immense pride welling up in her. She looked around shyly to see if the other women were watching Richard.

'I say, rarther a syooper garn you're wearing,' a lady in an expansive silk and taffeta creation said to her. Jennifer stared at her, trying to work out what language she was speaking. 'Paris?' she continued.

'Oh yes,' Jennifer latched onto a recognisable word and deduced that she was enquiring about her ballgown. She remembered the label inside it. 'It is from Paris.'

'Thought so,' the woman said over her shoulder as she swept away.

'All set?' Richard asked. She took a deep breath and nodded. 'Come on then. I'll show you the layout so that you don't get lost.'

'Is your friend here? The one with the donkeys?'

'Nessie? Yes, she's here somewhere. I'll introduce you later on. You'll like her. She's straight, like you.'

Straight like me? Jennifer hung onto his arm as he launched himself confidently into the bubbling crowd, occasionally acknowledging salutes from people whom he knew. He seemed to know a lot of these people but then, if he knew this girl Nessie, then they were probably her friends.

She stopped dead at the top of the steps at the entrance to the ballroom.

'What's the matter?' Richard asked. 'Not got cold feet?'

But Jennifer was transfixed by the sight of the couples swirling around the polished floor, the glowing, glittering, crystal lights, the huge mirrors, the tiny tables at the side, set into alcoves between the potted plants and the pillars and the stage at the end where the orchestra, not a band, but a dance orchestra was playing real music.

'No, I was just looking.' She turned to him. 'Oh Richard, it's like fairyland!'

'Think "donkeys",' he advised her as they began to descend the curving staircase. 'I don't believe that even you could get romantic over donkeys.'

But she was revelling in the unreal sensation of her ballgown swaying gently back and forth as she stepped daintily down towards the upturned faces below. 'Yes' she thought, 'you can all look at him. He is handsome. And I am with him.'

She did not realise that they were looking at her. At the silvery blue silk shimmering on a gown that had obviously been made for her, at the boldly held head of golden hair, at the fresh, open face and the wide, marvelling blue eyes.

Jennifer Pye had arrived.

Sitting in an alcove with her gown spread judiciously about her as instructed, Jennifer waited for Richard to return with her plate. They had circumnavigated the floor twice in an easy and crowded waltz; an activity which they considered had qualified them for nourishment, so they had then made their way to the banqueting room where they had jostled amongst the bare backs, bosoms and bustles whilst Richard ticked off Jennifer's choice on his fingers. At first she had cast about helplessly, the silver salvers and entrée dishes displaying foods that she had no hope of recognising and so she made a game of her ignorance and chose food to make an interesting mix of colours on her plate.

'Some of the pink over there Richard, two or three of the saffron, a dollop of the chestnut.'

The middle-aged lady in the gold sequined dress at the side of her had turned a startled eyebrow to her.

'One dollop,' Richard had repeated purposefully. 'Good evening Mrs. Paget-Brown, how is Leonard?'

The lady's mouth had opened and closed with no sound and then she had managed, 'Arr... Very well thank you Richard.' She had glanced at Jennifer and then back at Richard as if to check that they were together.

'Splendid! I recommend the prawn vol-au-vents.'

'Arr... Thank you. I'll try one.'

She had glanced again at Jennifer who by this time was struggling to keep her face as expressionless as possible whilst successfully stifling a giggle.

Then Jennifer had wondered who Mrs. Paget-Brown was and how Richard knew her.

'Hel-lo!' A voice jerked her from her thoughts. 'All on your ownsome?' The young man had blond wavy hair, eyebrows arched high over careless eyes and a purple satin cummerbund.

'Not exactly. My friend is just fetching me some food.'

'Rupert!' he said and suddenly thrust a hand at her. She was startled at the abruptness of the introduction and wondered if his name was really Rupert or whether he was making an obscure joke.

'Jennifer,' she said. 'Oh!' She jumped as he theatrically kissed her hand.

'Jennifer...' he mused. 'Jennifer all alone on a bench. Is there room...?'

'Buzz off Rupers, I saw her first!' Richard called. He was approaching with two plates laden with food. 'He's only after your seat, Jennifer. Don't give it to him.'

'Oh, Dennisy the Menacy! I might have know it would be you.' He turned a woeful eye on Jennifer, 'It seems fair lady that fate has intervened in our...'

'Hop it Rupers before I turn the hounds on you.' Richard handed a plate to Jennifer. The Honorable Rupert Blawe-Carding effected an insolently dignified withdrawal.

'Rapiers at dawn,' he hissed.

'Dawn?!' Richard laughed at his retreating back, 'You don't know the meaning of the word.'

'I thought he was rather sweet.'

'Yes, like syrup.'

'Why did he call you Dennisy the Menacy?'

'Ennessy Dennisy. Assonance, you see.' Richard tried not to sound too obscure. 'I went to school with him. Schoolboy humour. Nickname. That type of thing.'

Jennifer digested her food and this information.

Neatly avoided an awkward question there, he thought. He knew that he had taken a risk in bringing Jennifer into his milieu but damn it, she was outstanding and he wanted to be with her. Just to see her and hold her in this atmosphere. Something different from college. And he had calculated the risk. Even should they meet any of his acquaintances none would be likely to explain to Jennifer who or what he was because they would all assume that she already knew. Indeed the recent insurgence of Rupert had proved that.

But as he watched Jennifer tucking into her plate with gusto, he felt the first shivers of doom. A doom he knew was waiting unavoidably for them at some time if he persisted in wanting to be with her. He would not be able to keep up this deceit. He would have to tell her. But of course, that would only be necessary if he wanted to continue seeing her, otherwise they were just having a bit of fun weren't they? That is what they had agreed, wasn't it?

Was this then what the evening was all about? Was this its purpose? Was it to force him to decide whether or not he wanted to get nearer to this diminutive bundle of thought-provoking energy?

'Oh! The band has stopped playing.' Jennifer put her plate aside and drained her glass. 'Gosh I'm thirsty.'

'Let me get you another drink.'

'I'll do it. You've not had time to eat properly. And anyway I want a Coke or something and you would probably die of embarrassment to be seen carrying that.'

'Champagne not good enough for you?' Richard toasted her eyes which were sparkling like the chandeliers. She leaned across and put her hand on his arm.

'It's lovely, Richard. The whole thing, is... Just unbelievable.

Thank you ever so much for inviting me.'

'Oh don't be daft. Go and get your Coke.'

'Shall I get something for you?'

'No, I'll stick with my working class lemonade.'

He watched her swinging through the press of guests, not a few of whom turned their heads to glance at her as she passed. That gown did something indefinable to her. It was a sturdy, classical style. It did not thrust out bosoms or flash thighs it simply laid itself around her strong youthful body and then pretended not to be there.

'Richard!'

'Hello Nessie!'

Vanessa Clewe-Harting wore a tangerine dress which seemed to reduce the width of her shoulders and yet at the same time draw attention to the full firmness of her breasts.

'Quick Boy, I need you!' She waved him up from the bench.

'Nessie I'm with someone. I'm just waiting for...'

'Come on,' she said urgently.

He put down his glass and stood up. It was obvious that Vanessa was in a spot. He looked over towards where he had last seen Jennifer but there was no sign of her returning.

'What's the matter Nessie? Problems?' he said as he hurried to catch her up.

'The president's got the squits,' she replied and grabbed his hand.

'Well what do you expect me to do?'

'Daft old buffer. Probably been drinking stout again.' She was leading him towards the stage. Under a banner stood a tombola barrel. 'Just say a few words, Boy,' she pointed at the micrphone, 'and then draw the raffle.'

'I say, Nessie, that's a bit much. You know I don't go in for that sort of thing.'

She whirled him around, took his head in one hand and kissed him hard on the mouth. Somebody nearby clapped.

'Nessie!' he gasped.

'We're friends, remember? Now come up onto this stage with me and get me out of a fix. I'm a damsel in distress.'

Richard pushed his index finger down her cleavage and flicked her nipple.

'In distress? You're only just in this dress.'

'Richard!' she said sharply.

'Fifteen all?'

Jennifer was perplexed. She was sure that it was this bench that they had been sitting on. Yes, there was Richard's plate. She recognised his attempt at an origami sculpture with one of those paper collars they put on drumsticks. She looked around, glass in her hand. Where was he? Perhaps he had just popped off to the loo. She had better stay near here or they might never find each other again.

'Come on Zeena, they're going to draw the raffle.' The girl, who wore eye shadow to match her emerald dress and a sparkling tiara lodged in her black hair, dragged her friend along by the tartan sash on her gown.

'Soph, dear, do be careful with that. Angus will be frightfully upset if you insult his tartan.' She turned and appraised Jennifer. 'Hello,' she said.

Jennifer smiled uncertainly. 'Hello.'

A woman in a tangerine dress was calling for attention on the microphone. Jennifer felt herself being hemmed in by these gigantic coutured debutantes. She wished Richard would hurry up wherever he was. She comforted herself with the thought that with his height, at least he would be able to find her.

'Ladies and gentlemen. On behalf of the president I thank you for attending tonight and making this ball such a success. Without your support our League would be unable to achieve the many worthwhile projects that it does. Now it's time for the grand draw. I call upon the right honourable the Viscount Churle to say a few words and draw the winning tickets.'

Jennifer registered the name vaguely and then frowned.

'What was Richard...?'

'Thank you Vanessa. Ladies and gentlemen I suppose it is appropriate that to support the donkeys I have to stand up and make an ass of myself.'

The audience laughed. Somebody shouted, 'You usually do!'

Jennifer felt the blood pounding in her head. She did not understand.

'Thank you Alex. At least I don't look like a donkey,' Richard threw back at the heckler.

More laughter.

'Isn't he gorgeous Zeena?'

'Oooh I would even ditch Angus for him,' the girl sighed.

'Who is he?' Jennifer found herself asking the girl at the side of her.

'Glory!' she exclaimed. 'You don't know Richard d'Ennessy? Where on earth have you been?'

'Richard Dennissey?' Jennifer repeated stupidly. 'I thought they said something about Viscount something or other.'

'Viscount Churle, that's right. Eldest son of the Earl of Wisdene. He's the most eligible bachelor in the county. Come to think of it, his family owns half the county, isn't that right Soph?'

Jennifer stood stock still. She felt as if she had been struck down with paralysis. Viscount Churle? That was the name of the owner of his cottage. She remembered the letter she had picked up. Viscount Churle was Richard. The Earl of Wisdene? Wisdene Hall was the name of the big house on top of the hill in the park where their cottage was. That must be where they live.

'That's right Zeena. The most desirable single man under thirty this side of London, royalty excluded of course.' She flicked her hair from her face. 'I envy the woman that gets him, he's got everything. Nessie's had a try. So would I if I thought he would take any notice of me. He's off with some students up in Chelsea most of the time. You know, arty types. All long hair and torn jeans. He'll get it out of his system I suppose. Are you alright? You look a bit pale.'

'Could you tell me where the toilet is please?' Jennifer's voice came out in a feeble whisper. Her stomach felt hollow and her legs were beginning to shake. She just wanted to be alone for a minute. Just herself with her thoughts.

'The ladies' powder room is through that archway by the Greek statue thing. You look awful. Do you want me to come with you?'

'No thank you. I will be alright.'

She moved through the throng as if anaesthetised. Somewhere, a great distance away, Richard's voice was calling out numbers and making silly quips. Sound came to her as though she were under water. Muffled and meaningless. She stumbled on, fighting back the great gulp that would start her weeping. She ignored the powder room and wandered through the vestibule under the enormous glittering chandelier and out into the night. The carpet on the drive was still there. It led her to the cars.

She had not realised just how many limousines there would be. Here and there knots of drivers were smoking and chatting. Some were reading comfortably in the backs of their conveyances. Where was Winston? Some of the chauffeurs were turning now and looking at her. Straightening their uniforms. What was a little girl in a ballgown doing stumbling about amongst the cars? She saw a thin, gaunt chauffeur, stooping slightly to listen to a colleague.

'Harold!' she called.

The man straightened up, saw her and dropped his cigarette to the ground.

'Yes miss?'

'You are Harold aren't you?'

'Yes miss. What can I do for you?' His friend melted into the background.

'I'm with Winston. You know Winston don't you?' she asked desperately. 'You were just in front of us when...'

'Yes miss, I know Winston.'

'I... I can't find him. I need him.'

'Alright miss. Nothing to worry about.' He snapped on a flashlight. 'Come this way please. He's just over here.'

Winston saw them approaching and hurried towards them.

'Miss Jennifer! Is anything wrong?'

'Can you take me home please Winston?' She gulped a sob. Must not let them see her cry. 'Back to the cottage?'

'Right now Miss Jennifer?'

'Yes please.'

'And Master Richard?' She pinched her lips and shook her head. 'Thank you Harold.'

Harold touched his head and moved away. Winston opened the front passenger door.

'And you with no cloak! You will catch your death of cold Miss Jennifer. Sit in the front and I'll put the heater on for you.'

She climbed into the sanctuary of the gloomy car and shivered as her bare arm touched the cold leather seat.

'Just lean forward a little miss.' Winston tucked a travel rug around her. 'Wrap it around you miss until the heater warms up a bit.'

She nodded and then sighed silently as he closed his door and they were plunged into the safety of the dark car.

'Would you like me to collect your cloak miss?' Winston asked as they passed by the entrance. 'It wouldn't take a minute.'

But Jennifer was sobbing into the rug. Winston set his mouth grimly and drove on.

Gradually Jennifer's sobs subsided as the warmth and the rolling motion of the car soothed her. She slowly regained control, breathing in the damp mustiness of the rug. She ventured to look up and watched the long bonnet silhouetted by the light from the ear-like headlamps as the car swung gently through the lanes. Winston glanced across at her.

'We'll be there in about five minutes miss.'

Jennifer suddenly realised that she had to have a course of action. Up until then she had been merely running away from something unpleasant but now they were going to arrive at another stage. Decision time.

Richard had left the door on the latch so she went straight in to the cottage. Winston stood in the kitchen with a miserable expression of half guilt and half helplessness on his lined face.

'Could you phone for a taxi for me please Winston? I want to go to the station.' Without waiting for him to reply she hurried up the stairs. In the front bedroom, her bedroom, the one Richard had said she would like, the tears runnelled down her face as she hung the gown back on the door. She grimaced at herself in her racy underwear and grunted bitterly, 'You fool Jennifer Pye.' She pulled on her jeans and jumper, threw her things into her bag and grabbed her jacket. She laced up her sneakers and then carefully unhooked Cheryl's earrings and savagely pulled her hair down loose around her shoulders.

Winston was still standing as she had left him, fiddling with his cap.

'Did you manage to order a taxi?' she asked bravely.

He looked up and for the moment she thought that he had not heard her. 'It's what you want is it Miss Jennifer?' She nodded. 'Then I'll drive you.'

'No.'

'Are you going back to London, miss?'

196

'Yes.'

'Then I shall drive you to Reading station. It will be more convenient for you.'

'But you have to pick up...' She could not say it. 'You have to go back to the ball.'

'Plenty of time for that, miss.'

She took a last look at the cottage as they crossed the bridge. Winston tried not to notice and they drove on in silence.

As they came up to Reading station she said, 'You knew didn't you Winston?' And then she realised suddenly how absurd she must have sounded. 'Of course you knew. You are their chauffeur aren't you?'

'It was not my idea, miss. I did not agree with it and I told Master Richard so.'

She jumped out of the car before he could open the door for her.

'But you played the game! I thought you were a friend but you were only making fun of me as well.'

She never saw the anguish and distress on Winston's face. He sat there for half an hour until a drunk tried to get in to the car, having mistaken it for a taxi.

Only one light was showing at Cordoba Crescent. It was Cherryl's. She was no doubt waiting up to hear all about it. Jennifer pulled herself up the stairs, her mind still in a numbed torpor from shock. She stopped on her landing and then thought how stupid she was. Cherryl could not be waiting up for her because Jennifer was not supposed to be coming back tonight. That was the whole point of the weekend, according to Cherryl.

She let herself in to her room and dumped her bag on the floor. Jennifer Pye had returned.

She undressed mechanically and felt for her sloppy tee shirt under her pillow. It was cosy. It was comforting. Cherryl's light was still on. She crept across to the door. She could hear sobbing. She tapped softly.

'Cherry?'

The sobbing stopped and a muffled voice enquired,

'Is that you Jennie?'

'Yes. Open up.'

The door slowly opened to reveal Cherryl half undressed, her mascara and make up streaked down her face in violent rivulets, her eyes rimmed with red.

'You came back early?' she said.

Jennifer nodded. 'Can I come in?'

Cherryl wandered aimlessly back to the bed and sat down. Suddenly she covered her face with her hands and burst into floods of tears.

'Is it Keith?' Jennifer sat next to her and put her arm around her shaking shoulders.

'The ba... ba... bastard's married,' she wailed. Jennifer hugged her tighter, feeling her own fragile emotions being shaken again. 'That was why he couldn't see me at Christmas. He was with his kids.'

'Oh Cherryl! Cherryl!'

Jennifer could feel everything welling up in her again.

'What happened to you?' Cherryl's tear sodden face was close to hers, searching the sad eyes. 'Yours married?'

Jennifer could hold it no longer.

'No, he just wasn't the person I thought he was.' Hot tears thickened her eyes and blurred her vision.

They clutched at each other, rocking and gulping their private griefs, bound together in a common desolation and despair.

EPISODE FOURTEEN

Richard listened to the dawn chorus as he lay in the single bed in Bridge Cottage. He propped himself up against the head board. He had not slept well. In the fading gloom he could see his dinner jacket draped on the back of the chair and the rest of his clothes piled untidily on its cushion.

Around and around in his head ran the self accusation of his foolishness. However much he might have wanted to be with Jennifer, taking her to a ball where she might meet people who knew him had been a monstrously silly thing to do. He recognised, however, that this was not the heart of the problem. It would have been perfectly acceptable to have taken Jennifer to the ball had he been honest with her in the first place and told her everything about himself. That was the heart of the problem. He had not meant to be deceitful. The deceit had evolved as a policy designed to keep Jennifer interested and on the same footing as that upon which they had met. Their relationship had been fresh and untainted. He had seen his fair share of girls' eyes sparkle upon discovering his title and background. He wanted Jennifer as she was.

He did not blame Nessie, she could not have known. Ironically, on the frantic chase up to the stage she had remarked to him that she had not yet seen this golden haired girl in a blue dress that everybody was talking about. It was some moments before he had realised that she must have been talking about Jennifer.

Picking out the stupid raffle numbers from the barrel, he had had little opportunity to wonder how Jennifer would react but afterwards when he had seen the footman approaching, he had guessed that everything had gone wrong. 'A message from

Harold, Lord Tort's chauffeur, sir. The young lady has gone home with Winston.'

So that was that then. He had stayed and executed a few disconnected dances with young ladies of his acquaintance, exchanged some jesting comments with his male contemporaries and then sat somewhere quiet whilst he waited for Winston. He was certain that Winston would return to collect him and when he did, Richard sat in the front of the car and invited the censure that he felt that he deserved.

'O.K. then Winston, let's have it.'

In the darkness of the car he had heard Winston's measured voice, 'This evening, Master Richard, a young lady of whom I had very quickly grown fond, told me that she thought I had been a friend but had realised that I had only been playing a game. I trust you will never put me in that position again Master Richard.'

And that was all he had said.

Jennifer puzzled at the unfamiliar wallpaper on the ceiling. Then she felt the weight of Cherryl's arm across her chest and she remembered their crawling together into the warmth and comfort and crying themselves to sleep.

'Oi Cherry!. Shift your arm you're suffocating me!'

'Wha?' Cherryl rubbed her eyes and poked Jennifer with her elbow.

'Ouch. You are a brute Cherry.' She wriggled herself up onto her elbows. 'Not made for two is it?'

'Oh God! Is it morning? I don't want to get up. I don't want to do anything.'

'Come on Cherry, that's not the attitude.' Jennifer bounced off the bed and noisily rattled the kettle in the sink. 'Wakey wakey!' She made a pot of tea, poured out two mugs and then brought them to the bedside table. 'Now this needs a lot of care Cherry, otherwise we end up scalded.'

'You're not getting back into bed?!'

'Too right I am. Move over.' Jennifer squeezed herself back under the bedclothes, feeling quite slim alongside Cherryl.

'You know,' Cherryl took a sip at the tea and then continued, 'I should have realised earlier about Keith.' Jennifer said nothing. 'I mean, he was too good to be true. I thought we were going places but I was just his bit on the side. Trouble is, I still love him.'

'Oh Cherry you are daft! How can you possibly, after he has lied to you so much?'

'Well I do and that's that.' She flounced up her hair with her spare hand and nearly spilled her tea. 'Ooops.'

'You are dangerous in bed, do you know that Cherryl?'

'What a reputation to have, eh?' she giggled. 'Look, why don't we go out and celebrate for lunch? We could go down to the King's Head, they do a Sunday lunch.'

Jennifer was surprised at Cherryl's resilience. She was not certain what she thought she would be celebrating. Getting rid of Keith?

'Got no money love. I'm broke.'

'Yeah, so am I,' Cherryl admitted. 'We could share a take-away from the Indian?'

'O.K. But I must wash my hair this morning.'

'I'm gonna wash that man right out of my hair,' Cherryl sang.

The alarm clock rattled on the little cane table at the side of Winston's bed for some time before he reached out an arm and silenced it. He looked at it, wondering why on earth he had set the alarm on his Sunday off. He must be getting forgetful. He swung his legs out of bed and started his morning exercises. The hair on his chest showed white at the top of his pyjama jacket.

He thought of Miss Jennifer's impish grin when she had challenged him to drive the Yellow Peril and then contrasted the image with that of her leaving the cottage to go to the ball. The young lady just did not know what charm she had.

Images of Jennifer came back to him as he prepared his breakfast. The accusation she had levelled at him at the station haunted him. He felt quite upset that she could think that of him, although he understood why. The tragedy he felt was that he would never now be able to explain the truth to her. He did not think they would see Jennifer Pye at Wisdene again.

A movement in the mews yard attracted his attention. Master Richard was hesitating by the arch. Winston threw open his window and called out to him.

'Come on up, Master Richard. I'm just making coffee.'

'Err... Thanks, I will.'

Winston cleared away his dishes and brushed off the check table cloth then he put out two clean cups and saucers. Richard was standing in the doorway. He looked a mite subdued.

'Come in and sit down, Master Richard.'

'Thanks Winnie.' He sat on the kitchen chair, put his elbows on the table and rested his chin in his hands. 'I've come to apologise, Winnie.'

'Oh yes? What for?' Winston turned with the coffee pot in his hand.

'Getting you involved in all this.'

'In all what? I would not have missed meeting Miss Jennifer for all the world.'

'No,' Richard agreed, 'nor would I.'

'Do you think we'll see her again, Master Richard?'

Richard toyed with his teaspoon. Would he see Jennifer again? He would surely see her in college. Would she have anything to do with him? – that was more to the point. He thought of her temper, of her determination.

'I don't somehow think we will,' he answered.

'Now that is a pity.'

That evening, Richard drove slowly back up to town. He had felt empty all day. Everything seemed pointless. College, painting, there seemed no reason to carry on. He knew this was an irrational reaction, an observation distorted by his emotions but he still felt it.

Coming through Hammersmith he stopped and argued with himself as to whether he should go to see Jennifer. He was certain that he could find the block of flats he had dropped her outside when they had come back from Bristol. Bristol. The dance. Weston-super-Mare. The beach. And now he had behaved like a fool and spoiled it all. Or had it been doomed from the start? He let in the clutch and nearly knocked down a cyclist. The woman swore at him. He turned in to Half Moon Mews and put the car straight in the garage.

By the coffee percolator he found one of his sketches of Jennifer from which he had painted the portrait of her on the beach. All three paintings of her were now at the college. The sketch represented all that he had of her now. He had even lost the real thing.

Cherryl had not been able to maintain her bravado for long and had crumpled after their rather sordid take-away. She had retired to her room for some more weeping. Jennifer decided that it would be better to leave her to it.

She felt very angry still and also cheated in a way. She had not had a row with Richard. There had been no fight. She had merely left. It was an unsatisfactory way to leave things. Like a funeral with no body. Too many loose ends. When she unpacked her bag and found the little black evening purse with the blue satin panel which she had inadvertently brought away with her, she knew what she was going to do. She was going to return it. She would take it around to his cottage, and it was his cottage, she was not accepting any more of that 'friend lent it to me' rubbish, and she would have the whole thing out with him.

Could she do it? Did she have the guts? She doubted that she had. She put the purse gently on the bed and tidied away her clothes.

So Jennifer Pye was scared of him now was she? No she was not! She scooped up the purse, grabbed her jacket and started on her way to the tube station before she could change her mind.

The door buzzer made Richard jump. He must have been day dreaming. He glanced casually over to the closed circuit monitor and then jumped from his chair. There was no doubting who it was.

'Oh come in Jennifer!' he said and pressed the gate release. Then he ran down the stairs to meet her at the door.

'I've come to return the purse.'

'Jenni–'

'Thank you for lending it to me. I must have put it in my bag by mistake.'

'Jennifer.' She looked at him. 'Jennifer, will you come upstairs for a drink or something? Please?'

She nodded. This was not as easy as she thought it would be. In truth she had purposefully not thought past the front door otherwise she would have been too frightened to come at all.

She looked around the lounge and now saw the wealth for what it was. Nothing was make-believe. Richard was a seriously wealthy man. And he had been making fun of her.

'Look Jennifer, I'm sorry about the ball.'

'Is that all? You're sorry! You made a fool of me in front of all your friends Mr. Richard Ennessy or Dennissey or whatever.' She stuck her arms akimbo. 'Just what is your name, anyway?'

'It's Richard d'Ennessy. Spelled with a 'd' and an apostrophe.'

'So why do you call yourself "Ennessy"?' She threw the hair out of her face.

'Well, the reason was–'

'And what about this Viscount Chart or whatever?' She stabbed a finger at him. 'That's you as well is it?'

'Viscount Churle,' Richard sighed. 'Yes that's me as well.'

'And Daddy's an earl is he? I suppose I should bow down and call you "my lord" or something should I?'

'Not necessary.'

'You lied to me Richard.' Her face was becoming hotter. 'You told me it was somebody else, didn't you? Didn't you? Oh you've had a fine game at my expense haven't you? "Just got a country cottage lent to me by a friend." Was that what you said?'

'Something like that,' he mumbled.

'Yes, something like that. You could say anything to Jennifer Pye couldn't you? It didn't matter.' She didn't matter...' She could feel the tears running down her cheeks now. Tears of anger. Tears of sadness.

'That's untrue Jennifer.'

'Anything you liked and Jennifer would believe you. A cousin in America lent you this house. Remember?' She marched up to him and then turned away again, clenching her fists by her side. 'And even when I found a letter addressed to you, you had to make fun of me and pretend that it was for somebody else.'

'It wasn't like that, Jennifer, believe me.'

'Believe you? Believe you? Why should I believe you?' she hurled at him.

'Jennifer,' he shouted, 'I didn't want to lose you. I want you. Don't you understand? I was going to tell you but it all got too difficult too quickly. I fell in love with you that's why!'

But Jennifer was no longer hearing.

'I don't even know who you are,' she shouted and angrily kicked a cushion out of the way. 'You've been laughing at me all along! You've been playing with me. Just something to amuse you.' Cherryl's words came to her and she adopted them without questioning their relevance 'Your bit on the side.'

Richard stared in disbelief.

'I've only kissed you three times!'

'And whose fault is that?'

'Yours. You played hard to get.'

'I didn't play at anything,' she shouted as she ran down the stairs, her jacket trailing in her wake and her breath coming in sobs. 'I was serious.'

That told him. Now he knows.

Out of the front door. Sharp right. Shit! The electric gates. How do I get out? Headlights on cobbles. Car coming in. Run down the side of it. Feel the door mirror catch and rip at my jeans. Keep going.

'Jennifer! Come back!'

Half Moon Street. Down towards the lights of Piccadilly. Sneakers pounding on the pavement. Shadow from the street lamps lurching before and then disappearing behind. Couple of people staring at me. Don't care.

'Jennifer! Jennifer!'

An empty taxi! Brilliant! Jump in.

'Blimey! Where to miss?'

'Straight on as quick as you can!'

'Righto!'

Crouch on back seat, look through window. There he is, just rushing into Piccadilly. Looking left and right. Looking at the taxi. Trying to wave down another but it is hired. Richard getting smaller on the pavement. Staring at me driving away.

'Still going the right way miss?'

Jennifer's eyes darted to the taximeter in alarm.

'Drop me just here.'

'Right you are miss.'

She fumbled in her jacket and found enough money.

'Where am I?'

'Clerkenwell, miss. Is that where you wanted to be?'

'Yes,' she said vaguely. She watched the taxi drive away. Across the street she could see shadowy figures sitting in a steamed up yellow lit cafe. She walked slowly across and went in.

It was hot with the heating and bodies. She shrugged off her jacket and dropped it onto a hook with the others and then wandered up to the counter. A bald Italian-looking man grinned at her from behind a glass display stand of pies and cakes. Behind him the chromium urn was steaming gently.

'Tea please.'

'Cupporamug?'

'Mug.'

She took her mug to a table and sat down. Nobody took any notice of her. In the window, two men in overalls were polishing off plates of all-day breakfast. Their tow truck was parked outside. An elderly man in a dark grey, shapeless suit was sitting sideways, his bony legs crossed high on his thighs like a fashion model's, whilst he pencilled notes from the racing paper folded before him. He carefully licked the point of his pencil each time before he wrote. On the other side of the room, under a poster advertising a boot fair, sat a girl with a wan face and lank shoulder length hair. She had an empty cup and saucer before her and three plastic bags containing her worldly belongings beside her. She looked at Jennifer with eyes devoid of emotion.

Less than twenty four hours ago, Jennifer thought, I was dressed up to the nines in silk, chauffeured to a ball and accompanied by a handsome escort. And now I am sitting in a cafe somewhere near Clerkenwell.

Richard d'Ennessy, spelt with a 'd' and an apostrophe. Jennifer Pye, spelt with a capital 'P'. Come to think of it, they own half the county don't they Soph? Most desirable single man this side of London, royalty excluded.

The two men pushed their chairs noisily back on the lino and brought their empty plates up to the counter.

'Thanks Mario. G'night!'

The older man winked at Jennifer. She ignored him. The door banged as they went out and a waft of cold air swirled around her legs. The pale girl looked at her but glanced quickly away when Jennifer looked in her direction. Jennifer took a sip of her tea.

We're doing it for a bit of fun aren't we? And she had nodded. The Belle of the Ball miss. You'll be easily the prettiest girl there. It was not my idea miss. I did not agree with it. And she had said, I thought you were a friend but you were only making fun of me as well. She bit her lip.

Yours married? No he just wasn't the person I thought he was. Did it matter? Did it really matter? How can you still love him Cherry when he has lied to you so much? Well I do and that's that. Yes, I do and that's that. I love him. And he loves me. I didn't want to lose you Jennifer, don't you understand. I fell in love with you. Jennifer come back! Jennifer! Jennifer!

She looked up. She was alone in the cafe. The old man had gone. So had the girl. Mario was wiping the tables.

'Closing now miss.'

She took her mug to the counter. The tea in it was cold. She knew what she was going to do now. She was going straight back to Half Moon Mews. I've only kissed you three times! So he had counted! It meant that much to him.

She stopped at the door.

'Where's my coat? This isn't my coat!' she exclaimed.

'S'your coat,' Mario said.

She looked in dismay at the threadbare jacket hanging on the hook. The girl. The girl with the plastic bags. She had taken Jennifer's jacket and left her own.

'Who was the girl?'

'What girl? Closing now miss.' He switched off the light in the milk cabinet and the 'cafe' sign in the window.

Jennifer sighed heavily and lifted the coat from the hook. However disgusting it might be, she needed something to keep the cold away. She stepped out onto the pavement and found a jauntiness in her stride despite appearing like a tatterdemalion. She had resolved what she was going to do and the thought itself warmed her.

I love him and he loves me and that is all that matters. He is right. And I am going now to tell him.

Now, where's the underground station?

She never saw the car and it did not stop.

A man walking his dog heard the bang and phoned for the ambulance but looking at the little body crumpled by the kerb, there seemed little point.

EPISODE FIFTEEN

The phone was ringing. He pulled the duvet up around his ears and settled himself deeper into the bed. Why should he wake himself up now and answer the phone when it had taken him so long to get to sleep?

And all because of Jennifer. That dynamo of emotions and energy, storming about his house, red faced and accusing. And quite unjustified. If only she had been willing to listen to him. 'Believe you? Believe you? Why should I believe you?' Didn't she realise that he had done it because he did not want to lose her? And he didn't want to lose her because he loved her. Couldn't she see that? Obviously not.

And then that stupid chase down Half Moon Street into Piccadilly. He, tripping on the cobbled kerb of the mews and then running after her with one shoe off; she, racing far ahead, her long hair thrashing from side to side.

And then her white face getting smaller through the back window of a taxi and he spending the rest of the evening sitting in the armchair, kicking his foot against the stool and repeating her name.

The phone was still ringing. Something in his troubled semi-consciousness told him that he ought to answer it.

Why hadn't she just given him a chance to explain? He could have explained it couldn't he? He could have told her how he had been unsure of what he really felt about her and so had said nothing, not knowing whether the relationship was going to continue or fizzle away. She would have understood that surely? But no! She had to go charging out in a huff. Out of his house. Out of his life.

Bloody phone.

The bed had been lumpy. Then he had been too hot. Then he had been too cold. Then he was thirsty. Then he had put the radio on for a while. Then he had switched it off. Normally he slept easily but not tonight. He had tried reading but he kept seeing her face in the page. Eventually, from sheer mental exhaustion he had dozed off into a fitful kind of sleep and now this bloody phone was ringing.

He looked at the bedside clock. Half past four in the morning! Who the hell was ringing him at this time? They could go and take a running jump at themselves. It might be Jennifer. He leapt out of bed and snatched the receiver from the cradle.

'Jennifer?' His voice was thick.

''That you Richard?' His brother's voice, rendered tinny by the instrument, made the enquiry sound a little fatuous.

'Charles, for heaven's sake! Do you know what time it is?'

'It's father, Richard. He's ill. He's had a stroke. They are medivacking him back from Funchal.'

'They're doing what?'

'Medivacking him. Medical evacuation. He's coming home in an air ambulance. Mother is with him.'

Richard felt a turmoil of emotions and fears surge up in him. His father, their father. What should he do? What could he do?

'How bad is it?'

'They don't say but they are taking him straight to Hauberk's from Northolt.'

'Hauberk's? Is that the hospital at Mount Circus, just opposite the gardens?

'Yes, that's the one.'

'Where are you?'

'At home. Winston is going to take me to Northolt in the Range Rover in a minute to meet the plane. I don't know whether they will let mother go in the ambulance or not. At least we will have some form of transport.'

'Yes. Good idea. Good idea.' Richard thought quickly. 'Who's providing the ambulance at Northolt?'

'The insurance company. I've checked. It's already there.'

'What time are they due in? '

'About six.'

'Right. Can you cope all right at Northolt? I'll go straight to Hauberk's. You're sure it is Hauberk's?'

'Yes.'

'O.K. I'll check on everything at this end then.' There was a pause whilst they both thought, then Richard said, 'How did it happen? I mean, what was he doing?'

'Having dinner. It was in the dining room at Reid's. They were eating with the Palfreys.'

'Oh yes.'

'He was quite normal and then he started to stutter and hold his head and then he just fell off the chair.'

'I don't really know what a stroke is,' Richard admitted. 'It's not the heart is it?'

'No, it's the brain. Sort of seizes up I suppose.'

'Oh Lord.'

They both accepted that it sounded serious.

'Winston's here, I must go. See you later then.'

Richard put the receiver down and stared at it without seeing it. Father was not going to die was he? Not father. He was energetic and forceful. And anyway, he was only sixty, that is not dying age. He went to the front window and pulled aside the curtain. Peering upwards he could see a slight lightening of the sky, revealing heavy clouds, purple and massive in the thin light.

He pulled on his corduroy jeans and a mohair turtle neck sweater and then went upstairs to the kitchen. He ate a simple breakfast of toast and black coffee and made himself some sandwiches with the rest of the loaf and a tail end of brie that had been oozing off its plate. It made sense to have food with him. He did not know when he would next be able to eat.

Although he had pulled on a jacket, put the hood up and switched the heater onto full power, he still felt cold. Shock, he supposed. The streets were now greying in the light. At any other time he would have revelled in the uncluttered thoroughfares, the vistas and perspectives. He would have taken the corners just a little bit faster than he ought, he would have straddled the lane markings with impunity but this morning he did not even recognise the opportunity. At one point he drew up at the traffic lights behind a milk float and stared without interest at the mute pints stacked up before him. Only when across the junction did he think of pulling out to overtake.

He arrived at the hospital just before six. Far too early, of course. Even if the air ambulance landed on time, they were hardly likely to be at Hauberk's before seven.

'Good morning. Could you tell me please if you are waiting for an ambulance from Northolt?'

The nurse pulled a fax from the tray at the side of her VDU and scanned it expertly.

'What is your name sir?'

'D'Ennessy. Richard d'Ennessy.'

'Are you family?'

'My father, Alfred Ewin d'Ennessy. He's due in on an air ambulance from Madeira. He had a stroke.'

The nurse moved the fax to her side, out of his vision. She appeared unsure. 'Does he have another name?'

Another name? There can't be more than one d'Ennessy coming in from Northolt this morning, Richard looked at her blankly. 'Oh!' He gave a short laugh. 'Lord Wisdene. Is that what they've got him down as?'

'Yes. You see I didn't know,' she apologised. 'That's all I have. Could you give me his full name again please and I'll write it down.'

Richard repeated it.

'So you are expecting him?'

'Yes sir, everything is ready and waiting.'

'Should I phone my father's doctor for him to come?'

'We do have doctors here, Mr. d'Ennessy.' Her tone of voice implied that she wanted to add, 'We are a hospital'.

'Yes. Yes. Of course. And you have a room booked?'

'Yes sir, should he need it,' she added obscurely. 'Excuse me.' She turned to answer the phone.

Richard wandered away from the desk and sat on a seat by a plant. Away on the far side, a woman in green overalls was vacuum cleaning the carpet, dragging the machine behind her in little jerks as if trying to pull a dog from a lamp post. The air conditioning hissed. Somewhere a trolley banged out of a lift. Richard picked up a magazine on gardening and put it down. He stood up and went to the desk.

'Sorry to bother you again.' She smiled and he swept his eyes vaguely over her uniform for some sort of insignia or badge. 'Silly question, but are you a nurse?'

She grinned and tapped her left breast and then looked down in surprise.

'Oh, forgot my badge!' she exclaimed and pulled a plastic card from her pocket and clipped it on. 'Thanks for reminding me. Yes, I am a nurse.'

'Do you know anything about strokes?'

'Yes. What would you like to know?'

'Well, what happens in a stroke? My father has had a stroke, they think, and I don't really know what a stroke is.'

She looked at him and took a deep breath.

'Well,' she said slowly, her eyes flicking quickly back and forth across his face, 'The simplest way of describing what happens with a stroke is to say that it is when the blood supply to a part of the brain is interrupted by the forming of a clot or by a haemorrhage. It deprives the brain of oxygen, you see.'

'I see. What about recovery? I mean, after the patient has recovered, I presume there is some damage.'

'I think you should really be talking to a doctor about this. Dr. Bradden will be down in about half an hour, I am sure he could answer your questions with more authority than I can.'

'Yes. I just wondered, that's all. Will he be in a wheelchair?'

'Well, I mean I can't possibly answer for your father's case.'

'No of course not. Speaking generally.'

'Generally speaking, the percentage recovery really depends on the severity of the stroke, oh, and the condition of the patient's health before the stroke.' She pushed a wisp of hair back up under her cap. 'I mean, an athletic patient would probably recover more of his physical movements than an unfit person. And in the same way, someone who was a good speaker or say, someone who could speak several languages is more likely to recover his power of speech than one who doesn't, if you see what I mean.' The phone rang again. She gave a brief reassuring smile and then turned aside.

'Thank you,' he said and wandered back to his chair. He was imagining father, dumb and crippled, a cabbage in a wheelchair. No, not father. He was not athletic by any means and he was a little corpulent, but surely he would recover? Being honest with himself, he recognised that father ate well and exercised little but he could talk fluently and negotiate and conduct business so, according to the nurse, that would certainly stand him in good stead for recovery. It all depended on the severity of the stroke of course. It might have just been a minor blip and the insurance company had over reacted. He picked up the gardening magazine again but dropped it as if it had bitten him when he noticed the cover picture of a robust cabbage.

And what about mother? Heavens! What would she do with father around the house all day long? He tried not to think about anything more and started to count the ceiling tiles.

The ambulance arrived twenty minutes later. Two orderlies briskly pushed a stretcher trolley up to its back doors. Richard hurried out after them but stayed well out of the way. They knew what they were doing, he didn't. He did not want to hamper anybody. He could see the roof of the Range Rover some distance back. Winston could not come nearer.

Was this his father? A mummy on a stretcher, wrapped around in writhing tubes and wires? He could not even see his face.

'Richard, my dear!' His mother's angular form unfolded from a minute seat in the back of the vehicle. 'Richard,' she said again. She put out her arms and pulled him to her and clutched at him, her fingers claw like through his jacket. She was shivering.

'Mother, you must be freezing.'

He wriggled out of his jacket and pulled it around her shoulders as she turned to follow the stretcher which was already moving fast amongst a group of orderlies and nursing staff who were hobbling quickly alongside it as they held fluid filled bags and equipment aloft.

Lord Wisdene died ten minutes later.

'Pretty girl, probably,' Tara Hughes thought as she inspected the inert body through the glass screen. 'About the same age as me. Pity about her hair.' She looked at the girl's head which had been shaven to permit investigation of wounds and remembered the luxurious golden hair, tangled and clotted with blood and dirt. 'She won't half miss that when she wakes up. Supposing she does wake up.'

She returned to the paperwork. No consent form. Every patient having an operation should sign a consent form, or their next of kin should, but of course, this had been a life threatening situation and so all the usual procedures had gone by the board. It did not make her job any easier. She noted the folder.

The door opened uncertainly and a head appeared around it. It was the policeman who had been sitting outside. He had a fresh face, tousled hair and thick black eyebrows and he looked rather smart in his uniform trousers and shirt.

'They said I can't go in there.' He nodded through the glass screen at the intensive care department.

'I should think not!'

'Can you give me any details? Still unconscious is she?'

Nurse Hughes smoothed down her tunic. 'Yes. Come in.'

'My name's Andy by the way.'

'Hi. I'm Tara.'

'So what's the story then?' He unfolded his notebook. 'What's her name for a start?'

'Yeah, sorry we've kept you waiting so long. We haven't stopped tonight.'

'S'alright. I was glad to get the weight off my feet.'

Nurse Hughes squeezed past the policeman to the desk. She felt her buttocks tingle as they lightly brushed against him.

'Her name is...' She peered at a scrap of paper. 'Magdaline O'Neill. Sounds Irish doesn't it?'

'Any idea where she lives?'

'It looks as if her last address was the "Our Lady Hostel".' She handed him the piece of paper. 'It was in her coat pocket.'

Our Lady Hostel, Shoreditch. One bed. Magdaline O'Neill', he read. 'Was that all she had on her? No handbag or whatever?'

'That's the lot. And she had about two pounds in the pocket of her jeans.'

'Are those her clothes?' He pointed to a bag on the desk.

'Yeah. What's left of them. We had to cut them off.'

'Can I see?'

'Sure.'

'S'funny.'

'What is?'

'Her clothes. Not what I would have expected a dosser to wear.' He turned over the contents of the bag. 'They're not bad.'

'Oxfam. That's where they get them. Anyway, look at that coat.' Tara leaned across him and pulled out a ragged jacket. 'You can practically see through the elbows.'

'S'pose you're right. So,' he summed up, 'Magdaline O'Neill, no fixed abode, last known address, Our Lady Hostel, Shoreditch.' He scratched his head with his pen. 'Was she wearing any jewellery?'

'No, just a watch.'

He looked at the watch. It was just a watch.

'No crucifix? I thought all Catholic girls wore a crucifix.'

'I don't.'

He turned over a page on his notebook. 'Injuries,' he said. 'must be pretty bad. She looks worse than my car when it had its MOT, with all those tubes and wires on her.'

'Probably looks worse than it is. Always give fluids for shock. Blood – she's had two units.' Tara Hughes read down the sheet, muttering to herself. 'HB level 12? That's pretty good. Mind you the reaction probably won't show till tomorrow.'

'HB?'

'Haemoglobin,' she said automatically and continued reading. The policeman realised that he would not get the information he wanted in an understandable form until the nurse had read it first in the language that she understood so he waited quietly. 'Right,' she said. 'So it's concussion, obviously. Fractured collar bone, fractured femur, multiple contusions and abrasions. That's as far as we know. Little things like broken toes and that don't get found out till later. She was bloody lucky.'

'I wouldn't want her kind of luck.'

'No, I mean, as far as we know, she's got no internal injuries. God knows why not. No bleeding, or anything. No punctured lungs.'

'Has she been conscious at all?'

'No.'

'How did you know about her broken leg and collar bone? I mean, she couldn't tell you where it hurt.'

Tara looked at him, unsure whether or not he was pulling her leg. She decided to be charitable and suppose that he was pretty new to the job, after all, he did look rather dishy.

'Swelling usually gives it away. We can always check with an x-ray,' she replied. 'We've pinned and plated the femur. We don't do much for the collarbone. It will mend on its own if she lies still.' Tara looked through the glass at the girl again. 'It was a car accident, wasn't it?'

'Hit and run.'

'Poor kid. Do you think you'll get whoever did it?'

'Doubt it.'

'What if she dies?'

'Then somebody will have a bad conscience.' He shut his notebook with a snap. 'Any idea when she will wake up?'

'Could be the next minute, it could be next year. No way of knowing. I'm her designated nurse. I have to check her every fifteen minutes.'

'Oh. I can't sit outside until next year. We were rather hoping she would be able to make a statement. You'd better hang on to her clothes, or what's left of them, in case SOCO wants them.'

'SOCO?'

'Scene of Crimes Officer.' He looked at the bag and sucked his teeth. 'Shouldn't think it likely though.'

'Well I don't think she'll be using them for a while.'

'No, I s'pose not,' he agreed vaguely as he opened the door. 'I'm on till six. Let's hope she wakes up before then. I don't want to spend all my night duty here. Is there anywhere I can get a cup of tea, Tara?'

Tara pushed up her hair at the back of her head and said casually, 'If you want to hang on for ten minutes, Andy, I've got a rest period coming up. I'll take you along to the canteen.'

'That's an offer I can't refuse.' He grinned. 'I'll be outside.'

The village shop had long since disappeared from Easingford. It had become a private cottage and as if to celebrate the matriculation it had grown a hideously incongruous Georgian bow window. Where the distorted images of liquorice and gob stoppers had entranced the children of generations past as they pushed their noses to the rippled glass, now sat a man in slacks and a body warmer selling things in the City by means of the computer screen glowing before him. The slats of the vertical blind enabled him to glance occasionally out at the real world without it encroaching on his realism. He could view the triangular village green, still pock marked where the giant elms had been felled and grubbed out after the Dutch elm disease had got them. He could see the row of quaint cottages lining the far side, orange brick, tall chimneys, latticed windows and wicket fences. He could see the roofs of the cars shining above the straggly hawthorn hedge which surrounded the car park of the Wisdene Arms. If he swivelled his chair right around he could gaze upon the perspective of the rough gravel track which led up past the former village school to the church.

He frowned. Something was happening this morning. He had been distracted by the number of cars driving up that track and now the later arrivals were having to back down again and park around the green. He must put the plastic cones outside his garage. That was the problem with living in a calendar village, you got flooded out with tourists. A couple of special constables drove up in a police van and started to prop up direction signs and divert an increasing trickle of cars towards the cricket field.

At half past ten he got up to make himself a coffee as he had failed to make himself a fortune so far that morning. Standing in the kitchen, grinding the beans, he watched the visitors as they solemnly walked up to the church: sedate matrons in subdued colours, distinguished patriarchs in sleek, sombre suits and ruddy faced country folk ambling awkwardly in unfamiliar clothes. Occasionally a chauffeur-driven Rolls would hesitate alongside the policeman and then glide up to the church, returning empty a few minutes later.

He poured his coffee into a mug which bore the legend '*You need leather balls to play rugby*' and took it into the front room. He sat down and looked at his screen and then ran his fingers through his hair as he had seen people do in all the best films about market traders working under pressure. He must fix up another game of squash with Matthew. He made a note on his organiser and then gave his miniature stainless steel top a twirl and watched it wander about the engraved maze it lived in.

An enormous hearse moved slowly around the village green followed by a trail of black limousines. He gazed at it and thought it looked like some great conger eel coiling itself around something. He was not sure what eels coiled themselves around.

So that was it. Some bigwig had snuffed it. He wondered who it was.

'Lovely service, Richard.'
'Thank you Angela.'
'Your father would have loved it,' his cousin affirmed.
'Yes. It wasn't my idea actually.' He turned aside and took a glass from the tray. 'Thank you John. It was Nessie's.' He nodded across the room where Vanessa Clewe-Harting was talking to four lady relatives whose total ages under their veils amounted to over three hundred years. 'As you know, father knew

several bishops and traditionally one or other of them would always make themselves available for the service but Nessie said, 'Why not let the rector do it? It's his church. Your father always went there. It seems a bit unfair to pass him over when something important comes along.' So that's what we did. He needed a bit of persuading. He was a bit in awe at first, thinking that half the Church of England would be sitting in the congregation.'

'Well I thought it was lovely. He spoke like a man who knew your father, which he obviously did. And I noticed some of the tenants nodding agreement as they listened to his address.'

'Yes, he's a good man. In touch with everyone. I must go and talk with Courtney.'

Angela smiled and slipped away and Richard made his way across the room to one of the tall windows in front of which Courtney was standing. His back was turned to the room and he was apparently just waiting to get back to his estate work.

'Thank you for your arrangements Courtney,'

'Oh, Master Richard.' Courtney started slightly but was unable to hide the tear rolling gently down his left cheek. 'I was just thinking how much your father loved this park. Nobody realised but nearly all the good ideas came from him. He always regretted never finding enough time to spend in it. 'One day, Courtney' he used to say to me.' He swallowed hard. 'And now it's too late.'

'Yes. I didn't know.' Richard was at a loss to know what to say. 'Thank you for arranging for the security firm to look after the Hall and Park whilst we were all at the service. I must confess that I did not think of the risk.'

'Neither did I,' Courtney smiled gravely, 'it was Miss Vanessa who put the idea in my head. It had never occurred to me, I'm ashamed to admit.' He looked across at the group of men and women dressed in their Sunday best, who were talking amongst themselves self consciously. 'Will you see the tenants? I think some of them want to get back.'

'Of course.'

He walked over to the group. They opened up when they saw him approach and one of the wives pulled at the side seams of her skirt to straighten it.

'Thank you all for coming.'

'He was a lovely man,' a short, plump woman sobbed into her handkerchief. Her husband put his arm around her.

'Now now, Mary. His lordship wouldn't ha' wanted to see you a sobbing.'

Richard recognised Mary's husband as one of those who had challenged him to the treacherous game with the cricket ball at the Feasten and which had resulted in his being carried, corpse like, to the Hall. Neither man now showed any embarrassment.

'My father would have been very pleased to see you all there. He thought a great deal of you all.'

'We thought a great deal of him sir,' one of the men said and there was a general shuffling of agreement.

'We was wondering,' one of the others said, 'if you would mind us putting some of our flowers inside the railings.'

Richard knew what he meant. The family vault stood massively in the village churchyard but isolated from it by a fence of spiked railings. Inside the enclosure, alongside the vault, stood a sinister dark yew tree which always seemed to be dripping with moisture. Some said it was a weeping yew, mourning the dead.

'Of course you can. We would be delighted for you to do that. Go and tell the rector now that I said that you could put your flowers inside the railings and ask him to arrange with the church warden to open the gate for you.' He turned to indicate where the rector was standing and saw Vanessa coming towards them.

'Thank you sir, Thank you sir.'

Vanessa was wearing a dress of sheer black satin which hugged her figure but, overlaid as it was by a thick curtain of handmade black lace, it refuted any suggestion that it might be celebrating; it was indisputably mourning. She smiled discreetly at Richard and went up to a thin woman dressed in a navy blue woollen coat with a black chiffon scarf tied over her hair.

'Hello,' she said. 'My name's Vanessa.' She held out her hand.

The woman was too startled to do anything other than take it.

'I'm Mrs. Butcher,' she said, gathering her coat more closely around her. 'That's my Bert over there.'

The other tenants stared in simple, undisguised curiosity. The polarisation of the room into tenants and family had been normal, understandable and comfortable. It was quite expected that Master Richard would come over and talk to them, it was the kind of thing he would do, but what was happening with this lady?

'Mrs. Butcher, I've been admiring your brooch. Can you tell me something about it.'

How could this lady have know the anguish and the doubt that Mrs. Butcher had put into her dress? Her navy blue coat was the nearest thing she had to black. She had worried that the black scarf would make her look, well, poorly matched or ignorant of what to wear for a funeral and her Bert was no good with things like that. And pinning that brooch on her lapel had been for her the equivalent of an act of outrageous bravado. Everybody knew that one was not supposed to decorate for a funeral. She had seen Mrs. Perkins glance at it and purse her lips.

'It was my grandmother's,' she explained.

'Isn't it beautiful?' Vanessa said. 'It's jet of course. Is it Indian?'

'I'd never really thought about it. You know, it could be. My grandfather gave it to my grandmother when they were walking out together and his father, that would be my great grandfather on my father's side of course, he was on the railways in India.'

'It is lovely, and so appropriate. I would never have thought of wearing a brooch like that. What super dress sense you have.'

That's one in the eye for old Ma Perkins, thought Mrs.Butcher.

Richard had not been able to talk to everyone. Charles had introduced him fleetingly to his girl from the agrochemical empire and he had noted a young lady who appeared to be totally in possession of herself, neatly dressed, neat in movement and probably neat in thought.

His mother had retired early. She was still suffering from the shock and taking sedatives from their doctor. The stress and the pills combined to make her weary very quickly.

He looked about the room and saw one of his aged aunts signalling to him that she wished to leave. He knew that the imperiously waving arm meant, 'can you find somebody to get me my car?'. John, the butler was crossing the room before him. Ricahrd called him.

'Oh John?'

'Yes my lord?'

Richard stopped, his mouth open. 'Christ' he thought, 'I'm the ninth Earl of Wisdene.'

Mrs. Crowther stood at the foot of the stairs and listened, her frail head tilted to one side. Sandy followed her out of the parlour, his claws pattering on the linoleum.

'It does sound awfully quiet without the young ladies.' She addressed the remark to the Pekinese who, in lending her his attention, had tilted his head to one side. 'Ah yes, you clever little dog. You've noticed it too haven't you?' She stooped and picked the letters from the wire cage which was attached to the back of the street door. 'Miss C. Shapiro,' she read to the dog. He wagged his tail uncertainly. 'Ah now Miss Shapiro gave me the address of her sister so that I could redirect her mail didn't she? Now where did I put it?'

She paused with one hand on the banister rail. It was awfully quiet. The shock of Miss Shapiro suddenly leaving had upset her rituals and daily life. She had become accustomed to hearing the girls thunder down the stairs in the morning, or to hear them giggling or even sometimes singing and although she always remonstrated politely with them, and although they were always contrite, she actually did not dislike their little transgressions. They brought a life to the house.

But now it seemed that all life had been snuffed out. Should she go up? She looked up the stairs to where she had propped open Cherryl's door to air the room. She had not seen or heard Miss Pye at all this week and it was now Thursday. Of course, having recently adopted the genteel habit of taking a drop of whisky with her bedtime cocoa, Mrs. Crowther now slept a little later in the mornings. I suppose it was possible that she had just not heard Miss Pye every morning. But every evening as well?

'No, Sandy, stay there!'

She pulled herself up the carpeted stairs to the landing and then paused outside Miss Pye's door. She knocked gently.

'Miss Pye?' There was no answer. A van droned by in the street. 'Miss Pye? Are you in there?' Nothing stirred. Should she get her key and open the door? All kinds of things can happen to people. They can have accidents and not be found for weeks. She shuddered at the thought of finding a body. Then she shuddered more at the thought of Jennifer Pye coming up the stairs and catching her with the door open. No! She would leave it until the weekend. She was sure to see her then. If she did not, then, then... she would decide what to do about it.

She turned around and crept quietly back down the stairs.

EPISODE SIXTEEN

Richard watched the weak sun dapple the stone mullions of the window. Grey, greyer, a spot of mustard yellow lichen, a speck of brown moss. Wisdene Hall. His ancestral home.

His eyes drifted over the dark bookshelves of his father's library office. All the books he had loved, all the books he had put aside for his dotage and a comfortable chair by the fire. The chair was there, leather like a roast chestnut, carved wood, the colour of a night-watchman's face. The fireplace was there, a massive grey stone mantle under which some logs had been laid in preparation. The books were there, the chair was there, the fireplace was there. His father was not.

His fingers absently traced the tooled leather on the top of his father's desk as he gazed into the middle distance and saw his father's almost cherubic face. Why couldn't he have had some time for himself? Some time to do just what he wanted.

His breath caught in a sob as he saw his father's round hand-writing in the diary which was open before him. *'Courtney – timber Ackers Wood.'* What was father going to do today with Courtney at Ackers Wood? Should he tell Courtney? Did it matter now?

Nobody would have said of his father that he was not a man who did not go out and get what he wanted and yet, he had never retired to the armchair before the fire with a book on his knee. This was the only future that Richard could ever remember him declaring for himself and he had never achieved it. He should have just done it. He should not have waited until gout or sciatica or arthritis had earned him the points in his mind to qualify him for the corner by the fire.

Richard resolved that he would not make the same mistake. He would go out and do what he wanted but for the moment he must clear this desk. Anyway, he was not going to die yet, he had time. He stopped, his hand frozen on the drawer handle. He did not know if he had time. His father had thought that he had all the time in the world and he had been wrong.

He shook himself. This sort or reflection was daft and maudlin and unproductive. It was a reaction to his father's death, that was all. To work!

The drawer revealed a cheque book, some business cards, and an old race card for Chepstow. He looked at the race card. Why had his father kept it? Perhaps he should ask mother. He put it to one side and opened another drawer.

By the time that John arrived with the tray of morning coffee, Richard had arranged the contents of the drawers into neat piles on the desk top.

'I took the liberty, my lord, of adding a cup and saucer for–'

Vanessa Clewe-Harting strode into the room.

'What ho Boy! Busy?'

'–Miss Clewe-Harting my lord,' John announced rather stiffly as he straightened himself.

'Thank you John. You always were a charmer, Nessie,' Richard said at John's retreating back. He held out an arm to her and she slid alongside the desk and kissed him on the forehead. 'No sugar in mine.' Vanessa stuck out her tongue and bent over the low table. 'Not on the gee gee today, Nessie?' Richard idly watched her bottom as she energetically stirred her coffee.

'I came over specially to see you.' She handed him his coffee. 'How are you getting on?' she asked seriously.

'So so.' He indicated the piles of papers on the desk. 'Just doing some light clearing up.'

'Do you want any help?'

'Nessie, I can't thank you enough for all you have done. You've been an absolute brick this last couple of weeks.'

'Don't talk rot. What's all this?'

'I'm trying to sort out father's things. Some we need, others...' He faltered as he picked up the Chepstow race card. 'I don't know what I can throw away and what I dare not. This race card for instance. Why had he kept it? What did it mean? I've got a whole pile of things that seem to have no intrinsic value or relevance to his work but which possibly meant something to him.' He turned the card over and watched the outline stupidly as it blurred through his filling eyes. 'Why did he...? Why did he...?' he gulped.

Vanessa's arm came around his head and then suddenly everything seemed to let go within him and he was sobbing uncontrollably, his face buried in her bosom. He was the one member of the family who had not yet grieved. He had found an excuse in identifying the hundreds of things that needed doing for the funeral and making them his responsibility. He had stacked away his emotions for later. Each time they had approached him he had managed to erect a barrier to protect himself. He had had arrangements to consider and letters to write and announcements to make but now a stupid race card from Chepstow had beaten him. His father had kept a race card in his drawer. It had meant something to him; it meant nothing to Richard. No one would know why he had kept it.

'Alright Boy. Just let yourself go. Get it out of your system.'

He could vaguely feel Vanessa's hand soothing his hair as he tried to answer unanswerable questions. Questions that he could only express in meaningless half swallowed syllables and choked consonants. 'But he never... And anyway...'

'Alright Boy, Nessie's here.'

His shoulders heaved and he clutched painfully at Vanessa's torso as he pressed his mouth as hard as he could into her body in an unsuccessful attempt to stifle a wail of anguish. His tears, his dribbling, soaked the material of her blouse.

'I hadn't fi... fi... finished with h... him. I wanted to...'

The door opened quietly behind him. John had interpreted the wailing as a possible summons. Vanessa glanced emptily at him as she clutched the frenzied head of Richard to her belly and rocked him to and fro.

'Shush now, shush.'

John backed out, his face immobile.

'What are you drinking Tara?'

'Pint o' lager Andy. I'm going to bag that seat over there.'

Tara Hughes pushed her way across the pub to an empty bench by the window and flopped down onto it. Her raincoat flipped open and she mechanically pulled it closed. A coat should not be necessary in the first week of July but Tara always wore something to cover her tunic. The last thing she wanted was for someone to run in from the street looking for a first aider and to spy her in full regalia. She had finished for the day.

She watched Andy as he tried to grab the barman's attention. He was quite sweet really and she did not believe his line about 'just passing the hospital' because Julie had said that somebody had rung up that morning to ask what duty 'Nurse Hughes' was on. A man.

She smiled at him as he weaved his way through to her with the drinks. She had thought that he looked good in uniform. He looked pretty good in civvies too.

'There you are. Pint of lager.'

A man sitting behind Andy made a face to his mate.

'You got a problem, sunshine, with me drinking lager?' Tara challenged him.

'No, no,' the man replied in embarrassment.

'That's all right then. Cheers Andy.'

'Yeah... er. Cheers Tara.' He glanced behind him and then looked at her with wide eyes. 'Do you often come in here?'

'No. Usually go straight home. I'm knackered. 'You not on duty today?'

'No. Well, yes. Late turn.'

'Oh I needed that.' Tara plumped her half empty glass onto the table. 'What are you drinking?' She peered suspiciously at his glass.

'Grapefruit juice.'

'You're not sworn off it are you?'

'I don't drink before I go on duty. I might have a pint later.'

'So, what's it like being a cop?'

He winced and discreetly fluttered his hand on the table.

'Shh! That's the first thing,' he said, looking around the crowded pub. 'You don't shout it about.'

'Oh sorry. No I suppose not. Didn't think.'

'That's alright.' He smiled. 'You don't want to find me in one of your beds do you?'

She pouted provocatively. 'I might.'

'Don't know what you mean.' He took a sip at his drink. 'Oh, how is the sleeping beauty? Are you still with her?'

'Miss Magdaline O'Neill? Yes I'm still one of her designated nurses. She's still the same, in a coma.'

'That makes it six weeks. How long can she last?'

'Forever if she wants to. She's quite stable. Breathing on a ventilator, living on fluids. How's the investigation?'

'There isn't one. The trail's gone cold.' Andy took another sip at his drink then replaced the glass carefully on the beer mat. 'Actually, there was no trail. Nobody saw anything. Nothing to follow up. If she doesn't tell us, we won't know. What about her people? Have they turned up?'

'No. I don't expect they will. These down and outs have usually cut themselves off from all their family.'

'Or the other way around. The family has cut themselves off from them.'

'Comes to the same thing.' She eased her shoes from her feet and wriggled her toes. 'Ooh that's better. Don't you get flat feet in your job?'

'Not nowadays. Get piles from sitting in sweaty Fords and poxy Peugeots. What'll happen to that girl do you reckon?'

'Not a lot we can do till she wakes up.'

'Will she be brain damaged? You know, a vegetable?'

'No, not necessarily. Some of them just wake up one day and carry on just as if nothing had happened. It takes them a bit of time to adjust – losing a chunk of their lives – but they seem to cope all right.'

'Oh.'

'Don't worry about her.'

'I'm not.'

'You can't do anything to help her.'

'No, I know I can't. Can you?'

Tara Hughes pursed her lips and rolled her eyes to the ceiling. Then she let out her breath in a sigh of defeat.

'Not really,' she admitted.

In the dirty red brick building across the road, one of Tara's colleagues glanced at the wave line on the ECG monitor and verified the pressure on the ventilator, just as she or another of the team had done every fifteen minutes, night and day, since the immobile bundle of the girl had come down from theatre.

Winston nosed the Range Rover through the wrought iron gates of Half Moon Mews.

'Just up on the left, Winnie. Stop in front of the garage.'

'Yes milord.'

Richard remembered in time to say nothing. He had tried to get Winston to address him simply as 'sir' but the old chauffeur had taken it as an affront. He was proud of serving the d'Ennessy family and now that Master Richard had succeeded to the title, the devotion that Winston had been unable to express before, he could now display legitimately. To suggest that Winston, the chauffeur of the new Lord Wisdene, should not address his master as 'milord' was a heresy on an equal to opining that the Daimler ought to be scrapped.

'I say, I'm awfully sorry to hear about your pater.'

Richard glanced across the mews to where the blond haired heir to half of London was leaning from his window.

'Thanks,' Richard acknowledged him.

'I suppose you have to move into the ancestral pile now?'

'I'm keeping the flat on. I shall still need a base in Town.'

'Yar. Right.'

Richard unlocked the front door.

'This way Winnie. I've not got much to move, just some clothes and my art stuff.'

'Not a bad situation here, right in the middle of things,' Winston observed as he reached the top of the stairs. 'But I prefer my mews cottage to yours. It's quieter.'

'I had no intention of offering to swap. I tell you what, you make us some coffee whilst I pack my clothes up.' He ignored Winston's startled look. 'Everything is in the kitchen, Winnie, you can't get lost.'

'Well I don't know that I should,' Winston mumbled his discomfort and looked towards the kitchen as if he did not wish the boundaries between master and servant to become blurred, but Richard merely dismissed his half protest with a grin.

When, some time later, they had assembled Richard's moveable belongings at the top of the stairs ready for loading into the car, they needed no bidding to sit down gladly to drink their coffee.

'You look uncomfortable in that chair Winston, is it too low?'

'It's an unusual shape, milord.'

Richard laughed.

'That was quite diplomatic. It's an awful chair. I don't know why I bought it. Yes I do,' he contradicted himself, 'I liked the colour of the leather. I didn't think about sitting in it, that's all.'

'It's not the thinking about sitting in it that is uncomfortable,' Winston observed drily as he eased his back. 'Are you leaving it here?'

'Yes.' Winston's head moved in a discreet nod of relieved approval. 'I'll get Mrs. MacCallum to organize a regular cleaning so that the flat is ready whenever I need it. She can put in some dry foods for emergencies and I have left some clothes here. I expect that I shall be needing to spend the odd night in Town from time to time.'

'Your father certainly had a busy life and if you are taking over from him...'

'I am,' Richard said quickly. 'I have decided. I shall tell them at the meeting this afternoon.'

Winston greeted this confidence with a silence of contentment. Contented that the new lord was taking over from the work of the old and contented that he was still able to confide in Winston just as he always had done.

Richard looked at the motley collection of suitcases, bags, boxes and parcels. 'I think I'll make up another box of books,' he said. 'There are some more up there that I could do with at the Hall.' He nodded at the half empty bookcase.

'Well there will still be room in the car. I'll start loading.'

Whilst Winston carried the first two suitcases down to the car, Richard quickly selected another dozen books and slipped them into a plastic carrier bag. Then he grabbed an art folder and two bags and hurried down to avoid Winston having to repeatedly negotiate the staircase.

'I'll dump them here Winnie, you sling them in.' He bounded back up the stairs. When he returned with his next load, Winston was standing under the open tailgate and studying a piece of cartridge paper which he held in his hand.

'I was just looking at one of your drawings milord,' he said guiltily, 'It fell out of that folder.'

'Oh don't Winnie, you'll embarrass me.' He slipped the bags into the car behind the chauffeur. Winston was standing very still.

'I think it's Miss Jennifer,' he said.

Richard looked over his shoulder. He was holding one of the studies that Richard had realised in order to paint the ballgown portrait. Winston silently handed it to him. Jennifer.

Jennifer he had danced with, in the ballgown. 'I didn't play at anything. I was serious' Jennifer. Jennifer who had run out of his door and his life. He swallowed hard and cleared his throat.

'Yes that's Jennifer.' Winston nodded, his gaze focused on a window box, his eyes seeing another bloom. 'I was a bloody fool wasn't I Winnie?'

'It's a terrible way to learn milord.'

'I wonder if I have.'

Richard drove himself to his father's office in Reading. It would be some time before he stopped thinking of it as that. He took the Range Rover. He had not driven the Yellow Peril for some time now. He always seemed to be carrying something bulky or be travelling in a group which precluded its use. He had never questioned why his father had made his business HQ in Reading, it was not a particularly convenient journey from Wisdene Hall, but, like his father, he had no wish to run any part of the property empire from the family home. The Hall was for the estate and for the family and for friends. You made money in Reading, you spent money at Wisdene.

The offices were on the top floor of ancient bank chambers of a long forgotten bank; creaking floors and sash windows, dark stained doors and half panelled walls. Anatole Worstop, the company secretary, was waiting at the top of the stairwell for him. Richard knew him vaguely, having met him at some time or another. He was as tall as Richard, with white hair and a hooked nose. His pin striped grey suit was draped on his thin, angular body rather like a shroud on a statue waiting to be unveiled. His handshake, however, was as firm and vigorous as his voice.

Richard followed him into a long room with three tall windows down one side and a huge fireplace on the opposite wall. The walls were half panelled in the same dark wood as the other rooms but for some inexplicable reason, a tenant in the fusty past had painted the carved wooden mantle surround in a rich cream gloss. Above the shelf hung a gilt framed mirror which reflected the view of the railway outside through a vase of peonies.

The middle of the room was occupied by an oval wooden table garnished with blotters, notepads, pencils and water glasses. It was large enough to seat ten in comfort, but nobody was sitting.

'Let me introduce everybody.' Anatole Worstop indicated a

matronly woman in a printed cotton dress and cardigan. Her black and silver hair was tied up in a chignon and she wore a pair of spectacles which had been the height of fashion thirty years earlier. 'Lord Wisdene, this is Mrs. Dove.'

'Pleased to meet you Mrs. Dove.'

'Good morning sir,' she replied correctly.

'Mrs. Dove is the company administrator. She looks after the systems we use to run the company and makes sure that when we want something, we can be find it.' Mrs. Dove smiled slightly. Richard had a feeling that perhaps she was responsible for a little more than that and would tell him so when she had a chance. Worstop turned to a rotund man in his fifties. His ruddy neck was squeezed into the collar of a pink shirt and his paunch strained at the single button holding his sports jacket together over cavalry twill trousers.

'Harry Meachem. How do you do?' he announced before Worstop had time to label him. 'I do the surveying and draw up the plans, liaise with the architects and builders and stuff like that.' Richard shook his hand.

'And this is Piers Lansing.' Lansing was in his early thirties, which made him only a few years older than Richard. He had a square jaw and a heavy beard shadow and a pair of blue eyes which were so delicately pale as to be out of place in such an otherwise rugged face. He wore a well cut suit and a polkadot silk tie. His hair was brushed fastidiously back and his nails were manicured. 'Piers runs the lettings and does the research.' Worstop's explanation meant nothing to Richard but he realised that the moment was not right for clarification.

'Pleased to meet you milord,' Lansing said and then returned to stand behind his chair. They all looked at Richard.

'Well, good afternoon everyone,' he said. He looked around. They were waiting for something, he had no idea what.

'Shall we sit down?' Worstop suggested and showed Richard to the only chair with arms. They sat.

'I expect you are all wondering what is going to happen to the company and no-one wonders more than me,' Richard started. 'I understand from the family solicitor that succession to the earldom confers on me the control of the company and should I wish to have a hand in the day to day running, just as my father did, then I can. Not only that, but I have absolute executive power.' He stopped and looked at them. They were watching him as mice watch a cat. He began to realise what wielding power felt like; he was not sure that he liked the sensation. 'I have come today to meet you so that you get any news straight from the horse's mouth, so to speak.' They were holding their breath. 'I shall adopt the same role as my father did but I warn you that I am a different person and will probably do things differently. I cannot say how differently until I know how he worked and how I want to work. It will become rapidly obvious to you that I know nothing of the business or indeed business in general. I shall need you to help me.'

'I am sure you can count on all our assistance,' Worstop declared and the others nodded discreetly.

'Good. What I would like to do this afternoon is to see you individually within your own empires so that you can explain to me all that you do. I assume that you all have work in hand and do not need direction for the moment?'

He looked around them. Harold Meachem said 'Yup', Piers Lansing nodded thoughtfully and Mrs. Dove gave a little ironic smile and said, 'Oh yes.'

Richard stood up.

'Fine.' He looked at the company secretary. 'Can you give me some time to explain the set up of the company?' He turned to the others without waiting for acknowledgement from Worstop, 'Do not fret if I don't get around to you today, or indeed, this week. I am a notoriously slow learner.'

They sat in easy chairs in Anatole Worstop's office and looked at each other across a coffee table laden with box files.

'I suppose,' Worstop began, 'it would be easiest to explain what the company as a whole does.' Richard nodded. 'We invest in, and develop, land and property.'

'For what purpose?'

'Ultimately, profit.'

'And how do you, how do we do it?'

'We buy land and property into our portfolios. We sometimes just hold the land and then sell it later at a profit. We sometimes negotiate a planning permission on the land and then sell it. We sometimes obtain the permission and design a housing or industrial development scheme and then sell it as a package.

We sometimes do all that and then actually get the development built and sell it. We sometimes do all that and then don't sell it but hold it and let it.'

'And who decides which of these we do?'

'You do.'

'Ah. And what do you do?' Richard grinned.

'As company secretary my most important responsibility is to keep us within the law.'

'We're not doing anything illegal are we?'

'No. Certainly not, but in this world of company regulations it is frighteningly easy to step outside the law without knowing it.'

'So you will keep me legal will you?'

'I will keep all of us legal, milord.'

'Good.' Richard waved the annual report. 'I'll take this home with me and do some homework. Now I've transgressed on your time enough for the moment, can you show me where to find Harry Meachem?'

'Certainly. And at any time, I shall be at your disposal.'

Harry Meachem had discarded his jacket and was leaning his chair back on two legs with his own feet resting on the corner of his desk.

'That shuttering has got to be done by Monday morning, you know that,' he said and then turned to wave Richard to a seat. 'Ralph,' he said into the phone, 'Ralph, listen. Monday morning. No, Monday morning. That's your problem not mine. Well they will have to work on Sunday then won't they? Get it done Ralph. You can't afford to fail on this one.' He slammed the receiver down and lifted his feet from the desk.

'A problem?' Richard enquired.

'No, just normal. Builders don't like to get cold or wet any more. Right! You want to know what I do apart from swear down a phone all day long.'

'What was that call about then?'

'Manor Gate. It's a residential in Virginia Water.' He swung around on his chair and poked about amongst some plan rolls in the chest. 'Here we are.' He spread out the plan on his desk. 'Eighteen houses. Our own development.'

'One where we own the land, have designed the layout and are having it built?'

'That's right.' He put a nicotine stained thumb on the plan. 'Just there is a retaining wall which we need in place before we start to lay foundations.'

'And the builder hasn't got the shuttering in place ready for the concrete pouring on Monday morning,' Richard finished.

Meachem raised his eyebrows. 'Yup, that's it.'

'And are you, what do you call it, managing this project?'

'Just overseeing it. Ralph is my manager on site. He deals with the day to day running. Good bloke, only sometimes he needs a boot up the ar... backside.'

'And do we employ Ralph? Is he one of our employees?'

'No. Self employed like everybody in the building trade. We pay him a fee.'

'Have we got any other projects on the go like this?'

'Yup, two or three.'

'How do we decide what sort of property we want and what we want to do with it?'

'Ah, now you've got me there. Show me an old cinema and say you want to turn it into a supermarket and I'm your man. But you've got to know what you want first. Lord Wisdene used to do that. I mean,' he stumbled, 'your father, that is.'

'I understand.' He held up his hand. 'I think I've got enough to go on for the moment. I must not get in too deep to start with or I shall never see straight.' He smiled. 'I must see the others before I go.'

'Sure, sure.'

'Mr. Lansing is...?'

'Next door down on the left.'

'Thanks.'

The door to Piers Lansing's office was open so Richard walked straight in. Piers Lansing was sitting at his desk, deeply engrossed in reading a newspaper. He looked up.

'Ah. Lord Wisdene. How can I help you?' He adjusted the knot on his tie and indicated a chair. 'Do sit down. Or would you like the desk?' He bounced up.

'No, no I'm fine here. I want to know what you do. I'm afraid "lettings and research" meant nothing to me.'

'Oh that's quite understandable.' He took a pencil from the desk and fiddled with it as he walked across to the window. 'Well,

I manage the lettings, that is to say, the rents we receive from the property that we let or lease.'

'Do you mean that you go around and collect rents?'

'Oh heavens no! I would never be finished. We work through letting agencies.'

'Who presumably take a commission?'

'That is correct.'

'How many properties do we rent out?'

'I couldn't tell you that exactly without checking. Several hundreds.'

'And what is your role in this operation? I mean, if we use letting agencies to collect our rents, what do you do?'

'I make sure that the agencies pay us. That is quite important.'

Richard had forgotten that he represented absolute power and that by posing a question which implied that he thought that somebody did nothing, he would be making it look as if he wanted to get rid of them.

'I would think it was vital. Do they often default?'

'Some have a tendency to drag their feet and they do not always fulfil the service part of the contract properly.'

'What's that?'

'Many of our lettings are small residential units, flats in converted houses in city centres and such and they require a high level of maintenance. I negotiate a favourable and realistic deal with the agency based on their promised level of service, you know, "plumber within the hour" kind of response, but I have to check up to ensure that both we and the tenants are getting what they pay for.'

'I see.' Richard's eyes strayed back to the newspaper open on the desk.

'And that is the research side of the job.' Lansing lifted the paper to show the title banner. It was a local paper from Swindon. 'I keep track of how rents are moving in the provinces so that we can move into promising areas and so that our letting portfolio is correctly valued.'

'Do you sometimes see property advertised that you think we should invest in?'

'That is part of my job. Lord Wisdene gives... oh sorry.'

'Go on.'

'I get a monthly brief of the type of property we want and I look for it. I might be told to look for arable and grazing in the West Country, or student bedsits in university towns or something with water around it.'

'And my father used to decide what was in the brief.'

'I believe it was very largely he.'

'I see.' Richard gazed at the silver framed photograph of a lady and two boys which was propped up by the telephone.

'Do you live locally?'

'Caversham. My wife is Russian. She works up at the BBC monitoring station.'

Mrs. Dove glanced over the top of her spectacles as he entered the switchboard reception area.

'Ah. Lord Wisdene. I thought you would get around to me eventually.'

'Always leave the best till last, Mrs. Dove.' He had no idea why Mrs. Dove was so prickly. 'Now where shall we begin?' He threw the ball squarely into her court.

'Where would you like to begin?' She vollied.

He was tempted to reply with a forehand smash of 'at the beginning' but restrained himself just in time. For a reason which was completely obscured from Richard, she needed to win this match and he thought it politic to let her, this time. He heard a filing cabinet slam shut in the office behind her.

'Why not introduce me to your staff?' He nodded towards the door.

'As you wish,' she acceded and led him through to the other room. A lanky girl with straggly blond hair and thick lensed glasses straightened up from the filing cabinet and peered at them. 'This is Katrina, Lord Wisdene.'

'Hello Katrina. What do you do here?'

'Katrina is an audio typist and she helps cover the switchboard, don't you Katrina?'

'Yes Mrs. Dove.' Katrina nervously flicked a strand of hair from her face and then clasped her hands before her. Mrs. Dove swept past to the back of the room where a lad in jeans and a tee shirt was working at a photocopier.

'Just stop the machine a moment, Wayne.' Wayne turned a surprised face to her and then pressed the pause button. 'Lord Wisdene, this is Wayne.'

'Hello Wayne.'

'Hi!'

'Wayne is what you might call "the office boy". Thank you Wayne, carry on.'

The machine whirred back into its job as Mrs. Dove turned and said to Katrina, 'We will have tea in my office.'

'Yes Mrs. Dove.'

'Come this way, Lord Wisdene.'

Mrs. Dove's office was the interior design equivalent of her floral dress and cardigan. An embroidered cushion slumped in her swivel chair, although the chair was equipped with a lumbar adjustment facility; the windows were framed by curtains regardless of the presence of the venetian blinds and hanging on the side of a cabinet was a 'Picturesque Villages of England' calendar onto which she had duplicated appointments from her diary.

'This is the organigram of my department.' Mrs. Dove thrust a diagram into his hands.

'A what?' he said as he sat down.

'A diagram of how the department works.' She pursed her lips and folded her arms across her chest.

'I see.' Richard puzzled over the lines and boxes.

'I did a diploma in Business Studies,' she said as if this were an explanation in itself.

'So, all the correspondence comes through you.'

'In and out.'

'Er.... yes. And you are responsible for the record keeping and daily accounting, wages, heavens! even organising the servicing of the cars. However do you do it?'

Mrs. Dove glowed quietly and studied her finger tips.

'Well I do the best I can,' she admitted modestly.

EPISODE SEVENTEEN

'And there's a gorgon called Mrs. Dove,' Richard said.

Vanessa took another sip from her glass and curled her legs up onto the chesterfield.

'She can't be a gorgon with a name like that.'

'You'd be surprised. She goes around exuding this air of unrecognised martyrdom. You know, "the business couldn't run without me. I am the business" sort of thing.'

'I expect you've misunderstood her.' Vanessa put her glass onto a small table. 'She probably wants to mother you.'

'Ugh! I wonder if she wanted to mother father.' He paused and Vanessa held her breath anxiously. It was the first time that he had mentioned his father to her since his crying on her chest. Richard grinned. 'I suppose she sees me as an interloper.' Then he stopped, serious. 'You don't suppose she was sweet on father do you?'

'Almost certainly,' Vanessa maintained. 'And now she will fall in love with you and tumble over herself to serve you faithfully come hell or high water.'

'Ugh again.'

A bee droned in from the garden through the open doors and performed an erratic zig-zag reconnaissance of the room. From the lower lawns came the staccato chattering of the lawn mower as Blase, the head gardener, rode majestically to and fro, just his head appearing occasionally above the yew hedge.

'So what do you do all day long Boy? I can't see you in a pin-striped behind a desk.'

'Well that's all you know. I've got hidden talents.'

'Pompous prig!' Vanessa chided. 'Your talents are so well hidden that even you can't find them.'

'Last week,' Richard said airily, 'I called upon a plumber in Reading and asked him why he had not visited Flat 4 at 43 Montague Street and repaired their leaking U-bend.'

'You did what?'

'I am sure you heard me perfectly, Nessie dear, given the size of your ears.' Vanessa picked up a cushion. 'Ah ah,' Richard warned, 'Not while there are glasses in the firing line. Never hit a man with glasses. Haven't you ever heard that maxim?'

'I was going to hit him with the cushion not with glasses but now you have mentioned maxims I am not convinced that a Maxim gun might not be more appropriate.'

'Oh very witty. Quite the up and coming comedian. You should meet my plumber friend. He could give you a plug.'

'So why had not your plumber called at wherever it was?'

'He had not been asked to.'

'Seems fair enough. Why had he not been asked?'

'That is what I had to find out. As part of my apprenticeship to the helm I decided that I would work a bit in each department to see how the whole thing ran together.'

'Grass roots and all that.'

'Quite. We have this very dapper chap called Piers Lansing and one of his jobs is to check that the letting agencies are doing all that they charge us for. Miss Hextable or Ms, probably, as she has two children, had phoned us to say that...'

'Her U bend was leaking and would they send a member of the filthy capitalist land-owning aristocracy to fix it for her?'

'Something along those lines.'

'And?'

'Well, Piers and I checked up on the plumber first and he said that he had not been asked by the letting agency so then we went to the agency and they swore black was white that they had issued the instruction.'

'A breakdown in communication then?'

'No, a bare-faced lie and a straightforward attempt to pare down the services provided whilst pocketing the commission.'

'So what did you do?'

'I am ashamed to say that I did nothing. Piers did not let on who I was – they just saw me as a new boy learning the ropes.'

'Which of course you are.'

'How sweetly you put it.'

'My pleasure.'

'As Piers pointed out, we would never get to the bottom of the affair. All we could usefully do was teach them that if they didn't do their job then they would be called to account.'

'Oh, I bet that frightened them!'

'Your simple little brain has missed the point again, Nessie my dear. It is all psychological. If we make a nuisance of ourselves, more than the other landlords, then they will serve us properly if only for a bit of peace. I can see that you're not suitable for the cut and thrust of business, You'd better stick to your gee-gees.'

'Step outside and say that.'

'Don't be tiresome. It's too warm for cavorting on the terrace.'

Vanessa's grey green eyes swept over him. 'You are enjoying yourself aren't you?' she asked seriously.

'Yes I am, Nessie, I didn't think that I would, but I am. I can see now why father enjoyed it. It's not just the making of money – the sitting back and letting the filthy lucre roll in to the coffers – one is actually creating something. This development in the centre of Swindon for example. Well it's not exactly in the centre it's in an area of decayed Victoriana where the railway workers used to live. What father decided was that people should be encouraged to move back and live there. It's not just an arcade of lock up shops, there are flats and maisonettes. When it is up and running you will be able to go there after the shops have shut in the evening and still see and hear people. It won't be a dead, soulless selling point, there will still be life and movement. And another thing,' He continued enthusiastically, 'the proportions are to the scale of man. It's not a church, it's not a temple. We are not trying to intimidate or impress the populace, we are providing them with an environment in which they will feel safe and comfortable. It's a sort of sociological thing but it's creative as well.'

'Like the painting?'

'Yes. No. Well not in quite the same way.'

'You mean the business earns you your daily crust?'

'It's damn certain I could never have earned a crumb at painting.' Richard laughed. A little too easily, Vanessa thought.

'So no more painting? No more romping around in the lumber room looking for ballgowns?'

Richard threw her a sideways glance.

'I wouldn't rule out the latter.'

'What about the former?'

'The painting? It was good fun. I enjoyed it but now somehow, it seems just a little too...' he paused, searching for words, 'I suppose it is a little too self indulgent and in any case my time is taken up with my job.' Vanessa said nothing but turned her grave eyes upon him. 'I would never have been any good at painting.' He uttered a short self deprecatory laugh.

'Is that what they said?'

'Who?'

'Your tutors. Did they say you were no good?'

'Not exactly, no.'

Vanessa smiled and shook her head to herself.

'Did you ever use that ballgown?'

'What?'

'The ballgown we found in the lumber room. Did you paint the ballgown in your still life class?'

'It wasn't still life, it was figure drawing. Do you want another drink?'

'I haven't finished this one.'

He stood up and walked over to the French windows. He thrust his hands into his pockets and gazed out across the park.

'Well did you?'

'Did I what?'

'Paint the ballgown.'

He could just see the front bedroom window of Bridge Cottage. He waved his hand dismissively.

'Oh yes, I expect so. Yes I did.'

'Can I see it?'

And the track where Winston had taken her for a spin in his car. 'I haven't got it. All my stuff is still at college.'

Her golden hair.

'Don't you miss college?'

He turned sharply, breaking his reverie.

'Do you mean the plastic seats and the instant coffee?'

'No. Your friends, silly. You must have made some friends up there.'

'Well, not really. More... acquaintances. Not friends.'

'Not even one friend, Boy?' She was looking straight into his eyes, holding his gaze. 'One friend?'

'One friend.'

'Where is she?'

'I did something stupid and she walked out of my life.'

'Do you miss her?'

'Are you any good at shorthand?'

'Sounds like you are changing the subject.'

'Well are you, Nessie? You did a course didn't you?'

'That is a hurtful way of explaining away a comprehensive and intensive two years of my life.'

'Do you fancy a run out to Marlborough? There's something I've got to take a look at. I thought you could help me if you wanted to.'

'When? This morning?'

'Not this morning I've got to... I'm doing something else today. Friday?'

'I'll sharpen my pencils.'

A sore throat. Achingly sore. She swallowed and winced at the pain. Someone had left the light on. Very dim. She could just see it through her eyelids. Or was it the sun? Funny beeping noise nearby. Voices talking, fading in and out like short wave radio.

With the hood down the noise on the motorway was terrific. It was good to be back in his own car. Not as comfortable as the Range Rover of course, but more fun. Richard flicked his hair back out of his eyes and then crossed to the far lane to avoid a cloud of foul-looking black exhaust smoke which was issuing from the lorry he was overtaking. He squinted as the sun peeped over the screen at him. He put his hand in the door pocket for his cap and then bit his lip. He had just remembered what he had done with his cap. He would have to buy another one.

Soon he was coasting down from the elevated section, searching the streets for a clue to remind him. When they had come back from Bristol he had dropped her outside her flat, despite her protestations. He smiled to himself. Thank goodness he had insisted on taking her home. I bet she never thought that he would remember where she lived.

He recognised the newsagents on the corner and as soon as he turned into the street, he saw her block of flats. Risking the double yellows and with his heart pounding, he ran up the short flight of steps to the entrance. He pushed open one of the glass doors and entered the vestibule. This was going to be easy. No need even to study the letter boxes and bell pushes for here, of all things, was a hall porter.

'Are you visitin' sir?'

'Yes. Miss Jennifer Pye please.'

The grey haired man looked at Richard's light cotton trousers and silk shirt and then glanced through the door. 'Your motor?' Richard nodded with his eyebrows. 'Bit risky leavin' it there sir, if you don't mind me sayin'. Wardens are a blinkin' pest around 'ere.'

'I shan't be long I hope.'

'Suit yerself. Now who was it you wanted?'

'Jennifer Pye.'

The porter sucked on his teeth and slowly shook his head.

'Not got anyone called that. What number flat?'

'Well I... ha... I don't actually know. You must know her. She's a short girl with long hair. Golden hair. She's an art student, you've probably seen her carrying big folders and things.'

'Student? Don't get many of those. Got a young man studying law I think but he's working in Temple Bar.'

A flicker of fear flitted across Richard's mind. He looked about the hall. 1930's wood panelling and parquet floor. Not really Jennifer Pye.

'Perhaps she's moved. How long have you been here?'

The porter looked sourly at him. 'Eight years an' I don't remember a Jennifer Pye. You sure it was Anselm Court?'

'Anselm Court?'

'This is Anselm Court. You sure you got the right address?'

'But I know she lives here. I dropped her outside only a few months ago.' Even as he said it, Richard could see the flaw. So could the porter.

'But you didn't see her go in did yer? Oldest trick in the book, son.'

'Perhaps I have got the wrong block of flats.' Richard tried to save face.

'Yeah. P'raps you have.'

When he stepped outside the first thing that he saw was the entrance to the underground station and then he knew. But why had she done it? What had she got to hide?

As he sat in the stationary car he reflected upon the ironic injustice of the situation. She had been enraged because he had pretended that a flat which did belong to him, was not really his property and yet she had fostered a pretence of living in a flat which had apparently never seen her. The irony was almost unbearable. Where now?

Where he should have gone in the first place.

The Sloane College of Art and Design.

Can't swallow. Something gagging in her throat. Mouth like dry leather. Bumble voices. A hand touching her face, opening her lips, drawing something out from deep inside her. Scraping up her trachea with a strange roaring sound. Muscles in her diaphragm stretching and relaxing of their own accord. New air, not machine air.

It had not occurred to him that thus far into July, most of the students would have finished already. He went straight to the Registrar's office. 'I'm looking for a student.'

'Yes.' The woman's voice was utterly neutral. It gave him absolutely no indication of what she thought of his declaration.

'Her name's Jennifer Pye.'

'Ah ha.'

'Can you give me her address please? Her home address.'

'Ah,' she sighed with apparent contentment. 'No.'

'Pardon?'

'I said "no". We do not give out student's addresses.'

'Why not? I am a student here. I need to contact her.'

'You would not like us to give out your address to all and sundry.'

'I would not mind in the slightest.'

'That's as may be. The answer is still no.' She slid the glass door back into place and turned away from the counter.

Richard stood there, his fists clenching as the anger built up in him. He controlled himself and slowly let out his breath. Then he turned away just in time to see a vaguely familiar figure pass into the corridor.

'Oi!' he shouted and ran after her.

'Oh you made me jump out of my skin!' Patsy gulped.

'Oh er sorry. I was surprised to see you still at college.'

'We've got another week then we go.'

They stood aside as a technician pushed past them with a trolley laden with blocks of clay.

'All your course is still in college is it?'

'Yup. You must have finished very early. We haven't seen you about for months.'

'Oh I had to stop my course. A bit of trouble at home. Actually my father died.'

'Oh I am sorry.' Patsy impulsively put her arm on his then she snatched it back, blushing furiously. 'You'll never guess what everybody was saying.'

'What? About me?'

'Well, Ruth was saying it.'

'Oh yes, good old Ruth. Well if it was coming from Ruth it would have been scandalous and completely untrue.'

Patsy frowned.

'She said that you and Jennifer had run away together.'

For the second time that day, Richard felt a flicker of anxiety Almost a prescience of dread. He forced himself to appear calm and relaxed.

'Is Jennifer not in college then?'

Patsy peered intently through her spectacles at him.

'She's left. Just didn't turn in one day. I think she was getting a bit cheesed off. People do that.'

So that was it. She had stormed out of his life and then dropped out of college. She could be anywhere. He found his voice at last.

'Do you have her address?'

'No. Have you tried the Registrar?'

'Yes. They won't give it out.'

'Oh I know, they're terrible like that. Colin will probably have it. He'll be up in the library. You've met Colin haven't you? I'm sure they've been to the cinema a couple of times together. I think he's a bit sweet on her.' She confided and then put her hand to her mouth. 'Oh sorry!'

Unusual smells. A sharp chemical smell. A clinging, soft, glutinous odour. Reminded her of something. Or somewhere. Tired. Go back to sleep. Everything fading.

Richard squinted at the A-Z again and then threw it back onto the passenger seat. He drove to the end of the road and came up against a 'no entry' sign where he wanted to turn.

He swore under his breath. A tabby cat sitting on a garden wall stopped washing itself to watch him, ears pointing and eyes alert, as he turned the car around. Satisfied that he represented no threat, it continued its toilet. He retraced his track to the junction and then studied the map anew. 'Have to try from the other end,' he muttered. Another road. Another avenue of scraggy trees and concreted gardens. He turned left. An elderly woman bent almost double was trailing a wheeled shopping basket along the pavement. It had one buckled wheel which made it waddle and it rocked precariously over the paving slabs where they had been cracked by tree roots. Richard pulled up alongside her.

'Excuse me. Could you tell me if this is Cordoba Crescent please?'

She turned a wild, staring eye on him. 'Don't you speak to me you hooligan!' she wailed. 'I know what you're after. Clear off or I'll have the police on yer!'

Before he could gather his wits together, Richard found that he was fifty yards further down the street and still accelerating.

'Whoa there, slow down!' he chided himself, 'She was just a daft old bat. Nothing to get alarmed about. And anyway, there's Cordoba Crescent by that pillar box.'

He glanced at the scrap of paper that Colin had given him and then stopped in the street outside a large orange brick Victorian house. He reversed and parked in the only space available which was across the entrance to the house next door. In the drive he could see a rotting tarpaulin covering a mound of a car only identified by a rusty bumper and moss-covered tyres. Nothing would be coming out of that drive today.

He felt his heart beginning to thump again as he opened the garden gate. She might be there. If she has given up college then she would have had to get herself a job so perhaps she will be at work. Perhaps there will be nobody in. As he pressed the door bell he noticed the paint peeling from the sill of the front door and smiled ruefully to himself at his gullibility in thinking that she could have lived in that block of flats.

He waited. Perhaps, indeed, there was nobody in. He pushed

the button harder and this time he heard a faltering ring sound somewhere within the hall followed by the yapping of a dog. The net curtain in the bay window fluttered and he pretended not to notice. Through the coloured glass in the door he could just distinguish a shape approaching. The door was suddenly pulled briskly open and an untidy small dog issued from the gap and yapped at him.

'Sandy!' the elderly lady called sharply. 'Bed.' The dog ignored her and wandered off into the front garden to investigate a scent under the hydrangea bush. 'Yes?' she said to Richard.

'I'm looking for a friend and I've been told she lives here.' The old lady peered intensely at him with her thin blue eyes as if trying to guess the name of his friend before he could tell her. 'Jennifer Pye. She's shortish with...'

'Miss Pye. Oh yes, I know Miss Pye.'

'Oh good. Is she in? Can I see her?' He realised that he was beginning to sound a little too anxious but he could not help it. He was excited.

'She's not here.' Richard was aware of the old lady's bony hands wringing the front of her apron. 'I'm Mrs. Crowther, her landlady. Who are you?'

'My name's Richard d'Ennessy. A friend from college.'

'Ah yes,' she replied as if having confirmed something that she had always suspected. 'A student friend.'

'When will she be back?'

Mrs. Crowther said nothing but peered at his face closely. Richard glanced away slightly, embarrassed at the scrutiny. Perhaps the old lady was very short sighted. If she were, then it would be more enjoyable for her visitors if she wore spectacles instead of examining them like this. At length she replied, 'She didn't say.' Then she added an observation that suggested to Richard that she was perhaps a little confused. 'You've cut your hair.' Before he could react she added. 'You can come in. I am just having some tea. Will you have some?' She stepped aside and then called, 'Sandy, come inside you naughty dog.' Sandy continued to ferret. 'Biscuit!' she added. The dog scuttled out from under the foliage and jumped over Richard's feet like one of Nessie's steeplechasers.

She took Richard into the front room through whose net curtains she had peered prior to opening the door.

'Sit there on the sofa where I can see you young man.'

He felt like a distant nephew undertaking his obligatory annual visit to an aged maiden aunt. Once he was perched on the sofa, however, a discreet change came over her. It was as if she were reassured. As if she suddenly felt safe and determined in a course of action. She inspected him frankly. His face, his clothes, his bearing. She poured out tea into a china cup and handed it to him.

'My Terence introduced me to tea without milk. He was quite avant-garde at the time.' She took a sip. 'So much more refreshing, don't you think?'

'Yes.'

'So you are looking for Miss Pye?'

Richard did not like the sound of that.

'Does she still live here?'

'She used to. I had two ladies. There was Miss Pye whom you know and Miss Shapiro. Did you know Miss Shapiro?' Richard shook his head. 'I've been lodging ladies for a few years now. I used to have only professional ladies but they do not care to come out to Ealing now.' She sounded a trifle wistful. 'I try to give them a home from home. Somewhere where they know they can be themselves. Not,' she added sternly, 'that I do not have rules. One cannot run a tidy, happy house without rules.'

Richard wondered where this discourse was leading. Had Jennifer been evicted for breaking the rules? He remembered her fiery temper, her vivacity, her pure energy and could see that in this mothballed time-warp of a house, it could easily have got her into trouble. The hall clock solemnly chimed the quarter.

'I am glad you have come, young man, because I really need some advice. You look as if you have a sensible head upon your shoulders.'

'I will do what I can,' Richard replied with caution. 'Do you know where Jenn... Miss Pye went? Do you have a forwarding address?'

'Possibly, possibly.' She replaced her cup precisely upon the saucer and stood up. Richard also stood up. 'Will you come this way. I wish to show you something.'

'Certainly.' What had he got to lose? She might have her address. He imagined Jennifer's face as she received a letter from him. Or when he turned up on her doorstep.

'Now these are the rooms I let to my ladies,' Mrs. Crowther said as they reached the top of the stairs. 'This was Miss Pye's.' She opened a door onto a largish room equipped as a bedsit. A small square of linoleum sat in the fireplace under the gas fire. The window looked out onto the street in which he had parked. The bed was bare. The few ornaments that were there patently counted as fixtures and fittings.

He looked around the room and imagined Jennifer in that bed, alone. At that sink, washing her hair, maybe. At the cooker, making her breakfast. She watched him silently.

'You have no-one in here at the moment, then?'

'Not since Miss Pye went.'

'When did she go?' Richard was sure that he would know the answer. He was certain that Jennifer would have acted from blind impetuosity when aroused. He could still see her white face in the back of the receding taxi.

'Well, to be honest, I cannot say with any certainty.' Richard was surprised. 'I had gone to my sister's for the weekend, her Reggie was not too well, and when I came back Miss Shapiro was all in a state over something.' She pointed opposite. 'That was Miss Shapiro's room. I think she had boyfriend problems.' She made the observation quite ingenuously. 'And on the Tuesday, I think it was, yes Tuesday, she announced that she was going back to Essex and would I let her out of her month's notice? Well, you can imagine I was quite upset at her cheek but it was nothing compared to Miss Pye's.'

'Oh?'

'Now I would not have thought that of Miss Pye. We had a lovely Christmas together. She appeared to be quite an honest person. Would you not have said that?'

Richard thought of the way that Jennifer had tricked him into thinking that she lived in the flats.

'Oh yes,' he assured her, 'very honest.'

Mrs. Crowther's eyes held his for a moment, and he felt that she was trying to read the truth in them. She indicated the landing and showed him out of Jennifer's room.

'So what did she do?' he asked.

'You can imagine that I was a bit upset by Miss Shapiro leaving so suddenly and it was a few days before I realised that I had not seen Miss Pye since before the weekend. I sometimes sleep later in the mornings now that it is summer.'

'I see,' Richard said untruthfully as he followed her down the stairs, marvelling at the fineness of her white hair.

'They weren't bad young ladies, you understand, but they did make a certain amount of noise going up and down stairs and playing music and such like and I realised after Miss Shapiro had gone that the house was awfully quiet. Even Sandy noticed, didn't you my clever little friend?' She ushered Richard back into the parlour. He waited till she was seated before he reoccupied his place on the sofa. Sandy was utterly ignoring him now. 'And so I did an awful thing.' Richard sat, wondering. 'I took my spare key and I opened her room.' She watched him closely to gauge his reaction to this shocking news.

'It seems to me that that was the only sensible course of action to take.'

'Well I was worried.' Mrs. Crowther appeared relieved. 'She could have been ill, or worse.' She gave a little shudder. 'But she had gone. Just gone.'

'Had she left a note or anything?'

Mrs. Crowther made a little movement.

'No. Well not really. Not a note to me.' She sat back and took a deep breath. 'How well do you know Miss Pye?'

'I thought I was getting to know her,' he said cautiously.

'I don't wish to be indiscreet and, oh this is terrible really.' Her hands were wringing at the apron again. 'You see, she left her things behind and I packed them up into her bags.'

'All her things? Her clothes, books, everything?'

'They are behind you. Behind the sofa. I expected her to come back. At first.'

'How do you mean, 'at first'?'

'She once said something to me which I did not take much notice of at the time. That is to say, I did actually take notice of it but did not realise that she meant it. I thought it was just her way of talking. She could be a little, er, unusual in what she said.'

'What did she say?'

'It was at Christmas. We were having a lovely time and then straight out of the blue she said that she could just up and go one day. She could "leave everything and just get on a plane" I think she said.'

'Is that what you think she has done?'

'The last time I saw her she was walking out of the house with a bag in her hand. I had a strange premonition then. And there was this.' She stood up and went to the sideboard drawer. 'I'm sure you will think me an awful busybody but there was this letter on her table. She had opened it and left it there. It's from her parents. They are in Spain, you know.'

'Yes, she told me.' Richard looked at the sheet and hesitated. He did not know whether he wanted to read it or not.

'Quite a discreet young man aren't you?' Mrs. Crowther took the letter from his hand and perched a pair of specs on her nose. 'This is the important bit. *"Your Mam and I are really excited to hear that you're coming over."* She showed it to him and he waved his hand to say that he did not need to read it. 'Over to Spain, it means.'

'So that's where she's gone.' His voice was quiet. 'And there's no address on the letter? Oh I suppose she threw the envelope away. The address would have been written on the back.'

'Oh do you think so? What a strange idea. I never thought of that.'

They sat looking at each other, each with their own thoughts, not knowing what to say to the other. Then Mrs. Crowther got up and slowly went to the drawer.

'There was something else,' she said mysteriously. 'You are obviously a friend of hers so I will show you. It may help you to decide.' The wisdom of the world was lodged in her watery eyes but it did not appear that she was enjoying the tenancy.

He sat, holding it loosely between his hands, his eyes focused vaguely past it. It was the black and white photograph taken of him in the corridor at Bristol. Ruth must have given it to Jennifer. He recalled Mrs. Crowther's ardent inspection of him upon arrival and the subsequent change in her manner. Mrs. Crowther was nobody's fool and had recognised him from the photo. It was true, he had had his hair cut since then. She had deduced the relationship and they both recognised the importance of Jennifer having left the photo behind.

'What should I do with her things?' she asked. 'Can you take them?'

'It's not her belongings I wanted.'

'I think we have both understood that.'

A voice talking. Talking to her. A hand brushing her eyelashes. Making her blink. Annoying her. Wish it would stop. She would have to tell them. Tongue like a dry twig in a bird's nest. Won't work. Try again.

'Don't,' she croaked.

The teasing stopped. Shapes wavering. Blurry colour coming nearer. A face. A woman's face, lips moving. More bumble sound. She must have opened her eyes slighlty. A round face was looking at her closely. A woman with something white on her head.

'Hullo young lady,' it said. 'You've had a long sleep.'

'Drink.' Her voice grated in her dry mouth.

'I'll swab out your mouth for you. I expect you are a bit dry.'

'Drink,' she said again.

The face reappeared.

'You'll have a drink shortly. I'm going to open your mouth and just wipe it around inside to freshen you up.' She felt something deliciously clean and cool dabbing at parts of her palate and tongue. She still wanted a drink but satisfied herself for the moment with the improvement in her mouth. 'I shall wipe around your eyes for you. Can you see my finger?' She focused vaguely on a white stump held before her. 'Good, you can. That's lovely.'

She could feel a gentle dabbing at her eyelids. Her tongue was looser now. She swallowed and then groaned as the sharp pain hit her from deep inside her throat.

'Who....you?' she whispered.

The face smiled. 'My name is Tara. Hi!'

'What.... you.... doing.... my.... room?' she whispered.

'I am looking after you. You had an accident but you are alright now.'

'Accident?'

'Yes, but you are all sorted out now. All you need to do now is rest.'

'In.... hospital?'

'Yes you are safe in hospital and I am a nurse.'

'Throat.... hurts.'

'That is because we had to put a tube down to help you breath whilst you were asleep. In a minute I will see if I can find something to soothe it. Try not to talk for the present.'

Vague outlines of grey boxes standing around her bed. Plastic bags of fluid hanging above her. Wires and tubes. Dim lights glowing gold in the ceiling. Shapes and shadows of people moving quietly about. Soft voices, the gentle clinking of a metallic object as it was carried across the room. Safe in hospital. Had an accident. All right now.

It was easier now that he knew what he had to accept. He could get on with his life. He had not wanted his last vision of Jennifer to be her anguished face framed by the back window of a departing taxi but he could not change that now. The thing was done. He would have to try to learn from it. There would be somebody else one day.

She was gone that was all there was to it. He felt sorry for Mrs. Crowther, stuck with Jennifer's clothes and things but there was nothing he could do about it. They were not his and he had absolutely no wish to inspect or touch or cherish the artefacts of a relationship now dead. Such fetishism would only serve to stall his life around a period of a few lively and rewarding months. No good could come of that.

Winston was leathering the Daimler when he drove into the brick yard. A thin trickle of water was dribbling its unerring way towards the rhubarb as usual.

'Good afternoon Winston.'

'Good afternoon sir. Shall I pass a sponge over the Yellow Peril?'

'If it offends your sense of cleanliness then please feel free,' Richard replied jauntily. He jumped out and left the keys in the ignition.

Winston nodded. Richard was pleased that he had managed to persuade Winston to drop the 'milord' except when he felt that circumstances unavoidably indicated its use.

'You haven't been out in it for a while.' Winston passed his observation in a voice devoid of tone as if he were forcing himself for politeness' sake to talk about a subject which evoked painful memories in him whilst at the same time, trying to conceal this.

'Ah... No longer the carefree, irresponsible student!' Richard laughed.

EPISODE EIGHTEEN

It had been a strange night. Drifting in and out of sleep to the soporific muffled noises of the room and the indistinct shadows of movement. Occasionally she had realised that somebody was looking at her. A face would materialise out of the gloom above her and then smile reassuringly. As she lay there without moving, she could just see a nurse who bobbed about, attending to the grey boxes which seemed to surround her bed and from which a festoon of wires and tubes reached out towards her like tentacles. At one point she vaguely noticed her coiling up some wires or tubes, she could not distinguish which, and then piling them on top of the box before wheeling the entire contraption away. She surmised that she no longer had a need for that particular piece of equipment and that thought reassured her. If she were really ill they would be adding boxes to her bedside, not taking them away.

She needed reassurance. She felt an intangible fear like an infantile fear of the dark; irrational to an adult mind but oh so real to a child's. A monster, huge and terrifying, lurking somewhere behind her but every time she tried to give it substance it slipped away from her reasoning. She could not pin it down, draw its shape, define its parameters yet she knew it was there, waiting. She was frightened.

The hospital was waking up but here in her section the hubbub was non-existent. Her eyesight was becoming less blurred now. Over near the entrance a small group of nurses were taking over from the night staff. Listening soberly to reports and reading charts handed to them. Sometimes nodding, sometimes asking more questions. She could see her nurse from yesterday, what was her name? Tara, pulling her tunic briskly from below her belt buckle and checking her pockets. She would ask Tara. Tara would help her, she would understand.

'Hi!   How are you this morning?'

She must have dozed off again. She studied the smiling round face. 'Bit tired,' she said slowly. 'Your name Tara?'

'Right!' The face lit up. 'Well done. That's me, Tara. I have been looking after you with two of my friends.' She moved around the bed, inspecting the machines. 'Your throat still hurts a bit, I expect. Did that ice cream last night make any difference?'

'Yes. Lovely.'

'I'll get you some more today. As soon as we have got you feeding better we'll be able to take away some of these.' She waved vaguely at the tentacles and then picked up a clipboard from the chair. 'Now that you are back with us I've got some paperwork to do with you. It won't take long. I'll stop before you get tired. O.K.?'

The fear again. She wanted to say 'no'. She wanted to shout, 'no!' but she was not a child, just an adult frightened like a child. A child would refuse, an adult has to face up to the fear, to the dread.

'Yes, O.K.'

Tara hovered for a minute. 'I can come back later.'

'No. Let's get it over with.' Each word was an effort but not as difficult as it had been yesterday after having woken up.

'Right. O.K. then.' Tara pulled the chair around and sat close up to the bed and leaned over so that they could talk without effort. 'We were a bit rushed when you came in so we need a few details.' She looked at the clipboard. 'Your name's Magdaline O'Neill, right? Any other names?'

'Magdaline O'Neill.' She sounded the words silently around her mouth. 'Magdaline O'Neill.' She heard them in her head. Then that was her own voice saying the name. 'Magdaline O'Neill.'

Tara looked at her closely. 'So, no other names then?'

The monster was looming behind her, breathing down her neck. She would fend it off, keep it away for the another day.

'What happened to Magdaline O'Neill?' She said the name again.

'Do you remember what happened?'

'No.'

'You had an accident. A car accident.'

That was strange. 'Was I driving?'

'No, you were crossing the road. You were knocked over. By a car, we think.'

'By a car?'

'We think so. We don't really know. It didn't stop.'

'When? Last night?'

'Not last night, no. You've been asleep for a while.'

'Asleep? You mean unconscious?'

'Yes. You were brought in unconscious and we sorted you out and now you have woken up.'

'In a coma?'

'Yes, you were in a coma, if you like. It's the same thing.'

'How long?'

'Well you were brought in towards the end of May.'

May? May? That meant nothing without today's date. Fear bubbling up again. Why did she say 'May' and not 'yesterday'? Must ask.

'What is date today?'

'It's the 8th. of July. You were in a coma for about six weeks.'

Tara paused for a moment and thought hard. This was not reassuring the patient in any way, if anything it was having the opposite effect. She watched the blue eyes casting about the room. The last thing the hospital wanted was for her to relapse. Perhaps she should try later. 'Shall I leave it for the moment Magdaline?' Tara started in alarm. The girl's eyes had anxiety in them.

'Where was the accident?' Her voice was faint.

'I don't know. Somewhere in North London.'

'Tell me.'

'I honestly don't know.' Tara felt helpless. This was obviously important to the girl.

'I must know.'

'I'll tell you what I can do, Magdaline. I can ask the policeman who was involved in the case. He's on duty today. I'll ring him and ask him this morning. Is that O.K.?'

The girl closed her eyes in acquiescence. She began to nod off to sleep again. Tara checked her pulse on the monitor.

It was high. She walked over to the desk. One of her colleagues was reading a computer screen and hitting the keyboard in a desultory fashion.

'How's it going with Sleeping Beauty?'

'I'm not certain. She's not really with us yet. I must phone the police and find out where she was knocked down. It seems to be important to her.'

'Any excuse to ring your boyfriend, eh?'

'No. it's not that,' Tara refused to rise to the bait. 'I reckon she's in a trauma of some sort.'

'Hardly surprising. You'd better hurry, H. B. is coming in this morning to see her.'

'That's all I needed.'

H.B. Massingham was the surgeon who had operated. He was completely unlike the popular view of a surgeon. He did not appear erudite and with a delicate precision in his movements; he was big and bluff with a ruddy face and an old sports jacket. One would expect him to be more at home with a pitch fork than a scalpel. He was jovial sometimes to the point of nausea, as if convinced that his patients would heal quicker from his humour than from his hands. And he hummed. He hummed to himself when he was not talking. He hummed when he was operating. He drove any assistant to the point of murder. More than one anaesthetist had been tempted to give him a few puffs just to stop the unrelenting drone. Others had considered ear plugs. His initials, H.B., had earned him the soubriquet of Humming Bird Massingham. He was as blithely unaware of this, as he was of the effect of his humming.

Tara phoned Andy. He had given her a direct number to avoid her having to go through that infuriating central control room which re-routed the calls. She waited whilst somebody went to fetch him. In the background she could hear them calling him on his personal radio, asking him to come to a phone. She glanced back at the girl lying there amidst the paraphernalia of intensive care. Sleeping Beauty. She must have been pretty once and probably would be again but her cropped hair and drawn grey face would hardly attract a Prince Charming now. What was it like to sleep for six weeks? Sometimes when she came off duty she wished that she could do exactly that.

'Hi, Andy?'

'Speaking.'

'It's me. Tara.'

'Oh hi Tara. I thought it was official. You'll have to be quick.'

'It is official. You know the hit and run girl?'

'Oh yeah. The one in a coma.'

'She came round last night. Do you still need to talk to her?'

'I suppose so. Yes, we will do at some stage. There's not much hope of finding the driver now of course but she may give us something to go on.'

'You won't be able to see her until the doctor has agreed. That won't be at least until tomorrow.'

'O.K. I'll note her file. Will you let us know when we can interview her or shall we keep ringing?'

'We will let you know.'

'Thanks.'

'Andy? Could you do something for me?'

'Probably.'

'Where was she knocked down? She wants to know really badly. It's kind of upsetting her, not knowing.'

'Hang on, I think it was somewhere up in Finsbury. Near Clerkenwell Road or Farringdon Road. That sort of area. I can find out exactly and ring you back.'

'No that's all right. I think that will be enough for her. Thanks.' She replaced the receiver. Well that was something positive she could tell her. Let's hope it is what she wants to hear.

A farmer, peering at her. She must be lying in a meadow. Big bristly grey whiskers and a red face. Another face behind him. One she knew. What was that face doing out here? Thought she worked in a hospital.

'Tara.'

Big smile from the nurse.

'Hello Magdaline. You've had another sleep. This is...'

'Massingham,' the farmer said. 'Come to see how you are. You gave us a bit of a fright, young lady, sleeping for so long.' He was wagging his finger at her.

'How long?' How long for Christ's sake? Not another coma. How long this time? Was it still July? Which year was it now? Was she going to spend the rest of her life in comas? 'How long this time?'

'Six weeks, wasn't it nurse?' the voice boomed.

'Yes, but I've already...'

He didn't wait for Tara to finish. 'Mustn't do that again must we? Don't want to miss the summer! Right, lift back the covers nurse and let's have a look at this leg.'

Leg? Leg? Why not legs? Can't see under the cage. How many legs? God, they've cut one of my legs off.

'Just wiggle your toes, lassie.'

Wiggle all my toes. Both legs. See what they say to that.

'Splendid, splendid. Can you feel that?'

'Yes.' But why don't you touch the toes on the other leg? I can still feel that I am wiggling them but are they still there? It's well known that people can still feel that the limb is there even after it has been cut off. Must ask him. Not scared of monsters.

'Have I got...?'

'Yes, your leg was broken. I've put a plate in and you'll be hopping about in no time at all.'

Hopping? Hopping?

'Thank you nurse. Let's have a look at this collar bone.'

What about my leg? Tara doesn't look happy. Why is she upset? Why didn't she tell me? She knew. She knew all the time. Hands folding back covers. Wires on my chest.

'You can take the ECG off. No problem there now.'

'Yes sir.'

Big hands feeling my shoulders and neck. Big hands but gentle hands.

'A splendid set. Splendid. You've done well. Good. All you have to do now is do what the nursing staff tell you and you will get strong and healthy again and then we can get you back home as quickly as we can. That's what you want isn't it?'

Back home. Monsters. Monsters around me. Monsters snarling and lunging.

'I'll come and see you again soon to check how your are going along. Right nurse, ring up to Dalton's and tell them to expect me in ten minutes.'

Tara, come back. Don't leave me.

H. B. Massingham strode out of the unit, broadcasting his requirements right and left in a stentorian voice full of vitality and bonhommie. 'Tea, two sugars, in 117. And ring Dalton's.'

Tara turned to her companion at the desk.

'Ring Dalton's for me would you?'

'He told you to.'

'Just do it,' she commanded with such ferocity that the telephone was snatched on a startled reflex.

She could see the high pulse on the monitor even as she hurried back to the bed. If she didn't calm this girl down she would start to hyperventilate and heaven knows what complications would ensue.

'All right Magdaline, this is Tara.'

'Tara.'

'Yes, I'm here now.' The girl's eyes settled on her face. She was focusing a lot better today. Some colour had risen to her grey cheeks, giving them an unreal glow. Almost a luminescence.

'Who was the man?'

'That was our Mr. H. B. Massingham. He is a very good surgeon but a lousy psychologist.'

'What did he say about my leg? Where is the other one?'

'The other one?' Tara was confused.

'He said I would hop. He's cut one off hasn't he?'

'What? Of course he hasn't.' No wonder she was upset. 'Look. I'll take the covers off the cage. There. Isn't that two legs?'

'Yes.'

'Wriggle your toes. See, they are all working aren't they?'

'Yes.'

'And they are all yours aren't they?' Well at least that got the beginnings of a smile, she thought. 'Now what else? Come on, don't hold back. I can't help you if you don't help me.'

'What is the date today?'

'The same as it was this morning when I told you. The same day – the 8th. of July.'

'Promise?'

'I'll get someone else you can ask if you don't believe me.' She got up and bearded her long suffering colleague who watched her approach warily. 'Sorry I snapped, Sis, I had to get back to Magdaline as soon as I could. Old Humming Bird had left her in a terrible state, the ignorant slob.'

'Cream cake.'

'Cream cake,' Tara agreed the price. 'Can you just come over to Magdaline?'

'Now? What for?'

'She wants to ask a question. It's very important to her.'

The nurse raised her eyebrows and pursed her lips.

'O.K.'

They walked over to the bed. 'Now Magdaline, this is a friend of mine. She doesn't know what you are going to ask, do you Sis?'

'No. I don't know whether I will know the answer.'

'You should do. Magdaline?'

'What is the date today please?'

'Is that it? It's the 8th. July. Is that all you wanted to know?'

Magdaline nodded slowly.

'Thanks Sis. Cream cake.'

Magdaline watched the nurse go.

'Satisfied?' Tara asked.

'Yes.'

'Now you know you can trust me. What else do you want to know? I should think you must be bursting with questions.' Magdaline smiled again slightly. 'Now that's better. A smile makes everyone feel better.'

'Just one coma then?'

'Yes, you had just one coma. You were unconscious when you were brought in to Casualty. You had a broken collar bone, a cracked femur and you were bruised and grazed in several places. Mr. Massingham operated on your leg, putting in a plate to hold it together and we bound up your neck and shoulder to allow your collar bone to set itself which it apparently has done to the satisfaction of Mr. Massingham. So that is all good news, isn't it?'

'Yes.'

'Right. I am allowed to sit you up slightly so that you can see a bit more and I shall take these dots off you.'

'Dots?'

'These things with the three wires on. It's the ECG. It monitors your heartbeat.' She smoothly altered the angle of the pillow rest. 'But we don't need it now.' She began to peel the dots from her skin.

Magdaline looked around the room slowly.

'Is this an intensive care unit?'

'Yes but very soon you will go to the HDU, the High Dependency Unit, now that you are conscious. Depending on how quickly you get back your strength you will go from there on to the ward. That will be more fun. More people to see.' She wheeled the ECG monitor into a bay. 'Oh and I phoned the police about your accident. It was in Farringdon Road or Clerkenwell Road, somewhere near there. Does that help?'

'Farringdon Road,' she repeated without inflexion.

Tara looked at her carefully. Farringdon Road meant nothing to her. 'Because of your accident the police might want to come and interview you.'

'Interview me.'

'Ask you questions about what happened.'

'What did happen?'

Tara paused to think. It would be quite possible to do as much damage as Massingham had done if she were not careful. The patient was certainly in trauma and as Sis had observed, this was not very surprising. Waking up to find the world had moved six weeks further on would be a shock to anybody.

'Don't worry about it. We'll see what happens when the police do come.' She picked up the clipboard. 'Now let's do something useful. Because we knew nothing about you we haven't been able to tell your family or your friends and I am sure you would like them to come and visit you now, wouldn't you?' The girl did not answer but looked about her wildly. 'Or ring them? We can bring a phone to you. So, what about your mum and dad, where do they live?'

The girl looked at Tara as if expecting a clue. Then her eyes began to wander vacantly around the room.

'No,' she said.

'No? Do you mean no mum or dad?'

'I don't know,' she whispered.

'What about friends? Boyfriend?' There was no wedding ring in her belongings so she would not ask about a husband.

'I don't know.' Her eyes were frightened now. 'A mirror. I want a mirror. Please.'

'Right. O.K. I'll see if I can find you a mirror.'

She got up and went to the desk.

'Have you got a mirror in that cupboard, Sis?'

'Shouldn't think so for one minute. What do you want it for?' Tara nodded towards the bed behind her. 'Well she must be feeling better if she's worried about her appearance.'

'I don't think it is that. I've got a feeling it's something else.'

'Are you worried about her?'

'Yes. And intrigued.'

'Look you can borrow my make-up mirror. Any use?'

'Perfect.'

The girl accepted the mirror but held it face down on the bedclothes. Tara watched her, anxiously. 'Is that what you want? It's a bit small. Sis lent it to me. I shall have to give it back.'

Slowly the girl dragged the mirror up her chest and then held it away from her and solemnly inspected her face.

'Magdaline O'Neill,' she said. 'Magdaline O'Neill.'

The dowager Countess of Wisdene pinched the slice of lemon in a pair of silver tongs and placed it into her tea cup.

'Milk or lemon Richard?'

Richard dropped the country periodical to a dark wood table, tucked his thumbs into the belt of his summer flannels and turned around. 'Lemon please mother.'

He then collapsed noisily into a comfortable chair. His mother frowned but with a martyred indulgence, as a mother would to a talented child who occasionally displayed an annoying streak of impudence. She addressed her other son who was intently studying the park through one of the enormous windows.

'Charles?'

'Milk please mother. What would you say to a plantation of conifers just over the ridge by Spruce's?'

She finished pouring the tea and set the silver teapot down with great deliberation. It was heavy.

'Your father always said that he never wanted to see a conifer from the Hall.' She tried not to say it but she had to. When you have lived with a man for so long you knew what he thought and desired almost as soon as he did. You could not just wipe that out when he was no longer there. It was still a valid reason. More so, perhaps.

Charles nodded quietly to himself as he sat down.

'You would hardly see it. Just the bottom end,' he said.

'Why do you want conifers?' Richard asked.

'Quick growing. Timber. Money.'

'What does Courtney think, Charles?' The Countess fussed with a doily on the tray.

'I haven't asked him. Do you think I should?'

'We employ him as Estate Manager,' she reminded him a little acidly.

'Mother, if you eventually want me to take over the running of the estate you've got...'

'I want you to, Charles, not mother. I asked you to do it and you know why. It should be my job but I don't want it and you'll make a good job of it. Much better than I ever could. It's what you have always secretly wanted isn't it?'

Charles looked down at his foot which was tracing a pattern on the Persian carpet. He smiled almost guiltily.

'Yes. Yes, I always wanted to run the estate. From as far back as I can remember.'

'Well I have never wanted to run the estate from as far back as I can remember.

'Richard!'

'It's true, Mother, you know it is. Father knew it as well, deep down inside himself, didn't he?'

'Well I don't know.'

'I am sure you do, Mother. He was content for his elder son to waste his life daubing on canvasses in London for a while because he knew that his other son had long been training himself to take over the mantle.'

'Was it wasted then, Richard, your time in London?'

For a shocked moment he could see Jennifer's landlady's eyes in his mother's face. Pale blue and watery. Undecided, tired, saddened. He leaned across and took his mother's hands in his. They seemed to have become suddenly frail.

'In terms of the estate it was wasted. But I needed to do it for myself.'

'In that case, Richard, we will not consider it wasted.'

'Well, we shall see. We shall see. In the meantime we all have some adjustments to make but it will get easier. Charles will work with Courtney, won't you Charles?'

'I can do nothing without him.'

'And Charles will have his own ideas.'

'It's his ideas that we were...'

Richard held up his hand and his mother stopped.

'He will have his own ideas, just as father did,' he finished with emphasis.

'Yes, yes, I see.' She did not tell Richard that what she could see were the qualities of the father beginning to manifest themselves in the son.

'And so will I have my ideas and thanks to Charles taking over the reins here, I shall be free to try out my ideas and he will be free to try out his.'

'And what shall I do in this great scheme of things?' she sighed.

'You will box our ears when we go wrong, Mother, as you always did. Now, how did the fete go?'

'Just ten minutes Andy then I must go.' Tara Hughes nodded through the pub window at the barracks of the hospital. 'I'm on at three.'

'Yes, I must get back as well. What are you doing Saturday afternoon?'

'What are you offering?'

'Fancy a trip on the river?' he asked diffidently.

'Depends. Where to?'

'Barnes to Kew and back.'

'What for?'

'Met. v. City annual rowing race.'

'This is policemen is it?'

Andy grinned sheepishly. She liked his smile.

'Yes it's policemen. Metropolitan Police versus the City Police. From Barnes up river to Kew, round the island and then back again. Dinner and disco afterwards, if you fancy it.'

'What about this boat we will be on? Is it a proper one? Has it got seats and a roof in case it rains? And what about a bar?'

'The boat you will be on will have seats and an awning. There's no bar but you can take your own beer. The boat I shall be on will have seats, no cover and no bar but it will have oars.'

'You mean you are rowing in this race?' She imagined him in shorts. Thought of his legs and tried to guess how strong they were.

''Fraid so. Number three.'

'Am I allowed to cheer?'

'You're obliged to. You will be thrown to the sharks if you don't.'

'All right then, you're on.'

'Great. At least something has gone right today.'

'Oh?'

'Your Miss O'Neill,' he said ruefully.

'Oh you've been to see her have you? How's she getting on? I've been out on a course for four days.'

'Just saw her this morning.'

'She'd be in the ward by now. Where have they put her?'

'What?'

'Which ward is she in? They were talking of putting her in Women's Med. I think they were full in Orthopaedic.'

'I don't know, it had yukky yellow walls. Wherever she was she was not a lot of use. In fact, no use at all. She can't remember a thing about it. She just sort of looked at me and kept saying, 'I don't know. I can't remember' all the while.'

'Often happens. 'Don't know what hit me' they often say. 'One minute I was walking down the road, the next I was waking up in hospital'. It's fairly common. I suppose you'll just close the case now? You said at the start that you didn't have anything to go on.'

'Bit of a wasted journey, though.'

'Oh thank you very much! That's what you think of me!'

'Don't be daft. Anyway, you've got to go now or you'll be late. I'll ring you about Saturday.'

The girl in the next bed was reading a magazine. Magdaline watched her eyes flicking back and forth across the columns. She had unusual, slanty eyes. Brown, with long lashes. Her hair was brown also. Cut short and neat to her head. But it did not make her look boyish. Suddenly she realised that the eyes had stopped flicking and were looking at her.

'Oh, so you are awake then? My name's Lynne. What's your name?'

Magdaline shut her eyes quickly. No more questions. Please, no more questions. Too many questions with no answers.

Name? Magdaline O'Neill. Date of birth? Date of birth? I don't know. Everyone knows their date of birth, dear. Date of birth? 8th. July. Which year? 8th. July. Address? I don't know. You're not helping me dear, where do you live then? In hospital. Parents? I don't think so. Religion? I don't know. I'll put C. of E. then.

What make was the vehicle? I don't know. Was it a car? I don't know. What colour was it then? I don't know. Where were you going? I don't know. Were you alone? I don't know. Where do you live? I don't know. What work do you do? I don't know. Got any friends? Got any friends? I don't know. I don't know. I don't know.

What is wrong with me? Am I ill? Am I cured? Am I dead? Is this what being dead is like? Being somewhere that you shouldn't be and not knowing why you are there. Perhaps it is all a dream. Perhaps I am in hospital. Perhaps I have had an operation and I am dreaming under the anaesthetic. I shall wake up soon and... but that's no good. I'll still be in hospital and I won't know if I am dreaming or not. Everyone seems to expect answers from me but it is all about another time. What was the other time? Has there been another time with me in it? Have I gone back in time? Have I gone into the future? Am I living the life of my future grandchildren? If it is a time before, before what? Perhaps I am not dead, perhaps I have not been born yet. Is this how life starts? How can they expect all this knowledge from me if I haven't been born yet?

'I only came in for a twisted knee.' Magdaline opened her eyes. The girl, Lynne, was talking to her. 'I only came in for a twisted knee,' she repeated and slapped the magazine down on her bed. 'Playing squash. It should have been a let but I got all my feet tied up and went down with a bang. It didn't half hurt and then when they tried to sort my knee out they discovered that I had really buggered it up. "Tendons and ligaments and cartilage all over the place", they said.'

'Oh.'

'God knows what is happening to my flat. I've just moved. Two beds, dining, kitchen and bathroom. And some really clever fitted cupboards in unusual places. You know what I mean, really useful? I think that makes a flat, don't you? Of course, it's too much for me alone but I was going to advertise for a sharer but then this – wham!' She indicated her legs. 'Do you want the mag. to read?' She leaned over and offered the magazine. Magdaline reached out and took it automatically.

'Thank you.'

'It's the boredom that gets to you eventually. I was glad when you turned up. I thought, "at last, somebody under the age of ninety to talk to".' She looked pointedly around the ward and then back at Magdaline and rolled her eyes theatrically. 'You had a car accident didn't you?'

'Yes.'

'I saw the copper. He came to talk to you. Sexy wasn't he?'

Magdaline heard the dreaded phrase "I don't know" in her subconscious again and hated it. Then she checked herself. Why should she say "I don't know"? She did know. This was something that she did know. 'Yes he was, rather. I liked his long eyelashes.' She smiled.

'Gorgeous. We've got a messenger in our office like that. All casual and diffident but with gorgeous eyes. All the girls are mad about him but he doesn't realise.'

'Where do you work?'

'Janus and Janus. Advertising agency. There's a couple of ours in that mag. That shampoo one with the blonde swinging through the trees like tarzan, that's one of ours. Of course, she didn't really swing through the trees, it's all done with collage and airbrush. "Image manipulation" it's called.'

'Is that what you do?'

'No, not me. I'm not creative, apparently. I negotiate ad. space. Spend all my day on the phone arguing with newspapers, magazines, billboards and TV to try to get the best deal. What do you do?'

She could hear the nurse's voice. 'What do you want to know about yourself, Magdaline? We can't tell you much. You spent the night before your accident in a hostel for the homeless. You've got no possessions and hardly a penny to your name.'

'I'm not working,' Magdaline replied.

'Oh bad luck. I had a spell out of work, it was awful. Everybody I knew had money and jobs and I had nothing. Nothing to do all day long. The worst bit is feeling rejected all the while, isn't it?'

'Yes.'

'You keep applying and you're certain that you are the right person for the job and then you don't even get on the shortlist. Time and again it happens, it's awful. Still, you'll get a job when you get out. Do you do sport? Badminton? Squash?'

'No.'

'Only I thought with your hair so short like that you were probably well into sport or something.'

'I think they had to cut it here, in hospital.'

'You were in a coma weren't you?'

'Yes.'

'One of the nurses told me. Over a month wasn't it?'

'Six weeks.'

'What was it like? I suppose you don't know really.'

'No.'

'Like going to bed and waking up six weeks later. Weird!'

'Yes. Weird.'

'Still, you're alright now aren't you?'

'Yes, I'm alright now except that...'

'Except what?'

'I think I've lost my memory.'

'Wow! How romantic! Can't you remember anything?'

'I don't remember the accident. They said I was knocked down by a hit and run. I don't remember anything that happened before the accident. I don't know what I was doing, where I was going at the time or anything like that.'

'What about your family then?'

'I obviously don't have any. Nobody has claimed me.'

'Where do you live then?'

'I was living in a hostel. Look!' Magdaline carefully pulled out a slip of paper from the drawer in her bedside table. '"*Our Lady Hostel, Shoreditch. One Bed. Magdaline O'Neill*". And my entire fortune consists of this watch and two pounds thirty four pence. All my clothes were destroyed when they cut them from me. All I've got is this cap. I'd look fine walking down the street dressed in just that, wouldn't I?'

She was laughing but she did not know why.

EPISODE NINETEEN

'Thank you Mrs. Dove.' Vanessa Clewe-Harting took the tray and placed it on the boardroom table before her.

Mrs. Dove smiled thinly. 'There's hardly room for your coffee.'

'Yes,' Vanessa said, 'I'm a terribly messy worker. I wish I were neat like you.'

'Each to her own.' Mrs. Dove closed the door behind her.

Vanessa scratched her head, trying to puzzle out the meaning of her words but failed. She shrugged and pulled absently at the string of pearls at the neck of her suit and gazed out of the window. The sinuous snake of a train insinuated itself between some sidings, sliding its way to Reading station. She puffed up her cheeks and expelled her breath quietly. The oval shape of the table was buried under a mass of papers, folders and files. The door opened again. It was Richard.

'How's it going, Nessie?' He sat on the table.

'I see what you mean about your Mrs. Dove. She's full of resentment about something. I don't think she likes me here.'

'You're my personal assistant old fruit. Can't do without you. Anyway if Mrs. Dove was upset before she will be fuming in a minute. Anatole says that we must put you on the payroll or pay you a consultancy fee. Something to do with the insurance.'

'Nothing to do with my value, then?'

'None whatsoever. You know we could never pay you your full worth.' Vanessa raised a file, menacingly, waiting for the punch line. 'They don't make coins that small.' Richard put up a hand to defend himself. 'No, seriously though, Nessie, if you want to help me and you are still willing to give the time then we will have to officially appoint you as my PA.'

'Are you offering me a job?'

'I'm offering you the one you've been doing unofficially.'

Vanessa looked at Richard, perched on the corner of the table. He seemed to have quickly adapted to the role of entrepreneur-businessman. She wondered how long it would last.

'O.K.' she said.

'Great! I'll get Anatole to work something out salary wise and ask Mrs. Dove to do the papers. She'll need your National Insurance number and stuff like that.' He slipped off the table and strode over to the window. 'What do you think of the set up?'

'The set up?'

He turned and swept his arm around in an arc. 'All this.'

Vanessa's eyes wandered over the dark panelling, the cream gloss, the gilt mirror. 'It's a bit stodgy.'

Richard nodded. 'Just like the firm. Stodgy. Look at it! A few dusty rooms in the back of beyond.' He lowered his voice and glanced conspiratorially at the closed door. 'And the odd fossil or two.' He waved at the room again. 'We've almost certainly got better properties than this in our portfolio. We're a dinosaur sitting on a golden egg.'

'It would crack it.'

'You know what I mean. What sort of image do you think this projects?'

'What sort of image do you want to project? It depends whom you want to impress and what you want to impress them with. First of all, who comes here? Your clients?'

'No, probably not.'

'Well they can't tell what it is like from your address can they? Lots of businesses have great sounding addresses for their one room over the tobacconist's.'

Richard kicked absently at the leg of a chair.

'Yes, I suppose so. I just think that we should have a bit of a showcase office if we are a property company.'

'But that depends on how you see the purpose of the office. If it is there merely so that you can function as a viable business unit then surely it is already achieving that? Isn't it?'

'Well, yes. I suppose it is. We are still in the black. I haven't noticed any major cock-ups. Although,' Richard smiled, 'I'm sure they would be capable of hiding them from me.'

'No doubt.'

'Thank you.'

'My pleasure.'

'But are we to be just viable? "Just viable." It doesn't sound very inspiring. The thing is, Nessie, there doesn't seem to be anything going on here. It's like a morgue!'

'Many office workers would give their right arm to work in a quiet office like this.'

'Would they?'

'Yes they would. I know, I've worked in offices.'

Richard grunted. Vanessa watched him as he walked back to the window again. There was something about him. Some unease, some irritation. A frustration of some sort seemed to be pecking at him. Why did he appear dissatisfied with what his father had created? Was it a real dissatisfaction or did he feel the need to stamp his character on the business just as his father had done? She had no doubt that he would succeed in the firm, if he stuck at it. That was the problem, getting him to stick at it. Most people had expected him to take over the running of the estate. She approved of his arrangement with Charles for she had known them both a long time and Richard had always been careful to channel his own enthusiasm towards the less agricultural aspects of the estate such as the cricket match, the Christmas Feasten arrangements and such like.

What had he ever expressed an interest in? She supposed that the nearest that he had come was that flirting with the art set in Chelsea. She recalled the earnestness on his face when she had watched him painting the Monet. She was sure that he had been happy then, or at least, not agitated as he was now. Perhaps it was just his way of grieving for his father. It must be unpleasant to be reminded of the absence of your father in the hundred little details of your daily work.

'I was reading something in the Sunday colour section,' he said suddenly. 'About a chap who turned his business around.'

'Oh yes?'

'He got a Harvard Business School book and worked through it on his own. Apparently it worked a charm.'

'Is that what you want to do?'

'There was one thing he did which sounded like a dose of common sense to me. He analysed how much time his staff took doing certain aspects of the job. How much time they spent moving stuff from one bench to another. How much time lifting.

He found out that a lot of what they were actually doing was not making any positive contribution to the end product.'

'Americans were always keen on time and motion studies.'

'I have been thinking about what actually goes on here and how much of it makes the money at the end of the day. How long, for example, do you think that Piers Lansing spends every day in reading the local newspapers? What about Harry Meachem on the phone to foremen? If we are hiring a foreman shouldn't he be doing the sorting out of problems, not Harry? And what Anatole Worstop does all day long is a mystery to everybody, including himself, I sometimes think.'

'Do you want to find out?'

'It might be interesting. For me and for them.'

'Who is going to ask Mrs. Dove what she does all day long, you or me?'

'Ah. It's not easy being master of the ship, is it?'

'No capt'n.'

The occupational therapist had tried to interest Magdaline in making a basket but without success so she had left her a pad of paper and a ball point pen, in case she wanted to write any letters.

Who to? Magdaline thought. Who can I write to? Her pen doodled a sketched profile of Lynne's head as she pored over a magazine in the bed next to Magdaline. If I knew who I could write to I wouldn't be in this mess. What a position to be in! Imagine having pen and paper and no-one to write to. She flicked the pen slightly on the paper to make Lynne's eyelashes. I don't understand why I feel so resentful. I have lost something but I don't know what. For all I know I might be better without it. This is what I am. I must make the best of it. She hardened up the chin and marked a curve for the nostril. Anybody would feel the same if they had had their memory taken away. In Victorian times I would have been a rich princess found wandering and sheltered in some hovel where I would fall in love with the woodman's son and then I would be discovered and taken off to my kingdom but I would return and marry him against the wish of my father but we would live happily ever after and my people would see how love had triumphed over the difference in our backgrounds and they would be content. But that is a fairy tale. No one can live in a fairy tale. She dropped the pad to the top of the cupboard.

A nursing assistant in a yellow tunic bustled up to the foot of her bed. 'Right then, Maggie, I'm taking you to see Dr. Brady.'

Magdaline looked up, suddenly realising that the girl was talking to her. 'My name's Magdaline, not Maggie.'

'O.K. Magdaline. Do you want the chair or crutches?'

A nurse hurried past, talking over her shoulder to the assistant as she went, 'And after you've done that, see if you can sort out Mrs. Wood. She's complaining about her pillow rest.'

'I'll try the crutches,' Magdaline decided. 'Doctor said I was alright on them if I went slowly.'

'In that case it's the chair. I haven't got the time to go slowly.'

Magdaline opened her mouth to argue but the girl had already gone to fetch the wheelchair.

Dr. Brady was a portly man in his fifties wearing a grey suit which nearly fitted him. On his broad forehead was a red mark as if he had brushed back his hair with a paint smeared hand. She did not know whether it was a skin graft, a burn or a birth mark but she felt her eyes drawn back to it whilst he was speaking to her. He could have hidden it had he wanted, his greying hair was still thick enough to be combed down over the front.

When she was not looking at his forehead, she was watching him fiddle with a gold signet ring, pulling it up to the knuckle and then sliding it back down again as if deciding whether or not to pawn it. When he turned his swivel chair sideways, she could see where his trousers were creased behind the knees and his jacket folded across the back, proof of his sedentary life style. She could not remember his full title but it was something like 'clinical neurologist'.

He had already introduced himself to her in the ward. He had asked her a few gently probing questions which she had been quite incapable of answering and then they had played some boring games with words and numbers.

He pulled an open file across his desk and glanced at a note. 'Good morning, Miss O'Neill. Do you remember who I am?'

Panic. Do I remember? Of course I do. Why shouldn't I?

'Yes, you're Dr. Brady.' He nodded as he discreetly wrote a short comment on the file. 'Anyway, it's written on your door.'

He turned and looked at her and then at the door as if he had seen it for the first time. 'Hm. Quite. Well there's nothing wrong with your powers of observation.' He paused as if unsure where he was going. 'So how do you think you are doing?'

How do I think I am doing? Magdaline boggled at the concept. How do I think I am doing? How could I know?

'I don't know how I'm doing.'

'You're not walking yet?'

'I would be if I had crutches. I'm in the chair to save time.'

'Right. Right. Have you... er... recalled anything more?'

'I haven't recalled anything.' Magdaline could feel her voice rising in a beginning of anxiety. 'I've lost my memory haven't I? When will I get it back? When will I ever get it back?'

'Would you like a cup of coffee?' He pushed a buzzer on his desk. 'Or do you prefer tea?'

'No, coffee would be a nice change. We only ever get tea in the ward.' Magdaline found his manner distracting.

A young lad poked his head around the door. 'Ya?'

'Coffee for two please, Gerhard.' The door closed and Dr. Brady smiled. 'Wonderful thing the Common Market. Now we get students from everywhere.' He looked at her file again and tapped his pen decisively on the paper. 'When will you get back your memory, you want to know? Understandable. Of course you want to know. We don't know how much of your memory you have lost yet, if indeed it is lost. It rarely is completely lost, you understand, merely mislaid. It is quite common for a patient to lose some memory after an accident involving a blow to the head. Usually you cannot remember the accident. Sometimes you cannot remember what you were doing for a couple of hours before the accident, but it always comes back eventually.'

'But I cannot remember anything at all before the accident. I don't remember my family, where I lived – anything!'

'That is not strictly true as I will show you in a moment. Let me explain what I can do for you. I'm a neurologist. I deal with nerves, not with the mind. You had an MRI scan last week.'

'That was when I was put in that tunnel thing?'

'That's right. It takes a magnetic picture of your brain. I have seen the results and I can see no physical damage there.' She said nothing, calculating the importance of what he was saying. 'That is good news, Miss O'Neill.'

'Yes. Thank you doctor.'

He looked at her. 'There is an awful lot of rubbish talked

about amnesia, you know. I expect you've been to the cinema
and seen films where the heroine gets bumped on the head just
at the wrong moment and forgets everything until something
reminds her in the nick of time and it all comes flooding back?'

'Yes.'

'The problem is that we, the medical profession, we just do not
know what memory is or how it works. My medical opinion is
demanded,' he indicated the file before him, 'I would say that you
were suffering from retrograde amnesia caused by a blow to the
head. It's called retrograde because you cannot remember what
happened before you were hit on the head, can you?'

'No,'

'Do you remember the tests we did last week? The digit span
test when I gave you those numbers to remember? And the
words?' She nodded. 'That was to test what we would call your
"short term memory". And it was obviously all right, wasn't it?'
She did not know whether she had to agree or not. 'You could
remember the numbers and the words, couldn't you? She
nodded. 'But I bet you can't remember them now, can you?'

'Of course not.'

'Of course not. Neither can I. Because you don't need to
remember those numbers, you forget them. Or decide to no
longer remember them. That is your short term memory working.
Human beings use their STM, as we call it, to remember things
instantly, for example, directions on how to get to my office. You
remember them for the short time to enable you to get here.'

'The girl pushed me in a chair. I didn't have to remember.'

'No. I was just using that as an example. You remember a
thing in your short term memory and if you need it again, you
transfer it to long term memory. Now we don't know exactly
how this happens. It might be by repeating it. In this case, for
example, by coming here more often you would learn the route
and put it into your long term memory.'

'Oh.'

'You can remember what has happened to you since you came
out of your coma can't you?'

'Yes.'

'So you can remember things that you want to.'

He was fiddling with his ring again.

'Yes, I suppose I can.'

'Good. What is unusual in your case is that the retrograde amnesia has lasted so long. In many cases it only lasts for a few minutes, in some cases, a few seconds. Perhaps being in a coma has somehow reinforced the amnesia. Six weeks is a long period of unconsciousness for a mind and shows the possible severity of the trauma. Of the upset. In time we will see I am sure, that your LTM, your long term memory, is functioning but that your retrograde amnesic effect is preventing you from gaining access to a part of it. Do you understand what I am saying?'

'Not really. Do you mean that I will get my memory back?'

He swivelled his chair back to the desk, studied the file for a second and then pushed his chair away and got up.

'Nobody can assure you that you will get your memory back, but are you sure that you have lost it?'

'Am I sure...? What do you mean?'

He returned to the desk and looked at her file. The door opened and Gerhard carefully carried in a tray with two cups and saucers on it.

'Thank you Gerhard.' The lad smiled, glanced quickly at Magdaline and then went out. Dr. Brady turned back to her.

'What can you tell me about yourself? 'What is your name? Where do you live?'

'My name is Magdaline O'Neill. My last known address was the Our Lady Hostel in Shoreditch.'

'How did you remember this?' He handed her the coffee.

'I didn't. The nurse told me my name, and the address is on the label.'

'Good. So you recognise that all you know about yourself is what you have been told? You know nothing about yourself that you have remembered?'

'Nothing at all.'

'How is the coffee?'

Magdaline found his butterfly interrogation quite unnerving. She took a sip. 'Fine.'

He looked at her keenly. She could feel herself blushing.

'How did you know you liked coffee? I didn't tell you. You told me that you only got tea in the ward yet you knew you liked coffee as soon as it was offered to you. How did you know that you had been to the cinema and seen films where people lost their memory? It's not in your STM. You haven't been to the cinema since you've been here.'

'Well I... I just know.'

'Exactly! You just know. You are accessing your long term memory for some things but not for others. You know this is a hospital and that I am a doctor.'

'Well yes, that's obvious.'

'Not to somebody who has entirely lost their memory. So you see that you have not entirely lost your memory. You remember simple operations like cleaning your teeth and you remember the deep and complex learning processes to enable you to read.'

'Yes, yes that's true.'

'I don't want to burden you with lots of heavy words and ideas because we don't really know a lot about the human mind. My analysis is that you have a residual post traumatic amnesia, caused by the six weeks you were unconscious, we do not know what you were forgetting during that time, and profound retrograde amnesia which, for a psychogenic reason, has not cleared.'

'What does all that mean?'

'It means that there is an influence other than an organic one which is preventing you from remembering.'

'I don't understand.'

'Who are you?'

'Magdaline O'Neill.'

'Where were you going when you were knocked down?'

'I... I...'

'You see, if I ask you something that makes you think of being knocked down, your mind prevents you from accessing the information. It is protecting you from reliving the pain and trauma of your accident. The impact was a tremendous physical shock to your body and being effectively switched off for six weeks for was an equally great neurological shock. I know from your scan that there has been no damage to affect your neuronal connectivity. Your amnesia could now have changed from the organic to the purely psychogenic.'

'You mean, it's all in my mind?'

'Under the circumstances, an ironic way of expressing it, but yes. And that takes it outside my competence. I am referring you to a colleague of mine called Melanie Millson. She is a psychiatrist who has a particular interest in the subconscious. An extremely clever lady. You'll like her. If there is a way of sorting you out, she will find it.'

Lynne had a visitor sitting at the side of her bed whom Magdaline assumed to be her father. Lynne looked across as if to draw her attention and chat but Magdaline averted her eyes and concentrated on getting herself into bed with the minimum of pain and discomfort. She still got a dull ache from her neck and shoulders if she stretched too far; no doubt her newly mended collar bone complaining, but putting weight on her leg was quite unpleasant at the moment. The nursing staff and the doctors had both said that they were pleased with her progress but they all meant progress on the physical side. What about her mind?

She lay, staring moodily at the top of the curtain rail and the wire which hung from the ceiling to support it at the corner. There was a maintenance hatch of some sort in the middle of the ceiling with a hasp and padlock on it. She laughed to herself, imagining that the lock was to prevent the patients from escaping. If any of them were capable of dragging a table underneath the hatch, placing a chair on top of it and then clambering up the pyramid to climb through the hatch then they would not have been in hospital in the first place.

A psychiatrist. Psychiatrists were for neurotics. Or mad people. Was Dr. Brady just trying to be polite? Did he really think that she was just plain mad? A bag lady with no money and no friends and no home. But! But one who knew that she liked coffee and knew that she had been to the cinema. She knew it.

She was aware of voices raised in farewell and noticed the shadow pass across the ceiling as Lynne's visitor left.

'Hey Magdaline!' Lynne called. She tried to ignore her. 'Magdaline. Come on, I know you're not asleep.'

She sighed heavily and turned towards her.

'What do you want?'

'How did you get on? What did the specialist say?'

'He's sending me to a psychiatrist to sort my mind out.'

'Have you lost your memory then?' Magdaline nodded. 'What all of it? Don't you remember anything?'

'Some things. It's all a bit complicated.'

'What things do you remember?'

'Oh, silly things. Things that I don't realise that I know. For example, I knew I liked coffee without tasting it.'

'What does the doctor think about it?'

'He thinks my mind is locked up by something, a sort of safety valve to protect me from nasty memories.'

'Wow! This is exciting! I've just thought of something. Remember when we were talking earlier, I mentioned your hair and asked if you did any sport?' Magdaline nodded again. 'Well that's another thing you know. You said you don't do any sport. That's something from your past. You could probably find out all about yourself. Like, who's your favourite pop star?'

'Lynne.'

'Or what is your favourite food? Do you like curry? Do you eat tomatoes?'

'Lynne!'

'What?'

'Don't. Just leave it.'

'I was only trying to help. Anyone would think that you didn't want to find out. Anyway, I don't see why you can't get a job if you can draw like that.' She handed the writing pad back across to her. 'I showed it to my boss and he thought it was jolly good.'

Magdaline looked at the pen sketch she had made of Lynne. It was quite good. And the pen had felt right in her hand. She carefully pulled herself up in the bed and scrabbled for the pen. Flipping over to a clean sheet, she looked across at the old lady opposite, asleep with her mouth open, and started to draw.

Mrs. Dove bustled into the boardroom like a busy hen.

'I'm sorry I'm late sir. A minor crisis I had to attend to.'

She took her place at the table alongside Harry Meachem who was picking his teeth with a matchstick and looking for all the world like a seedy bookmaker.

Richard smiled encouragingly at her and waited. Across the end of the table Piers Lansing was talking sotto voce with Anatole Worstop and moving his finger down a list they were both scrutinising. Mrs. Dove pushed up her sleeves in a declaration of preparedness and inspected the point of a pencil which she hovered over an open pad.

'Right,' she said brightly. This signified to Richard that he could now begin.

'Are Katrina and Wayne on their way?'

Mrs. Dove blinked at him. 'Here?' She was unable to keep the incredulity out of her voice. Richard nodded. 'Oh I can tell them of any developments affecting our department.' She waved her hand dismissively. Harry Meachem sucked noisily on his match.

'I'm sure you can Mrs. Dove but could you ask them to come along please?'

'Well I suppose Wayne could come but I've left Katrina in charge of the switchboard. She can't possibly leave that.'

'Do we have an answering machine?'

'Well yes, but it's not very–'

'Shall we use the answering machine then?'

'Well if you say so.'

Richard nodded again. Mrs. Dove raised her eyebrows to show that if the firm was plunged into receivership because Katrina had been called off the phones, then We Would All Know Whose Fault It Was. Below the table, Vanessa's fingers tapped a warning against the side of his knee. She apparently thought that he was near to overstepping the mark. Mrs. Dove returned quickly, dragging a myopic Katrina and a bemused Wayne in her wake.

'Take a seat everyone,' Richard suggested and casually waved his arm at the empty chairs. Katrina sat where Mrs. Dove showed her to sit. Wayne sat next to Vanessa and said 'Hi!' to her.

'Hi,' she replied, ignoring the searing look that Mrs. Dove was directing at Wayne.

'Good morning everyone,' Richard began. A chorus of good mornings stuttered around the table. 'We have several things to do in this meeting and I shall keep it as short as I can. First let me introduce Miss Clewe-Harting here. You have seen her around for the last few days, no doubt making a nuisance of herself on my behalf. As from today Miss Clewe-Harting will work as my personal assistant.

'I will quickly cease to be a nuisance to you all,' Vanessa said, 'providing you address me as "Vanessa".'

'Hi Vanessa.' Wayne grinned and extended his hand. 'I'm Wayne.'

'Hello Wayne,' she laughed easily and shook his hand.

'There you are, you see: Vanessa is completely harmless,' Richard observed flippantly.

'Where will Miss... Vanessa work, sir? I mean, this is the board room usually.' Mrs. Dove liked things to be ordered.

'Oh I shall hardly require much space, Mrs. Dove. I shall be out and about with Richard most of the time and when not, I shall just squeeze myself in where there's a desk or table.'

'I see. Thank you.' Mrs. Dove did not sound placated.

'I told you when I started that I knew nothing of the job and I trust I have not disappointed you with my ignorance. Over the last few weeks I have been forming an idea of where I want the company to go and I will need your help to tell me the best way to get there. But before that, I need your help to tell me where we are at the moment. So what I want you to do this morning is to go back to your offices and draw up your own job descriptions; to write down all the tasks that comprise your responsibilities and then estimate the percentage of your time you spend on each. Don't struggle to make it up to one hundred percent. I am not chasing decimals, I just want an estimate. Any questions?'

Vanessa thought that they all looked too stunned to ask any questions.

'Good. I shall come around to each of you after lunch and chat with you about what you have found out.'

'Mmmm, that'll get my old grey matter churning,' Harry Meachem said to nobody in particular.

He held the door open for Mrs. Dove who sailed through, followed by Katrina and Wayne. Piers Lansing appeared as if he was about to say something but, noticing Anatole Worstop hovering, decided to follow the others.

'I have had a certain amount of experience, in previous appointments, of management systems analysis, milord, would you like me to help you in collating the results?'

'Thank you Anatole, but not at this stage. As you have had experience I should imagine that you will be pretty quick with your job description so I'll come around to you first after lunch, say two o'clock?'

'My job description?' His voice jerked. 'Of course. Yes, that would be fine.' He turned to Vanessa and gravely inclined his head. 'I look forward to working with you, Vanessa.'

'And I do with you, Anatole.'

He paused at the open door. 'Related to Lord Harting?'

'My father.'

'Ah,' he nodded with satisfaction and went out.

'Well what do you make of that?' Richard said.

'I think you've stirred up a hornet's nest.'

'Let's get out of here quick then. Grab your handbag. I want to go over to Virginia Water and have a look at Manor Gate.'

Richard drove them over to Virginia Water in the Range Rover, remarking that the air conditioning was a different system to that of the Yellow Peril where, with the hood lowered, you froze whilst driving and fried as soon as you stopped.

The troublesome retaining wall had long since been erected and the eighteen desirable residences of Manor Gate were already represented on the ground by concrete foundations gleaming white and the beginnings of brick walls. The 'harmonious landscaping' was a spread of dusty rubble, bits of pipe ends, empty oil drums, piles of sand and gravel, broken palettes, odd ends of wood and a woollen sock.

Richard picked his way about the site, pausing every now and then to consult the plan and then point out some feature to Vanessa. The workmen ignored them for a time. Eventually a bare chested Irishman swaggered out of a temporary hut to investigate the intruders. He was, he said, the foreman and who might they be? Local planning department would it be? Once Richard had gently disabused him of this idea he went away around the site cajoling the builders into supreme efforts as the 'the man himself' was inspecting.

As soon as he was out of sight they crept quietly away and walked down the road to a pub which a couple of centuries earlier had been a simple house but had now grown a plethora of gables, roof extensions and Tudor beams. Once they were inside, they had the impression that the clientele had been supplied by the pub renovation company as a job lot. Richard sipped at his beer and prodded his Ploughman's.

'I've decided we'll sell the houses.'

'What was the other option?' Vanessa picked a lemon pip from her mouth and flipped it into the ash tray.

'We could have let them for a few years until the value had gone up but,' he looked about the pub, 'anybody who could honestly think of this as their regular would easily pay the price we want now. We'll sell.'

'Fair enough. Do I have to finish this sandwich?'

'Of course. What would the neighbours say?'

Anatole Worstop had produced his job description written in a firm hand on one side of paper. He went through it with Richard, answering questions with a courtesy that served to hide any indignation.

'So when you say that the machine does the accounts,' Richard said slowly, 'You meant the daily money in, money out sort of thing? Because you draw up the balance sheet don't you?'

'Yes. We all have our input into the daily finance model on the computer, most of the information is entered into the machine by Mrs. Dove, but the trial balance and annual accounts, I, in effect draw them up and they are then audited.'

'So you must know quite a bit about capitalisation and reserves and such like?'

'I've had a wide experience, milord.'

'What do you do in your spare time?'

Anatole Worstop dragged his job description towards him.

'Well...' he began.

'No, I mean outside of work. What do you do when you are not working?'

'I watch cricket and grow orchids,' he replied stiffly, as if resenting the intrusion into his private life.

Harry Meachem was anxious.

'I've not really had the training like the others. I'm more sort of hands on, if you know what I mean.' He brushed some pencil shavings from the desk into the waste bin. 'But that is as near and as comprehensive as I could get it.'

'It's not easy,' Richard sympathised.

'I'd never thought about what I did, I just did it. I mean the way I drew that up,' he jabbed a stubby finger on the pencilled scrawl that he had submitted to Richard, 'was by going back through my diary and sort of listing and timing out all my meetings and visits. I couldn't see any other way of doing it.'

'I'm sure that's what I would have done.'

'Oh good.'

'I went out to Manor Gate at lunchtime. What do you think of the foreman there?'

'Ralph? He's as good as any. He needs a good kick every now and then.'

Piers Lansing's job description had covered three sides of typing. It was neat and meticulous.

'Probably some of my tasks I could have amalgamated,' he explained, 'under one heading.'

'This is always the difficulty.' Richard marvelled at his confidence in making this observation.

'I'm sfraid it does make it look as if I do an awful lot of work.' He pulled at his shirt cuffs in his jacket sleeves.

'I think you all do, but I've saved you some work. We won't be letting Manor Gate. That won't come onto your books. We'll sell. Do you think we'll get our asking price?'

'Two seventy five and three two five?' Richard nodded. Piers Lansing reflected for a second. 'Possibly, possibly. The market is fairly resilient there.'

'Well, we shall see. Some time this week could you get me out the details of any office accommodation or potential office accommodation that we have in our portfolio within, say, a ten mile radius of Reading?'

Piers Lansing wrote 'Reading office' on a scrap of paper, drew a ring around it and added the figure 'ten'.

Mrs. Dove looked up quickly from her desk as Richard entered. Her cardigan hung limply in its accustomed place on the back of her chair.

'That's all right Mrs. Dove, don't disturb yourself if you're busy. I'll just go and see how Wayne and Katrina are getting on with their job descriptions.'

'I have only just finished mine.' She indicated the papers on her desk. 'I haven't started theirs yet.'

'Oh heavens, Mrs. Dove, they can do their own. It's not for you to do.'

'I hardly think they can, sir.'

'Well, shall we let them try?'

'I don't really think they are up to it.'

'I'd like to give them the opportunity.' Richard insisted gently. 'It will be good practice for them.'

Mrs. Dove pursed her lips and said nothing.

EPISODE TWENTY

Mrs. Armitage in Hospital Admin. grabbed the ringing phone as she walked through the door. With the other hand she slung her umbrella and bag to the floor and then stabbed at the switches on her computer.

'Admin.' Whilst she listened to the caller she flicked over the catch on the sliding window above the counter and pulled it open. 'It's on order,' she said and cradled the receiver into her neck as she pulled a box file from cabinet beneath her desk. '10,000 litres. Ordered at the end of last month.'

A messenger unloaded a bundle of post from his trolley and dropped it to the counter.

'There y'are darling. All yer luv letters.' She gritted her teeth and nodded, having heard the same greeting every morning for five years, and the man went off down the corridor, whistling.

'O.K. I'll tell them it's urgent.' She replaced the phone on the cradle and wrote herself a note about the delivery of heating oil. As the phone rang again the door behind her opened and a young woman bustled in, greeting her as she drop kicked her soft bag under the table and then spun the tap on the sink to begin filling the kettle.

Mrs. Armitage acknowledged her with a nod and picked up the phone again.

'Admin.' She covered the mouthpiece with her hand and said to her colleague, 'New box of tea bags in the cupboard.' She returned to the caller. 'I can check for you doctor.' She spun on her chair and flipped over the pages on a diary. 'Next Tuesday is the special meeting of the housing committee. No, it's over in Manchip's at 14.30. My pleasure.'

She replaced the phone, muttering to herself, 'Why don't you use your bloody secretary, doctor? That's what we pay them for.'

A man appeared at the window.

'We're two drivers short on the transport roster this morning. If you can get any of the distant ones to take a taxi it would be quicker.'

'O.K. Joe.' She pulled down the clipboard with the day's intake and began to peruse it as the phone started ringing again. 'Oh Nikki,' she said to the girl, 'before I forget, there's a patient down in Women's Med. Name of...' she forraged for the note from the previous day, '...name of Magdaline O'Neill. She's got no clothes.'

'Got no clothes?'

'We burned them. Ring Mrs. Nugent and see what she can do.' She picked up the phone again. 'Admin?'

Mrs. Nugent was one of those bustling, nosy, irritatingly energetic women who always got themselves onto the Hospital Friends committees and then took them over, swamping any objections and ignoring any criticism. The type of person whom nobody loved but nobody actively disliked and whom nobody helped but nobody positively obstructed. And the Mrs. Nugents of this world thrived on the blathering indifference of humanity and, rolling up their sleeves, just got on with the job.

Magdaline sat in the chair at the side of her bed, looking at her white knees sticking out from under the flower print skirt. She had a pair of brown flat heeled shoes made of real leather and a cotton blouse with a pretty lace ruff. In the cupboard was another skirt, two shirts, a pair of slacks and some more underwear still in its wrapping. She did not know that the clothes felt right on her but at the same time, she did not know that they felt wrong. They just felt different after so long in hospital nightdresses and towelling dressing gowns. What she really needed was somebody to give her an opinion. She glanced across to Lynne's bed and sighed. The gnarled yellow face was not Lynne's. Lynne had been discharged nearly a week ago but Magdaline still missed her every day.

Now that she could move about, Magdaline tried to occupy herself with little errands; collecting newspapers from the booth for other patients, helping with the tea trolley and such like.

Life out of bed was better than in it, but it lacked a purpose. It lacked a stimulus. Mrs. Nugent's arrival with the bag of clothes had been like Christmas. She had felt quite giggly but after Mrs. Nugent had bustled out of the ward, she had asked herself what she was going to use the clothes for. And the fear began to return. What would she do when they discharged her? Where would she go? Back to Our Lady Hostel in Shoreditch?

'Buck up Magdaline, you've got a visitor!' A nurse broke into her reverie. 'Don't look so surprised. You are allowed visitors you know, it's not a prison.'

'But who could...?'

'Hey Magdaline!'

'Lynne!'

'Hey, you look great!' She pinched the chair from the old lady's bed next door and sat down. 'You look different dressed.'

'So do you.'

'Oh well... work clothes, you know.' She was wearing a sober two piece suit. 'But you look, well, more alive.'

'Oh thanks a million!'

'You know what I mean.'

'So what are you doing here?'

'I'm visiting you, you idiot!'

'Oh, I thought you were back in for a check up or something.' The idea that somebody should come on purpose to visit her had not occurred to Magdaline; it touched her.

'My boss let me have a couple of hours off. He's not a bad old stick. Of course it was easy 'cos he remembers you.'

'Does he? Oh from when he came and visited you.'

'Yeah. So how's the memory?'

'Don't start that again.'

'Well I'm going to test you.'

'Lynne, don't.'

She fished in her bag. 'Do you like chocolate?' She put a box on the top of Magdaline's locker.

'I...'

'Do you like grapes?' She pulled one from the bunch and popped it into her mouth. 'I do,' she admitted. 'And romantic slushy novels?' She threw a lurid paperback onto the bed. 'Page ninety three is the naughty bit.' She grinned up at Magdaline but stopped quickly as she saw the tears running down her cheeks.

'Magdaline, Magdaline, I'm sorry. I didn't mean to upset you.'

'It's not... you haven't...' Magdaline gulped. 'I'm not used to the kindness, that's all.'

Lynne took her hand and squeezed it. 'Hey now, don't be daft. Have a grape.' She shoved the book across to her. 'And read page ninety three, it'll do you good.'

Magdaline smiled. 'Tell me about your job and that.'

'Janus and Janus? It's not bad. Actually they're quite good. Old Mr. Janus, we call him 'old' cos he's at least forty, he doesn't come in much now. I think he plays golf all day.'

'That wasn't old Mr. Janus who came to see you, was it?'

'No that was Dominic. He's head of the creative side. Strictly speaking he's not my boss but I get on better with him than the accounts side of the company. He's got a Porsche. And a wife.'

'Oh dear.'

'No, not really. She's very nice, I've met her. At an office party would you believe? Do you know anybody who takes their wife to an office party? "Lynne, this is Amanda, my wife". I thought he was joking. She was very nice though. Not at all put out by all the horseplay that was going on. You know the sort of thing.'

'What sort of thing?'

'You know... Have you never been to an office party?'

'I don't... I can't...'

'Never mind,' Lynne said quickly, 'If I told you what people got up to at office parties the nurse would throw me out.'

'I wish they'd throw me out,' Magdaline joked and then shivered as the cold wave of fear ran through her. Out where?

Lynne looked at her closely. 'Are you all right?'

'Yes. Yes. How long have you worked at Janus and Janus?'

'About four years. I started out as an assistant buyer and then when the woman I worked for got pregnant and left, they just told me to carry on by myself. So I moved onto her desk before anybody else thought of using it. It gets the sun in the afternoon.'

'And what do you buy?'

'I told you before. Space. Advertising space. In magazines, newspapers, radio, television, billboards. You name it, I buy it.'

'Is it difficult?'

'It's not difficult exactly but it takes a lot of wheedling and negotiating to get a good price.'

'Oh I would have thought that the magazines and newspapers

had all their prices already sorted out.'

'They do, of course, but my job is to get a cheaper price. Anybody can pay the full price.'

'So how do you get a cheaper price?'

'Lots of ways. I can say "how much if we pay in thirty days instead of sixty?" or I can say "for that price can you put our ad in the middle of your main feature in the colour supplement?" or, "four for the price of three?" I'll try anything.'

'Sounds like hard work.'

'It is. It is. But I enjoy it. After work I go and thrash about on the squash court or pedal my bum away in the gym.'

Magdaline looked at her glowing face, the neat brown hair and the sensible suit. 'You look quite the successful business executive,' she said.

Lynne stared at her thoughtfully. 'Give me your comb.'

'I haven't got a comb. I borrow one from the ward.'

'You haven't got...? Have you got a brush?'

Magdaline shook her head. 'I've got a toothbrush. They gave me that.'

Lynne was searching in her capacious handbag.

'Sit still a minute,' she said and she pulled out a long handled comb. 'Now let's see what we can do with your hair.'

Magdaline dutifully sat still whilst Lynne whisked the comb back and forth in her short hair. She watched her eyes frowning and then opening wider again as she worked.

'That's better. You need to let these bits grow a bit and then if you trim down there and there it'll look really smart.' She gave her a small mirror from her handbag. 'Take a look.'

Magdaline saw quite a serious face staring back at her, the short hair combed and arranged neatly.

'I'm afraid you will have to leave now. Visiting time is well finished.' It was the nurse who had been standing at the doorway.

Magdaline saw her own face in the mirror crumple into anguish. Lynne jumped up. 'Keep the comb and the mirror.'

'Will you...?'

'I'll come again,' Lynne assured her and then winked. 'Page ninety three,' she said.

Magdaline watched Lynne's trim figure in suit and high heels as she clicked down the ward, pausing to wave at the door before disappearing into the corridor.

'Friend from work?' the nurse asked. 'Cheered you up no end didn't she?'

'Yes she did. That was my best friend Lynne. She works at Janus and Janus you know.' The nurse nodded. That was easy, Magdaline thought. Nothing to it.

'Tell me some more about this company you propose to float.' The Dowager Countess of Wisdene deftly flicked a wasp from the table with her fingers. 'That is always the trouble with planting dahlias near a gazebo, they do attract the wasps.'

Richard gazed serenely out over the park to where the massive oak trees were dark with heavy summer shade.

'Are you sure that they attract wasps?' he asked. 'I thought they would be more likely to attract bees.'

'Are you doubting the word of your mother, Richard?'

'I think it is more likely to be the temptation of the jam pot than the dahlias,' he observed.

'You ought to learn a little diplomacy, Richard. You never know when you might need it. Especially now that you are in business.' She almost winced as she said the last word.

'I already know diplomacy, mother, I just do not bother to apply it.'

'And why not?'

'I don't need it. People do what I want already.'

'That sounds a deal too callous for my liking.' She sipped from her cup.

'It's realistic. But just to show you that I can also be ruthless,' he waved a beckoning hand to Blase the gardener who was squeezing through the overgrown doorway in the wall of the kitchen garden, 'I'll get a second opinion.' Blase stumbled up the lawn. He touched the brim of his straw hat.

'Milord?'

'Blase, tell me, in your opinion, would these dahlias here be more likely to attract the bees or the wasps?'

'These dahlias here milord?'

'Yes. Are they going to attract bees or wasps?'

Blase looked from one face to the other. He sucked his top lip and then his gums. 'Earwigs,' he said.

'Splendid, Blase,' the Countess laughed, 'Splendid.'

'See here ma'am.' He peeled apart the petals of a dahlia head and pulled out an earwig and held it up. 'Little nippers,' he muttered and threw it to the lawn. 'They get right inside.'

'Thank you Blase, that was most instructive.' The Countess turned a dazzling smile onto her son who was grinning back at her, quite unperturbed. 'Most instructive,' she added.

'Thank you ma'am. Hmm, right,' Blase said and turned to go. 'If it's wasps that are worrying you ma'am, it'll be the jam pot they'd be after.'

'Thank you Blase,' Richard said and once Blase's back was turned, he made a face at his mother.

'That was quite uncalled for, Richard.'

'Yes wasn't it? Satisfying though.'

'Drink your tea and behave yourself. You still haven't told me about this company you want me to invest in.'

'I might not let you, mother,' Richard said haughtily as he speared a piece of Victoria sponge.

'Might not let me buy shares in our own company! The very idea! This executive power buzz, I believe they call it, this buzz, must have turned your brain, Richard. I'll go direct to Anatole.'

'It was Anatole who told me.' Richard was smug.

'It was...? Anatole Worstop? Words fail me.'

'No they don't, mother. Ever. But to be fair to Anatole he did not suggest that I prevent you from subscribing for some shares–'

'I should think not!'

'–he merely pointed out that I could veto any application for shares. Indeed, the invitations to subscribe would only be sent to persons nominated by me, so you must learn to cherish me a little more, mother dear.'

'Cherish? This viper!'

'Or perhaps, learn a little diplomacy.'

'You know you can be infuriating sometimes Richard.'

'Yes I know. It's amusing isn't it?'

'You are amusing yourself with Churle Investments aren't you dear?'

'Yes mother. I can guess now with some insight what father got from the business. I think I probably get different things but it is satisfying all the same.'

The Countess put her hand on his.

'I am pleased, Richard.'

'And it's hard work.'

'That pleases me even more.' She smartly smacked his hand. 'It was about time you started to bend your back a little.'

After her husband's death, she had avoided any allusion to Richard's 'arty' period; almost as if she had held her breath in case he went back to college. By the time that they had re-established some sort of life, a life without the smiling cherubic figure they had all supposed to be immortal, then the memory of London, Chelsea and the students had seemed so far away that one could have thought that it had also been buried.

The pain would never be over. She would always miss him in his hundred little ways, some endearing, some annoying. Sometimes she longed to hear him click his tongue as he always did when he saw horses. When he was alive this habit had irritated her beyond relief; now she missed even that irritation.

Lately, a different emotion had accosted her. Since Richard had started the custom of telling her what he was doing in Churle Investments, she had begun to look forward to the little snippets of information. She did not understand all of what he told her but she loved him telling her. She was living it. Alfred had never done that. 'Don't you worry your pretty little head, my dear,' he used to say. 'Its legal and profitable, that's all you need to know.' He was not being secretive. He was not dismissing her. He had really believed that it was better for her to remain in ignorance so that she could not worry. But now she found that she enjoyed knowing and that was the problem. She felt guilty because she was enjoying something that Alfred had chosen not to give her. And then when she thought about feeling guilty, it made her feel even more guilty. She must be more positive.

'You still have not told me about this investment, Richard.'

'Ah. Well it all came about after a little enquiry that I did into the running of the company.'

'Enquiry?'

'Yes. I wanted to know what Churle Investments was all about. Not just the accounts and balance sheet, but the people, what they were up to.'

'Did you suspect them of some subterfuge ?' The Countess was shocked at the thought that anybody would dare to misbehave in a company which had been set up by her Alfred.

'No, nothing like that. I suspected that they had not thought about what they were doing.' He looked carefully at his mother before speaking. 'I think father may have been domineering at work. No, perhaps 'domineering' is not the correct word. I think that perhaps he did not let his employees do enough of their own thinking. He wanted to do everything himself, if he could. This meant that people did what they were told but sometimes stifled suggestions because father always had ideas and was always telling them what to do, so they did it.'

"I don't follow you Richard. It was your father's ideas that kept all those people employed.'

'Father is not here anymore. I need all the ideas I can get. In no way can I hope to emulate father in that respect. So I will listen to their ideas, if they have any. At least I can promote an atmosphere in which they might feel that it would be worth expressing ideas.

'I asked them to write me their job descriptions. I think they were all worried that I was looking for redundancies but they had to learn to trust me. Wayne for instance, he is the office junior, you can't get any lower than him in the hierarchy. When I went through his job description with him we discovered that he spent ninety minutes per day, on average, photocopying. So I asked him if he liked photocopying. "Not particularly," he says, "but it takes such a long time because you have to feed the sheets in one at a time." So I told him to find a solution. The next morning he came to me with brochures from three companies, all featuring machines which are far more advanced than ours, will save us hours of his time and, here's the surprise, will probably cost a little less to run if we rent the machine instead of buying it and then depreciating it to zero.'

'And did you ask everybody to do this job description thing?'

'Without exception.'

'Even Anatole?'

'Even Anatole.'

'I suspect that he found it unpleasant. Poor old Anatole.'

'"Old" is the word. Do you know how old Anatole is?'

'Sixty three next April.'

'Er. Yes, you're right. Well, I don't know about next April.'

'I do, dear. I've known Anatole a long time. Longer than your father. He proposed to me once.'

'Anatole Worstop?' Richard's mouth fell open. 'Anatole Worstop proposed to you? When?'

'Before your father, Richard. Have some sense. He was not likely to have done it afterwards was he?'

'Why did you turn him down?'

'Would you rather I had married Anatole Worstop, Richard?' Richard shook his head. 'Then we are both happy.'

'Did father know that he had proposed to you when he took him on?'

'Of course. But he had been married thirty years by the time that he came to work for your father. Do stick to the point Richard, what was the outcome of this job description exercise you were telling me about?'

'I think Anatole found it rather embarrassing. It must have been obvious to him that much of the time he actually had no work to do, and that is what he said.'

'Yes, that sounds like Anatole. It is not honesty, you understand Richard, it is an astonishing paucity of original thoughts. He was always crippled by an utter lack of imagination. He could not think of any other way of putting it, that was all.'

'Well it worked out well for him, in fact for all of us.'

'Oh Richard, just tell me what happened, I have not the patience to listen to your self congratulation.'

'You still wish to invest in this venture do you?'

'Richard dear, if you are going to use blackmail and coercion as part of your stock in trade then you must learn not to smile when you threaten your subjects, they will simply not take you seriously.'

'Sorry mother. I asked him to tell me honestly how many days he actually needed to come to the office each week and he said, two or sometimes three. So I suggested that he attend the office two or three days a week if he thought that he could do the work in that time. As long as we knew beforehand which days he would be coming in, he could spend the rest of the time looking after his orchids and watching cricket.'

'Yes, that was one thing about Anatole. He always sent me gorgeous bouquets of flowers. What did he say to your idea?'

'Once he understood that I was not making him redundant but rewarding him for his service and that his salary would not be affected in any way, he seemed to brighten up a lot. And so did the others in the office when I told them.'

'Yes, I can imagine they would. How did they get on with their job descriptions?'

'Do you remember me telling you about Mrs. Dove?'

'The "man-eating cardigan" I believe you called her?'

'Yes. She is in charge of Wayne and Katrina. Except that Wayne is so laid back that–'

'So what?'

'Mother, if you are going to ask me these questions you must be prepared to do a little homework on the jargon. You know very well what "laid back" means. Anyway, if she thinks she frightens Wayne then she is deceiving herself. She does dominate the audio typist, Katrina.'

'Oh get to the point Richard, or the summer will be over.'

'Mrs. Dove's job description was full and bulging; I could never have challenged it with any authority. The point she was making was that she was Very Important because she made the entries on the accounting computer and so she really needed another assistant to cover the other tasks. I think she just wants to build herself a little empire to run, heaven knows why. Unfortunately for her, Katrina proved not to be so downtrodden when it came to expressing herself on paper and she had made a very good case for herself to be trained to use the computer. I sat them together at the same table to talk it through and instead of Mrs. Dove finding herself with another minion to boss about, she has discovered that someone whom she thought was beneath her could eventually threaten her position. It should be interesting to watch. I just hope it does not all end with fireworks.'

'It sounds most unsavoury and Machiavellian. What about the handsome young man with the Russian wife? He came here once to deliver some papers. He has lovely blue eyes.'

'Piers Lansing. Well, he got a shock. I had put Nessie onto some statistical analysis for me and when he looked over the results with me he had to admit that eighty per cent of his time is spent in an area which earns us nine per cent of our turnover – the flats, houses and maisonettes which we buy, rent and sell. That is just plain stupid in anybody's language.'

'Did he have any suggestion to make?'

Richard thought for a second and changing his tone he said, 'I don't really like the power. No, that's not true. I like the power to do what I want to and what I think needs doing. What I don't like is the effect that this perceived power has on others.'

'Yes,' his mother said as she fiddled with an immaculate pleat on her skirt. 'Your father was always aware of that. It is good that you feel it too. Power is not an easy tool to wield. It can so easily become a weapon.'

'That was what I felt with Piers Lansing. I could see him looking at me as if I had laid him on the altar slab and was sharpening the knife.'

'So what did you tell him?'

'What I am going to tell you now. We are going to sell our stock of small, fiddly lets. Lansing would be good at that. He knows the entire market . The disadvantage is that we would lose a steady, if small, source of income. The benefits are that we gain an increase in cash reserves and give Piers Lansing a bit more spare time. Churle Industrial is our company which holds leases and owns a few freeholds on factory and warehouse units. We are going to use it to take over an industrial company which has not revalued its property portfolio.'

'I am not certain that I am following you, Richard.'

'O.K. You know that companies declare how much they are worth every year on their balance sheet?'

'Yes, I understand that.'

'Well, some companies have not identified the full potential of the buildings and land they own. To put it brutally, in some cases the best thing that could happen for the shareholders would be that the company ceases trading and sells off everything it has. They would earn far more from that than they ever would from holding on to shares and hoping for a dividend. The one thing that Piers Lansing is good at, is research and investigation.'

'That is two things, Richard.'

'I'll ignore that interruption. I have given Piers Lansing the job of finding the target company. When he does, then I shall invite selected favourites of mine to cough up their thousands and Churle Industrial will buy it out. Anatole will have something worthwhile to do. Organising a share flotation, albeit in a private company, is just up his street. Piers Lansing can then start to learn Anatole's job. He is ambitious enough to study and take exams if he thinks they will get him somewhere and Harry Meachem will be able to yell down the phone at really big construction companies instead of bawling at little Irishmen.'

'And Mrs. Dove?'

'I shall have to find her an olive branch I suppose.'

'How much money will you need to raise, Richard?'

'Probably about fifteen million, it depends on how much we manage to raise on our portfolio of flats and such.' He looked back to the house at the sound of horseshoes on stone. He watched as Vanessa slipped lithely from the saddle and handed on her bay to Winston. 'My PA has arrived mother.' He got up. 'I've got work to do.' He stretched and then set off full of purpose up to the house.

The Dowager Countess watched the Right Honourable Earl of Wisdene marching towards the steady grey green eyes of the daughter of Lord Harting of Plethero and she thought what a vibrant couple they would make.

The rain was drizzling down the plate glass doors at Casualty. Outside, Magdaline could see grey figures scurrying about under umbrellas and the yawning rear of an ambulance by the sliding doors. The foyer was choked with spartan grey tubed wheelchairs, hospital ownership crudely daubed in thick white painted letters.

She was standing to one side of the flower stall which had been set up by the tea bar. From here she could watch. She could survey. She would not look out of place. Nobody would know that she was not about to order tea or buy a bunch of carnations.

The top of a Belisha beacon winked at her, orange over a red brick wall. Now you see me, now you don't. An ambulance backed up to the door and lugubriously lowered three elderly patients on a platform to the ground. One lady had spots of rain on her hair like silver sequins. A young lad cycled slowly past in shorts and tee shirt, drenched to the skin by the summer shower. That was outside. They were outside. In the world. They did not look any different from her. In her slacks and sloppy shirt she could just walk out and be one of them, merge into the crowd.

'Magdaline.'

She turned to a short woman with white hair and sparkling blue eyes set in a pink face. She was wearing a navy blue track suit which had a lime green elephant patched onto the front. She probably worked in the children's ward. 'Magdaline O'Neill?' she said. Magdaline looked at her. Why was she asking for Magdaline? Must be some other Magdaline. She looked back through the weeping windows at the world. Full of people. People with memories. 'You were supposed to come and see me. Were you unable to find the room? I am Melanie Millson.'

No, she had not been 'unable to find the room'. She had found the room as directed with no difficulty whatsoever and had walked straight past it and to the entrance of the hospital. She tried to convince herself that she had almost walked outside into the world but she knew it was not true. Her footsteps had faltered long before she had reached the door.

'You can hardly believe it's August with this weather can you?'

'How should I know? I can't even remember this May let alone last August.' She knew she sounded bitter. She was bitter.

'We might as well sit down if we are going to watch the rain.' Melanie Millson walked across to one of the low chairs, turned it around to face the window, sat down and propped her feet up on the guard rail. The receptionist frowned disapproval. Magdaline continued to stand. The rain continued to fall.

Psychiatrists were for people who were mad or had too much money for sense.

'People are funny,' Melanie said to nobody in particular. 'Take Dr. Loose there, the man in the grey suit trying to keep out of the rain. If he was not so stuck with this idea that he is God's gift to women then he would not mind sharing the cleaning lady's umbrella but as it is, he cannot imagine himself consorting with a lady of the same age as me and so he gets drenched. Daft really, it makes him look quite unattractive with his hair plastered down on his head and his shirt sticking to him. By blindly sticking to the promotion of the image he is trying to create he achieves exactly the opposite image in the minds of those he is trying to impress. Shall we have a cup of tea if we are staying here?'

Magdaline nodded. Melanie got up and walked over to the tea bar. Magdaline watched her talking to the lady at the counter and then she pulled up a chair next to Melanie's. She sat down and looked out of the window. Melanie returned with two plastic cups and a packet of biscuits.

'Garibaldis,' she said. 'We call them squashed fly biscuits.'

'Ugh that's horrible!' Magdaline retorted and put her feet up on the rail like Melanie.

'You see that man in the orange shirt?' Melanie pointed with the jagged end of a half eaten biscuit. Magdaline nodded. 'I'm going to make him step in that big puddle by the skip, you watch.'

She screwed her eyes up and concentrated her gaze on him. 'It's called psychokinesis. Making something happen by willing it.' She wrinkled up her face again. The man stepped with dainty care around the puddle. Magdaline laughed. 'Of course, it doesn't always work every time. Now you do one.' It's easy. You just decide what you want to happen and then concentrate on it.'

'Just like that?'

'Just like that.'

'And it may work or it may not?'

'You've got it.'

'Right then.' Magdaline looked out of the window. 'The man just getting out of the taxi is going to scratch his nose.'

'You have to screw up your eyes and make it look good otherwise nobody will believe you.'

'Right then.' Magdaline screwed her face up in concentration. The man stared through the window at her. Magdaline lost her concentration and as her breath burst from her mouth, a shower of biscuit crumbs pattered against the window. The man hurried away in consternation. They both dissolved into giggles.

'Not bad for a first attempt,' Melanie pronounced. 'I bet he's scratching his nose furiously just around the corner.'

'Do you think so?'

'Indubitably. Let's take our tea back to my room before we get chucked out.' She stood up and Magdaline followed her back up the corridor. Melanie pushed open the door with her foot. 'Make yourself at home, I've got to put this laundry away.' She went in. It was a small, impersonal room with a pair of easy chairs and a coffee table at one side of the doorway and a cupboard and bookcase at the other. 'It's not very cosy. I am only in the hospital for one morning every fortnight and I share this room with so many other agencies that it just has to be kept anonymous.' She slammed the cupboard door. 'I don't expect you will come here many more times. You will probably be discharged soon, as you know. Then you will be able to visit me at my house. That will be far more comfortable.'

'I don't know whether I want to come and see you. I don't know whether I want to be discharged.'

'It took a lot of courage to say that, didn't it?'

'I suppose it did.'

'That is a good way to start.'

'I feel so angry.'

'I noticed.'

'Angry and frightened.'

'The two emotions often go together. Do you know why you are angry and do you know what you are frightened of?'

Magdaline was silent whilst she thought. Melanie waited, sipping from her plastic cup. 'I am angry because somebody has stolen my memory. I am frightened of going out into a world of strangers. A world where I know nobody.'

'Brilliant!'

'What do you mean, brilliant?'

'You are so clear and so positive. You know why you are angry and why you are frightened. Not many people can say that. Did you ever get the impression that we thought you were mad?'

'No, never,' Magdaline said quickly. Melanie's bright blue eyes gazed into hers. 'Yes,' she admitted. 'I did.'

'Well you are definitely not mad. You are saner and more rational than some of the consultants here. Don't expect too much, too soon from your mind, Magdaline, it has suffered a terrific shock. What we can do to start with is to try to attenuate your anger and to find you reassurance to counter your fear. How does that sound?'

Magdaline looked at the lime green elephant, the white hair and the pink face. 'O.K. as far as it goes,' she said cautiously.

'It goes as far as you want it to. You are in charge.'

I am not going to be bullied by a woman with a ridiculous green elephant on her sweater.

'In charge of what?'

'Of your life, Magdaline. Many people would envy you.'

'Envy me? Why on earth?'

'You have been presented with an exciting opportunity. The type of opportunity that comes to one in ten million. You can be whatever you want to be. You are not clutered with memories of past failures or successes. You have a clean slate. You are an intelligent and pretty young lady with an exciting future.'

'With a tin plate in her leg and six weeks taken from her life.'

'Anger is a terribly destructive force. This is what I want you to do before we meet again. I want you to think about anger. Think about a target for your anger. Will you do that?'

Magdaline said that she would.

EPISODE TWENTY-ONE

Harry Meachem, Piers Lansing and Richard sat in the Range Rover and silently perused the dilapidated building across the street. Two girls clomped by on platform-heeled sandals; their heads nodding on drooping shoulders, they seemed to personify the depression that was Halifax. One of them turned to look at the men and then nudged her friend. She also turned and stared. Piers Lansing cleared his throat quietly and tugged nervously at his collar. Harry Meachem put Lansing's fears into words.

'If we sit here much longer we'll have the cops on our backs for loitering or, worse still, kerb crawling,'

Richard laughed silently and nodded at the building.

'Well, what do you think of that one then Harry?' he said.

'Worst of the lot I'd say. Only good for demolition. Nobody would convert that. It's a sloping site – it'd cost the earth to redevelop and look what you'd end up with.' He gestured in despair at the neighbourhood of industrial obsolescence.

'Piers?' Richard said.

'I am at a loss to know how to put it.'

'It's not worth the seven hundred and fifty thousand that they have put in their books, you mean?' Piers agreed. 'How much then?' Richard said.

'Two hundred and fifty would be generous. As Harry said, just look at the area. The whole place is depressed. Even if you could find a use for the mill, where would you find the user?'

Where indeed? They had thought that the purpose of this new venture of his was to identify companies that had undervalued their property, not overvalued it but as yet, they were not privy to Anatole Worstop's actuarial analysis. Worstop himself, was like a man reborn. Converting Churle Industrial into a predatory force had brought a sparkle to his eye and a spring to his step. Amongst the target companies that Piers Lansing had suggested had been an old, family run, light engineering company with a tangle of underfed subsidiaries which had no logical thread to hold them together. A company which had grown over the decades. When bits flourished, they had been watered; when they languished, they had still been watered, but with no result. There had been no cutting back, no grafting on of new talent and no replanting.

The takeover had created redundancies. You cannot combine the business of four disparate workshops into one without cutting labour. The workforce had grumbled but within themselves had realised that they had been living on borrowed time. To develop the original workshop, now in the centre of a thriving suburb, Lansing had negotiated a 'change of use' with the town planning department and then Churle Industrial had sold it on to a super-market chain for five times the original book value. One of the other factories had been stripped and, once the useful machinery had been transferred to the still functioning factory, it had been let as a warehouse on a short lease to a charity involved in the Third World. Churle Industrial had already broken even on the deal and it still had one more workshop to develop.

It was when Richard was ploughing through the complexities of the subsidiary companies with Anatole Worstop that they had uncovered a loan that the company had made to another firm. Athough the loan had been secured on property, rather like a mortgage, the interest had not been paid for eighteen months. Worstop had checked and re-checked. There was no doubt about it. He had been scandalised by the discovery but the only information they could obtain from the company's auditors was something to the effect that it was a gentleman's loan to a business associate. 'The family did things that way.' Whether the business associate was family or friend had not interested Richard, it was the name of the company: Priestman's of Halifax.

He had put Piers Lansing onto some detective work and he had come up with an ailing textile company run by a Walter Priestman with the other members of his family co-opted to the board. Ten years ago it had been flourishing with a contract to supply a high street clothing chain with own-branded clothes. Five years later the contract had gone to the Far East but

Priestman's had carried on, brazenly borrowing from whoever it could, plastering its name widely across the north of England. It seemed that there was not a market stall anywhere that did not have 'genuine seconds' of Priestman's products. They had tried ready-made curtains and spent half a million stocking a super-store with goods that nobody bought. In desperation, they had even tried exporting to India.

Priestman's of Halifax. It had to be the one. He thought of Bob Priestman, his angry red hair and his crush on that girl in Bristol... what was her name? But even as he was searching his memory, it was Jennifer's face he saw. Jennifer dancing with him at the disco. Jennifer slapping his face and then looking shocked when he had slapped hers. Was that why they were here now, in Halifax? Was it to get closer to people who had known Jennifer? That was not a rational way to take business decisions but it was Anatole Worstop who had unwittingly given him the excuse.

'With their debt that we bought in the takeover, Priestman's is practically ours for the asking.' Then he had grimaced. 'Heaven knows what we would do with it, should we ever want it, of course.'

'What happens if we do nothing?' Richard had asked.

'We will eventually have to write off the bad debt. Two and a half million.'

'Right then, so we are agreed are we? King's Mill is the best proposition?' Richard put some briskness into his voice. It woke the others from their moroseness.

'I think so,' Piers Lansing said and turned to Meachem in the back seat for confirmation. Meachem nodded.

'Shan't be a minute,' Richard said suddenly. He had just seen a movement behind one of the ground floor windows. 'Just going to have a look around. There's somebody in there.'

Before they could say anything he had slipped from the seat and was walking through the open iron gate into the cobbled yard. As he approached the building he could see a light bulb dappled through a frosted glass window, and the white shape of a person within. He looked right and left and eventually located a green painted wooden door which led into a small vestibule of wood block flooring and dust marks where bolted down furniture had been removed. This was presumably the offices. A rattling noise was coming from a room down the corridor.

'Hello?' He was aware that he was technically trespassing. 'Hello?' he called again. The rattling stopped, a door was yanked open and a young man's head shot out horizontally.

'Hi!'

Richard looked at the white pasty face with large dark eyes and thought of the does up at Long Covert on the estate.

'Hello,' he said again. 'I was... just looking around.' He thought it sounded particularly lame and possibly suspicious but these judgements apparently never entered the disembodied head for it merely grinned and said, 'Come in,' and with a kick of unseen legs, it drew the chair back into the room on its castors.

It must have been one of the offices. The door was half glazed with frosted glass as were the two tall windows opposite. At the bench which ran down one side of the room, sitting in front of a computer was the complete body, in a white lab coat which was unbuttoned over faded jeans and a tee shirt.

'I'm Greg. Who are you?'

'Richard.'

'Pleased to meet you Richard.' He offered his hand. 'What can I do for you?'

'Is this Priestman's.'

'Aye. Sort of. Buying or selling?' He grinned impishly. 'Selling, I should think, in that suit.'

Richard laughed. 'What are you doing?'

'Old man Priestman thinks I'm looking after his bloody derelict mill for him, just in case somebody breaks in and leaves something worth more than the freehold, like an empty fag packet for instance, but I'm actually looking after myself. If Priestman's are going down the chute there's no reason why I should go with'em.' He looked at Richard again with more care then sucked on his lip. Having reflected upon his behaviour and possibly considered that it had been a little too familiar he now tried to repair the damage. 'Of course,' he began formally, 'if you really want Priestman, Mr. Priestman the owner, like, well you'll need to go up to the head office in Commercial Street and speak to his secretary.'

'Has he got a son?'

'You a friend of Bob's? From London, I bet. Tell by yer accent, you know.'

'I studied with him for a while.'

'Oh one of them arty types.' He theatrically looked Richard up and down again, the amusement bubbling in his eyes, 'I heard they dress differently.' He spun his chair around to the computer. 'Well if you're an arty type then you'll like this.'

'What is it?' Richard bent to the screen.

'Its some software I've got to design patterns on cloth. You see, you can make a design, any design you like, something geometrical for example,' he worked at the mouse and a triangle took shape, 'Now I can make that any size, twist it around, double it, overlay it, anything. But here's where the clever bit comes in.' He rubbed his chin. 'I'm still working on it so just be patient if it doesn't work out. I can tell the pattern to reproduce itself to a certain length of roll. Say I wanted all those triangly things to stretch out to two point four metres and reproduce thereafter,' he tapped some keys, 'then that is what it will do, look!'

Richard watched the pattern resolve itself into the desired length and breadth of the cloth.

'Is this what they use at Priestman's?'

The look that he received he told him that they did not.

'I'm still working on it. That's why I took this job instead of redundancy. I can use Priestman's machine and his electricity. Actually it's not even his computer it's an ex-lease machine that got lost off the inventory. I had my mate upgrade it – there's loads of room in these old chassis, you know.'

Richard nodded as if he did.

'So is this a commercial package of software is it, that all companies use?' Greg gave him another one of his looks. 'Does that mean 'yes' or 'no'?' Richard smiled.

'It means that I think you're taking the piss. This is my software.' He emphasised his proprietorship. 'Nobody else has got it because I haven't finished writing it yet.'

Richard was startled as the door behind him suddenly crashed open. A glowering bundle of a stocky man stood there, his feet planted firmly apart in the classic Henry VIII pose. His wiry red hair had mellowed to rust and the sideboards which ran down to his thrust forward chin were silver. He wore a suit which, although of a similar grey, could never have been the twin of Richard's. It was baggy, it was shiny and seemed to be held together across his girth by a Victorian watchchain. Greg appeared utterly unmoved.

'Good afternoon Mr. Priestman,' he said.

'I'll give you "good afternoon Mr. Priestman"!' He strode into the room, grabbed the power cord and yanked it from the socket. Greg sighed with the expiring computer. Priestman spun around and turned a pair of angry eyes on Richard, looking him up and down. 'And who the hell are you?' he shouted.

With as much disdain as he could muster, Richard silently inspected the knurled finger which was prodding his chest. So this was Bob Priestman's *pater familias*? No further explanation for Bob was necessary.

'He's a friend of Bob's,' Greg said neutrally.

'Nobody asked you, Sharman!' he spat at Greg. 'And if I catch you playing silly games again on my computer... my computer... I'll have 'power cut off.'

'And the electric pump will stop and the basement will flood.' Greg shrugged. 'Please yourself, it's your mill.'

'Aye, you're bloody right there lad, it's my mill and what I say, goes. You'll laugh on t'other side of your bloody face when you're down on the Social like the others.' He spun around to face Richard again. 'Who are you and what the 'ell are you doing here? Friend of my lad's did 'e say?'

Richard returned his malevolent stare with as much ambiguity as he could muster. He was boiling inside. He wanted to thrash out and punch. He wanted to damage and maim. The physical power emanating from the man was massive and intimidating. Behind Priestman's back he saw Greg half close his eyes and slowly shake his head as if he had read Richard's thoughts and was dissuading him.

'It was nice meeting you Greg, I'll be in touch,' Richard pointedly ignored the simmering volcano that was Priestman. He saw Greg's eyebrows rise in question.

'You're not leaving here till you give me an explanation of what you're doing on my property, interfering with my staff.'

Richard opened his mouth wide as if to shout back but merely whispered, 'Goodbye Mr. Priestman. I'll be in touch with you as well.'

She knew that this was worse than the first day at big school. Knowing that you were soon to be pitched in amongst a crowd of strangers who would all seem to know each other and only you would be alone. When you went to big school at least you came home to familiar surroundings at night. Magdaline looked around the ward. The brown linoleum, pockmarked by bed and chair legs; the walls, painted two shades of green; the curtains which clacked on overhead rails – this was the only home that she knew, these were familiar surroundings and she was leaving them. The day she had feared had arrived. She was being discharged.

She sat in the chair at the side of her bed. Her bed. It would be somebody else's bed tonight. Her clothes nestled in a grey plastic bag at her feet. She waited, dreading. She had signed papers with a careful *'Magdaline O'Neill'* in round handwriting. Now she was waiting for the machinery of hospital administration to compute and release her. A list of her next appointments was being drawn up. Melanie Millson's arrangements to treat her outside was being finalised. Her accommodation was being organised with the local authority. A travel voucher would be issued. Then she would be spat out.

She felt utterly alone. Completely and utterly alone. Nobody could understand what it was like to know absolutely nobody, not even yourself. Gripped in her left hand was a scrap of paper. Crushed with the intensity of her attachment to it, it was creased from the number of times it had been consulted. She opened it out, spread it on her knee and read it although she knew it by heart. *'Our Lady Hostel, Shoreditch. One bed. Magdaline O'Neill.'* Her link with the life she had lost. On her wrist was her watch. It had stopped. It needed a new battery but she would not change it. That battery had worked in her old life and her new life. It had bridged the gap just like the piece of paper. It might be able to tell her something one day. And she had the denim cap. These were the only artefacts that she had. Even her clothes were not hers really, they had been foisted upon her.

An orderly paused at the door and looked around the ward. With her heart thumping she shrank into her chair, hoping he would not see her. He smiled at her pleasantly, picked up a plastic box from the desk and continued on his way. He was not for her. She relaxed but another figure appeared in the doorway and she tensed up again like a hunted creature.

'Magdaline!' It was Lynne.

'Lynne! Oh Lynne!'

She swirled in and bounced on the bed. 'You look as if you're waiting for someone,' she said. She leaned forward and took Magdaline's hands in hers. 'How are you?'

'Oh Lynne! I am pleased. I am very pleased to see you. Very pleased.' She could feel the tears filling the backs of her eyes. 'I was so... so...' She pulled a hand away and groped for a tissue in the box on the table.

'Hey, hey, hey! What's all this? Hmm?'

Magdaline swallowed hard. 'I'm being discharged.'

'That's great! When?'

'Today. Some time today. That's what I am waiting for.'

'That's brilliant. Are you all cured then? I mean...'

'Well I can walk, I can breathe, I can feed. I've got to come back for some check ups and the psy... er, one of the specialists will continue to treat me when I get outside.'

'Oh that's great! I am pleased. Look I brought you another book, it's the sequel to that other one. What did you think of it?'

'A bit naughty,' she replied vaguely.

'Yeah, good wasn't it?'

Magdaline sighed, unable to completely stifle a sob.

'So why the long face if you're getting out of this dump?' Lynne said. 'Surely you don't like it here do you?' Magdaline was looking at a scrap of paper on her lap. 'What's that?' She asked.

'It's me. It's my history. Magdaline O'Neill, destitute, down and out. No family, no friends, no home.'

'So where are you going to live?'

'They are putting me on the local council. I don't know where I'll end up, I suppose there must be hostels for people like me.' She laughed bitterly. 'Our Lady Hostel, Shoreditch. One bed. Magdaline O'Neill.' She carefully folded the paper and put it in her pocket. 'I was alright here. You see, this is the only home I remember.'

'Yes.'

'No.' Magdaline shook her head sadly. 'No you don't see. Just before you came in I was hoping that they would forget me and I would be left here and forgotten. I was thinking about how, going out there,' she waved at the window, 'going out there would be worse than going from lower school up to the big school. Do you know what I mean? Do you remember the feeling? All those enormous children, taller than you and the strange buildings and staircases everywhere.'

'Oh yes, I remember.'

'But you see the school when you remember. You know what you are talking about. I only remember the feeling. I have no idea what the school was like. I have no idea whether I went to school or not. I only recall a feeling and for all I know, I could be making it all up.'

'But you must have gone to school,' Lynne insisted. 'You can remember it.'

'No I can't remember it!' Magdaline snapped. 'That's the point. I don't remember it. And soon I've got to go out there and nobody will understand what I will feel like.'

'When are you being discharged?'

'I don't know, I'm waiting for... well, actually, I signed the papers this morning so I suppose I'm discharged already. But I can't go yet. I'm waiting for them to decide where they are going to send me.'

'Haven't they told you where you will be living?'

'No, not yet. They probably don't know yet. They'll send someone along when they do.'

'Well how will I find you? I must give you my address.' She began to delve into her handbag. 'You must write to me. Call me. Come and visit me.' She stopped searching. 'You could stay the night sometimes. I've got a spare room. It would make a change from a hostel.'

Magdaline felt sadness welling up in her again. 'I would like that, Lynne,' she said, carefully, daring to hope at a proposition of friendship. 'That would be very nice.'

But Lynne was tapping her foot on the floor and not listening. 'What's in the bag?' She pointed at the plastic sack.

'My clothes and things.'

'Everything?'

'Including the comb and the mirror you gave me.'

'Do you fancy a walk?'

'Well there's not much to see. I can show you the–'

'Bring your bag.' Lynne stood up and pulled the hem of her skirt down. 'Come on slowcoach!'

She led off down the corridor.

'That's where I see my specialist, in there,' Magdaline explained. 'She wears a tracksuit with a green elephant on it.' They came to the foyer and Lynne took her elbow firmly.

'I can hold you there can I? No mended fractures?'

'No that's alright.' Magdaline continued her guided tour commentary. 'Those seats by the window are where we sat and watched everybody get wet in the rain.'

'And this is the front door,' Lynne said, 'and we are walking through it. Magdaline O'Neill is not going to a hostel, she's not going back on the streets. Magdaline O'Neill is going to share a flat in Lewisham with her best friend, Lynne Hall.'

Mrs. Armitage gulped her mouthful of tepid coffee and took the phone from Nikki who was making anguished faces.

'Mrs. Armitage.' She put down her beaker and waited for the talking to die down. 'Why can't you put them at the back of the kitchens where you usually do?' She leaned over and prodded Nikki in the back with her pen and then stabbed it in the air towards a notice board. 'Yes, yes. I gave them permission to park there.' She nodded confirmation as Nikki took down a list and passed it to her. 'Well you will still have to speak to me because I am in charge of it.' She initialled the list and passed it over the counter to an orderly. 'But they are working on cables and that is where the manhole cover is so they have to park their vans there. Yes, well put them in front of the boiler room door temporarily. I know it is but I'll take responsibility for that.' She replaced the receiver. 'All sweetness and light,' she muttered and pulled a fax from the machine.

'When you've done that Nikki can you put a new roll in the fax machine? It's coming up with a pink stripe.'

'O.K. Did those sharps come through for Surgical?'

'It should be on this fax... No. Tomorrow morning at the earliest. Ring Surgical and ask them if that will do.' She swung back to her desk where the phone was ringing again. 'If not, get them to courier them over.' She picked up the phone. 'Admin?' She twisted through ninety degrees to her computer monitor. 'I'm working on them now sir.' She stabbed the keyboard and the printer in the corner began to whir out a sheet of paper covered with figures. 'But they are only go as far as the first of the month,' she said as she leaned back and pulled the sheet out. 'I'll send them down by messenger. My pleasure sir.'

'Did the council get back to us about that girl for discharge on Women's Med?' Nikki asked as she threaded the fax roll through the rollers.

Mrs Armitage pressed the buzzer for the messenger and folded the sheet of statistics into an envelope. She gave her reply over her shoulder. 'I haven't taken the call but they may have gone straight through to the ward. Can you check when you've done that?' She turned around and caught Nikki making a face. 'Alright, I'll do it.'

'Messenger!' a thin voice piped from the corridor. She held the envelope over the counter and it was taken from her hand as she lifted the phone with the other.

'Women's med? Hello, has the local authority come back to you with the address for your discharge today? No that's alright, I can wait.' She pulled an enormous diary across towards her, turned several pages and made an entry. 'I've put the glass inspection in for next month,' she said to Nikki, 'You'd better warn Watkins because it falls on a Friday afternoon and you know what he's like before the weekend.'

'O.K. I'll send him a fax,' she grinned. 'Then he won't be able to say that we didn't tell him.'

'Good idea. Hello, yes, Oh really? No that's all right, makes our job easier. Thanks.' She turned to Nikki and sighed. 'She went before lunch apparently. Obviously they found somewhere for her. I wish they'd trouble to tell us instead of leaving us chasing around all day long.'

'It's a pain, isn't it?'

EPISODE TWENTY TWO

Magdaline paused with the spoon halfway to her mouth. 'It's coconut, isn't it?'

'Yup,' Lynne agreed.

'Now I would never have thought of putting coconut in porridge. I like it.'

Lynne made a mime in the air of writing on a notepad.

'One more for my epitaph,' she said. '"I would never have thought of coconut." What a slogan! Perhaps I could sell it to that dishy Davros in the Creative Section.' Magdaline laughed at her. 'Your turn to do the dishes,' Lynne added.

'Good.'

Magdaline was pleased with the domestic exigencies of flat sharing. In a strange way they gave her confidence. She was doing things that other, normal, people did and if washing dishes made no more sense to her than it made to anybody else, then that made her normal. At least by doing it she was partaking of the nonsense. She glanced at the calendar hanging above the bread bin.

'It's almost the end of October. I can hardly believe I've been here already seven weeks. So much has happened.' She looked gratefully at Lynne who was flipping the pages of a magazine, her coffee cup poised in mid air, precariously hanging on one finger. Lynne sensed the warmth in the glance and looked up.

'Get on with the dishes, slave,' she growled.

Magdaline smiled broadly. 'Yes master.'

Just seven weeks ago she had been at the bottom of her life, as far as she could see. The only place of refuge that she had known was throwing her out. She had no friends, no home, no job, no money. Then Lynne, marvellous Lynne, she who plays squash and twists her knee; Lynne had come along and suddenly she had a friend and a home.

Lynne had taken her along to the right offices and insisted with officialdom until they had found Magdaline an emergency National Insurance number and an entitlement to some form of supplementary benefit. Not content with that she had come home one evening and announced that Dominic wanted to see Magdaline on the morrow to check whether she could really draw and by the end of that day, Magdaline had a job. Dominic had seen her in hospital and having been fully appraised of her situation by Lynne, had instructed Personnel that she was to be paid weekly until she felt more established. So now she had money. Not much, but it was hers. She had earned it herself.

Dominic had also listened carefully to her explanation of who she was and how insecure she felt and mixed up and angry and lost and cheated and he had proposed that, if she thought she could cope with working with the others in the office, then nobody but he, Lynne and Personnel need know her story. And that was how it was. She arrived at Janus & Janus with Lynne every morning and quickly graduated from 'Lynne's new flat mate' to 'Magdaline', a person in her own right. 'Magdaline', not 'Maggie', the office had learned very quickly. Magdaline, the girl who was a whizz with a soft pencil and a smearing thumb; particularly good with fashion detail on figures.

She stood with her hands in the sink of warm water, waiting for Lynne to finish her coffee. From the window she could just see the stark limbs of a black tree in the back yard of another house in the terrace. The phone rang, she ignored it. That was one area where she had not yet made an impact, of course. There would be no phone calls for her. Lynne got up to answer it and Magdaline hoped that it was not one of her friends suggesting they do something this Saturday morning because Lynne had already promised her that she would come with her to the shops and help her spend some of her money on a decent set of clothes. Something she could wear to the office.

Magdaline bit her lip as she realised how selfish she was being. After all that Lynne had done for her, she was already begrudging her some life to herself. She must not make herself jealous of Lynne's friends nor resent the time that she wants to spend with them. So far, the problem had never arisen because Lynne had taken Magdaline everywhere with her and had introduced her to all of her friends – partly because she wanted her to have a good time and this was the quickest way of assuring it and partly, Magdaline was ashamed to admit, because at first Magdaline would not go out except in Lynne's company.

'Magdaline! Wake up! I'm talking to you.'

'Sorry Lynne, I was day-dreaming. What did you say?'

'It's for you.'

Magdaline looked at the telephone receiver in Lynne's hand.

'What do you mean?'

'The telephone. It's for you.'

Blood began to pound in Magdaline's ears. She heard her tiny voice saying from a long way off, 'Who is it?'

Lynne pulled her mouth sideways, shifted her weight onto one foot and rested her elbow on her hip.

'I don't know who it is.'

'How do you know it is for me?'

'Oh for heaven's sake, Magdaline, they said, "can I speak to Magdaline O'Neill please?" That's you isn't it? I'm damn certain it's not me.'

'Yes, I am Magdaline O'Neill.' Lynne handed her the phone. 'Where are you going?' she was alarmed. 'Don't leave me.'

'I'm going to wash my coffee cup. I'll be over here. See.'

Magdaline nodded. Lynne turned her back. It was her way of telling Magdaline to get on with it and not be such a baby. She put the receiver to her ear. 'Hello?'

'Is that Magdaline?'

'Yes.'

'At last.' Her heart started thumping. The voice was familiar. 'You're a difficult girl to find, Magdaline.'

Lynne was taking a long time washing that cup.

'Am I?'

'It's Melanie Millson.'

'Yes of course.' She closed her eyes and let out her breath slowly. The psychiatrist. 'Hello Melanie.'

'I want to hear your news. When are you coming to see me?'

'I don't know if I can. I mean...'

'You don't know if you want to?'

'Not exactly that. It's the time.'

'No time like the present. Why don't you come over today?'

'We were going to Oxford Street to buy some clothes this morning.' She looked around at Lynne who nodded.

'Perfect. That's only just around the corner from me. I live in Paddington. Come along after lunch, say two thirty?'

'I'm not sure.' She sought guidance from Lynne but Lynne had not heard the suggestion and could only shrug in ignorance.

'Your friend can come along as well if you like. We have a small garden; if the weather stays fine it's lovely sitting out. This is the address. Have you got a pen and paper?'

Magdaline copied the address onto the shopping list board and then put the phone down.

'That was Melanie Millson. From the hospital. Well, not from the hospital, she was phoning from home.' Lynne nodded. Magdaline continued. 'I said I would visit her this afternoon. 'She lives in Paddington. She says it's not far from Oxford Street.'

'Fine. Don't look so serious. She can't do anything to you.'

'I was just thinking about my escape from hospital.'

'It wasn't an escape. Not in that sense anyway. They had already discharged you. You were free to walk out. The reason you were waiting was because you had nowhere to live.' She put her hands on Magdaline's shoulders and looked into her eyes. 'You've done nothing wrong, Magdaline.'

'No, I suppose not.'

'Of course you haven't. Now buck up and get your coat. That's the first thing we'll remedy. It looks as if it came from Oxfam!'

'It probably did.'

They marched up the north side of Oxford Street and back down the south side. Lynne would not permit them to stop for coffee until Magdaline had purchased a coat to keep her warm through the winter.

'Take the blue,' Lynne insisted.

'Do you think so?'

'Yes, the blue. It brings out your eyes so.'

She purchased the blue coat, handing over the notes to the cashier. Her money that she had earned and now it was buying her a coat.

'Put it on,' Lynne said.

'What now?'

'Of course. That's what you've bought it for isn't it?'

'Yes. Hold my bag.'

She slipped the coat on and the assistant hurried out from behind the counter with a pair of scissors and snipped off various labels. 'Keep your receipt ready madam, just in case the store detective stops you at the door.'

Once outside Lynne said, 'Why are you carrying that thing with you?' She took the old coat from Magdaline's arm and pushed it into a rubbish bin. 'Good riddance, I say.' They both laughed. 'And what about that old cap? You're not keeping that are you?'

Magdaline's hands flew to her head in alarm, clutching the denim cap to her scalp. 'Not the cap,' she said. 'It's my cap.'

'So was the coat.'

'This is my cap, Lynne. Don't you understand? My cap. I had it before the accident. It's my cap. It belongs to my life before.'

'O.K., O.K. Sorry. I didn't think.'

'My cap, Lynne,' Magdaline sobbed. 'Don't take it from me.'

Lynne put her arm around her shoulders and guided her out of the view of the staring shoppers.

'Come on, Magdaline. Coffee time, we've earned it.'

Melanie Millson opened the door herself. She was wearing pink trousers and a yellow floppy jumper.

'Magdaline! Come in, come in.' She ushered Magdaline down the passageway. 'Go straight through the kitchen. Keep heading towards the daylight,' she said. From a room at the side came the sound of an ignored television and squabbling children. Melanie poked her head through the doorway. 'Samuel! Jonathon! Television off if you are not watching it.'

'We are grandma, we are!' youthful protestations assured her.

'Little tikes!' she muttered. 'They ought to be out in the park.'

'Your grandchildren?'

'Two of them,' she said. 'We've got seven.'

'Grandma, can we have a drink please?' One of the boys stood in the doorway.

'Yes but say hello to Magdaline first.'

The boy stood on one foot, put his head askew and stared at her. Magdaline stared back. He had dark brown skin and black, tightly curled hair. 'Hello,' he said.

'Hello.'

'There,' said Melanie, handing him two glasses. 'Take that one to Jonathon. Magdaline and I are going to sit in the garden. If I hear any more arguing coming from you, there will be no more cricket.'

With big serious eyes concentrating on the brimming glasses, the boy carefully turned back to the television room.

'Tea, coffee, beer?' Melanie asked.

'Coffee would be lovely thank you.'

'Go out and push the chairs into the sun.'

Magdaline stepped into the small courtyard garden. Three sparrows flew off the garden wall, chirping noisily at the intrusion. She moved the chairs around until they benefited from the triangle of sunshine that was slanting onto the concrete. She sat down, closed her eyes and let the sunshine make pink patterns on her eyelids. She could just hear the distant rumble of Saturday afternoon London wafting intermittently over the garden walls. The sun was warm for October. Perhaps this would compensate her for the six weeks of summer she had lost.

With the thundering weight of black dread she brutally recalled that she had lost more than just six weeks in summer. She had lost, she did not know how many, years of her life.

'Right, here we are.' Melanie put the tray on a large upturned flowerpot between them. 'Help yourself and tell me what you have been doing with yourself and how you are getting on.'

Magdaline picked up her coffee. 'I am sharing a flat with a girl called Lynne. She was in the bed next to me in hospital.'

'Oh yes and you live down in Lewisham don't you?'

'Yes. How did you find me? I mean, I wasn't trying to hide. I didn't have time to tell the hospital where I was going. It all happened on the spur of the moment.'

'Yes, it must have been exciting – suddenly finding that you did not have to go back to a hostel, or out on the street.'

She sensed that Melanie was watching her as she spoke.

'I didn't want to go to a hostel,' she admitted quietly. 'At the time, I did not want to leave hospital. I felt safe there.'

'That makes good sense. It was the only environment that you knew by remembered experience. Of course you felt safe there. What made you change your views? How did Lynne get you to go with her?'

'I don't know really. Force of character I suppose. And I wanted to go with her anyway. I like her. She's been very good to me. Very good. You know, she won't let me help with the rent until she is satisfied that I have all that I need for myself.'

'How are you supporting yourself then? We know that you were on the Benefit to start with because they phoned up the hospital to check on your story. That was how we found you, by the way. Somebody in the admin. office remembered your name and put two and two together.'

'Oh. Lynne took me to the Benefit Office and explained it all to them. It took ages and she had to have time off work to do it but she was magnificent. She just kept at them until they agreed. But the best news is that I've got a job.'

'A job! Oh Magdaline that's brilliant! What do you do?'

Magdaline pulled her new coat around her. 'I work in the same office as Lynne. Well, that is to say, I work in the same company. I am not in the same office because Lynne buys advertising space and I help in the graphics department.'

'What does that mean?'

'I draw for them. The clever people on the creative side think up an advertisement, either a TV ad. or perhaps a magazine ad. but not many of them can draw very well so they tell me what they want and I sketch it out on the pad. It's a doddle.'

'You find that easy?'

'Yes. I seem to have the knack.'

Melanie looked at Magdaline who was sitting on the edge of her chair, bubbling with sparkling eyes. 'Life is exciting isn't it?' she said. 'Do you remember me saying to you that many people would envy you because you could go out and just do what you wanted to do; be who you wanted to be with no complexes and memories to hold you back? Start anew?'

'Yes, I do. But I didn't believe you. I am still not certain whether I believe you now.'

'But you recognise the opportunity?'

'Yes, sort of. I was very lucky to get the job. I had no references or certificates to show. Dominic just gave me something to draw and I did it.'

'You can be what you like, who you like.'

'That's a bit frightening.'

'Are you sure it is frightening or is it more exhilarating?'

'A bit of both really.'

'Are you still angry?'

'Yes. Sometimes.'

'What are you angry with?'

'Sometimes I am angry with the anonymous person who caused the accident.'

'That could have been you. We don't know what happened.'

Magdaline stared at her. 'I had never thought of that. When you wake up like I did, finding all your previous life wiped clean, you automatically feel the victim. It can't be any other way. It should not be allowed to happen.'

'What else do you get angry at?'

'Just the injustice of it all. There I was, living my life, no harm to a soul and bang! I'm suddenly here without a "by your leave" or whatever.'

'You don't know what life you left behind you.'

'I know I don't.'

'Are you happy in your present life?'

'I suppose I am. I ought to be jolly grateful. I've got a great friend, a good job and a nice flat.'

'Which we suppose you did not have before.'

'Why do we suppose that?'

'You must know, Magdaline, that all the evidence points to the fact that you were probably homeless and unemployed.'

'We don't know we've got all the evidence.'

Melanie leaned forward and took one of Magdaline's hands. 'A friend, a job, a flat. If you had a friend, Magdaline, why did nobody claim you in hospital? If you had a job, why did none of your colleagues come around? If you had a flat, why did not your neighbour or landlord remark upon your absence?' Magdaline could see a sort of weary concern in her eyes. 'I think you are getting close to the truth.'

'What do you mean?'

'What did Dr. Brady tell you about your illness?'

Magdaline thought back to the German student bringing in the coffee and the portly man with the red mark on his forehead.

'He said lots of stuff I didn't understand. Then he said he could not help me any more and he would send me to you.'

'I am helping you because Dr. Brady diagnosed that your amnesia was only partial–'

'Only partial? But, I can't remember a thing about what happened before.'

'You can, Magdaline. You know you are in England, you know how to catch a bus, how to read, how to count, how to shop. You remember lots of things that you knew before the accident.

'Oh yes, that's right.'

'Dr. Brady and I both believe that there is something psychological preventing you from remembering what happened before. It is a sort of safety switch for the body. It decides that the memory of what happened is so painful, so traumatic that you will stand a better chance of recovery by not considering it at all.'

'You mean the shock of having the accident?'

'Not necessarily. There might have been something before the accident that you do not want to relive. It might be your subconscious saying to you, "you never wanted to be a homeless down and out and now is your chance to change it." It is quite possible, Magdaline, that you were ashamed of your life as it was.'

'And that is why I don't want to remember it?'

'I am not saying that you are refusing to tell the truth. I am saying that your mind is protecting you. It's giving you a chance.'

'In that case I will never get my memory back. I will never want to remember. Do you think I will get it back?'

Melanie put her coffee cup on the balanced tray.

'Nobody can answer that question truthfully. What I will say is this: you are approaching it in the right way.'

'I am?' Magdaline was surprised. 'What am I doing right?'

'You are getting on with your life. You are living.'

'And that is the right thing to do?'

'Yes, I think so. Your body and your mind are getting stronger all the while that you are occupying yourself with your present life. Once your body considers itself strong enough, then you have the greatest chance of recovering the access to that part of your memory that is denied to you at present. If you go looking for the memory, if you rack your brains trying to recall things, then you will worry yourself, tire your body and push your memory recapture even further away.'

'How will it come back? If it does,' she added hastily.

'Impossible to say. You can't force it. Whatever you do, don't try to bump yourself on the head again. That only works on TV. Your brain does not need any more physical shocks to its system. Trying to trip your memory will cause you intense anxiety and have no effect, or worse still, an adverse effect.' She sat back and picked a leaf from her trousers and played with it absently. 'You might just realise one day that you can remember more and more. You might wake up one morning and find that everything is back to normal.'

'And I might not,' said Magdaline.

'And you might not,' she agreed.

Mrs. Dove's cardigan drooped lifelessly on the back of her empty chair. Wayne was sitting on the corner of her desk, flipping over the pages of a motoring magazine.

'What do you think of the Loch Ness Monster then?' he asked Katrina.

Katrina pushed away a crossword puzzle book and peered up at him through her thick lenses.

'The what?'

'The Loch Ness Monster. Miss Vanessa. Haven't you heard him calling her "Nessie"?' Wayne's face broadened into a wide, innocent grin.

'Wayne! You shouldn't say things like that. You should show respect. Anyway, I thought you liked her.'

'I do. In a way. What about you?'

Katrina turned her eyes towards the ceiling as if searching for inspiration in the plaster cornices. 'She's a bit hoity-toity. No, I don't mean that. She isn't a bit hoity-toity she just speaks like it. Did you know her dad was a Lord?'

'How do you know?'

'I heard old Doorstop talking to her.' Anatole Worstop would have been mortified had he known of his nickname.

'Funny place this, isn't it?' Wayne said.

'How do you mean?'

'Well...' he began. 'We've got Richard, who is a lord but he doesn't act like one and the only person who calls him "milord" is the Doorstop. We've got the Loch Ness Monster whose father is a lord which must make her something but she doesn't act it either. The only person here who looks and acts like aristocracy is the Doorstop himself.'

'Yes,' Katrina agreed vaguely. 'My mum asked me once what it was like working for a lord and I couldn't really tell her. He's just a person like anybody else really. She thought he would be sitting here in a carmine cloak or something.'

'Ermine.'

'What?'

'It's not carmine, it's ermine.'

'Well whatever it is.'

Wayne looked out of the window. 'There's Richard and Vanessa. I wonder where the Vulture has got to.'

'I don't know but I wish she would hurry. I've got work to do.'

Richard tried not to look at Vanessa's bottom as it wriggled up the stairs before him but the suit she was wearing did fit her rather well.

'Good morning Harry,' he called at an open door as he walked down the corridor.

'Morning Richard. Have you got Vanessa there?'

Vanessa stopped and turned back. 'Harry?'

'Could you show me that thing with the graph you were teaching me yesterday? I haven't quite got it.'

Good old Harry, Richard thought, no complexes there, just get on and do it and never mind what the others might think of you. He had assumed that because Harry was working in a male dominated atmosphere, requiring him to be tough with tough people, he would patronise Vanessa as a feeble woman. He had been surprised to discover that Harry was quite open to suggestion and willing to learn from whoever. Richard realised that he was learning a lot about himself, about his own prejudices as well as those of others. He turned in to Piers Lansing's office.

'Ah, um good morning.' Lansing half rose from his desk.

'Stay as you are,' Richard said easily. He pulled a chair across to the desk. 'How are the liquidations going?'

'That is what I was working on now. Um, quite well, quite well.'

'Any sticky patches?'

'Cavenhan Terrace. He tapped a town plan. I don't think we will get anywhere near my estimate. I popped down there to have a look on the way home yesterday.'

'On the way home?'

'Well, not quite on the way home. The area has gone to seed a bit and the council is buying up properties as and when they become available.'

'Will we lose in this sale?'

'That, or break even.'

'What happens if we don't sell?'

Lansing fiddled with his pencil and then smoothed down his hair. 'Well, the value of the area is going down steadily and so too will the level of rent that we could expect to receive. We will come to a point when the council will have to show its hand and then make a compulsory purchase order for the remaining properties that it requires in order to do whatever it is planning.'

'What do you think we should do?'

'Me?' Lansing seemed surprised. Richard nodded. 'Sell now for whatever we can get.'

'And put it down to experience?'

Lansing smiled thinly.

'Yes, and put it down to experience.'

'Fine. I'll leave it to you then. I must go and get some figures from Katrina.'

Richard stopped in the doorway and looked, bemused at Katrina and Wayne. They were quite patently doing nothing.

'Good morning sir,' Katrina greeted him. Wayne waved a hand from the low filing cabinet upon which he was sitting.

'Good morning. Katrina, could you get me the figures on Priestman's of Halifax?' He nodded at the computer.

'Well, I can't for the moment sir,' she apologised, 'Mrs. Dove is not in yet.'

'That's all right we don't need Mrs. Dove for that. You can use the computer, you've had your training haven't you?' He recalled Mrs. Dove's tight lipped assent to the training of the person whom she had considered as her office girl, in the mysteries of the company's administration software.

'Oh yes sir. Anyway that is not on the admin system it's in the Current Ops. File.'

'Fine,' Richard said encouragingly.

'But I need the hard disk.'

'I thought the hard disk was part of the computer.'

'Oh no sir, not this one.' Katrina's eyes were enormous. 'For security reasons it has a removable hard drive. We take it out every night so that if somebody breaks in and nicks the computer we don't lose our records.'

'That sounds quite wise. Where is it then?'

'In Mrs. Dove's cupboard.' She indicated the corner of the office behind Mrs. Dove's desk where a small, grey cupboard squatted. It was made of gunmetal steel, with shielded hinges and a serious lock.

'And Mrs. Dove has the key?' Richard asked. Katrina nodded. 'Where is Mrs. Dove?'

'She's not in yet sir.'

'Her old banger's probably broken down. It was smoking something awful when it left yesterday. Head gasket I shouldn't wonder.' Wayne proffered his suggestion with the authority of a car enthusiast who could not yet afford a car.

'Is there another key?' Richard asked.

Katrina shrugged. 'Not that I know of.' She looked across at Wayne. He shook his head.

'And I can't unlock the filing cabinets or switch on the photocopier,' he complained.

'Because...?'

Wayne silently pointed at the locked box surrounding the mains plug for the photocopier. At that moment, Mrs. Dove hurried in, her coat flapping and the hair straggling away from under her headscarf.

'Oh I'm sorry I'm late sir, I don't know what happened to my car, it suddenly went bang in a cloud of smoke on the bypass. I had to come on by bus.'

'Big end, thought so,' Wayne muttered from his filing cabinet.

'That's alright Mrs. Dove, Wayne and Katrina have been keeping me entertained.'

She shot them a puzzled glance as she tugged her scarf from her head.

'Where is your car?' Richard asked. 'We can get a garage to tow it in. Or Harry and Wayne could go in the Range Rover.'

'Please don't trouble sir, I'll phone Pinner's, they'll know what to do.'

'As you wish. We are rather glad you've arrived. We need the hard disk for the computer. I believe it is in your cupboard.'

'The hard disk. Yes,' she said, looking at Katrina. Katrina gazed blankly back.

'And we would like to turn the photocopier on,' Richard added, his voice full of meaning. 'And unlock the filing cabinet.'

'Yes, yes, of course.' She opened her purse, took out a keyring and unlocked the cupboard. She silently handed the hard disk to Katrina.

'I am sure that you can see that this system, although designed for security, is a little inconvenient for us in times such as this.' Richard made the observation with as little intonation in his voice as possible. He knew he was on dangerous territory and resented the feeling. This was obviously Mrs. Dove's way of retaining control; of ensuring that the office revolved around her.

'But I am never late sir. This is the first time in years,' she protested hotly as she put the keys back in her purse. 'And I came as quickly as I could.'

'And I am very relieved to know that you are unhurt. We were worried that something nasty had happened to you.' He looked around at the others who took up the cue with concerned faces. 'How many keys are there to the cabinet?'

'Just the ones that came with it.'

'How many is that?'

'Three.'

'I think it would be wiser if they were distributed wider in the office to avoid incidents such as this.'

She subconsciously clutched the purse to her. 'But this was an exception. I can hardly be blamed for this.'

'I am not blaming anybody, Mrs. Dove, I am merely trying to ensure that the company can continue to run when one of our number fails to attend the office.' He held out his hand.

She looked at it then fumbled, red faced in her purse.

'Well I... I...' She took out the ring and removed one of the duplicates. 'That one is mine,' she said defiantly.

Richard smiled pleasantly as he detached another key.

'And this one is Katrina's,' he said, handing it to the open mouthed girl. 'I'll label this one and put it in the key safe in Piers' office then anybody who knows the combination can get it in an emergency.' He put the key in his pocket. 'Now Katrina, can you find me the figures I want?'

Katrina shut her mouth and powered up her machine.

Magdaline acted on the spur of the moment. She had come home early from work because Dominic had said that they did not need her that afternoon. He had packed her off after lunch with a, 'Take the afternoon off. Go home and put your feet up. You deserve a rest.' He had not added that he thought she looked tired and had probably been working too hard.

And now she was standing in the kitchen of Lynne's flat, biting her lip with indecision. Should she or shouldn't she? Melanie Millson had said that she definitely should not. It would all come back in its own time and if she tried to force the pace she would regret it. That was all very easy to say but not so easy to do when you were faced with situations such as had occurred this morning.

It was just the sort of trivial thing which would not affect a normal person. She had just come out of Dominic's office carrying a storyboard of a series of about a dozen small sketches depicting the running of a television ad. in its chronological sequence. 'Man goes to front door; inside house, flowers being put in vase; on doorstep, man rings bell' and so forth. She had not invented the story line – that had been done by one of Dominic's protegés – she had merely filled in the boxes on the sheet with a rough interpretation of what was supposed to be happening. One of the other juniors had walked by, glanced at the board and complimented her on the drawing.

'You're good at that aren't you?'

'Am I? I don't really know.'

'I think you're good. Do you like doing it?'

'Yes, I suppose I do.' She realised that she sounded vague but could do nothing to alter it.

'I wish I could draw like that. You make it look so easy. Which college did you go to?'

Magdaline had started in horror.

'I don't... I didn't go to college.'

'You must have gone to art college to learn to draw like that. You must have.'

'I don't think so.' She looked around frantically for Lynne, but Lynne worked in another part of the office.

'Well you must have been doing it a long time. Where were you before Janus?'

'Oh... nowhere.' She had put the board down hurriedly. 'I must go to the loo!' She had rushed off leaving the girl gawping after her.

And then she had started to ask herself questions. Where did I learn to draw? Did I go to a college? No, I was a vagrant living on the streets. I don't want to return to the streets. Where had I learned to draw? Had somebody taught me or was I just a natural? What was I doing before? Just living on the streets, I know that, so why did this girl think that I had been doing this job somewhere else? Had she seen me there? Does she know something about me? But all she could do was ask herself questions. She could not find any answers to them and then her head had started to ache and Dominic had sent her home.

And despite all that, or maybe because of it, she was now standing in Lynne's kitchen, holding her piece of paper and trying to decide whether it would be a good thing to go back to the Our Lady Hostel in Shoreditch to see if anybody remembered her. The aching in her head told her it was a silly thing to do. Melanie Millson had advised her against any attempt to jolt her memory but Magdaline felt that she wanted to. She needed to.

She made up her mind, pulled on her new coat, crammed her denim cap down over her ears and went out.

'We're not open yet, ducks. Not till five.' The portly woman continued to swab the tiled step, swinging her wide bottom from side to side as she wielded the mop.

Magdaline looked at the red brick porchway. Above it, on a grubby keystone she could read the date, '1882'. Inside the porch, on one wall, hung a glass fronted notice board. The door was a double door like a church hall, painted dark red. The tall Victorian window frames were painted the same colour. She stared at it. Was this the last doorway through which she had walked to be knocked down in the street? Had this same woman cleaned away her footprints on that very day?

The woman leaned heavily on the mop, squeezing the last drops of grey water into the bucket, then she rubbed her hands on her overalls and turned around to look at Magdaline. The new blue coat and smart skirt obviously impressed her.

'I beg yer pardon, miss, I thought you was one of our ladies. They always try to slip in early to get a good place.'

'No, I'm not... Not one of your ladies.'

'What can I do for you? Is it Sister Connie you're wanting?'

'Sister Connie?'

'She'll be in her office. It's her you'll be wanting?'

What did she want? What was she doing here? What did she

hope to find? Melanie had specifically told her that this was a dangerous thing to do and so here she was, trying to do it.

'Yes, Sister Connie,' she confirmed. The name meant nothing to her.

'Go down the side there.' The woman pointed with a hand brush. 'You'll see a door by the bins. It's got *"office"* on it.'

'Thank you.'

'It's a red door. Like this one.'

Magdaline found the door and knocked hard to show that she was not scared.

'Come!' came the order from inside. Magdaline pushed the door but it did not move. 'Give it a shove, it sticks!' came the instruction.

She put her shoulder to it and burst, stumbling, into the room. 'Sorry!' she excused herself a little breathlessly.

'Sit down now that you're in.'

Sister Connie was sitting at a laundry table which obviously served as her desk as well. She was a chubby middle-aged woman in blue stretch trousers and a blue pullover. She was long-sighted and her spectacles gave her eyes a magnified importance completely out of proportion to the rest of her round pink face. Magdaline sat on the kitchen chair by the boiler.

'What can I do for you?' Sister Connie said.

Magdaline had thought out a plan on the short walk to the office but now that she was sitting there it did not seem so good. She was going to pretend to be looking for a friend but in the end she merely said, 'Do you have a book with the names of people who stay here?'

'Yes we do. Are you looking for someone?'

'I'm looking for a name,' Magdaline replied vaguely. 'The name of someone who stayed here in May.' It suddenly occurred to her that neither the cleaning lady nor Sister Connie had shown any recognition at seeing her again. Perhaps they saw so many people that the faces all merged into one. Perhaps it was as Melanie Millson had said, she could be whom she wanted to and now that she was dressed smartly she did not look like a vagrant and so was not recognised as one.

'We've got plenty of names.' Sister Connie pulled open a drawer in the table and tugged out a register. 'Now when was it you said?'

'May.' She looked hard at the top of Sister Connie's bowed head.

'And what was the name?'

She cleared her throat.

'Magdaline O'Neill.' He heart was thumping. She was waiting for Sister Connie to say 'Oh yes, I remember Magdaline O'Neill' and then she would take off her hat and show her face properly and Sister Connie would tell her all about herself and it would all come flooding back and she would know who she was.

'Here she is.' She turned the book around for Magdaline to read. The page divided into columns. Names, dates, places. She saw her name, *'Magdaline O'Neill'* written in the same hand as the others. A bold, round cursive script.

'Yes that's m... her. What is this column here? *"Hinslop House, Hinslop House, Dartford Sanct."*?'

'That is where the girls were going after leaving us. We used to phone ahead but it was a waste of time. They rarely told the truth, you see.'

Magdaline nodded dumbly, her eyes focusing with difficulty on the page, blood thumping in her temples.

'She hasn't got anything against her name,' she said. 'Where was she going when she left you? Where was she going?' She could hear her voice rising.

'Bless you my dear, I don't know. If they don't tell us, we cannot know.'

'But don't you remember?' she whispered.

'I only came in July. This is Sister Andreas' writing.'

'Can I speak to Sister Andreas?' she pleaded. 'Please?'

'She transferred. I took her place. I'm not sure where she went, it may have been Norwich.'

'Norwich?'

'The best thing I can do, if it is that important to you, is to find out where Sister Andreas is and get her to write to you. How does that sound? If you give me your name and address...'

Name and address. Magdaline O'Neill, Our Lady Hostel, Shoreditch. Name, Magdaline O'Neill. Address, Our Lady Hostel. Name.

'No.'

Address, Our Lady Hostel, Shoreditch. Lady Hostel, Shoreditch.

She turned for the door.

'No.'

Name, Our Lady Hostel. Address, Magdaline O'Shoreditch.

'Well just give me your name and I'll tell... Are you all right my dear?'

The door. Pull hard. Get out.

'Just your name then.'

The tarmac pounding beneath running feet. Startled lady and mop. Just my name. Who am I? Who am I?

I'm nobody.

Nobody.

EPISODE TWENTY THREE

Winston brought the car to a stop as if it were the Daimler pulling up before the Ritz and not a rather travel stained Range Rover stopping in a shabby street in Halifax.

'Thank you Winston,' Richard said. 'I don't think any of us would have wanted that drive this morning.' He looked up at the signboard. 'This is it. Priestman's head office.'

'It doesn't exactly exude prosperity,' Vanessa observed from the back seat.

'Good job you haven't seen the mills,' Richard said. 'You would think this a thrumming hive of capitalism by comparison.'

Vanessa made a face.

'You are sure of this, milord?' Anatole Worstop made a final check on Richard's resolve as they got out of the car.

'You are sure of your figures?'

'Absolutely.'

'Let's get going then. And Anatole, I shall rely upon you to keep me legal. I'm not used to board meetings.'

'You will have no problem milord.'

Richard grunted non committally. 'You know where to go now Winston?'

Winston paused just a fraction before assuring him.

'Yes milord.'

Richard noticed the irony.

'Sorry Winston. Off you go then.'

Richard was not feeling very sure of himself. He could not forget his previous fleeting encounter with Walter Priestman and his overbearing aggression.

'You go first, Anatole. You're better looking.'

Walter Priestman fiddled irritably with his watch chain and scowled down the boardroom table.

'And remember. We stick together. Whatever they are after, they pay for. Top wack. You take your lead from me. Some o' these London companies think themselves really smart. They think we don't know the value of what we've got. But we're not being hoodwinked. Lord Wisdene or no Lord Wisdene.'

He scowled again at his board, measuring them up as he did so. Roderick Priestman, his younger brother. Sitting there as if he would rather be anywhere else. Well he probably would but this was a Special Meeting. All hands to the pumps. Bill Press, his brother in law. Going bald and worried about it. God! What his marriage had landed him with! Aunt Jane. Not his aunt, his wife's. She had always looked seventy all the time he had known her. An interfering old busybody with nineteen per cent of the shares. Must try to keep her sweet so that some of her money comes to his missus when the old biddy pops her clogs, but she didn't make it easy. And William Hepple, the company secretary. A small man, in a small suit who took himself far too seriously.

'By God this might be just what this firm needs to pep it up a bit.'

'How is business?' Aunt Jane enquired, her clear voice modulated with the gentle wavering of age.

'Well I'll not hide it from yer. It could be better.'

'I noticed that you've closed Top Mill.'

'Aye we're restructuring.'

'Quite a few redundancies, my daily told me.'

'Your daily don't know owt about business.' He swung around as the door opened. 'How many times 'ave I told you to knock?' he threw at the girl who visibly shrivelled before him.

'Th... th... they've come.' She nodded her head to a group of people behind her.

'Well let them in yer daft girl.'

She stood aside. Walter Priestman stepped forward to the tall, distinguished man in an impeccable dark suit.

'Please to meet you Lord Wisdene, I'm Walter Priestman, chairman and managing director of Priestman's.' He turned to the others at the table. 'This is...'

'No, no, I'm Anatole Worstop, Mr. Priestman.'

'Anna what?'

'I am the company secretary to Churle Industrial.'

'Oh are yer?' Priestman looked past him at the two others. 'I was told Lord Wisdene were coming.'

Richard took a deep breath, put on his sunniest smile and stepped forward.

'How do you do, Mr. Priestman. I am Lord Wisdene.'

Priestman looked accusingly at Anatole.

'Are yer?' He inspected Richard from head to foot, patently not remembering him from their previous short encounter. 'I were expecting someone older.'

'Oh I shall get older,' Richard assured him. 'And this is my assistant Miss Clewe-Harting.'

Priestman ignored her. 'Come and meet the board then. This is Will Hepple, company secretary, Bill Press, marketing director, Roddy Priestman, he's the production director. Oh and that's Aunt... Miss Amos.' They greeted each other vaguely across the table. 'Well sit down then and let's hear what you want. We're a busy company you know. Time is money up here.'

'I will come as directly to the point as I can,' Anatole Worstop said in a measured voice. He was visibly shaken by Priestman's aura. He probably had never imagined that a person could be so rude. 'We are Churle Industrial, a private company owned largely by Lord Wisdene. We specialise in developing smaller industrial companies.'

'Oh aye. Are yer thinking of putting some money into Priestman's then?'

'Not exactly.'

'Well what then? You Londoners only come up 'ere when yer smell brass.'

'I suppose, strictly speaking, we are after money, yes. That is our purpose.' Anatole was hedging, looking at Richard for help.

'I thought as much. Where do yer see brass up 'ere then? What have we got that you want?' He looked at Worstop. 'What's the matter? Ave I offended yer sensibilities? Listen, I don't mind telling you I'm a Yorkshireman and a Yorkshireman speaks his mind. That's how we do business up here.' He suddenly softened, as if a fleeting suspicion had crossed his mind that was not being the perfect host. 'Any road I expect you could do with a drink.' He nodded down the table at Vanessa. 'The lass can get coffee. You'll find cups an' that through there.'

Vanessa smiled sweetly.

'That's quite alright Mr. Priestman, I am flattered by your attention but I assure you that I can perfectly well wait and have my coffee with everyone else. It's so much more sociable isn't it?'

'Eh?'

'Hah!' said Aunt Jane.

'Tell me,' said Richard, 'Have you ever met a man called Beardsley? John Beardsley?'

'Beardsley,' Priestman jerked back in his chair and looked up at the ceiling. 'Can't say that I have,' he ruminated. 'What's it go to do with you anyroad?'

'Wasn't Beardsley the...?' William Hepple began.

'Shut it!' Priestman interrupted his company secretary.

Richard looked across at Anatole and said nothing.

'Could you tell me, Mr. Priestman how you financed your expansion into curtains?' Anatole asked.

'I could, but I don't see why I should answer yer bloody cheeky question. Our company business is private.'

'Oh I can tell you that,' Aunt Jane proffered.

'Aunt Jane, be quiet! We don't discuss our affairs with strangers.'

'How dare you talk like that to me, Walter!'

'It's for your own good, Aunt Jane. Do as I say, I'm the chairman, don't forget.'

'And I hold nineteen per cent, don't you forget, not counting the non-voting rights issue you raised.'

'I told you to be quiet!'

'So you used a rights issue?' Anatole Worstop showed surprise. So did Richard.

Priestman stood up. 'Look, what is it you want? I'm a busy man. I've got a company to run. Now if you haven't got anything better to do than ask a lot of damn fool questions you can clear out. There's the door,' he shouted. 'Why don't you use it?'

'I'll tell you what we want.' A tinge of colour was showing in Anatole Worstop's usually pale cheeks. 'We want our money, Mr. Priestman.'

'Money, what money?'

'Eighteen monthly interest payments of twelve and a half thousand pounds each and the principle of one and a half million pounds.'

'Is the company in debt, Wal?' his brother looked worried. 'That doesn't sound too good.'

Priestman strode around to Anatole, clipping his brother on the back of the head as he went. 'What are you talking about?' he said. 'We don't owe Churle Investments a brass farthing.' He turned on Richard, 'And if you repeat that accusation outside these four walls I'll sue you for every penny you've got. Lord or no Lord.'

Aunt Jane's quavering voice rang out. 'Do sit down, Walter, you're making a spectacle of yourself.'

'Aye, that's all you ever worry about isn't it? I'll run the bloody company and you worry about which hat to wear.'

'How much money do we owe, Wal?' his brother insisted.

'Look! Will you get it into your thick skulls, all of yer,' he swept his angry eyes over his board, 'that we don't owe these crooks a tuppenny nickel.'

'Well why do they say we do?' his brother whined.

'Lord Wisdene,' Aunt Jane said, 'Why do you say that we owe you money?'

'Aunt Jane, I told you to shut up!'

'A few months ago,' said Richard, 'John Beardsley sold his company to Churle Industrial.'

Priestman stared. 'What, all of it?'

'Lock stock and barrel. Including the debts.'

'He never told me.'

'Why would he if you've never met him?' Anatole Worstop asked quietly.

'What? I never said that!' Priestman clenched his fists.

Vanessa quietly turned back a few pages and read from her notebook. 'Lord Wisdene: Tell me, have you ever met a man called Beardsley? John Beardsley? Mr. Priestman: Beardsley? Can't say that I have. What's it go to do with you anyroad?'

'Has that lass been taking down everything we've been sayin?' Priestman's face was contorted in anger.

Vanessa smiled her sweet smile again. 'One hundred and forty words per minute,' she said. 'And I can also make coffee.'

Priestman threw himself down in his chair, his jaw muscles chomping in tension.

'I wish somebody would tell me what's going on.'

Aunt Jane looked to Anatole Worstop as being the kind of

person whose utterances she would be prepared to trust.

'And me,' said Roderick Priestman.

'We, that is, Churle Industrial have bought a company. About three years earlier, one of its subsidiary companies lent Priestman's one and a half million pounds under a singularly irregular arrangement. No interest payments have been paid by Priestman's for the last eighteen months. We purchased the company and with it, the debt. That debt is now owing to us.'

'Is this true, Walter? Is it?' Bill Press asked as he self consciously smoothed his thinning hair.

'How much do we owe, Mr. Worstop?' Aunt Jane asked.

'Approximately one million, seven hundred and twenty five thousand pounds,' he replied correctly. 'The bank will calculate it exactly.'

'Is it true, Walter?'

Priestman sat quietly in his chair, his ridiculous watch chain stretched across his gut and a smug expression on his face. He looked around the table.

'What if it is?' he said. 'What can you do about it?'

'We can insist upon payment,' Worstop said stiffly.

'Insist all yer like, you won't get it. We haven't got it. Can you prove that we had it? Can yer?'

'Mr. Hepple, as company secretary of your major creditor, I am requesting you, "requesting" at this stage, please note, that you show me the entries in your accounts relating to the loan to your company of one and a half million pounds by our subsidiary.'

'Yer wasting yer time,' Priestman growled.

William Hepple puffed himself up and, taking his cue from his chairman he said, 'I note your request Mr. Worstop and will communicate with you upon it in due course. Could you give me an address at which I can contact you?'

'I see,' Worstop said quietly. Just two words, but they had the menace of cold steel held at an unprotected throat. He took some papers from his battered leather case. Somehow that case had taken on the character of a campaign veteran. He passed copies across the table to the members of the board. 'These are extracts from the journal of our subsidiary. I would draw your attention to the entry that I have ringed. You will see it is a transfer of one and a half million pounds to the account of Mr. Walter John Priestman in Halifax. The second sheet is the collateral upon which he secured the loan. You will note that it is on the freehold properties belonging to Priestman's of Halifax.'

'I can see that,' said Aunt Jane. 'What is the importance of it?'

'Should I presume that you, as the board of Priestman's, agreed to the chairman arranging this loan?'

'Well I don't understand half the things that we vote on,' Roderick admitted.

'You don't understand any of them,' Priestman observed sourly. 'What are you getting at, Worstop? Isn't it time you left?'

'If I leave now, the next person through that door will be a high ranking officer in the Fraud Squad with a warrant for your arrest. All of you,' he added.

'All of us?' Bill Press squeaked.

'You are all, apparently, parties to the fraud.'

'Fraud, what fraud?'

'One upon our subsidiary.'

'But that was a loan. You have the collateral. You've showed us here.' He tapped the paper.

'There is no collateral, Mr. Press. Firstly, the properties mentioned are not worth their stated value. We had them valued independently at one tenth of your balance sheet figures.'

'Yes but there is always room for difference in these things.' Bill Press was clutching at straws.

'And secondly, the properties do not belong to Priestman's.'

'They don't...?' His last straw capsized and sunk.

'Copies of the Land Registry Certificates,' said Worstop as he passed them across the table. 'Every building the company owned is mortgaged to the bank. They have first claim and they will be making that claim on Monday morning when we tell them that you cannot pay your debts.'

'Lies! Poppycock! You can't know what the bank will do!' Priestman spluttered.

'Well we can, actually, Mr. Priestman,' said Vanessa. 'My Daddy owns it.'

Priestman stared open-mouthed at Vanessa.

'But that's a breach of banking confidence!'

'And then there is the question of how the chairman has defrauded the shareholders,' Richard continued.

'But we are shareholders as well,' Aunt Jane quavered. 'I've got nineteen percent. Has Walter defrauded us?'

'Don't listen to 'im!' Priestman said.

'The money which was raised on the supposed assets of the company Priestman's of which you are the board, went into the private bank account of the chairman, Mr. Walter John Priestman. You voted to defraud yourselves but it is you who will have to pay it back.'

'Walter! Is this true? Have you pocketed the money?'

'I haven't pocketed any money,' he said wearily.

'Where is it then?'

'Yes where is it?' his brother in law chimed in.

'You can shut up Bill, you've got no part in this. You're not blood family.'

'Thank God.'

'Where is the money?' Roderick said. 'I'm your brother.'

Priestman looked at him as if noticing him for the first time. He was sagging in his chair now, his shoulders drooping, his hand gestures, vague.

'Aye, you're me brother. It's gone, Roddy. I've spent it. Every last penny is gone.'

'What did yer spend it on for God's sake Wal?'

'The business, Roddy, the business. The sheeets. The ready made curtains. The wages. The bills.'

'But why did it go into your account?'

'Oh I don't know. Pride. Didn't want anybody to know the trouble we were in. Beardsley agreed with it.' Priestman addressed Richard. 'Did he get a good price for his company?'

'He got a fair price,' Richard said.

'Aye, 'e would.'

'Where does all this leave us?' Aunt Jane demanded. 'We have a right to know.'

'You've got nineteen percent of a one and a half million pound debt and no assets,' Priestman snapped. 'Don't you understand English, woman? We're broke!'

There was a silence.

'You mean our shares are worthless?' His brother in law was aghast. 'Not worth a thing?'

'I'm not very happy with you Wal,' Roderick said.

'Aye,' Priestman said.

'What's going to happen now?' Bill Press said. 'What do we do?'

'As your chairman intimated some time earlier, it is not in our interest to let you go under. We won't get our money back that way,' Richard explained.

Priestman's eyes flickered with shrewd interest. 'So you'll put money in to the firm then?' he asked hopefully.

'On our conditions, yes,' Richard said.

'And your conditions are?'

'The first is that you resign as chairman,' Anatole Worstop glanced at a sheet before him.

'Why should I resign as chairman?' The possibility of extra funds was restocking his indignation.

'Because,' Anatole said in a clear, careful and crisp voice, 'you are unfit to run a public company and you have lost the confidence of every member of your board.'

Priestman looked around the table.

'Hasn't any of you got anything to say?' he demanded.

'Yes,' said Aunt Jane, 'I agree with Mr. Worstop. You are unfit to run a company, Walter, and I have no confidence in you. I want you out.'

'What about you, Press? Worried what your sister might say if you sack her husband?'

'Not in the slightest, Walter, I've never trusted you.'

'Oh aye. Big words little man.'

'What about you Roddy?'

'I think it would be best if you went, Wal.'

'Well that seems settled then doesn't it? My entire board has given me the heave-ho.'

'Not quite.' Richard turned to catch the imperceptible nod that Vanessa gave him as she came back into the boardroom from outside. 'We are missing Mr. R. Priestman. According to our records he is also on the board.'

'That's my son, Bob. I don't want him mixed up in this.'

'You don't have much choice. You elected him to the board.'

'I don't want 'im mixed up in this!'

'Do we take it then, Mr. Priestman that you have resigned from the position of chairman and managing director of Priestman's?' Anatole Worstop asked him formally.

'Aye.'

'Thank you Mr Priestman. Now would you please make over your shareholding to Lord Wisdene?'

'Yer what?'

'Or do you want to be held liable for one million, seven hundred and twenty five thousand pounds?'

'You can't just do it like that. You need forms don't yer, Hepple?'

Anatole Worstop silently placed the forms before him.

'You're a great help, Hepple, thanks very much,' Priestman said laconically. Hepple shrugged.

'Please send in the share certificates as soon as you can,' Anatole Worstop said.

'As your new chairman,' Richard addressed the others, 'I formerly request the company secretary, Mr. William Hepple, to stand down.'

'But I...'

'Just do it, Hepple,' Priestman said. 'Use what little brains yer've got. If your name gets into the papers you'd never get another job.'

'And your one per cent shareholding will go to the new company secretary.' Richard pushed the forms across. 'For this post I propose Mr. Anatole Worstop.'

'I second that,' Aunt Jane said energetically. Worstop inclined his head towards her.

'You can go now Mr. Hepple.' Richard nodded towards the door.

'Just like that? After all I've done for the firm!'

'What is it exactly that you have done for this firm, Mr. Hepple?' Anatole Worstop's voice was like ice. 'As company secretary you were in a position of trust and great responsibility. You betrayed the trust your board put in you. You connived in a sordid attempt at fraud.'

'I deny that. I knew nothing about that loan.'

'Yer bloody fool,' Priestman said quietly.

'It would be impossible for any company secretary who was performing his duties correctly, not to know about the loan. Are you also pleading incompetence?' Worstop asked.

'It wasn't fraud.'

'Perhaps you would like to argue that in a court of law, Mr. Hepple?'

'You wouldn't dare.' Hepple tried to brazen it out.

Anatole Worstop's pale eyes bored unblinkingly into his.

'Try me,' he said quietly. 'It would give me great pleasure to ensure that you never went near another company for the rest of your life. You are a disgrace to our profession. I shudder to think that anybody could associate me with your incompetence and peculation. Bring me the company seal and leave your keys.'

Hepple looked at the impassive faces of the others.

'Right, well if that's the way you want it.' He left the room and came back with a polished wooden box and a bunch of keys. 'You haven't heard the last of this.'

'I hope for your sake we have,' Anatole Worstop observed.

'You'll see,' he said and walked slowly to the door as if he hoped that somebody would call him back. Nobody did.

There was a silence as they all assessed the position. It was eventually broken by Priestman himself.

'I suppose that I had better go as well. I've got no place here now. Thanks to you lot.' He glared at his former board.

'You can stay if you wish, Mr. Priestman, as my guest,' Richard said. 'I can understand that you would still be interested in the future of the company, if we can find it one. If you wish to be present when I discuss it with the board you may do so, but you will have no opportunity to speak and indeed, no voice.'

'Aye. Well, alright then.'

'Your son is outside, Mr. Priestman.'

'Bob? Here? He should be up at Top Mill. I said, I don't want him mixed up in this.'

'I've invited him as a member of the board. As far as he needs to know, you have sold the company to Churle Industrial and retired. I have taken over as chairman. Are we agreed on that?' Richard looked around the table and received thoughtful assents from all present. Vanessa got up and went over and opened the door.

'Please come in Mr. Priestman.'

The red hair looked a little less unruly but it was still the same Bob Priestman. He was wearing worn jeans and a thick knitted jumper decorated with a bold, modern pattern. With a sudden stab of memory, Richard realised that it was the kind of thing that the students designed for themselves back at art college. He came into the room with the ease of familiarity. He was on his own ground.

'Hallo Dad. It must be important if yer sent a car for us.'

'A car? Oh aye.' Priestman looked mystified.

'Hello Aunt Jane.'

'Hello Robert.'

'Uncle Roddy. Uncle Will.' They nodded.

'Bob... er lad, I want yer to meet Lord Wisdene.' Priestman gratefully took the initiative that Richard had left him.

'Hallo Bob,' Richard said.

Vanessa and Anatole looked up sharply. Walter Priestman stared hard.

'But... Richard. How the 'ell are yer?' They shook hands. 'Wha' yer doin' here? It's great to see yer. Worra surprise!' Bob Priestman turned to the astounded company. 'I were at college wi' Richard. In London,' he added, accentuating the importance of isolated Yorkshire.

'I've got yer,' Priestman said victoriously, pointing at Richard, 'I knew I'd seen yer before. You were with that lad who...'

'Yes that's right Mr. Priestman,' Richard interrupted him.

Bob turned to his father. 'Who did yer say 'e was?'

''E'd best tell yer. Seein as 'ow y'er pals.'

Richard tried a disarming smile.

'Bob, you know me as Richard.'

'Aye, Richard Ennessy. Paints pictures of girls who slap his face.'

Richard shut his eyes momentarily as Jennifer's face flashed before him. 'Yes, well I am also known as Lord Wisdene.'

'Gerraway!' Richard realised that with his return to his native county, Bob Priestman's accent had relapsed into a relaxed informality that he had never heard. 'What, a real lord? Well I never knew.' He looked about the room. 'Nobody did,' he added, as if trying to excuse his lack of perception.

'This is my assistant, Vanessa Clewe-Harting.'

'Oh. Pleased to meet yer, miss,' Bob shook Vanessa's hand, blushing furiously.

'And my company secretary, Anatole Worstop.'

Bob shook hands with Anatole.

'Company secretary?' he said.

'I'm here on business,' Richard explained. 'This is actually a board meeting.'

'What do you want me for?'

'You are on the board.'

'Well, I know but Dad always...'

'Sit down Bob and listen,' his father said.

They sat down.

'What's this all about Dad?'

'Your father has retired, Bob.'

'Have yer Dad?'

'Aye.'

'You must have known that the company was not doing all that well,' Richard said.

Bob Priestman looked across at his father, not wanting to be disloyal.

'Well, it just needs a bit of a shake up, that's all.'

'I am going to give it a shake up,' Richard said.

'You are? Why you?'

'My company has bought Priestman's.'

'Robert, the company is bankrupt,' Aunt Jane said. 'Lord Wisdene is bailing us out.'

'Dad?'

'It's true son. We're mortgaged up to our ears and we've got no work in hand.'

'What about the army contract at Hanner's?'

'Stitching tents? It's losing us two thousand a week.'

'So what's going to 'appen?' Bob Priestman had been brought up to believe that he was going into the business and now it appeared that there was no business to go into.

'That is the purpose of this meeting,' Richard explained. 'I am now the chairman of Priestman's, your father has retired. Anatole is the new company secretary. The board is as you see it now. There is no point in beating about the bush, the situation is very grave. You, the board, have shares in an apparently worthless company and I am putting money into it. It is in all our interests to work together now. This is what I propose. Firstly, we make over all our freeholds bar one, to the bank.'

'Repossession?' Roderick Priestman said.

'In a word, yes. With a normal repossession, the bank sells the property and any surplus is returned to the mortgagee. I do not think we should hold out any hope of receiving a surplus. We will be hard pressed not to avoid penalties.'

'You said 'all the freeholds bar one'.'

'Clarice Mill we will keep. Churle Industrial will pay off the mortgage in total so that we hold the entire unencumbered freehold. This is the only property we hold that has any potential whatsoever. Bob, this is what I want you to do. You remember that warehouse in Bristol that you drew?'

'Oh aye, with the 'ammerbeam roof.'

'And the sketch of Harrods?' Bob Priestman nodded. 'I'll send my surveyor to you. His name is Harry Meachem. We are going to convert Clarice Mill into flats and maisonettes. He knows the structural stuff, you do the drawings for him. I'm not talking of technical drawings, I'm talking about artist's impressions and fairly accurate sketches to assist with the initial enabling works. Can you do that?'

'Sounds like real fun.'

'Just a minute,' Bill Press said. 'If we are selling or giving away our mills, what happens to the workforce?'

'How many have we got?'

'About seventy five now, that's all,' Priestman said. 'We used to 'ave over three thousand.'

'How much work have they got?'

'Only the army contract.'

'On which we are losing two thousand a week?'

The board looked at each other glumly.

'Might I make a suggestion milord?' Anatole Worstop's use of Richard's title jerked them back into reality. 'Mr. Meachem was in the army. If anybody could renegotiate that contract, he could. But after that...'

'After that, we would not need them,' Richard said. 'They will have to be made redundant.'

'But they're skilled workers!' Bill Press said.

'Stitching tents. We don't need their skills. Priestman's won't weave another roll of cloth or stitch another garment.'

'But Priestman's have always been in cloth,' Bob Priestman protested.

'And look where we are now,' Richard replied. He turned to Vanessa. 'Can you get Greg in?'

As she stood up, Priestman also got up.

'I don't know about you, but I'm parched,' he admitted and then added self consciously, 'I'm gonna to make us all some coffee.' When he reached the door he started at the sight of the young man with Vanessa. 'What are you doing here Sharman?'

Greg Sharman, whom Richard had last seen playing with a computer in one of Priestman's redundant mills, had taken off his white lab coat and in his green track suit and white sneakers, looked just ready for a jog over the moors.

'Hallo Mr. Priestman. I was asked to come. I thought you wanted me.'

Greg Sharman walked into the room and looked at the people sitting around the table.

'No I asked you Greg,' Richard called.

'Oh it's Bob's friend from art college. How're yer doin?'

'I'm fine, thanks.'

'Oh hello Bob, didn't see you there. So what's this all about?'

'Your software,' said Richard. 'What resources do you need to put it on the market and earn some money for Priestman's?'

Richard lay prone and groaned slightly as the strong fingers kneaded the knot of muscles in his back and shoulders.

'Are you groaning because you want me to stop?' Vanessa enquired.

'Oh no, please don't stop. It's heaven. Where did you learn to do this?'

'From looking after horses.'

'Oh. That was some meeting! I wouldn't want to go through that again.' Richard was fervent in his assertion.

'Anatole was magnificent. He scared the pants off me.'

'You did pretty well yourself, – "And I also make coffee".'

'Oh wasn't he an awful man?' she laughed. 'I didn't think such people existed. His poor son! How on earth do you cope with a father like that?'

'I think Bob does pretty well. He annoyed me intensely when we first met. In fact, I think we annoyed each other.'

'Unavoidable really, given the differences in your upbringing and backgrounds.'

'Yes,' Richard said absently and then added, 'just a bit lower to the right. That's it. Aaah, lovely.'

'Who was the "lass" he asked you about?'

'Oh just someone I knew.' He shut his eyes. He could see smiling blue eyes. He could see angry blue eyes.

'He seemed to think that you and this someone would be together.'

'Well we are not.' Richard sat up.

'Were you?'

'No, not really. No.'

'Did you want to be?'

'I think she might have wanted it.'

'Did you?'

Richard stood up.

'Nessie, thanks for all you did today. You were brilliant. The best PA I've ever had.'

'Glad to be of service.'

'Yes well, we've got that job tied up quite neatly.' He put out his hand and pulled her up to stand before him. He looked her directly in the unwavering eyes and said quietly, 'There's only one more thing to sort out now, isn't there?'

EPISODE TWENTY FOUR

'Dominic, could I have a word please?'

'Come on in Lynne. The policy of Janus and Janus, as you know, is that the manager's office door should never be shut to the staff.' He delivered this dogma with a measured irreverence which did not, however, invalidate it, for he believed in the principle; he just did not like the supposition that he needed to be told to do it.

'Thanks. The open door, can I shut it?'

'Ah. Yes. It's like that is it?'

''Fraid so,' Lynne smiled guiltily and closed the door, isolating them from the bustle and the ears of the office.

'What's the problem?'

'Well...' Lynne paused. She had not really thought this out properly and now she realised that it might be impossible. 'I really want to know how you think Magdaline is getting on? What is your opinion? If you can't tell me on account of staff confidence and all that I quite understand,' the words tumbled out. 'But if you can, it would help. Might help.'

'Right,' Dominic said briskly, 'you are absolutely correct – I am forbidden from disclosing details of her personnel file to you but then, I don't have access to it in any case.'

'Oh, I see.' Lynne looked at the desk top. 'I just thought–'

'However,' he continued, 'we both know things about Magdaline that others don't and we are both mixed up in it all so why don't you tell me what's troubling you?'

'I'm worried about Magdaline.'

'Go on.'

'Something happened before Christmas and, I mean, I thought since then she had been getting better and better.

347

I thought that she had really... stabilised.'

'What is she like at home? I see her in the office and she works steadily, quickly and with flair. She is quite a talented girl.' He grunted ironically. 'To think that she was out on the streets, what a waste!'

'That is the point,' Lynne insisted obscurely. 'We don't know for sure and nor does she whether she was out on the streets or not.'

'But you said she had come from a hostel for the homeless.'

'Well, yes, she did. But where did she learn to draw like that?'

'It could be natural, quite easily.'

'But the problem is, it makes her wonder what she did before.'

'God! I should think that she wonders that all the while. I know I would. Have the others noticed? Is that the problem?'

'No, not really. They notice that she gives strange answers sometimes. She has to. Anybody can ask her a quite innocent question and it can make her utterly panic stricken because she has no idea of the answer. She worries because she looks stupid when she can't give a proper reply and then she worries herself to try to work out the correct answer.'

'I can't stop people from talking to her.'

'No, I know that.'

'It would probably be the worse thing to do.'

'Yes.'

'What do you want me to do?'

'Oh I don't know.' Lynne felt the desperation.

'You are a good friend to Magdaline, you know,' Dominic said suddenly.

'In a funny way, she is a good friend to me. I just don't like her to get upset but I don't know how to stop it. A few months back I came home from work...'

'Yes?'

'Have you noticed any change in her recently?'

'Well she has her ups and downs, we know that, but her work is always competent and often inspired. Everybody has off days.'

'She still goes to the psychiatrist. To help her cope with her lost memory. She tried to explain it to me. She hasn't lost all her memory, you know, if she had, she wouldn't be able to do basic things like feeding herself and that. What's happened is that her brain has stopped her from getting to the part of her memory that contains the stuff which it thinks is harmful to her. Trouble is, this is the bit which tells her what she did before the accident so when she gets it back, if she ever does, she knows that it's going to hurt her. Except that her brain won't let her access it whilst it can still hurt her, if you see what I mean. Am I making sense?'

'Perfectly.'

'Oh. Good. Her psychiatrist told her not to do anything silly to try to jog her memory back, like banging herself on the head or whatever.'

'No, I should think not!'

'Well, a few months back, it must have been in November, she had come home early from work. I think she had been feeling off colour or something. When I got in, I found her in the dark, curled up, hugging herself and saying, "I'm nobody" over and over again. "I'm nobody," she kept crying. It was horrible.' Lynne sniffed into her handkerchief, unsuccessfully trying to disguise her own tears.

Dominic waited in silence. He could imagine the girl in the physical position but realised that he could never imagine her mental anguish. Nobody could ever understand what it must be like in her mind. 'Had she been like this before?'

'No, not really. As you said, she does have her ups and downs. I hadn't told anybody about it because, well, I haven't got anybody I can tell, except you. She's so fragile. Little things can upset her. She won't go anywhere without that cap.'

'Oh yes, I've seen it.'

'It is the only bit of clothing that she's still got from her old life. She has gone all over that cap minutely for clues. But you know, it's only a denim cap. That day I was talking about, she had done exactly what the psychiatrist had told her not to do. She had tried to jog her memory.'

'How? Not banging herself on the head, I hope?'

'No. She went back to the hostel where she spent her last night before the accident. She saw the matron.'

'And?'

'The whole place meant nothing to her. It was an absolute washout. And that was why I found her in the dark saying she was nobody.'

'Silly girl!'

'Don't say that.'

'No, sorry. I didn't mean it like that.' He leaned back, cupped his hands behind his head and sighed heavily. 'It's a tragic situation, Lynne. I like Magdaline a lot. She works hard. She's been here, what – six or seven months now?' Lynne nodded. 'And she has definitely made her mark. She's got a future here, I don't mind telling you that.'

'Have you noticed her upset in the last fortnight?'

'No, I don't really see enough of her to notice.' He reflected for an instant, then looked apologetic. 'I suppose I don't really see enough of any of my staff, and that is an awful admission. Do you think she is still upset by this hostel business?'

'No it's not that. Well, I mean, she's obviously still upset, but I think there is something else. I can't put my finger on it.'

'Well I can only promise you to keep my eyes open and let you know if I notice anything.'

'Yes.' Lynne looked at him and realised that they had finished talking. There was nothing else to say. 'Thanks.'

She got up and went out, leaving the door open.

'Oh Richard, what on earth were you saying to Vanessa when they took the photograph?'

'It is probably better that you remain in ignorance, mother, the photographer caught me by surprise.'

'But you look so peremptory with your lips twisted like that. You really could have made a nicer shape with your mouth.'

'I had no idea that the confounded little man was going to jump out at me.'

'Was it just by chance that they saw you then?'

'No mother, it was not just by chance. Somebody from the paper got wind of the announcement, phoned up the office, spoke to our Mrs. Dove and said that they needed to contact me urgently, where could I be found? So she told them. She managed to tell three different newspapers before Wayne began to suspect something.'

'Oh, how indelicate.'

'And of course they hit the jackpot because I had my PA with me so they killed two birds with one flashbulb.'

'But Richard, why did you choose to stand in front of scaffolding? It's so ungenteel.'

'On a building site, mother, it is often difficult not to stand in front of scaffolding. We should thank our lucky stars that in order to fit this photo to the page they had to crop the bit with the portable toilet on it.'

'Oh Richard, please!'

'Sorry mother.'

'Has Vanessa seen it?'

'I rather think not. When she reads, *"Property Lord To Wed Secretary"* she will select the stiffest crop from her rack and call on the editor.' He took the daily paper from the tray, skimmed the article briefly and sighed in exasperation. 'The stately home does not stand "in a one thousand acre park", we do not possess, to my knowledge, "a stable of Rolls Royces", unless Winston has stashed them away somewhere...'

'Winston does not like Rolls Royces.'

'He should do, they are old enough. Not as old as Daimlers of course, but fairly ancient.'

'When are you seeing the *Tatler*?'

'They are coming on Thursday.'

'Good. They will make a proper job of it. We must sweep out the orangery, the light will be perfect in there for Vanessa's tiara. So luminous.'

'You amaze me mother. I did not know you were such an expert on photography.'

'Don't be facetious, Richard, you know perfectly well that I know nothing of photography. What I know about is diamonds.'

Ruth Robey smoothed a hand down her tights and tossed her head, hoping to catch the eye of the Mediterranean looking student who was part of a group talking in the far alcove of the college library. She failed.

'Oh come on Ruth,' Patsy pleaded, 'you're supposed to be doing the bit on Valentino.'

'Oh him!' she said lethargically. 'Couldn't I crib off you, Colin?'

'Now that would be news!'

She ignored Colin's sarcasm and pulled his notepad across to her side of the table. She scanned through a couple of sheets, her forehead creasing in a frown.

'You'll get wrinkles before your time if you do that,' Patsy nodded at her and her glasses slipped down her nose as they always did. 'Bloody things,' she muttered as she pushed them up.

'Language!' Colin scolded, his head still bent to his book.

'But I can't find a thing on Valentino,' Ruth complained. 'Where is your Valentino stuff?'

'Ah,' said Colin, 'I haven't got any.'

'Why not?'

'We're doing Schiaparelli.'

'But I thought it had to be Valentino.'

'No. He only used Valentino as an example. You should read the assignment properly. It says *"an Italian designer".'*

'Oh bum!'

'Language!' Colin repeated.

She pushed his notes back across the table and picked up a discarded newspaper from the table behind her.

'Holy shit! Look at this!' she exclaimed. Before Colin could say a word she had spread the paper across their work.

'Oh Ruth!' said Patsy. 'You are the limit!'

'Never mind that. Look!' She stabbed a scarlet nailed finger on the paper. 'Isn't that Richard Ennessy?'

Patsy pushed her spectacles up and scrutinised the picture. 'I think it is. Yes it is. Doesn't he look posh in a suit? Why is he in the paper?' She tried unsuccessfully to pull her work out from underneath but Colin had leaned across to read.

'Property lord to wed secretary. Richard d'Ennessy, the rich and ninth Earl of Wisdene is to marry his secretary and childhood sweetheart, the Honorable Vanessa Clewe-Harting, daughter of Lord Harting of Plethero. Lord Wisdene succeeded to the title on the death of his property-dealing father earlier this year. He had long been considered the most eligible bachelor in the Home Counties. Disappointed daughters and frustrated mothers will surely be venting their grief county wide at having missed the stately home set in a one thousand acre park, the stable of Rolls Royces and of course, the status of "her ladyship, the Countess of Wisdene." Are you sure it's him?' Colin asked.

'Oh yes, that's him,' Ruth confirmed.

'They've spelt his name wrong. Typical.'

'No they haven't.' Ruth remembered the incident at the Ritz when she had made up a story about knowing the golf coach who had then come over to speak to them. "D'Ennessy" he had called Richard. She had thought at the time that he had said

"Tennessee". 'No,' she said, 'D'Ennessy is his name. He... er... told me when he took me to tea at the Ritz that time.'

'But you never said,' Colin objected.

'He didn't want anybody to know,' Ruth said airily. 'He asked me to keep it a secret.'

'Oh poor, poor Jennifer,' Patsy said quietly.

They stared at her.

Now that the engagement had been announced, Richard realised that there was one thing that he had left undone. He had always meant to sort it out but each time he had thought about it, his courage had left him. He now had no excuse, indeed, his very situation pressed him into action. He picked up the phone.

'Could I speak to Dr. Sullivan please?'

The hall clock clunked resolutely in the dim desert of the passageway. Sandy pricked up his ears at the slight movement in the parlour, assessed it as uninteresting, and closed his eyes again.

The clock ticked on.

'Well I never.'

He opened his eyes again but his mistress was not talking to him, so he closed them again.

A paper rustled. He ignored it. He knew that it was not the type that brought forth biscuits.

'Well I never did.'

She got up. Ah, this held more promise. He stretched and yawned and wagged his tail. She went to a drawer and took out something. He lifted his black snout and sniffed.

'Oh you greedy little dog,' Mrs. Crowther scolded him, 'that's all you think of.' He wagged his tail hopefully. 'It's only a photograph.' The tone of her voice indicated that there was no interest for him.

He lay down on his belly again and snorted rudely.

The paper rustled.

The clock ticked.

'Well, well, well. I wonder if Miss Pye knew he was an earl. Such a nice young man, so discreet.'

'Calm down, Boy!'

Richard looked down at Vanessa's hand which was tapping his

thigh. 'They had no right!' He gritted his teeth and angrily stared at the back of Winston's head as the Range Rover weaved through the London traffic. 'No right at all.'

'But how long had you left them there?' Vanessa said. 'It must have been months.'

'That's not the point, Nessie.' He tugged peevishly at the grab handle above his door.

'Of course it is. They can't be expected to store every student's daubs indefinitely. Be reasonable, Richard.'

'I am being reasonable. I don't see how they could possibly convince themselves that they had the right to do that. They are my paintings!'

'Which you abandoned there.'

'I did not abandon them.'

'Well what could they have thought? Didn't they try to contact you?'

'They say they did.'

'Had you given them your address?'

Richard hesitated. 'The college had my address. Half Moon Mews. And Mrs. MacCallum has been forwarding the mail, though why she bothered I don't know, most of it is junk.'

'So you could have thrown away a letter from college without opening it?'

'Oh don't be silly.'

'Here's the gallery milord.'

'Right. Thanks. Er... can you wait here Winnie?'

Winston's practised eyes swept around the square.

'I'll be over there, milord, keeping an eye open for the traffic warden. I will be able to see the front door from there. You can signal when you need me.'

'Thanks Winnie. Come on Nessie.' He jumped out of the car and bounded up the steps, leaving a more sedate Vanessa, reflecting thoughtfully as she followed him.

Lynne stood motionless on the stairs, her eyes level with the floor of the landing above. She could just see Magdaline. She was still at her drawing board but was now pulling on her cap. She would then come out of the office door and go to the lift. Lynne would run down the stairs and see which way she left the building. Then she would follow her. It was deceitful. It was sordid, but she had to find out where Magdaline had been going these last few lunchtimes. Wherever it was, it was not doing her any good.

Footfalls below her announced somebody climbing the stairs. What was wrong with the lift for God's sake? Too many fitness freaks in this company, that's the trouble. She snatched the newspaper from the top of her bag and pretended to study it.

'Lucky bitch!' the climber said.

'What?'

'Her with the nose like a paper dart.' The girl prodded the photo that Lynne had not been looking at. 'Lucky bitch, I say. He could have had me for a few millions less, no trouble.'

Quite true, Lynne thought. Several in the building had already had her for nothing. Mind you, he was some catch, even if he did look a bit daft with that scaffolding pole sticking out of the top of his head. A thousand acres? Room to run about there. She quickly pulled the paper up in front of her face as Magdaline disappeared into the lift then she turned and ran lithely down the stairs, two at a time.

Vanessa held his arm and gazed up at the pictures. They were actually very good. She had only seen some of Richard's sketches and his half finished painting of the Monet. Somehow they had never really talked about his actual artistic achievement, he had always seemed a bit coy about showing her his work. Now she was seeing it for real and it frightened her a little. He could paint. Her life had always been bound up with horses, estates, the countryside and, latterly, property development. What would she do if he suddenly decided to go off to Tuscany or wherever it is artists go? Come on Vanessa, buck up! You've cleared the last fence this time. You've jumped a clear round. All you've got to do now is trot off to the prize giving.

'That's the blue ballgown.'

'Yes.'

'Oh Richard. Naughty naughty. Girl with no clothes on.' She nudged him saucily. 'Oh and isn't that your sweater that this one is wearing on the beach?'

'Yes.'

She looked hard at the golden hair. She looked back at the other two paintings. 'It's the same girl in each picture, isn't it?' she said slowly.

Richard shook his head. 'She never wanted this. She never wanted this. They should have asked me. They had no right.' Then he added,' Thank God I painted out that hair. She would never have forgiven me.'

'This is the girl, isn't it?' she asked softly.

He did not reply and then she knew that, framed on the wall and depicted in oils was her last fence. It was not behind her.

Winston glanced in his mirror again. Not a peaked cap in sight. He returned to his book. General Gordon at Khartoum, that was the stuff. A coach lumbered up to the front of the gallery and a crowd of blue tunics and straw hats began to clamber in. If Lord Wisdene and Miss Vanessa came out now he would be quite unable to see them. He tut-tutted to himself. No point in moving the car. He would just have to keep his eyes open.

Suddenly he jerked as if stung and then leaned forward, staring at the figure of a young woman wearing an incongruous cap above her neat business suit. Without taking his eyes from her, his hand fumbled in the door pocket. In an instant the binoculars were at his eyes. Never mind parking tickets, this was important. He dropped the glasses into the footwell as he slammed the door and locked it. They could tow the car away for all he cared.

The anguish of Reading station was ever present in his respectable mind. 'I was not making fun of you miss,' She had to know that. He hurried across the road.

'Well fetch the director then,' Richard said. 'I'll wait.'

'Do you have an appointment sir? He's a very busy man.'

'He's a busy man?' Richard exploded. 'Is he the only busy man in London? What do you think I do all day long? – Sit and twiddle my thumbs?'

Without blinking an eyelid the woman picked up the phone from the counter.

'Who shall I say is calling, sir?'

'Lord Wisdene.'

She spoke into the phone and listened to instructions. Vanessa patted his arm and said, 'Don't take it out on her. She's doing what she is allowed to do.'

He shook her off irritably and strode over to a chair.

'The director will be down in fifteen minutes Lord Wisdene. Would you like to look around the gallery?'

'If the director is not down here in five minutes, I'll have the police here in ten and he will be at the station in fifteen,' Richard boiled.

Vanessa blew out her breath noisily.

'I'm going to look around the gallery,' she said.

Why those three pictures? Lynne wondered. Magdaline had been staring at them for ages. Did she want to draw them? Lynne edged closer to her, deciding that if Magdaline saw her now she would just have to admit that she had followed her there from the office but she need not have worried, Magdaline was oblivious to her presence. Lynne watched her carefully and did not like what she saw. She was breathing hard and her lips were moving as if she were saying something. Now she was passing her hand over her head, pressing that cap to her temples as if in pain. That decided Lynne, time to act.

'Magdaline.'

'Snug in his jumper. His jumper. Why his jumper? Where is he?'

'Magdaline, it's me Lynne.'

She took hold of Magdaline's arm. It was shaking.

'You can't dance in bare feet. You can't dance in bare feet.'

'Magdaline! Magdaline!' Lynne looked around. 'Can you help me please?' she called. The attendant slipped from his stool and came over, shaking his head.

'Are you with her?'

'She's my friend. She's ill.'

'I thought she was. She always stops at those three pictures. Strange I call it. I'll go and get her a glass of water and some aspirins. Perhaps this lady will help.'

'Oh could you?' Lynne turned to the lady with relief.

'If I can,' Vanessa said. 'What's the matter?'

'It's Magdaline, she's... she's...' The girl stopped. Something had just occurred to her. 'What is it Magdaline? Is it the pictures?'

'It wasn't like that,' Magdaline said. 'He's changed it.'

'What does she mean, "he's changed it"?' Vanessa looked sharply at Lynne.

'Oh Magdaline, love, who's changed it?'

'The hair. The private hair. It's gone. I told him I didn't like it. He's changed it.'

'Who changed it, Magdaline?'

'I don't know.' The voice was whispered in desperation. 'I don't know. You can't dance in bare feet.'

'Can she hear us?' Vanessa said.

'I don't think so,' Lynne replied. 'She... look I shouldn't tell you this but she had an accident and lost her memory. She doesn't know any of her past. She was told not to try to look for it. They said it would only cause her problems, and now this has happened. I followed her from work because she has been really strange these last few days. I knew something was going on, I knew it. She must have been coming here.'

'When did this happen? The accident?'

'Oh... er... last year. Let me think. I'd done my knee in. Last May or June.'

Last May or June. Vanessa looked at the cap. Richard used to have a cap just like that. He kept it in the door pocket of the Yellow Peril. And under the cap was short hair but it was golden, like on the ballgown. Those eyebrows had been plucked, but if you looked carefully you could see that the nose was the same, and the mouth and the eyes. Oh yes, Richard could paint.

'I'll get help,' she said.

'I wonder if you could help me.'

Arthur Northgate stopped with the glass in his hand and looked at the elderly gentleman with the silvery hair.

'Yes sir, if you're quick.' He nodded at the glass. 'Bit of an emergency.'

'I'm looking for a young lady who came in here. I've been looking all over the gallery for her. She is shortish, and she had a cap on. One of those floppy blue things that youngsters wear nowadays.'

'Oh yes I know the type of thing you mean. That sounds like the young lady I'm getting the water for. Just had a queer turn. Come with me sir.'

Richard was impatiently tapping his hand on the arm of the chair.

'Look,' said Vanessa. 'Why don't we just go home?'

'Not without my paintings. Even if I have to unscrew them from the wall myself. They should not be here.'

'Let's leave them here. You can always do other paintings. Any painting you like.'

'Not like those.'

'What's so special about them?' Vanessa was remarkably offhand. 'Few pictures of a girl that's all. Plenty more like that.'

'No there isn't! That's the point. She was special,' Richard said hotly.

'She doesn't look very special to me.'

Richard stared at Vanessa. 'Well she was.'

'Huh!'

'What did you say?' Richard's voice was cold.

'I said "Huh". Special? You went to bed with her, that's all.'

'I did not!'

'I bet you did,' she taunted him. 'I bet you were in love with her.'

'O.K. O.K. If you want the truth Miss Clewe-Harting, I was in love with her. More than with anybody else I have ever met. But she just walked out of my life. O.K.? Satisfied? She dumped me.'

'I think you still love her.'

Richard rubbed his hands over his face briskly as if trying to wash away the conflict he felt.

'Look,' he began. 'Look, I don't know what's got into you. Are you jealous? Because if you are, it's a bit daft. But you might as well know that I loved Jennifer Pye, I still love her, and I shall probably always love her.'

'So you love this Jennifer Pye?'

'Yes I love Jennifer Pye.'

'Even though she dumped you? How pathetic!'

'Yes even though she dumped me.' He stood up and wildly waved his arms. 'What do you want me to do? Shout it out so that everybody knows? I love Jennifer Pye.'

He did not recognise the gleam in Vanessa's eyes.

'Yes,' she spat at him. 'Why not? Shout it out. Go on. Tell the world now you've told me.'

He drew in his breath.

'All right Magdaline, just keep calm. Everything's going to be alright.' Lynne held her arms around the trembling shoulders and looked about her. Why was there never anybody there when she needed them? She could hear voices somewhere, they sounded angry.

'His jumper,' Magdaline muttered.

'Oh Magdaline, Magdaline, why did you?' She could feel her own tears trickling down her cheeks. 'They told you not to.'

At last! The attendant man was coming back with a glass. He had an older man with him. Probably a doctor.

'I LOVE JENNIFER PYE!'

The shout canonned around the galleries, freezing everyone into a tableau of shock, indignation, outrage, confusion. Lynne felt Magdaline go rigid in her arms, then suddenly she was struggling. She had the strength of a bull.

'Richard!' she shouted. 'Where are you?'

'Magdaline,' Lynne said. 'What's the matter? What is it?'

More shouts.

'Jennifer! Jennifer! Where are you?'

Running feet echoing through galleries. The attendant started forward and then looked quizzically at the older man's hand on his arm, restraining him gently. Suddenly she was free and running, her handbag clattering to the tiles and shattering chattels widespread. A man skidded into the doorway and with a scream she was in his arms.

'I came back to tell you I love you too.'

Rooted to the spot for the instant, Lynne now ran towards the couple. This was somebody from Magdaline's past. It had to be! They told her not to do it but she had ignored them. Good old Magdaline!

The lady had come back. Magdaline was still swallowed up in the man's hug.

'She's found someone,' Lynne told her ecstatically, brushing the tears from her cheeks with the back of her hand. 'She's found someone she knows!'

'Yes, I can see,' the lady said.

Lynne looked at the man. The face was familiar. She caught her breath and then tugged the newspaper from her bag and showed it to the lady.

'Look!' she gasped. 'It's him. In the newspaper. Lord Wisdene.

Magdaline knows Lord Wisdene.' She shook the paper at the lady. The lady with the nose like a paper dart. Lynne's mouth dropped open and her head jerked back to the photograph. The fiancée. 'Oh!' she said. 'Oh. Oh.'

'I think your friend's name is Jennifer,' the lady said.

'Oh I'm sorry,' Lynne stammered. 'I didn't realise... I didn't know who...'

The lady was still looking at the couple, a deep satisfied sadness filling her grey green eyes.

'I rode deliberately into the last fence,' she said. 'I could never have cleared it.'

Arthur Northgate moved his stool back into the alcove and then turned and surveyed his now quiet domain. The gallery had sunk into its usual torpor of muffled somnolence. This was how he preferred it. He could do without all that excitement. He wandered over to the west corner and stood looking at the three paintings. They were alright, he supposed, in their way. Not his kind of thing, though.

What he liked was a picture with a story to it.

MARTIN LLOYD

The Trouble with France

Martin Lloyd's new international
number one blockbusting
bestseller

"...makes Baedeker's look like a guidebook..."

When Martin Lloyd set out on his holiday to Suffolk why
did he end up in Boulogne? What caused Max the Mad
Alsatian to steal his map and what did the knitted
grandma really think of his display of hot plate juggling?
The answers to these and many more mysteries are to be
found in THE TROUBLE WITH FRANCE

THE TROUBLE WITH FRANCE contains no recipes and
no hand drawn maps. It does not recount how somebody
richer than you went to a part of France that you have
never heard of, bought a stone ruin for a song and
converted it into a luxurious retreat which they expect
you to finance by buying their book.

Nor is it the self satisfied account of another ultra fit
expedition cyclist abseiling down Everest on a penny
farthing but Martin Lloyd attempting an uneventful ride
on a mundane bicycle through an uninteresting part
of France... and failing with outstanding success.

THE TROUBLE WITH FRANCE is destined to be a worldwide
success now that Margaret's Mum has been down the
road and told her friend Pat about it.

Published by Queen Anne's Fan ISBN: 9780 9547 15007

*Martin Lloyd has recorded THE TROUBLE WITH FRANCE as
a talking book for the blind. RNIB catalogue no: TB 15323*

The Trouble with Spain

MARTIN LLOYD

FROM THE BESTSELLING AUTHOR OF
THE TROUBLE WITH FRANCE *COMES*
THIS EAGERLY AWAITED SEQUEL

"...makes Munchausen look like a liar..."

Still smarting from his brutal encounter with Gaul as detailed in his much acclaimed book, THE TROUBLE WITH FRANCE, Martin Lloyd drags his bicycle over the Pyrenees to pursue the twin delights of sun and breakfast.

What factor will defeat his proposed headlong plunge into raw hedonism? Will it be his profound and extensive ignorance of Spanish history or perhaps his coarse insensitivity to the culture of the peninsula?
Or would it be the damning condemnation that he is just too lazy to learn the language?

Read THE TROUBLE WITH SPAIN and you will discover nothing about bull fights and enjoy no colourful descriptions of sensual flamenco dancing but you will learn why you cannot train goldfish to be guard dogs and you will clearly understand why even Martin Lloyd's trousers ran away from him.

CAUTION
This book contains moderate use of humour, some expressions in foreign language and a short but ultimately frustrating scene in a lady's bedroom.

Published by Queen Anne's Fan ISBN: 9780 9547 15014

The Chinese Transfer

Martin Lloyd

The

Chinese Transfer

a thriller romance that you will not
want to put down

"...this is storytelling as it used to be..."

Paris in the 1970s – student demonstrations, union strikes
and oppressive heat. Coach driver Simon Laperche is sent
to Orly Airport to pick up a Chinese group and take them
to their hotel in the city. A run of the mill job. He could
do it with his eyes shut. It was a pity about the guide,
but then, he could not expect to please everybody.

Abruptly, things go wrong. The plane is diverted to Lyons
and Laperche is ordered to drive his coach south to
meet it... and he has to take that infuriating guide
with him. Unknown to them both, a terrorist unit has
targeted their group and is intent upon its destruction.

Stalked by the terrorists, the driver and guide continue
to bicker as they struggle to bring their group safely to
Paris. Will the mutual respect which eventually begins
to grow between them prove strong enough
when the test comes?

Published by Queen Anne's Fan ISBN: 9780 9547 15021

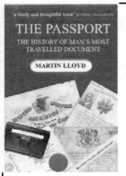

THE PASSPORT

The History of Man's Most Travelled Document

SECOND EDITION, REVISED AND ENLARGED
with 246 pages and 80 illustrations

The passport is a document familiar to many, used and recognised worldwide and yet it has no basis in law: one country cannot oblige another to admit its subjects simply by issuing a document. But the state, by insisting on the requirement to hold a passport, provides for itself a neat, self-financing data collection and surveillance system.

This well illustrated book tells for the first time the story of the passport from its earliest origins to its latest high-tech developments. Handwritten documents adorned with wax seals, modern versions in plastic covers, diplomatic passports and wartime safe conducts, all drawn from the author's collection, complement the exciting exploits of spies and criminals and the tragic real life experiences of refugees.

Whether recounting the birth of the British blue passport of the 1920s or divulging the secrets of today's machine readable passport, Martin Lloyd has written an informative and engrossing history book which is accessible to everyone.

"...a lively and thoughtful book..."
Sunday Telegraph

Published by Queen Anne's Fan ISBN: 9780 9547 1503 8

Martin Lloyd has recorded The Passport as a talking book for the blind. RNIB catalogue no: TB 14107